GRAND Romantic DELUSIONS AND THE MADNESS OF Mirth

PART TWO

MEGHAN CIANA DOIDGE

Library and Archives Canada
Doidge, Meghan Ciana, 1973 —
Grand Romantic Delusions and the Madness of Mirth/Meghan Ciana Doidge — PAPERBACK

"My Magic Girl" lyrics by Michael James Horrocks (used with permission)
Cover design by Alicia McFadzean (aka Serif and Somnia)
Scenery illustration by Kateryna Vitkovska
Other graphic design by Eternal Geekery
ISBN 978-1-989571-77-4

MEGHAN CIANA DOIDGE

AUTHOR'S NOTE: CONTENT

The Mirth duology is set in a secondary world that shares many common traits with our own. The divergences in language, governing bodies and countries, technology, and geography are all intentional choices by the author.

Content of note: Grief, loss of a sibling, violence, explicit language, and sexual situations. Discussions of suicide. Casual drug use. Kidnapping of minors. Child trafficking. While choice vs. duty is a strong theme in the Mirth duology, Mirth herself doesn't have to choose between her suitors, and they are more than happy to lend a helping hand to each other as well.

READING ORDER

The Mirth duology is set in the Conduit World. While it's not necessary to read all the interconnected series, the ideal reading order is as follows.

- Awry (Conduit 1)
- Grand Romantic Delusions and the Madness of Mirth, Part 1 (Mirth 1)
- Grand Romantic Delusions and the Madness of Mirth, Part 2 (Mirth 2)
- Snag (Conduit 2)

Content notes and a list of tropes can be found on MCD's website: http://www.madebymeghan.ca/mirth-part-2

FOR MICHAEL

My soul-bound mate. Through all our lifetimes together.

INTRODUCTION

I walked away from my own matchmaking event, leaving behind me the men who I was beginning to believe might be mine. The ones I was even starting to hope were my soul-bound mates.

I know now that hope was wrong.

I also know what I need to do to move forward. To say goodbye to my beloved brother, to accept the duty I was born and bred to undertake — to hold the intersection point and rule a realm.

Love, compatibility, and companionship aren't factors in my future. But I need just a moment, a few days, to accept everything else that comes with my blood and my position. I need to embrace my fate as if it were my choice — even if it never really was a choice. Any of it.

And that includes finally accepting the deadly power I wield.

But apparently, my would-be suitors have a different future in mind for us all. And though I'm not running — or at least not running from them — they're primed for the chase.

A good thing, too. For there are children who need our protection ... and a last layer of secrets to be uncovered.

1

Mirth

NOT EVEN TWENTY-FOUR HOURS AFTER I WALKED away from my own matchmaking event, I'm sliding out of the converted classic Rolls-Royce Phantom that I absconded with from my father's collection of cars. With a brief stop for some food and to stretch our legs, Roz and I have driven all the way from Waterfell Castle, my father's seat of power, to Prague.

And yes, this pampered princess can actually drive. Fleeing kidnapping or assassination attempts would be rather difficult if I couldn't, according to the head of the royal guard. Though Anne, my father's chosen mate, had seriously freaked out when Raoul got my brother Armin and me both learning to ride motorcycles even while we were technically too young to have our licenses. Raoul and Anne hadn't been bonded then, as they are now with each other, my father, and Eleanor — the two of them exchanging bites in the shifter way. And Anne had pretty much lost her mind seeing us grapple with bikes far too big for us.

Speaking of disgruntled protectors, my royal guard, Roz, slams the passenger door shut and crosses around to the front of the car to join me. Even while doing more than her share of the driving, my combat mage has had her lips perpetually pressed together in disapproval the whole trip. Ignoring the fact that I could have wandered off without notifying her at all, as I had done countless times before, trailing in Armin's wake. Granted, he and I didn't usually drive partway across Europe without letting anyone know where we were.

It's midmorning. We've arrived earlier than I planned. Though the former estate is set on the edge of the city, the sound of the bustling metropolis is muted by the tall walls and the even taller, ancient-looking trees sporadically growing all across the front of the property.

Roz sweeps a dark-eyed gaze around the mostly empty visitor car park, then scans the ostentatious brick building set back on the property.

The Prague Phrontistery. Well, the main building, at least.

"It's still spring break," I say, only slightly exasperated as I retrieve my black designer backpack from the back seat. "They have security." We had to cross through the wards at the gates.

Roz only grunts in response. Her thumbs are already flying over her phone as she sends out updates, most likely to my other personal royal guard, Greg, as well as their supervisor. The cat shifter is still in London at my request. Getting a phone to the children, Tommy and Kitty, whom I've inadvertently — and possibly inappropriately — taken under my protection. I should know the name of Greg and Roz's royal guard supervisor, but I don't.

Though I have a sense that Roz might report directly to Raoul.

"The guard at the gate didn't even ask you for ID," Roz says sourly, not looking up from her phone. "And he's new since we did our last security checks."

"Well, that's probably a good thing," I say casually. "Since I don't actually have any ID. In the traditional sense."

Roz throws me a look. I just grin at her, then deliberately point to my thick-framed black designer sunglasses, indicating the purple-hued eyes hidden behind those vintage shades more than the glasses themselves.

She grimaces, her own dark-brown eyes only partially shaded behind sleek aviators. "Sorry. We've never traveled like this before." She sweeps a hand down her body. She's not in her royal guard uniform. Her casual outfit — dark jeans, leather jacket over a thin sweater, and kick-ass boots — was what she was wearing when I gave her exactly no notice before I stole the car.

In my defense, I was rather ... distracted.

Right after I stole Armin's ashes from my father's study.

Right after I realized all the ramifications — or at least all the ones I hadn't already spelled out for myself — of being my father's only heir. All the reasons that I needed to accept and bond with a well-established bond group. I would need to help my father hold the intersection point. I would need to be grounded and steady enough to hold that point myself when the time comes. Because an imbalanced intersection point has worldwide ramifications. It's a massive responsibility. One I was born and bred to undertake.

Honestly, giving Roz any notice at all was rather generous of me. Especially given that I took off from Lake

Thun Castle without her, forcing her to race after me to Waterfell.

I sling my backpack over both shoulders. It's comfortingly heavy. Anchoring. Still, it seems as though carrying a marble urn around in a backpack should be disconcerting.

I'm wearing a black cashmere-and-wool duster that falls to my lower calves and comes with a glorious cowl hood, over perfectly stretchy, straight-legged dark-wash jeans. The duster is more of a coat than a sweater, and I've layered it over a cobweb-thin, long-sleeved, tight-fitting sweater, then paired the entire outfit with sleek, square-toe ankle boots with a generous heel. I had found the entire outfit in prettily wrapped boxes in my rooms at Waterfell and thrown it on before I left. Clearly, the clothing was another courting gift from Sully, either sent to the castle before or during the matchmaking event so I wouldn't be overwhelmed by too many gifts from him all at once.

And yes, despite leaving Sully and all my other suitors behind without a more formal goodbye, I greedily accepted the absolutely perfect outfit.

My heirloom pearl necklace lies warm against my skin. Armin's emerald ring weighs down my right hand. But I already know I'm no longer the princess to whom both were gifted years ago. I'm also not all shiny and new.

I'm floating in the *becoming* between my recent past and my near present.

And that is ... okay. I can slow down — my mind, my heart. I can take the time to ... grieve. Hopefully in a healthier way than I've been doing so far. If only for the few days I promised my father.

A narrow garden — more a series of interconnected pathways than greenery — separates us from the main building. The huge double entrance doors are situated above a short set of steps, just beyond a low fountain that never freezes thanks to layers of essence-wrought spells. Even now, I'm sure some creature is living within the shallows — an essence-crafted creation from the Phrontistery's upcoming graduates. The staff plays along with such pranks until summer break.

Not that all the students leave for the summer. Or even spring break, for that matter. Sully never did, not unless he was with Armin or Bolan. And me, of course. His so-called guardians were mostly estate lawyers and extremely distant relatives who pulled allowances from his inherited estate, but who never bothered visiting. So even though Sully technically owned houses all over the world at the time, he had no home to go to.

The last time I allowed my power free rein had been on these grounds. Not that 'allowed' is the most accurate description of that involuntary unleashing, and all the far-reaching ramifications of that extreme manifestation.

The unreciprocated kiss with Bolan ... the terror of hurting people ... the defense of my brother ...

The deaths I caused that still haunt me. So much so that I locked all that power away and refused to deal with the aftermath — for far too long, it now seems.

The entrance doors, carved in an intricate design featuring multiple lynx, fly abruptly open. Tereza Landenberg hustles through them and down the stairs in our direction. The golden-haired lynx shifter is dressed much more formally than either me or Roz.

I find myself hoping I haven't pulled Tereza away from anything more important than my visit, because I can feel her anxiety from all the way out in the car park. And not just because my hold on my own essence gifts has become more ... unbound of late. By choice.

That makes me dangerous, it seems.

But I might need to be a little dangerous, and much

more unpredictable, to get through … well, formally mourning Armin in order to somehow embrace my predestined place in the world.

Though I know that the grief of losing my brother — my crux, even if we weren't soul bound within the essence of the universe — will never truly leave me.

"I thought we were expected?" Roz says. The combat mage tucks her phone away, stepping up to stand just behind my right shoulder. The stance — behind me instead of in front — is another of our compromises. We've been compromising for the entire trip. Roz would have preferred for me to not leave any of the royal properties at all. I would have preferred to sneak away without her.

I smile at Tereza, striding forward so she doesn't have to cross all the way to the car park to greet us.

The lynx shifter shakes her head, tossing golden curls all around her neck and shoulders. Then she visibly reins herself in, pausing a few steps beyond the stairs, hands clasped before her, back stiff. A chilly breeze lifts the pressed collar of her gold silk blouse. She's paired the blouse with wide-legged wool crepe pants, a statement gold belt, and spiked heels.

"Tereza," I say as we near, hoping my informal use of her first name will set the tone. "Thank you for seeing me at such —"

Tereza curtsies. Deep and low.

I sigh — though only internally. Because despite my wardrobe and my hopeful attitude, I'm still a fucking princess, aren't I? "Please, Lady Landenberg. We're all friends here, yes?"

Tereza raises just her head, blinking up at me. That's when I notice the red-edged eyes she's mostly disguised, rather expertly, with makeup. She's been crying … because of me? Because of me making the appointment with her?

Tereza slowly straightens, glancing at Roz and then behind us, as if expecting us to be flanked by more of the royal guard. As if she's anticipating further ramifications because her two chosen, Lukas and Radek, playfully — and most ill-advisedly — attempted to kidnap me during our courting.

"I'm earlier than expected," I say pleasantly, trying to ease Tereza's tension. "I thought about stopping for a hot chocolate in town, but decided that you wouldn't mind if I wandered the property for a bit before lunch? I don't wish to be a bother."

Tereza's anxiety finally ebbs, enough that it's no longer pressing against me. An unfortunate side effect of my power that I'll have to compensate for if I'm not going to be bottling everything up so tightly.

"You're welcome to wander where you will, Your Highness. Always welcome."

"Just down to the lake house," I say. "And perhaps ... a glimpse into my old rooms? If they aren't occupied?"

"Moravia Hall isn't currently in use," Tereza says, still clasping her hands together just a little too tightly. "We're ... the roof is leaking, unfortunately. We've temporarily patched it, of course."

"But you're looking to renovate."

"We're just two months before the summer break." Tereza turns slightly toward the door in a clear offer for me to follow her into the main building. She flashes me a smile that is far more in character than the hand wringing. "And about to reach out to our parents and donors."

I laugh quietly. "Well, let's see if I can be of any assistance."

"I wasn't able to get all the paperwork in place —"

"Really?" I ask playfully, cutting her off. "With less than a day's notice and during spring break?"

Tereza's gaze and tone are terribly serious as she steps slightly closer, towering over me in her heels. "Anything the Line of Landenberg can do, Your Royal Highness. We're in your service."

"No need for oaths of fealty, Tereza. We are friends."

She swallows, then nods stiffly.

I place my hand on her arm gently, knowing my energy might be off-putting, but still not liking the concern lurking behind her red-edged eyes and woven within her anxiousness. "If I'm not too much trouble," I add teasingly.

Tereza's eyes crinkle at the edges. "I've never been concerned about a little trouble, Your Highness."

I laugh quietly, allowing my hand to drop away from her arm. "Where and when shall I meet you for our lunch? The dining hall?"

Tereza hums. "I thought the staff lounge. Do you know where it is? And in forty-five minutes?"

"I'll come through the lakeside gardens," I say, already turning away. The weight of Armin's urn across my shoulders is a reminder of the main reason for my visit. "Thank you for coming in on what I assume was supposed to be ..." Realizing what I'm saying as the rote pleasantries fall from my mouth, I don't finish the thought.

Tereza and her two chosen would have blocked this time off for the matchmaking event, not simply spring break from the Phrontistery. And they were expelled from that matchmaking event by my father. Not even twenty-four hours ago. I know that the elders of the Line of Landenberg won't have taken that expulsion ... easily. Hence, the red-rimmed eyes.

Tereza fills my pause without hesitation. "I'm at your disposal, Your Highness."

"You're lucky I'm not the kind of royal to take advantage, Lady Landenberg."

She laughs involuntarily. "I think the open invitation precludes any possible ... exploitation."

Offering her a slight smile, I pull the duster's hood over my head, occluding my peripheral vision but also most effectively hiding my face.

Then, instead of entering the main building, I take the side path leading around it. Roz falls back a few steps to follow. We haven't discussed my true intentions during our drive, though she's overheard any voice messages I sent. But the way she instantly gives me space makes it clear that she's easily guessed why I'm here.

I zigzag around the lake house that houses staff members not assigned to one of the student residences, cutting along the pathway at the edge of the narrow beach until I reach a well-known after-hours hang-out spot just beyond a stand of trees starting to leaf out. A few students cross between buildings, mostly coming and going from the dining hall and the main library, but none pass close enough to notice me or trigger Roz.

I have no doubt that little happens on campus that the staff and guards don't know about, including the lakeside hang-out spot. Unless one of the students is an expert in essence-shielding. But such things are indulged at the Phrontistery to some extent — at least in Prague. Mostly because the relationships formed here among the student body — a mix of mages, shifters, and a few awry — are almost more important than the education itself.

"You were here on scholarship, weren't you?" I slow my pace to speak to Roz. Because even as the justification of all the casual rule-breaking my peers and I engaged in while attending school flits through my mind, I have no doubt that her experience was much, much different. And that's relevant to why I've scheduled a lunch with Tereza instead of just doing what I came here to do and moving on. "A year ahead of Armin and Bolan?"

"Recruited by Raoul for the royal guard when I was sixteen," she says proudly. "But I stayed for another two years. All expenses paid. My family cut me off, preferring to be assholes about me taking a working-class position rather than admit they were so far in debt they couldn't have paid for two more years here anyway." She snorts, quietly derisive. "First time the press published a shot of me with you, they were suddenly all supportive."

While I was in school — along with Sully, I attended until I was twenty-one, both of us opting for advanced degrees — I had older guards who mostly coordinated with school security. But once I needed to be in public more often, Raoul paired me with younger guards. Supposedly to blend in, though this is the first time Roz and I have ever been in public without her in uniform.

I pause to look over the lake, cinching my duster around me against the chill. A scarf and gloves would have been a good idea. Not that I'm staying for long.

"We used to come down here," I say. "Bolan entertaining us with his guitar, taking requests when he felt like it … or quietly working in one of his notebooks." I don't articulate the rest of the memories flitting through my mind out loud, including that one early morning when I'm fairly certain Armin and Sully shared their first kiss. I'd been reading by firelight, desperately trying to not gaze adoringly at Bolan, only to look up across the fire to find my brother and my best friend wrapped together, sprawled across the sand.

About two weeks after that, I was bold enough to kiss Bolan myself —

I shove the thought away. My heels sink into the soft sand as I stride toward the water's edge. That memory isn't at all important in the now. And I understand that I've let it, that I've let the fallout from Bolan's rejection, rule me — and how I interact with my essence and the world around me — for far too long.

Roz lingers behind me along the path as I take Armin's urn out of my backpack — and inadvertently dispel the essence-wrought sealing spell on the lid. Which is annoying, because I have no ability to cast such a spell myself. The marble lid isn't hinged, nor does it screw in place. So I'm going to have to find some tape or something ...

Hugging the cold white marble to my chest, I settle the backpack across my shoulders again instead of putting it down in the sand. Then I allow myself to just gaze out at the lake, listening to the wind rustling through the trees at my back and the chittering of nearby birds, watching the gentle lap of the water. Armin and I spent most of our childhood on this campus. Mostly sheltered, but hyper-aware of our ... function in the real world at the same time.

I'm not entirely certain how long it takes. My nose and cheeks are numb, and my fingers feel frozen against the marble urn. But when my head is finally empty, I tuck the lid of the urn in the pocket of my duster. Then, not thinking about anything at all, I dig my hand into the loose ashes in the urn and pull out a handful.

The wind instantly tries to take that handful of Armin's remains from me, but I tighten my hold.

Just for another moment.

I think of my brother.

I picture him in my mind, smiling, laughing, with his

purple eyes glowing. I see him alive and happy in my mind's eye.

Then I open my fist and allow the wind to scatter the remainder of the ashes I'm holding. Some ash sticks to my hand. I brush my fingers together to dislodge it.

I'm crying.

Silently weeping. But still. I don't want to have tears streaming down my face. I want to celebrate my brother. Yet tears continue to fall.

I should have words … I should have words to say — an invocation, a benediction, or even a lament — but I don't. Not yet. Maybe never.

So I simply try to hold the image of Armin's smile in my mind's eye and the sound of his laughter in my heart.

I let the last of him go.

Just a handful.

For now.

That's all I can bear to lose.

SALVATORE STRIDES DOWN THE NARROW STONE path toward me. I'm cradling Armin's urn against my chest as I walk, because I'm worried it will spill if I return it to my backpack without a properly sealed lid. I've managed to move away from the lake edge and wipe the tears from my cheeks. But … I'm not really back in the present yet. My mind … lags.

The moment I lock my gaze to Sully's concerned gray eyes, I instantly feel more grounded — yet lighter at the same time. He's wearing a dark-blue suit and a crisp white shirt that has way too many buttons undone to be at all proper.

Roz, casting her gaze around the otherwise empty campus, slows her pace so she falls farther back behind me.

I practically barrel into Sully's arms. He hugs me to him, too tightly. The marble urn between us is seriously uncomfortable, but I ignore it to tilt my head so I'm pressing my face into his warm neck.

He huffs — likely in response to my frozen nose — but then just tightens his hands around me while shoving his own nose into my windswept hair.

I don't ask why he's here, or how he found me. We've exchanged a few texts in the last twenty-four hours, but I didn't mention my plans. And I thought he was headed to Zurich for some yet-to-be-disclosed reason.

Completely irrationally, struggling to not burst into tears all over again, incapable of greeting him properly as I should, I cry out into the warm skin of his neck, "I broke the sealing spell on the lid."

Sully pulls back just enough to gaze at the marble urn held between us. He swallows harshly. Skin-to-skin, and with only the loosest of reins on my own power, I can feel the underlying simmer of his grief.

I try to pull away, reaching up to straighten my askew sunglasses, but Sully keeps me tucked against his side with one arm curled around me.

He raises his hand. Slowly, as if he thinks I might stop him.

I don't want to stop him.

I never want to stop him.

He brushes his knuckles across my cheek, leaving a touch of his essence in the wake of his caress. Then he lowers that same hand between us, places those same fingers to the lid of the marble urn, and seals it with another touch of his essence.

"You should be able to open and close it now," he murmurs quietly. "With just a touch of intent."

I sniff noisily. Instead of bursting into more tears.

Sully gently tugs the urn out of my hands.

The wind catches in my hair, whirling it around us. But I don't do anything to try to tame it because I can't do anything but look at Sully.

Our shared grief weaves between us, tightening everywhere we still touch. As if it's tying us together rather than tearing us apart.

I let Sully take the urn.

I let him slip around behind me, unzip my backpack, and place the urn within it.

His touch is gentle, skin warm as he runs his fingers down my arm to take my hand, tugging me toward a perpendicular path that leads to the nearest building.

I should be asking questions ... or at least talking ... but I just curl my fingers around Sully's, watching him instead of noting where he's leading me. Watching him instead of letting the grief have me, own me.

Sully opens a side door of whatever building we're closest to with another press of his essence. Then we're stepping into the warmth within. The lights are on, but the wide halls are empty.

"We need a moment," Sully murmurs politely to Roz behind us. But my guard is already settling back against the wall next to the exterior door and pulling out her phone in anticipation of just that.

A few more steps down the hall and Sully leads me into a bathroom. Its placement and set up — three sinks across from three stalls, and half-height tiled walls all in shades of cream and chrome — instantly orient me to the fact that we're in the humanities building. I took the bulk of my literature and language classes here, from my teens into my early twenties.

Sully seals the door behind us with a flicker of his power.

I still don't speak. I don't question him.

It feels as if we're wrapped in a protective bubble, and I don't want that quiet, that understanding between us, to be confused with conversation. Don't want it broken.

Sully tugs off my backpack, setting it on the counter. He's not smiling or smirking as usual, but he's not … sad. His essence is vibrant, filtering through to me with every brush of his fingers.

A brush across my shoulders as he sweeps my hair back. A brush up the back of my neck as I lean against the counter, letting my head fall back to gaze up at him.

"Sunglasses," I say, making it a request even though I'm really just acknowledging where this is going between us. Where I want it to go. My voice is husky with restrained grief.

Still cradling the back of my head, Sully reaches up and removes my sunglasses. I blink against the brightness of the bathroom, feeling oddly exposed for a moment.

That feeling fades almost instantly, withering under the brush of Sully's gaze across my face. His gray eyes gaze steadily into my own. His grief still simmers just under his skin, along with a weary acceptance. But …

He looks at me as if I'm precious to him.

Salvatore, my Sully, always looks at me that way. And not only when he's smiling and playful. Even when the world frustrates him, or when he needs help with some class or understanding a confusing interaction. I've seen him in pain — both emotional and physical. I've seen him on and off meds that made him manic or depressed, before I — we — convinced him that he should be the one deciding how he wanted to live, rather than any medication making that decision for him. That we would happily navigate the world with him, as he wanted, as he saw it.

I've seen him angry. I've hauled him away from beating the shit out of multiple people. Including Bolan once. Even through being berated as I washed the blood off his knuckles, he looked at me as if I was ... precious.

And I had simply accepted his friendship. Accepted that look as the love between friends. Because he was also Armin's. He was Armin's more than he was mine.

But ... Armin is dead.

"He left both of us," I whisper.

"Yes." Sully sighs.

Holding his gray-eyed gaze, I deliberately arch into him, brushing my chest up against his taut body. Then I tease my lips against his in invitation, in welcome, in reverence.

He shudders, likely in response to the touch of my essence.

He groans into my mouth when I lick playfully at his bottom lip.

Desire crashes through me abruptly, painfully.

I'm suddenly not grieving or playful or poised at all.

I simply need.

Energy tangles between us. There has always been friendship and laughter and shared experiences between us, but it's all tighter now ... woven together by our shared grief.

And I need.

"Sully ..." I cry, aware that I'm not remotely articulating myself as I fist my hands almost helplessly in his shirt.

But Sully understands me. He's always understood me.

His mouth crashes over mine.

Maybe he's always wanted this between us, and I've

been the fool who didn't understand. Or maybe losing Armin has fundamentally shifted something in who we are.

I'm suddenly, almost viciously alive in his arms. Not able to touch enough of him at once, wanting more even as he gives all of it to me. Our tongues dance. Our energy, our essence, entwines. Desire pulses between my legs. I'm warm and wet.

I can't reach enough of Sully's skin. The buttons fly off his shirt, one actually hitting me just below my right eye.

Yanked out of the moment by that pinpoint of pain, I hesitate for a breath, worried I've lost too much of myself, unleashed too much.

But Sully doesn't pause. He palms my ass, bending his knees to press his hard cock right between my legs before lifting me up on the counter. Kissing me fiercely as he works his hands up under my thin sweater, not bothering to remove my duster.

I allow myself to relax into the energy weaving around us, shoving his jacket and ruined shirt off his shoulders so I can reach more of his skin. He groans as I tweak his nipples. Then he's arching over me, kissing down my neck with a hand holding me steady on my lower back. He gives up trying to get my sweater up and simply nips at my breast and nipple through all the fabric between us.

Another fierce wave of desire and need shoots through me, then I'm pushing him back from the counter and scrambling to get his belt undone. He's panting, alternating kissing me, tangling my tongue in his, with sucking lightly on my neck. While massaging my ass hard enough to bruise me.

Utterly irrationally, I want those marks on me. I want to claim Sully, make him mine even if he isn't actually mine. Even if he was supposed to belong to Armin. We're both untethered. And though Armin wasn't my soul bonded, I know he was Sully's.

So ... why can't we try to claim each other now?

I get Sully's pants undone, reaching in to palm his cock through his blue silk boxers. He bucks his hips, muting his shout against my neck.

"Is this okay?" I ask. I remember to ask. Consent goes both ways.

Sully cups my face, taking a moment and a shaky breath to simply gaze down at me. "I want you. I always have, and ... I ... I didn't want to lose you if you didn't want me back."

"I ... we can still be friends even if we fuck, yes?" I'm feeling undone, exposed, even as I'm cradled within the weave of essence around us. So I understand his caution. "I can't lose you, Salvatore. I've ... I know it's my fault, but I've been so lost ..." My voice cracks as grief and a whole lot of self-recrimination threatens to break into our perfect, thoughtless bubble.

"I'm not going anywhere," Sully says.

I pull his head down so that I'm kissing him instead of trying to formulate more thoughts, pile on more concerns. He presses against me just as eagerly.

I free him from his boxers. He's warm and thick in my hand. And ...

"Um, is that a piercing?" I pull slightly away to try to get a look at what I'm feeling.

"Don't worry about it right now." Hands under my sweater, his essence kisses my rib cage as he gives up trying to get my bra off using the clasp, instead cutting it off me with a lick of his essence. He palms my breasts as they fall free from the bra's loosened confines. He teases his thumbs over my ridiculously hard nipples, drawing a shudder from me.

Groaning himself as I stroke his length with a twist of

my wrist, he tugs down my pants enough to free one leg, then lifts me back up on the counter. His hands, his essence, are everywhere.

I'm on the verge of coming just from these fevered touches. On the verge of insanity as I tug him closer to me by his cock, lining him up and wrapping my legs around his hips.

"Fuck, fuck," he groans, shaking his head as if to clear it.

I get his tip notched within me, linking my ankles over his hips and urging him forward with my legs.

"Fuck," he pants. "I don't have a condom."

"You just got tested for Lake Thun. And I've only been with Rian, and we use condoms."

"Mirth ... fuck ... birth control?"

I ... I ... I can't remember if my birth control is still good. I've lost complete track of it, except I haven't menstruated in months, so it has to still be somewhat effective.

"I just want to be fucked, Sully," I whine, utterly irrationally.

He groans as if pained. But finally easing into me, he teases in and out to coat himself in my wetness. His piercing hits me in places I hadn't realized craved such attention — along with a touch of his essence, which might well be the point of the enhancement. Then he thrusts, settling fully within me.

The stretch of him is everything I want.

"I'll pull out," he breathes into my ear. With one hand on the small of my back to hold me steady and one hand palming my breasts and tweaking my nipples, he sets a rough, almost erratic pace.

I cling to him, riding the rush of yet another heady flush of desire. I open myself up to all the essence twisting around us, threading us together. And I know I'm not really comprehending more than the cadence of his voice or the passion stuttering through each ragged breath.

I'm here in this moment with Sully.

We're not becoming one soul or anything overwrought like that. We are two people breathing in each other, entwining essence, and acknowledging the need, the desire, and the playful passion that's always been within our grasp.

We only had to reach for it.

Mewing quietly and panting, I wrap my arms around Sully's neck, plastering myself against him as I become unable to focus on kissing him properly. He thrusts in and out of the slick friction between us. My thankfully blunt nails dig into his skin as I release everything ...

I let all my own expectations drop away, willfully succumbing to the fierce, almost painful desire streaking through me.

Sully slips his fingers between us, finding my clit with his thumb. But it's the press of his essence that forces me, tumbling, over the crest.

I cry out, head flung back, losing control of my limbs, my body, as my orgasm shudders through me.

Sully anchors me until I settle into the moment. But then his hips jerk, completely off pace. Without warning, he pulls out of me.

I shout. Actually hating the feeling of him ripping free from me. I shove him back a step, falling to my knees on the hard tile floor before I even make the decision to do so.

I slide my tongue over his cock, sucking the pierced tip into my mouth. He's still holding himself at the base, likely intending to stroke himself through his own orgasm. But I dig my fingers into the back of his thighs as he tries to pull away — or perhaps he's still stumbling from my push — knocking his hand away and replacing it with my own.

Then his hands are in my hair. Holding me almost harshly at the angle he wants me, he thrusts — shallowly and just once — into my mouth, spilling his load with a shout.

I swallow eagerly, sucking all his come from his cock and teasing my tongue over the metal piercing until his fingers twist in my hair, letting me know he's getting too sensitive.

He's braced his free hand on the counter, chest heaving as he looks down at me … as if … as if he's overwhelmingly … in love with me. So much so that his own emotions have shocked him.

Of course, it could also be the image of me on my knees, looking thoroughly fucked with his slowly softening cock in my mouth.

I release that cock with a playful pop, slightly thrown by my own actions. "I'm sorry, but you weren't going to come in me, and I'm not sure why, but I … I needed —"

The fingers still buried in my hair tighten, then he's practically dragging me to my feet and kissing me with the same passion as before we fucked. Not simply chasing the taste of himself on my tongue, but … acknowledging that this desire, this need, isn't going to be satisfactorily fed in a single fuck.

He lifts me back up onto the counter, going down on his own knees and tucking my legs over his shoulders. Settling himself between my thighs, he hums quietly and flicks his tongue over my clit. Gentle, teasing licks.

With barely time to brace myself, I orgasm as if I haven't just already come so hard that my reasoning dropped into I-just-need-Sully's-come-inside-me levels.

He clutches my ass and licks me through the lingering shudders of my second orgasm. Then he straightens, kissing me — on the mouth this time — with a gentle sweetness.

The grief we were both projecting previously has been fucked away. For this moment, at least.

"Mir ..." he whispers. Then he laughs quietly against my lips. "I wasn't supposed to ... I didn't come here with the intention of ..."

"Fucking me?" I ask teasingly. "And why not?"

He kisses me, groaning quietly as if he adores hearing me say 'fucking.'

Before he can answer my first questions, which are more playful than necessary, I ask, "Did you come here for me?"

He grins at me saucily, presumably at the implied double entendre. "A happy coincidence. I called ahead ... well, texted. I'm crashing your lunch with Tereza. But ..."

Ignoring the fact that his own clothing is all but torn apart, his pants and boxers still around his own ankles, he runs his hands through my hair. He instantly tames it with a touch of his essence before moving on to repairing my bra and straightening my clothing. "I could feel you the moment I stepped through the wards and onto the property. I thought Bolan was bullshitting about that aspect of ... being yours. That's how he can always track you down."

"Being ... mine?" I echo. "I thought ..."

"You thought you'd decide for us?"

I open my mouth. But though I'm still settled in my skin, my mind isn't ready to push into all the reasons why I shouldn't ... I can't —

Sully kisses me, sucking my lower lip into his mouth. "You claimed me, Mirth. With that kiss in the hot tub. With this fuck. With you coming on my cock, on my tongue. With me exploding in your mouth, coming down your throat. I'm yours now. And you are fucking mine."

I can only blink at him, because ... no matter what list of names I might have written under the influence of the intersection point after my father announced the matchmaking event he planned to host ... no matter what I think that list ultimately means ...

This is what I want.

Six names on that list, including my dead brother and my best friend, Sully.

Five potential suitors. All but one of whom I walked away from less than twenty-four hours ago because I didn't believe that they were meant to be mine. Not universe destined, at least.

But Sully ... Sully wants me just as much as I want him.

He continues straightening my clothing, then moves on to his own, letting me just look at him. His smirk teases his lips now, gray eyes amused. He knows how pretty he is.

With his buttons repaired and his suit smoothed of wrinkles, Sully lifts his fingers to my face and wipes away all the lingering tracks of dried tears, refreshing the bit of makeup I slapped on when we arrived at the Phrontistery just to be presentable. Thankfully, I always carry the basics — lipstick, mascara, and a brush — in just about every bag I own.

Salvatore is so fucking striking. Utterly unique. I can't look at anything but him. His essence caresses my skin, shivering through me and causing my nipples to peak. A low, heavy ache gathers between my legs. I'm panting, ensnared by his gray eyes, already addicted to his touch.

A self-satisfied smile sharpens his expression. Then, just as I think he's going to pull away, he slips those fucking magical fingers into my pants, into my underwear, and into my renewed wetness.

I try to stifle a moan, my hips jerking, as he easily finds my clit. Again.

"One more, Princess?" he whispers into my neck, sucking gently behind my ear. "Then lunch? Then if you need more words, we'll talk."

"Yes," I moan. "Yes, Sully. Please."

He hovers his mouth over my ear, his breath warm and almost invasive, overwhelming and delicious. "Say you are mine, Mirth. When you come. Say you're mine, say my name."

I wrap one hand over the wrist of the hand he's using to pleasure me. My other hand goes around the side of his neck because he's covered the rest of his skin. I lift his chin with my thumb, staring him straight in the eyes. I keep his gaze locked to mine even as pleasure streaks through me, even as he has to pin me against the counter with his body so my legs don't give out.

He looks deep into my eyes — and doesn't falter in response to whatever I reveal to him. He looks at me as if I'm everything. Everything he wants. Everything he desires.

As I orgasm, suddenly and almost painfully, my grip on his neck tightens. I don't drop his gaze, and I don't question the desire, the need, as I say, "You're mine, Salvatore. I claim you. I claim you."

The weave of essence still threaded around us — a connection born through a lifetime of friendship and solidified through shared grief — tightens over us.

"I love you, Euphrosyne," Sully whispers, cupping my pussy tightly as the lingering sparks of my orgasm fade.

Something more than skin deep snaps into place between us. As if just for the next breath, our souls splinter into each other, resolving into one whole. Together.

Sully brushes his lips against mine.

And we're two people again.

A tiny sliver of the empty space that Armin's death has left in my soul, the space I acknowledged as I released a single handful of his ashes to the wind, isn't quite so empty anymore.

"Mine," Sully murmurs.

"Mine," I agree. "Forever, now."

"No, Mirth." His tone is deadly serious. "It's always been forever between us. I tried to be Armin's, but it was you I needed. It was always you. And if I have to spend the rest of our life together proving it, I'll do so gladly."

Reality tries to intrude, and a sharp pain coalesces in my chest. "It's not just me and what I want … which is most definitely you. This is about the intersection point, and …" I swallow harshly, struggling to hold his gaze even as I can feel the protective bubble surrounding us slowly dissolve.

"I know," he says simply and definitively. "And we're going to prove that we're the best choice overall. Even if you don't want to fuck all of us." Grinning saucily, he pulls his hand free from my panties, then sucks on his middle finger and forefinger.

I blink at him. "We?"

"Yes." He does up my pants, stepping back to run his gaze over me. Then, seemingly satisfied, he holds his arm out. "I believe we're late for lunch now."

I slap his forearm instead of taking it. "Sully!"

He grabs my hand, kissing the back of it tenderly, then twining his fingers through mine. "I'm not supposed to be chasing after you. Yet. It's not only my secret to tell."

I narrow my eyes at him even as a completely different warmth slowly spreads through my chest. It feels a lot like hope and contentment, where before I felt only resolve and a sense of duty.

He laughs at my expression, snagging my backpack and swinging it over his shoulder as he leads us toward the bathroom door.

Roz is waiting for us, gazing out the exterior door at the end of the hall.

We've exited the building before my well-fucked brain clicks together the little hints Sully has teased.

"You think … you think I can have you and still do my duty?" I whisper, almost too low for my own ears.

But Sully hears me. "It's not just me. And yes, I know it."

"AH, SALVATORE!" TEREZA SAYS, STRIDING purposefully toward us as we step through the open patio doors that lead into the teacher's lounge. "You found Her Highness. Lovely."

"Lord Savoy," Sully corrects her stiffly. His arm tenses under my touch as he casts his gaze around the cozy room.

High-backed, well-worn brown leather chairs and low oak tables dominate the space. A few huge paintings gifted by famous alumni line the walls, and a linen-and-silver-swathed table has been set up for our luncheon. A fire crackles quietly in a stone fireplace with a wide hearth.

I've never set foot within the Phrontistery's staff lounge. I actually haven't returned to campus since I left almost five years ago. And Tereza has only been overseeing it all — for her family — for the last year or so.

Tereza's step hitches, and she clasps her hands together, shifting her gaze between us uncomfortably. "Lord … Savoy?"

My stomach sours a little at the confirmation that Sully has decided to claim his maternal lineage. In order to be with me, I have no doubt.

Tereza's questioning glance bothers me just a little more than Sully claiming that title, though.

"Official paperwork filed this morning," Sully says with a shrug, placing his hand on my lower back and guiding me around Tereza toward the table. "Not that the title hasn't always been mine."

Tereza blinks at that for a moment, her mind obviously working overtime. In the same moment that she realizes the previously unclaimed title is inherited, I realize that she thought I had bequeathed it on Sully to make him more eligible. Or rather, that my father had bequeathed it at my request.

I instantly bristle. It's funny how such slights bother me only when they're directed at someone I love.

That's such a short list. Even shorter than the list of names I wrote under the influence of the intersection point —

Sully's hand slips to my waist, squeezing, then pulling me against his body. And I realize that my essence has risen along with my ire.

Tereza's gaze is firmly fixed to my feet now, her hands twisting together tightly enough that her knuckles have whitened.

"It's through my mother," Sully says smoothly, though it's uncharacteristic for him to bother with being ... diplomatic. "Everyone will know soon enough. Assuming the clerk at the courthouse hasn't already leaked the information to the media." He smirks in my direction. "Eli already has me running errands. First, Zurich early this morning ..." Then he snaps his mouth shut as if catching himself from saying too much.

I narrow my eyes at his obvious teasing, even as a little thrill of ... something ... shimmers through me. Elias ... the Earl of Hereford, who also holds a seat on the World Council, and who was one of the names on my apparently not-hallucinated list. Elias is involved in whatever Sully has —

"Well," Tereza says, stiffly but vigorously, as if she's grasping for the graceful exit that Sully has flung her way.

She skirts the table to take the seat opposite the one Sully has pulled out for me. "That sort of leak can be mitigated. I know the editor-in-chief of —"

Sully waves a hand in her direction, sliding into another chair. "No need."

I see four place settings, but I'm not certain who else is to join us. After closing the patio doors behind us, Roz has quietly taken up position next to them. She won't eat. Not even if asked. And Tereza knows better than to ask.

Tereza lifts her golden-hazel eyes to meet my own, and I politely remove my sunglasses. Though only because Sully has seated me with my back to the windows. She clears her throat. "Your Highness ..."

Sully shifts his chair so he's close enough to curl his foot around my own, our ankles touching. Not even attempting to do so with any subtlety.

The contact settles me back into my skin, and I flush a little at the sharpness of his gaze. He doesn't seem to remotely care that Tereza will read into that look and know ... know he's in love with me? Overtly obsessed with me?

Tereza's gaze flicks between us. As I assumed it would.

Sully smirks — of course and always — at my reaction, then slumps back in his chair with his typical feigned disinterest. His gaze, hooded and playful now, still rests on me, though.

Refusing to be flustered, I ignore the flush across my face — and in other areas — and take a sip of the water set to the side of my plate. "I appreciate you making time for me, Lady Landenberg." My use of her title is intentional, and I side-eye Sully to make certain he notices.

His smile widens in delight.

"It's my pleasure, Your Highness." Tereza pulls her phone out, pressing a few buttons, then sliding it into her lap. "Though a few of the kitchen staff have remained over the break to see to the students who stay on campus, I ordered —"

"The unwanted brats," Sully interjects, his tone flat.

Tereza clears her throat, more annoyed than flustered.

Sully has a way of bringing that out in people he doesn't particularly care about. And his list of loved ones is even shorter than mine.

Actually, I think our lists would be an almost perfect match save for one new addition on my part. Rian.

Oh, fuck.

I told Rian that I wouldn't take any chosen without talking to him first. Shoving the mild panic away, I take a breath, forcing myself to tune back into the conversation.

Tereza is talking.

"Students stay for a variety of —"

"And one of those reasons is no one gives a shit about them." Sully sneers dismissively. "Or the assholes who occasionally feign to give a shit are too busy to play at it. I know, don't I?"

Tereza sighs.

I rescue her. "I'm certain lunch will be lovely. Also unnecessary. I just thought it would create a more comfortable atmosphere."

"After Bastian almost executed Radek and Lukas for the treason of touching you?" Sully asks me while looking pointedly at Tereza. It is neither a question nor a condemnation of my father. "You're lucky Mirth is so forgiving, Lady Landenberg. Soul bound or not, losing your chosen, no matter how stupid they might be, would be —"

I breach all sorts of protocol to lay my hand on Sully's wrist. His gaze instantly snaps to me. The frown marring his forehead eases until his eyes are once again crinkling at the edges. Not smiling, but pleased that I'm touching him.

"I am blessed by Her Highness's intervention," Tereza

says quietly, though I know by the set of her shoulders that she's hiding her clenched hands in her lap.

"A misunderstanding," I say smoothly, speaking to Sully and knowing he has only Bolan's accounting of events to go by. "As I'm sure you heard."

Sully twists his lips, not outright disagreeing with me. Not while in public, at least.

The door opens, and two staff members enter with covered plates. We sit in silence — me smiling politely — as we are served, and the trays are removed to reveal a chicken breast stuffed with spinach and wild rice. I hum appreciatively as Tereza waves off the staff.

I carefully slice off a bit of chicken, dipping it in the creamy sauce that also coats the stuffing. I eat it, chewing thoughtfully. Tereza and Sully both start eating after I do.

I set my knife and fork down, taking another sip of water. "We aren't waiting on a fourth?" I ask.

Tereza's gaze flicks to the fourth chair. "No, Your Highness. I wasn't certain who you would have accompanying you. Even after ... Lord Savoy messaged."

I typically never went anywhere unaccompanied by a friend or family member. Honestly, I never went anywhere with less than twenty-four hours' notice. At all.

"As I broached in my email, I want to discuss the establishment of a perpetual scholarship ... two yearly scholarships, to be specific. To be paid for by the foundation I'm establishing for Armin. He ... we ... spent the bulk of our lives here, learning who we ... were ..."

Tereza nods politely, ignoring that I can't speak about Armin in the past tense without my heart cracking, just a little. "Of course. I've got the preliminary paperwork ready for your lawyers. Specifically, what the Phrontistery requires to help you establish and maintain the scholarships. But if the sponsorship is coming from a private foundation, then you, rather than the school board, oversee the yearly allotments."

"Yes," I say, still a bit shaky. "Or ... I'll likely find a director or two with more experience. But it's the criteria that I'm ... it's not just grades and an entrance exam, correct? I assume that the Phrontistery must have requirements or a way to assess ... essence ... abilities?" I feel absolutely stupid, asking about things I should probably already know or inherently understand. My place in this school would never have been questioned, even without the color of my eyes proclaiming me as one of the awry since birth.

"You have kids in mind, Mirth?" Sully asks almost gently.

I nod. "Two. I'm not certain of their designations, but I believe they are both awry blooded. Would you require them to be tested?"

Tereza pauses thoughtfully. "The Phrontistery isn't ... and especially not here in Prague ..." She rethinks what she wants to say a second time. "You might not know, Your Highness, but —"

"The rich shits that go here are fucking brutal to anyone who isn't powerful enough to put them down." Sully leans back in his chair, crossing his arms. "Even worse if they don't come with the right pedigree."

"Or have powerful friends," Tereza says, eyeing Sully right back.

He snorts, but more in acknowledgement than derision. Then a sharp-edged smile overtakes his face. "The Savoy bond group will fund the refurbishment of Moravia Hall."

Both Tereza and I blink at the fabricator mage.

Sully predictably smirks back, mostly at me. "You'll rename it Savoy House. And Mirth's scholarship kids will be among the first residents this fall."

"The Savoy bond group?" I ask quietly.

He nods. "Elias says going around and getting our name on shit is part of establishing ourselves. I was pissed he sent me. But then I found you here, my darling Princess."

Tereza's gaze rapidly flicks between us once more. Then she laughs, sharp-edged and completely delighted. "Gods. The Mertons are going to be fucking pissed."

"That they are," Sully drawls.

I shoot him a quelling look, feeling out of depth but ... in an almost delightful, heady way. Not unlike Teresa's own bond group, the Line of Merton is comprised of two generational tiers, with the elder Lord Merton as their primary crux. Like Elias and my father, Vincent Merton holds a hereditary seat on the World Council. His presumptive heir, Archie, is the head of the younger bond tier, comprised of his half-sister Isla, a savvy lawyer who is on the board of my literacy charity, and their recently bonded — Noah, an awry. The Mertons participated in my matchmaking event ... and they are still the most solid, the most established choice. Likely the best choice to help me hold the intersection point.

"Are you adopting the kids?" Sully asks me, curious and just a little bit pleased. And not only with himself. He's just ... enjoying sharing this moment. With me.

"No, they have a family ... I'm ... I think ..." I glance over at Tereza. "I just wanted to have the conversation, understand the parameters. This isn't something I want to hand over to a board. I understand if there needs to be an assessment. Or other ... tests. But ... I know you have other scholarship students."

"Yes," Tereza says kindly. "The Phrontistery scholarships are merit based."

I nod, thinking furiously. I know next to nothing

about Tommy and Kitty. Just because Tommy came to a literacy event doesn't in any way mean he has special needs. But if he did? Or if Kitty needed a different kind of school? Well, I could come up with another plan if that was the case.

"I'll have the preliminary paperwork sent to your lawyers," Tereza says. "For two students. I'll include the school's scholarship requirements, just so you have them. And everything we'll need to establish and renovate the Savoy House residence hall." She flashes a grin at Sully. "Ready to spend some of daddy's money?"

"It's not like you care how filthy it is, Tereza."

That wipes the smirk off the lynx shifter's face.

I stifle a sigh, then politely eat another small piece of my chicken.

Playful with me or pissy with Tereza, leaking so-called secrets or not, Sully still has his foot wrapped around mine under the table. I rub my foot against his ankle, getting a heated look in return.

And just for a moment, I allow myself to forget the urn in my backpack and to think only of the tentative steps I'm taking into my future. Whether or not I sound like an idiot asking questions I should already know the answers to, or having the realities of the life of scholarship students pointed out to me.

Because knowledge can be gained. Hurdles can be overcome.

Only Armin's death is irrevocable.

Sully ghosts his fingers over the back of my hand, breaking protocol. Though I touched him first. "The scholarship kids? Will you tell us about them?"

I smile at Sully gratefully. "Tommy and Kitty. Or, properly, as Tommy informed me, Thomas and Katherine Walsh. I'd like you to meet them. We've been texting every few days. They send me pictures, some selfies, and the best updates ..."

The smile that Sully levels on me is so bright it sears right through to my soul, taking my breath with it.

Tereza chuckles to herself. "I wish I could be in the room when Isla lays eyes on the two of you and realizes you've finally admitted that you've been crazy about each other from the moment you met. Or, even better, Lord fucking Merton himself."

Sully laughs, and I have a difficult time quashing an inappropriate smile.

Even though I haven't actually decided to turn down the Mertons' suit. Not yet.

BACK IN LONDON, WITH SULLY GLEEFULLY AND noticeably ignoring his text messages, a brown-paper-wrapped parcel awaits my return on my entranceway table. It's rare for me to receive packages directly, but after I open the attached card, I immediately understand why the royal guard accepted it on my behalf.

The sender has already been more thoroughly vetted than just about any other person in my sphere.

Christoph, the Duke of Hapsburg, also known as the Archduke of Austria, has sent me the most delectably scented peaches-and-cream candle. It's hand-poured into an adorable antique crystal dish — a repurposed small pitcher typically used to hold milk or cream. Its mage signature is so distinctive that I'm worried about touching the candle for fear of dispelling whatever essence was used to create it. The candle is accompanied by a matching sugar dish filled with similarly scented bath salts.

Sully peers down at the half-unwrapped package, then eyes my lightly flushed face. Yes, apparently, anything having to do with peaches is going to trigger a recollection of trading slices of the peach Christoph previously gifted me at breakfast. Hence, the blushing.

Sully hums knowingly. "Seems I have to up my wooing game."

I laugh a little breathlessly. "I'm dressed head to toe in your handpicked outfit, Sully."

He flashes me a wicked grin. "But not the bra and panties."

I huff playfully, pulling the pretty crystal-encased candle out of the box and smelling it. Dislodged from the tissue paper, a small embossed card falls to the counter.

Biting his lush lower lip, Sully winks at me. Then he wanders into the living room to throw himself on the long couch. Holding his phone over his head, he starts to answer his messages. Or perhaps he's shopping for lingerie.

I retrieve the card. The duke's name, Christoph Williams, is the only thing on the front, embossed across the thick white paper in black ink. On the other side is a short note, carefully hand-printed in capital letters, and a phone number.

Just in case you ran out of peaches.
Text me?
– C.

I shouldn't text Christoph. I walked away from the matchmaking event. I have fairly serious plans to accept the Mertons' suit, but ... I'm feeling just a little weak-kneed from the reasoning behind all of the duke's peach-themed gifts. Specifically, his confession that my ass looks like a peach to him.

And it would be terribly impolite not to at least thank Christoph for the sweet gift.

I open my message app and start a text thread.

Lord Williams, thank you so much for the lovely gift.

Sully is smirking over the back of the couch at me.

Setting my phone facedown on the counter, I narrow my eyes at him, then lift my chin offishly.

He chuckles, then says, "Let's order in Indian for dinner."

"Yes," I say, perfectly polite. "That sounds lovely."

My phone buzzes on the counter with a text message from Christoph.

>Have dinner with me this week? I'll be heading to London in the next couple of days.

I stare at the message for a moment, completely conflicted.

"That was a quick answer," Sully says playfully. "Think he's been watching his phone since he had the gift delivered?"

"Sully ..." I murmur, half-heartedly chastising him.

"Mirth ..." he purrs back, sliding off the couch and prowling toward me.

"We haven't talked about all of this ..." I say, swallowing and glancing down at Christoph's message on my phone.

Sully rests his chin on my shoulder, watching as I take a deep breath, then text back.

I'm uncertain of my schedule this week, Lord Williams.

>Please keep me in mind, Your Highness.

"That's not too much to ask," Sully whispers against the sensitive skin behind my ear. Then he slides his hand up under my sweater to cup my breast, flicking my quickly hardening nipple through the fabric of my bra. "Is it?"

"No," I groan, pressing back into his hold. "That's not too much to ask."

"Text the poor duke back then, Mir." Sully kisses me, lightly sucking his way down my neck.

I text back, *I will.*

"Such a perfect princess," Sully croons, sliding his other hand down the front of my jeans.

I misplace my phone somewhere between the kitchen and bedroom. And we have to heat the Indian food up ... a couple of hours after it gets delivered.

It's still dark beyond the drawn curtains as I slip out of my bed, leaving Sully sprawled across the other side. He's nude, barely covered in a sheet. Forcing myself to keep moving and not just gaze at my best friend like a complete and utterly infatuated idiot, I grab some clothing from the closet.

The two of us finally collapsed into bed — to actually sleep — only a few hours ago.

I shower quickly, avoiding getting my hair wet, then slap on just enough makeup to counter the I've-only-had-three-hours-sleep-because-fucking-my-best-friend-is worth-the-exhaustion bags under my eyes. I tug on some dark-gray, straight-legged jeans I've owned long enough for them to go out of style, yet haven't really worn long enough for them to not feel overly new, and a long-sleeved, tightly knit merino sweater. I'll add Sully's gifted duster and boots over top of it all.

Plus my backpack containing Armin's ashes.

I slip back out into the dimly lit bedroom.

I've let myself get distracted. Not that I could have emotionally handled multiple stops the previous day, and not that I regret any moment I spend with Sully. But —

"You're leaving me behind?" Sully asks in a gravelly tone from the bed.

I instantly drop the boot I've been pulling on, spinning back to the bed, and leaning over to brush a kiss across Sully's lips. I'm not sure how awake he is, and I don't want to wake him further if —

His arms close around me as he yanks me across his chest, then rolls over me on the bed.

The kiss is edged in anger and just a bit of betrayal — of him, not from him. And yes, I'm so in tune with him, skin-to-skin, that it's hard to kiss and not pick up his emotions.

I soften under him, completely submitting even though it's not in my nature to do so. Sully's kiss softens, turning playful.

When he finally lifts his head just enough to allow me ownership of my own mouth, I say quietly, "I thought I might be back before you woke."

"Where are you heading?"

"The Yates country home."

Sully blinks down at me for a moment, easing back enough to settle beside me instead of pinning me to the bed with his body. "He's not there."

"I know."

"How do you know?"

I grin at him saucily. "I do have access to that sort of information gathering."

Sully snorts. "And since when have you used it?"

I sober slightly. "Since I'm not ready for the confrontation Bolan is craving. But I want ... to leave a bit of Armin where we spent a lot of happy times."

"By the pond," Sully murmurs, searching my gaze for something. "And you want to go alone."

"I'll drag Roz with me. But yes." I hesitate for a moment. "I've asked Greg to stay with you."

Sully frowns, confused.

I add, "Lord Savoy."

He huffs. But I know he understands that suddenly declaring himself to be fourth in line to the throne to the United European Nation — even if it's mostly a figurehead position these days — is going to come with a lot of unwanted attention.

I look at him, waiting.

"Mirth ..." he mutters. "I've got a few more days, at least." Then he falls back and rubs his face. "Shit, I need to get Fluff and Fizz in the loop. And there is going to be more fucking paperwork to sign."

"Probably daily for a while," I say quietly.

His gaze cuts to me, not liking whatever he's heard in my voice. Then he's up on one elbow and cupping my face. "I love you."

I part my lips, slightly surprised. Not at the sentiment, but at the sudden change in —

"I love you," Sully repeats, his tone hardening. "I fucking love you, Mirth. I don't want there to be any more space or time lost between us. If that means I need to be Lord Savoy on paper, then so be it. I ... love ... you."

"I love you," I whisper back. I've said it to him before, many times. But this time, he looks at me as if I'm saying it for the very first time. And maybe I am.

We just linger there, holding each other's gazes, his hand cupping my cheek gently. Then he slowly lowers his head — I meet him halfway — and we brush our lips together. Pure, undiluted energy passes between us — his and mine. As if maybe we're not just pressing flesh to flesh but breathing soul to soul.

"Fine. I won't ditch Greg," Sully says, playfully grumbling. "But if I get my stupid shit done ... I swear fucking

Elias keeps adding to the list ... and you aren't back in town, I'm coming after you."

"Fair." I playfully raise an eyebrow and ask, "What list?"

Sully hums quietly, delightedly. "I see I need to distract you just a little longer ..."

I shake my head at him. Though I quite enjoyed his method of distracting me when I kept prodding him about the newly minted Savoy bond group yesterday. Not that I haven't put a few of the pieces together myself. Such as ever-so-slyly noting the text exchanges between Sully and Elias, as well as Sully, Bolan, and Christoph. Not that I read those messages, just the names of the senders.

Speaking of which ...

"Do me a favor?" I ask.

"Anything."

I crawl out of bed, retrieving my phone from the charging station out in the hall, then climbing back into bed with Sully. He's sitting now, sheet demurely tucked across his lap, but his tan-skinned chest is beautifully bare.

I cuddle next to him, shoulder to shoulder, then hold my phone aloft so we're both framed within the screen. Then I thumb my contact for Rian.

"Really? Now?" Sully flashes a gleeful smirk at me.

Rian answers before I can respond to Sully. The light is low enough around him that all I can see is that he's walking down a wide corridor. Then he raises the phone to frame his face, already smiling as he fits an earbud into his ear. He's wearing a collared lightweight jacket over a thicker knit black sweater, with a backpack slung over one shoulder.

"Mirth." Despite the low light, Rian's smile blazes bright. Then that smile turns slightly questioning as he takes in Sully — who looks completely nude at this angle.

"Rian," I say, "you've met Sully."

Sully smirks — of course and always — then nods at Rian.

Rian nods thoughtfully back, then shifts his gaze to me.

"You're not in Lake Thun," I say.

"Heading to Dublin. Just arrived at the airport, Heathrow. You?"

"London."

Rian's gaze flicks to Sully, then back to me. "You've made your choice … I thought …"

"Both of you." My interjection is clumsy, and blunt, but I don't want the conversation to head off in the wrong direction. "If you'll have me. If you'll —"

"Yes," Rian says.

"No question," Sully murmurs.

"Just …" Rian's gaze flicks between me and Sully again. "Just us?"

"No," Sully says.

"Nothing else has been decided on," I say, knowing this conversation is necessary but also premature.

"But we're the only people Mirth is currently fucking," Sully says, not entirely playful.

Rian nods. "To be determined, I guess."

"Is that an issue for you?" I ask frostily. Because I might not know all the choices I need to make in the next few weeks, but I'm certainly not going to be told whom I can fuck. "For either of you?"

Sully raises his hands, still not entirely playful.

Rian exhales, scrubbing his free hand over his face. An announcement comes over the airport speakers near him. "I'm stalking my fucking mother, who won't take my calls. I'm sorry if I'm acting … I'm all in, Mirth. I have been since the moment you looked my way. I understand it can't just be me. That …" He looks at Sully.

"We're strongest together," Sully says.

Rian tilts his head again, listening to the next set of announcements.

"Your flight?" I ask.

"Yes. Mirth, I —"

"You sort out everything you need to sort," I say gently. "Text me."

Rian flashes me a grin. "What kind of texts?"

I laugh.

"Are there pictures?" Sully asks, always quick to pick up any and all innuendo. "I need to see pictures!"

"Absolutely not," I say.

"I'll send you one of Mirth," Rian says at the same time.

"What?!" I cry. "Absolutely not —"

"Got to go! Love you, Highness."

Rian ends the call. I blink at the blank screen for long enough that Sully's shoulders start to shake against mine in silent laughter.

"Is it the 'love you' or the promised exchange of sexy pictures that's tripping you up, Highness?" he teases, hitting Rian's pet name for me hard.

"That's none of —"

Sully makes a grab for my phone, no doubt to search Rian's text messages. Or get his phone number. We wrestle for it. Sully quickly gets the upper hand, managing to pin me down.

I distract him just as well as he distracted me last night.

I end up having to shower a second time.

And missing breakfast.

2

The Yates country home is about an hour outside of London by train. Though we were usually driven there by the royal guard whenever we visited during school breaks. Roz dozes beside me in the passenger seat of the Phantom as I slow to turn onto the long drive. I know she's not sleeping properly at night because of me, but it would likely be worse for her if I took off on my own.

I haven't called ahead. And maybe I should have because I don't actually know what's going on with Bolan and his mother — what with the reveal of Bolan and Rian's shared parentage only two days ago. But even though I'm not entirely certain of my welcome, I needed to come.

Armin was happy here. We were allowed to just be children here, then to just be teenagers here, treated the same as family. Not prince and princess. Not presumptive heir and spare heir to the realm.

I know that leaving a bit of Armin behind will help heal the gaping wound in my chest, but calling ahead would have formalized all of that.

The grass that spreads out from either side of the driveway is a vibrant green and in need of edging despite it barely being spring yet. The windows and doors of the red-brick house need a fresh coat of paint. It rained overnight, but the sun is currently peeking through the clouds overhead.

I'm acutely aware that I've left Sully behind. Reminding myself that he has his own responsibilities to deal with today — a list of 'secrets' that apparently includes purchasing some ridiculously pricy art that's not actually for sale, given the peeved tone Sully was using while haggling on his phone as I left him.

I'm not certain what collecting rare art has to do with establishing the Savoy bond group. I just know that Sully has a list of things to spend massive amounts of money on, and he's the one with the contacts in the art world.

The odd ache in my chest from leaving Sully behind eased as we drove out of London, thankfully getting out of city traffic and onto the motorway quickly. But I can still feel an echo of it if I let myself focus on it. As if I've tethered myself to Sully, but it's ... new, even tentative, and it feels too early to be testing the boundaries.

All silly thoughts. Distractions, really. So I don't have to think about the next task on my own unwritten to-do list.

I've barely pulled up to the front of the house before Adeline is throwing open the front door and striding across the wide front patio. Tall, white-blond, and blue-eyed like her son Bolan, she's still drying her hands with a tea towel. But her blazing grin tells me I'm welcome.

I exhale some of the stress I've been carrying. While she's always been lovely to me, I wasn't certain how Adeline would have reacted to my silence since Armin's death. And then the reveal of Rian. That I'm with the child her dead husband had with another woman while they were still together. Or at least that's the story as far as I know.

Adeline might still care for me, cared for Armin, but

she loves her children fiercely. She might view Rian as some sort of interloper, just as she might see me as betraying her family.

Dramatic, I know.

But those thoughts have been haunting me, just a little.

There are no wards on the estate, no wards on the house. Which made the royal guard nervous when we visited. But despite Bolan's fame, he's been adamant about keeping his family sheltered from the public. Adeline, his sister, and his half-sisters are all wolf shifters and more than capable of taking care of themselves and each other.

"Mirth!" Adeline cries, tucking the tea towel in the back pocket of her jeans and spreading her arms out in greeting as she traverses the wood front steps and then the gravel drive in bare feet.

Roz is barely out of the car before I'm barreling straight into Adeline's arms. Bolan's mother is only slightly taller than me, but her arms band around me tightly. She kisses my temple as if my energy doesn't bother her in the least. She smells like fresh bread. I've come on a baking day.

"Are you just with Roz?" she asks.

I nod, still holding her almost as tightly as she holds me. "I'm sorry for not calling ahead —"

"You never need to call," she says. "Though I ..." She pulls back from me slightly, trying to look me in the eyes despite the shading of my sunglasses. "I've been worried."

I nod again, feeling like a complete asshole. Not only for not being in touch for over seven months, but because I doubted my welcome. "I'm so, so sorry ... I just ... haven't been able to ..."

Adeline nods, almost briskly. A flicker of her aged but still deep-seated grief filters through to me — picked up inadvertently because of our close contact.

I don't think about how I could take that flicker of

grief, twist my essence around it, and transform it into a false joy.

Not any longer than it takes me to step back from her hold, at least.

That's the problem with me letting my power have even just a little give. It makes me aware. Aware of everything I could wreck and ruin. But if I don't have Armin to balance me, and if I have the intersection point to take more responsibility for, then this state of awareness is going to have to be my new normal.

"Will you ... stay?" Adeline asks almost tentatively. "The girls aren't up yet, but they'd love to see you. For a late breakfast at least, darling girl?" She clears her throat quietly, uncomfortably. "Bolan isn't here."

I smile. I can't remember Adeline ever treating Armin and me any differently than her own children. I suppose if we'd ever been in public together, she would have been forced to use more formality when addressing us, but that wasn't what our visits here were about.

We could be almost normal here.

The royal guard still patrolled the property, of course. And the neighbors to the east were encouraged to take vacations — not that I knew about that when we were young — so that the guards could use their home as an outpost. "Pancakes? Or ...?"

Adeline laughs, sliding her hands up my arms and squeezing my shoulders gently. "I have leftover sourdough starter. Come inside. I'll get you some juice. And I'll whip up some pancakes."

"Do you mind if I take a walk first?"

Adeline tilts her head thoughtfully, quirking an eyebrow. "Alone?"

"If you don't mind."

"Of course not ..." But she hesitates, glancing over at

Roz. My guard has remained by the car, her eyes on the house, her body language relaxed. Adeline lowers her voice. "Is there something you need to tell me, Mirth? About ... Bolan? Or the matchmaking event?"

I shake my head, attempting to ignore the sinking feeling that Bolan hasn't spoken to his mother. About Rian. "No. I haven't seen Bolan for a couple of days. And ... I ended the matchmaking fiasco."

"You've made a decision?"

"Not ... formally."

"But ... not Bolan?"

My chest tightens. With anxiety? Or trepidation? "You haven't heard from him?"

"Should I have? I thought you were ... did you reject his suit?"

Even with my sunglasses as a barrier between us, I have to look away for a moment to steady myself. Bolan is an asshole. Bolan is always an asshole. But putting me in this position — whether or not he knows he's done it — just reinforces all of that. I either have to tell Adeline about Rian, or I have to lie by omission. "Everything with Bolan is ... difficult."

Adeline snorts playfully. "How is that any different than it's ever been?"

I look back at her, suppressing a sigh. "It isn't."

She grimaces, then wipes her already dry hands on the front of her jeans. "Take your walk. We'll talk more over breakfast."

A slight reprieve is generous of her. Also, out of character. Adeline never relented when we were younger. Not that it was ever me on the wrong end of one of her disapproving looks or biting chastisements or 'no dessert' punishments. I'm fairly certain that Armin sometimes broke little rules — doing things like tracking mud through the house —

because he loved being treated the same as Bolan and his sisters.

I, of course, wasn't ever going to jeopardize a single dessert.

"The pond is pure swamp," Adeline says, proving yet again that she has some level of psychic ability. Or maybe she's just that good at reading me. "Come grab some wellies from the mudroom." She doesn't wait for me to answer, simply sending Roz a look over my shoulder, then striding back into the house.

"Want me to wait here?" Roz asks quietly. "You'd know … wouldn't you? If anyone but the Yates family members were on the property?"

Stepping back to the car to retrieve my backpack and Armin's urn within it, I don't answer for a moment, rolling the implications of that statement around in my head. Loosening the rigid hold on my power hasn't gone unnoticed by Roz. And why would it? She's a combat mage deemed powerful enough to protect one of the direct heirs to the realm.

The sole heir now, marked by my purple-hued eyes. And also by decree of my father.

"I could check in," Roz adds to fill the silence. "Greg is pissed we ditched him a second time, and that Lord Savoy has multiple errands in London in multiple unsecured locations. Plus they've never worked together."

Settling the backpack across my shoulders, I take the intended rebuke, not reminding Roz that I could have left her to run around after Sully instead of Greg. Or that both Sully and I could have just gone off on our own, sans guards altogether.

Roz grimaces at my silence, which feels like its own sort of chastisement. The trust and respect between us is necessary for our relationship to function, but we can't be friends. No matter what I might want. I'm also not really Roz's employer. She's assigned to protect me, but she has no authority over what I do. Or who I choose to spend time with.

Instead of apologizing for overstepping, which in turn would force me to apologize for there even being anything to overstep, she finally says, "Plus, Raoul is insisting on hourly proof-of-life updates."

I laugh quietly, hoping she's exaggerating. Otherwise, she really isn't getting any sleep. "I'm just going to walk down to the pond. And yes, alone. With the way the property slopes, you should be able to see me from the back patio. Though I might walk a little farther through the wooded area ..."

Roz struggles to not look completely put out. Or maybe she's just uncomfortable with ... me? With the shifting in my relationships and my position? She referenced my ability to know if anyone was nearby. I never thought that the potential of what I can do, what I can destroy, might worry my guards. Mostly because I've kept it all so tightly tamped down for so long.

Grinning playfully — because I can't focus on another set of potential problems right now — I tug my phone out of my pocket and wave it at her. "You've got me tracked every minute of every day."

"It's not like that," Roz grumbles.

I laugh. Then I head into the house to grab some boots.

THE YATES COUNTRY HOME — AN ODD NAME, because the family doesn't have a city home — didn't originally include the section of property that contains the pond, replete with duck house and a multitude of ducks, or the wooded hectarage that spreads out beyond the three-level red-brick house. Three levels if you count the attic, anyway. Those sections of property had been sold off years before the current generation of the Yates family settled here. As far as Bolan understood, his mother repurchased those sections after his father's death. She also paid off the remaining mortgage on the house with the money from her husband's royal guard life insurance.

Tuition funds were set aside for Bolan and his sister Olivia as well. Bolan was immediately enrolled in the Prague Phrontistery, joining Armin and me in our first year there. The deliberate intent to pair Bolan and Armin, whose life Bolan's father had died protecting, was now obvious from my adult perspective. But not much thought about by my seven-year-old self.

Olivia, more commonly known as Livi, is three years older than Bolan. She was already an accomplished dancer at age twelve when their father died. She enrolled in a private, extremely competitive conservatory instead of the Phrontistery. Now a lauded ballet dancer, Livi lives at home between performances, her studio tucked away on the western edge of the property.

The two much younger half-siblings, Sophia and Emily, use their father's surname, Harris, not Yates. Age twelve and fourteen, the sisters currently attend a local school. I'm not certain their father and Adeline were ever formally married, or even mated in the shifter way through exchanged bites. As far as I know, they haven't been romantically involved since the girls were quite young. David Harris was never a prominent figure in Bolan's life, and therefore not in Armin's or my life either, though they got along well enough. Bolan's father, James — the father he shares with

Rian — had been dead for over five years before Emily was even conceived.

All of that ancient history flits through my mind as I wander down toward the pond, wellies squelching in the wet grass and Armin's marble urn weighing down the backpack on my shoulders. I pause near the water's edge, scanning the long reeds, still thick and green along the circumference, for swans or ducks but seeing none.

I can feel the house at my back. Or perhaps that's Adeline's and Roz's gazes resting upon me? Either way, it's ... slightly ... disturbing. More an itch than anything nefarious, but it keeps me moving. I skirt around the pond toward the wooded area, the reeds snagging in my duster as I traverse a narrow foot-worn path. We paddled around the pond in an old rowboat when we were younger, though the wooden boat launch we also used for sunbathing has been removed for the winter. Or maybe removed altogether, along with the boat.

I haven't been here for longer than a quick visit in years. Bolan moved out when he left school, taking early graduation to focus on his music.

I should be focusing my thoughts on Armin. On why I felt the need to leave a piece of him here, one of the places he knew only pure happiness. Adeline did her best to treat us the same as her own children, and Bolan — even when he was Oliver — always outright refused to use our titles or treat us any differently than anyone else.

When Bolan wasn't being epically charming to everyone, he was a complete asshole. There was no in-between. Offish. Angry. Dismissive.

Except ... not to me.

He and Armin fought. But like brothers, it always seemed to me.

The path cuts deeper into the woods that encase the far

side of the pond. Tall, slim trees close around me, and I breathe deeply, mindfully. Buds are just starting to form on the silver birch that are well spaced apart in this section of the wooded area. It's newer growth, though old enough that the white, papery bark is peeling on most of the trees. Adeline had the birch planted when she reclaimed the property.

Keeping the pond vaguely to my left, I leave the main path to walk among the trees for a few more minutes until the itch between my shoulder blades eases. I note another foot-worn trail — or rather, worn by wolves' paws — leading back to the pond and a gap in the reeds edging the water. I allow it to pull me back to my purpose.

Crouching, I tug off my backpack and place it on some already flattened reeds in an attempt to keep it out of the mud. The still water is green and not remotely clear. As I watch, delicate rings punctuate the surface in a few places. From fish coming up for air or to eat a bug. Still no swans or ducks, though. Maybe they're happy in their house. Or Adeline has gotten rid of them.

I pull the marble urn out of my backpack, cradling it to my chest, and just ... aching. It's a strange ache, though. Pervasive, but almost tender. Poignant.

I carefully open the lid of the urn, thankful that Sully's sealing spell doesn't disperse under my touch. I pull out a handful of ashes, losing a bunch as I stretch my clasped hand out over the water.

I realize that I'm mourning more than just Armin in coming here. I'm saying goodbye to our shared childhood and the friendship and love that might have been so much more —

I feel him a moment before I realize he's standing on the far edge of the pond with the house at his back. That unwanted awareness I always have in his vicinity.

Bolan.

He stands with his head cocked to one side, bright-eyed gaze riveted to me and glimmering with the essence of his wolf. One of his hands is shoved in the front pocket of his torn, age-worn black jeans, while the other hangs loose at his side. His black sweater is also worn, fraying at the hem and neckline, and long enough to cover his knuckles.

My chest starts aching in earnest. Something torn and ragged lurks in the depths of that pain. Still crouched with my handful of ashes clutched in one hand, I press the urn against my rib cage with the other. Grinding the marble between my breasts as if it might shield me.

But the pain only sharpens, jagged and torn. That soul-deep agony has grown so much worse since Armin died. Worse each time I'm near Bolan, as if Armin was a buffer between us. I don't understand why except … except …

No. I know why.

I know why.

I know that Bolan —

No. I know what Oliver did. All those years ago.

I know.

I've just been in denial. I didn't want to acknowledge it. Because it's so, so much worse than a simple kiss or a childhood crush.

Across the water from me, Bolan stiffens, pressing a hand to his chest and grunting quietly in pain. The sound travels across the still water.

A terrible anger, edged with despair, explodes through me, emanating from my chest and through my limbs. I squeeze my eyes shut, shaking under the onslaught of my own emotions.

I know this is an overreaction, verging on unhinged, but I —

Bolan is suddenly behind me. I don't open my eyes, but I can feel him, even as I try to regain some control of myself.

"Mirth," he murmurs.

I don't answer. The pain writhing in my chest won't let me speak. Crouched with one hand still extended over the edge of the pond, I clutch the pitiful handful of Armin's ashes so hard that my nails feel as if they're cutting into my skin. My entire arm is shaking.

Then Bolan curls around me, his chest to my back. His knees in the mud, legs brushing against mine. He reaches forward, not otherwise touching me, until he curls his fingers under the wrist of my extended hand.

He holds me there, steadies me.

My arm stops shaking.

I manage a ragged breath.

So, so slowly and gently, his other arm comes around me, finding and pressing his hand over my other hand as well, so that we're both cradling the urn to my chest.

I take another breath, feeling my back expanding against his chest.

He's warm.

The pain and anger retracts just enough for me to unclench my jaw and open my mouth. "Let's be done with it," I say, not quite knowing what I mean even as I voice the words.

"If ... if that's what you want," Bolan whispers back.

I can feel his grief. He has it tamped down, practically smothered, but it threads through his words.

I open my hand over the water's edge. Armin's ashes coat my fingers, but I've managed to protect the tiny mound in my palm. Bolan keeps his hand under mine, but I can feel the tremble that runs through him now.

"I have to tell you something," he croaks quietly.

"I already know."

He stiffens as if steeling himself against a physical blow, then shakes his head. "Not ... that. This is ... you need to know this to ... keep moving forward. I think. I ... know ..."

"Then tell me, Bolan," I say, surprised I'm capable of snapping at him while I'm holding a handful of my beloved brother's ashes.

"I know ..." he whispers, close enough that I feel his breath stir my hair and fan across my ear. "I know why."

I freeze, literally numb but completely understanding what he means. *Why.* As in, the *why* that's led to me holding a handful of my brother's ashes in the *now.*

Bolan continues, "I know ... how."

I squeeze my eyes shut, as if I might block out his words even though they're already echoing through my mind, embedding into my brain.

"Tell me," I rasp, forcing myself to open my eyes, to keep breathing, my chest so tight and breath so shallow that I can barely articulate the words.

He swallows harshly, then hesitates.

"Bolan!"

He takes a shuddering breath. "It's just, you ... I can't lose you more than I've already —"

"Tell me, Bolan."

"There's this new drug ..." he whispers.

I close my eyes again, and I'm light-headed suddenly. Actually swaying on my feet. Bolan tugs me a little closer so I don't fall over. It's an instinctual protective reaction, I think, because his tone is remote, almost empty.

Bolan's voice is never devoid of emotion. Never.

"There's always a new drug," I murmur back, waiting for his next words to embed even more shards of pain into my heart. "But the awry aren't affected by ..."

Bolan nods, then swallows again. I still have my eyes shut, still primed to weather whatever he has to tell me. So I feel the movement, the sides of our faces almost pressed together, rather than see it.

I wait in the *before* because I have no choice. I have to survive whatever revelation Bolan needs to tell me.

I've already fallen apart.

I cannot completely disintegrate.

Pampered princess or not, I don't have that particular luxury.

So I hold myself in the moment. I anchor myself, my feet in the mud, the marble urn pressed against my chest ... and within Bolan's arms.

"This one, this drug, is different." Bolan's tone and tenor firm, as if he needs to get the words out, to be done with the secret he's been carrying. "There's been a few variants of it because most dealers have been cutting it with something else. Another suppressant. The original drug was medical grade. Rumor has it that there was some sort of big heist rather than a leak or a single disgruntled chemist. It was developed to ..."

"Take down an awry," I say, opening my eyes to a view of the pond, already knowing the direction of Bolan's tale. "To contain awry."

"Well ..." He clears his throat. "Powerful essence-wielders at least."

"You sourced this for Armin." I make it a statement, not a question.

Bolan flinches. I'm still holding the ashes in the palm of my hand. He's still helping me keep my arm aloft.

"Tell me."

"I got some of the cut stuff from a mage with a potions specialization I buy regularly from. I ... I'm always looking to suppress the wolf."

"And Armin didn't want any of it," I say flatly, as if I'm

simply reciting facts. "Any of the power that teemed within him. Or any of the responsibilities that came with it."

"He just needed an occasional break, Mirth."

"Don't defend him right now," I whisper without heat. "I ... we ... need to ... survive this, don't we? I need to know and to acknowledge the truth of it all."

Bolan inhales shakily. "The stuff I sourced barely dampened Armin. His essence just ... burned it off. I literally could feel heat coming off him moments after he took it."

"The awry are immune to a certain extent to most essence-based spells or potions or ..." I sigh. "But you know that."

"Yeah, I buy from mages or other shifters, mostly. No point in bothering with human or null-made drugs, really. Except for a minor buzz."

"Armin didn't want a minor buzz."

"No."

"He got his hands on the medical-grade stuff," I say quietly. "The uncut, human-made stuff."

"Mirth ..."

"And he took it during your ski trip."

"I ..." Bolan breathes in deeply, his arms tightening around me. "Yes, we took it that night. I ... it honestly scared the absolute shit out of me. I do a lot to suppress the instincts of the wolf when necessary, but I felt ... it was too much. Even for me."

"But not for Armin."

"I don't know. All I know is I woke up late the next morning feeling like my heart had been ripped from my chest. Completely fucking incapacitated. I stumbled into Armin's room, saw his empty, still-made bed. And I knew ... some part of me knew. I tried to track him down, but I couldn't even find his guards. I didn't know what the fuck had happened. I convinced myself that he'd just taken off ... even though he ..."

"Left his luggage at the chalet."

"Yeah. But ... he's done that once before, and I ..." Bolan doesn't finish the thought. Not because he doesn't know what to say, but because he doesn't really want to acknowledge it himself.

"There were no drugs on him," I say, shading around the edges of Bolan's recounting of that morning with everything else I already know. "Unless someone managed to hide them before I arrived to claim ... him ..." My voice cracks.

I felt hollow by that point, after also feeling like my heart had been inexplicably shredded within my chest. Just as Bolan described it. I felt hollow as I was ushered into that cold room to identify the corpse of my brother. "It would be a serious risk for one of his guards or even one of the paramedics to hide that kind of evidence from me, from my father. I suppose it could have been lost in the avalanche, or ..."

"No. There were only three pills," Bolan says. His tone isn't devoid of emotion now. A bright, pulsating anger wars with his grief.

I can feel it battering against me, against all the shields I hadn't quite realized I held between me ... between me and everyone else. Beyond simply suppressing my own essence. This is an emotion-evoked shield that has only thickened, even hardened over, since that night with Oliver — that kiss and rejection and everything that happened after. Born from an overwhelming need, the belief that I had to control myself, myself and everything around me.

"We took two that night."

I clear my throat, focused on anchoring myself in this

moment. This is why I stole Armin's ashes. I need this to move forward. But it … hurts.

It hurts to confirm what I already knew.

Armin made a choice.

"And?"

"And the container was empty the next morning. Armin took the last pill."

"He took a pill that completely suppressed his powers. Then went skiing. On an unplowed run in avalanche conditions."

"It wasn't suicide."

"Then what would you call it?" I snap.

Bolan chokes back a sob, and only then do I realize that he's been doing so over and over since he wrapped himself around me. "It was … we didn't talk about it. For me, it was the worst I ever felt. Almost the worst …" His voice trails off, and his arms tighten around me. "I felt empty, like I'd lost half my soul. I was fucking freaked out of my mind about it, locked myself in the bedroom to ride it out. Alone."

The wolf, he means. The wolf is the other half of his soul, no matter how much he tries to suppress it.

"But Armin?" Bolan shakes his head. "For Armin, I can only guess that it felt like …"

"Freedom," I whisper, focusing on the ashes in my hand. "Skiing always did for him as well. On a smaller scale. It felt like freedom."

"I should have been with him," Bolan croaks. "We were supposed to do that run together."

"I should have been with him," I murmur, brushing my ash-coated fingers together. The small mound of ashes in my palm crumbles at the edges and falls into the water. I fight the instinct to close my hand around the remainder. I have to let it go. I know I do.

"You weren't your brother's keeper. He should have been protecting you. He left you —"

"He left us." I force myself to tip my hand over, allowing the remaining ashes to fall into the pond. When I turn my hand back over again, some ash remains, clinging to my skin. But before I can make the decision to brush it off, Bolan runs his thumb across my palm, across my fingers, brushing away the remnants.

His touch is warm and solid. Comforting.

It's everything I've ever wanted.

So I pull my hand away.

I pivot to put the urn back into my backpack, effectively breaking Bolan's hold on me to do so. Though he still crowds against my back.

"Do you think it's possible for you to ever forgive me?" Bolan asks.

I don't look at him. "Did you shove the pills down Armin's throat? Ever?"

"No, I —"

"Armin made his choices, Bolan. You two might have influenced each other, but ... if I blame you for not being on that ski run with him, then I have to blame myself, right?"

"It's not the same thing —"

I sigh heavily, straightening and leaving Bolan kneeling behind me. The bottom of my duster slaps against my calves, heavily coated in mud. I ignore it, gazing out over the pond for a moment. "It's done. It has to be done now."

"I know."

I pick up my backpack, swinging it over my shoulder. "I can't stay for breakfast. Will you let Adeline know that —"

Bolan wraps his hand around my knee, stopping me from stepping around him. Then he drops even lower in the mud, head hanging forward.

"Bolan ..."

"I need to say the words. I need to —"

"It's done," I say again.

That twist of pain is back in my chest, writhing around my heart. With all my grief over saying goodbye to Armin, of having the simple truth of his senseless death confirmed, I didn't realize the sensation stilled while Bolan held me. That realization comes with an extra slice of agony, right across my heart. But I shove it away. I steel myself against it, as I would if it were a malignant spell or even a knife.

Deflect. Fortify my defenses.

"I know," I whisper.

Bolan's head snaps back. His shoulders stiffen, twisting my way. He gazes up at me with essence-bright eyes. His wolf is present, if not verging on dominant, and his voice rasps as if his vocal cords aren't completely human anymore. "You don't know it all."

I try to move away, but his hold tightens on my leg. "I don't need to hear it."

"I need to say it."

"What will it change?"

"Everything? Nothing?" He shakes his head. "I came after you that night. After you kissed me. I knew I'd made a mistake right away. I knew what I wanted before that kiss, during that kiss, but the wolf ..." He swallows. "The reaction, my reaction ... scared the fuck out of me. I didn't know why ... no. I didn't know for certain. And I had to sort out my head, get the wolf under control. Try to stop myself from just claiming —"

"Would you at least stand?"

He laughs harshly. "I know my place. I know where I belong. On my knees, begging —"

"I'm not interested in your dramatics —"

"Fucking listen to me, Mirth!"

I make another bid for freedom, yanking on my captured leg so hard that I stumble back and almost fall.

Almost fall. Because in the midst of my falling, Bolan springs forward, grabs my hips, and gently lowers me the rest of the way to the ground.

On my ass.

With him now looming over me.

I shove at his chest. My heart is beating wildly.

"Don't run from me," he growls. "I can't handle it a third time."

"Or what?" I snap.

"I'll fucking chase you," he says. A warning, low and deadly. "And if I chase, my wolf will rise. And my wolf wants you. My wolf wants you any way he can have you."

My heart does this weird squelching thing, tripling its intent to seemingly burst free of my chest. Then the truth of his words sinks in.

"Your wolf," I sneer. "But not the man."

Bolan, still anchoring me by my hips, still looming over me, tilts his head in that shifter way. Listening to ... my heartbeat?

He bares his teeth. It's not a smile. "You want to be chased, baby girl?"

"Fuck you, Bolan."

He chuckles darkly.

I get right up into his face and snarl back. "You wouldn't know what to do with me if you caught me, asshole."

His wolf-bright eyes flick to my mouth, then up to ensnare my gaze. Then he slowly, deliberately, peels his fingers off my hips and settles back onto his knees.

On his knees between my legs. And looking at me as if he's in just as much pain. Radiating grief and anger, but waiting for his moment? To reach for what he wants?

My heart thrums against my rib cage as I slowly pull my legs away from him, then get my feet under me. Bolan's head tilts. His pupils are blown out, cobalt-blue eyes edged with the essence of his wolf as he focuses entirely on me.

He watches me as if nothing else exists in the world but each movement I make, each beat of my heart. I'm not entirely certain what's in the process of shifting between us.

Except that pain in my chest? It's warming and expanding.

It's anger, yes. But it's also need. Want. And … hope.

A terrible, potentially soul-destroying, desperate hope.

"You run and I'll follow," Bolan growls. "I'll fuck you where I find you. Then I'll bite you, make you mine. Because I'm tired of denying who I am to you. I'm not remotely worthy of you. I can't do anything to change the circumstances of my birth or the stupid choices I've made out of fear. But the fucking universe says you're mine. You're my soul-bound mate."

I'm not breathing properly. I'm light-headed from it. Or from trying to contain everything … all this emotion. Or maybe from trying to deny everything …

"Don't you fucking run."

I run.

3

OLAN

M IRTH ABANDONS THE BACKPACK, PIVOTS, PLANTS one hand in the mud. Then she fucking springs to her feet and dashes into the woods as if she was born to run.

As if she was born to be chased.

By me.

The wolf slams into me in a desperate attempt to take over, to chase his mate, shoving me forward onto my hands. I'm already on my knees. And I plan to stay on my knees for as long as I need to be there, as long as I need to convince Mirth I'm willing to do whatever it takes to regain her trust.

I lose a few moments in a struggle to gain control of myself. I'm not entirely successful, because my fingers are suddenly tipped with wicked claws, and my incisors are cutting into my bottom lip. The wolf's instincts, his desperate need, flood my mind.

Drug-free for the first time in years and with the wolf

ascendant, I can smell Mirth. The combination of her anger, grief, and need is like a sledgehammer to my brain.

The wolf is convinced we can soothe everything for our mate.

But first she has to be ours, completely.

Not only claimed, but with that claim accepted, reciprocated.

I ease onto my feet, still warring with the instinct to run on all fours.

I can hear each of Mirth's footfalls. Her little gasps and huffs as she inhales and exhales.

I yank off my sweater, then my boots and socks, wrestling the wolf further back instead of also removing my jeans. Then, setting out at a light jog, I follow Mirth deeper into the woods.

I find her long sweater-jacket abandoned about a minute later, snatching it up while still moving steadily after her. I bring it to my nose to scent her. Mirth doesn't wear perfume, she never has. But there's shea butter and jojoba in her skin cream, along with that indescribable but unmistakable scent that is just Mirth. And her essence.

My brain ever-so-helpfully flashes to watching Christoph delicately feed my Mirth slices of peach — to the memory of her bringing the peach to breakfast in the first place — like it was some sort of slow tease between them. As if he weren't the archduke of illegal bareknuckle fights well before his more recently acquired royal titles. I wonder if that's how the hulking bear shifter interprets the sweet tang in her scent. Ripe peach.

Mirth has changed direction. She dropped the sweater in an attempt to confuse me. But I don't need eyes or ears or a sharp nose to find her. She thrums through my chest. She's in my erratic heartbeat, which steadies the closer I get to her.

Deep within the birch trees and well out of view of the main house, Mirth's breathing is ragged as she finally slows her pace to a walk, looking back over her shoulder for me. But I've skirted around her, stalking her to satisfy the wolf ... just a little. Her shoulders stiffen, and she slowly pivots to scan the trees encircling her.

She can feel me.

I've always noted how I can get into her space without her noticing. How Sully could too. I thought it was just pure trust, but now I know for certain it's something else.

Our souls were divided from the same section of the universe. Our destiny is to find and fortify each other on this plane of existence. Through every lifetime.

Whether or not I'm actually worthy of that.

Mirth stills, looking right at me now, though I know the shadows between the trees hide me from her sight.

She could reject me.

The chase, this chase, and the ultimatum could trigger her to fully reject me. And that would be the end of it. Because I've already damaged the bond between us. I can feel it all twisted in my chest. A rejection from Mirth will sever it completely.

"That's it?" she asks softly. Then with a quiet, bitter laugh, she pivots sharply away, heading back toward the house.

That pained laugh knifes through my chest, so harshly that I stumble under the assault and have to stifle a moan.

On the edge of the moment, I've fucking hesitated. Again.

I always have to find the right thing to say. I always need more time to put the words together in a way that doesn't just piss her off —

The wolf surges forward, taking advantage of my confused state to take me over completely. I stumble a few more steps under the internal onslaught. Then I throw my head back as a strangled, grief-filled howl rips through my entire self, my entire being, and out my throat.

My mate.

My mate is rejecting me.

The change from man to wolf floods through me, dangerous and abrupt. The pain is so incapacitating that all I can do is writhe on the muddy ground and endure it.

To my utter horror, when the wolf gains his feet, I'm no longer in full control. I'm shoved into the back of my own mind. The wolf is ascendant and so, so dangerously unchecked.

And Mirth. My darling, perfect Mirth, has run back to us. Run back at my howl. When she should have been fleeing in the opposite direction.

The wolf leaps, easily closing the distance between us and Mirth. He knocks her onto her back, then pins her down with a large paw spanned across her chest. No claws, but the wolf could crush her.

Mirth's purple eyes widen as her concern transforms into panic.

Stop. Stop. Not like this, I scream in my own head.

The wolf doesn't listen. I've denied him for too long, dampened his urges and instincts with a steady diet of mage-wrought drugs and alcohol. He wants his mate. Even though that mate is one of the awry and not another shifter, he's wanted her for even longer than I have — the self-deluded human half of our whole.

He looms over our mate, exerting dominance and baring his teeth. He slowly lowers his huge head. An unvoiced growl vibrates through his chest.

Mirth is too tiny like this, too vulnerable.

He's going to bite her, and —

"Absolutely not," she snaps, coldly fierce and utterly ticked off.

The wolf huffs. But he hesitates for just a moment. Listening. Because he likes Mirth like this — with the perfect-princess mask and the perfectly-in-control tone even while pinned to the ground with an abnormally large wolf salivating over her.

He likes it just as much as I do.

Mirth reaches up, wraps her hand around the wolf's jaw, then clasps his mouth closed. She's so petite compared to my beast that her hand spans only half of the wolf's jaw and nose. But she still grips him firmly, then angles the wolf's head so she can look him deliberately and directly in the eye.

Exactly everything you aren't supposed to do with a wolf shifter.

"You want me, Bolan?" she says firmly, still acting as if she hasn't even noticed the fucking huge beast pinning her to the ground. "You use your words. Or better yet, your fucking mouth. On mine. On me. No games. Just the truth of it all. Make a fucking choice."

Then she addresses the wolf, and yes, there is a difference in her tone, in her intent, even though we're the same being. "I haven't given you permission to touch me."

The wolf exhales in clear dispute. In his mind, he needs no more consent than what's already been granted from the universe.

She narrows her eyes at him. "Either give the man back or go for a run."

Utterly inexplicably, the wolf concedes, stepping to the side. A deep, ferociously pleased contentment sinks into me. The wolf likes our mate's dominance. And ... her acceptance? The wolf doesn't feel rejected at all.

And that ... all these years ... was it the wolf who held

my end of the bond, shredded but not broken? Because Mirth never outright rejected us. Only me, the human part of myself, tried to reject her. More specifically, to reject our bond.

I'm honestly not certain she ever knew what I was to her all those years ago ... what I still am to her.

Mirth gets to her feet with a huff, brushing off her mud-soaked pants as if doing so will improve their condition in any way. Ignoring the wolf, she walks stiffly over to the pile of clothing I left behind when I transformed, and grabs her sweater.

The wolf abruptly retreats from my consciousness, from controlling our form. The transformation floods my limbs, my body, my mind, with utter agony. My spine snaps and reshapes itself until I find myself in control again.

Mirth keeps her back to me as I change, sliding her arms into her long sweater. But she glances over her shoulder, her dark lashes fanning against her cheek, when I'm finally crouched on human feet again, sweating and panting from the change.

She raises her chin. Her nostrils flare as she readies some poised and perfect retort. Some sure-to-be-ball-withering rejoinder already primed on her lips.

I straighten.

She blinks, taking me in. I'm completely nude, wearing nothing but the tattoos that scribe my arms and chest — and completely erect. Totally hard and ready to take up the challenge she issued. To use my fucking mouth on her if I can't find the words that I need to say and she needs to hear.

Her lush lips part as I stalk toward her. Sharp sparks of the transformation from wolf to man still run across my skin. Whatever she was about to say dies on her tongue. Perhaps at the sight of my bobbing cock.

So I take that mouth, those lips, for myself.

Threading my fingers through her already mussed hair, I cradle her head in one hand and her hip in the other. I crush her against me. And I just fucking kiss her.

I kiss her like I should have kissed her in the fucking rowboat eleven years ago. Even if I'd never admitted it to myself before Mirth kissed me, I knew what I was doing, what I wanted, when I brought her out on the lake and played her that song.

I kiss her like I should have kissed her the next day, when I knew deep in my soul that I'd made an epically stupid mistake. But when I asked around, no one had any idea where she and Armin had gone. Or why they'd left school so abruptly.

I kiss her like I should have kissed her a thousand times between then and now.

I kiss her like I should have after Armin's death.

I should have been the one to go to her. I should have risked the outright rejection I knew I deserved. I should have waited outside her apartment. Or at the gates of whatever castle walls she was sequestered behind.

I try to pull back. Just enough to give Mirth some of the words, to articulate some of the feelings rampaging through my brain. But she wraps her arms around me, twisting her fingers in my hair and kissing me back like I'm the only thing holding her together. Like she needs me more than oxygen, more than anything.

And I can do that. I've been shit at everything else she's needed in our life together. But I'm capable of holding her, touching her. I can help anchor her in the moment, to just feel.

I palm her ass, bending my knees enough to grind against her core. Just in case she missed how much I want her. She gasps into my mouth, eyes half closed, fingers twisting harshly in my hair.

"No more games, Bolan," she says, sucking lightly on my bottom lip. My cock twitches as if her hot mouth were sucking on it instead. "If you want me, you follow through now."

Not totally clear if she's being explicit, explicitly specific, I shake my head a little to clear it. It doesn't help. "Now?"

"Yes." She says it in that perfectly poised and cool tone that makes my balls ache. In need of her. "Fuck me now, here, or walk away one last time."

"Here ...?" I echo like an idiot. "I can't fuck you in the woods, Mirth. You are —"

She grabs my hair hard enough to yank my head to the side. "Then don't make any more promises you can't keep!"

Her bright, potent anger is like a sledgehammer square to the chest, over my heart. She loosens her grip on me, stepping away and leaving me chilled without her.

I've missed something. Again. I try to think through the lust, through the haze of transforming twice in a row, of almost losing myself to the wolf.

Mirth must notice my confusion, because for once in our long years of terrible communication — all of that my fault — she offers clarification. Though not without a mockingly arched eyebrow and a now-ball-chilling look. "You said that if I ran, if you caught me, you'd —"

"I said ..." A grin spreads across my face. I can actually feel the arrogance well up to radiate from me. "I'd fuck you where I found you."

She takes a measured step back — taunting, eyes gleaming in challenge. "Liar, liar, Bolan."

I lunge.

She pivots, trying to run again.

I get a handful of her long sweater, yanking her back against me. She throws her head back, trying to smash my face with her skull. She hits my shoulder instead. Wrapping a hand loosely around the front of her neck to secure her against me, I press my rock-hard cock to her ass.

She gasps. With desire.

Instincts still riding me hard, I nip the bare patch of skin between her neck and shoulder. Hard in reprimand, but not breaking the skin.

She shouts in surprise and tries to twist out of my arms.

I thrust my hands up her top, palming her breasts roughly while squeezing her nipples through her bra with my fingers.

Her mew of protest turns into a groan as she arches, pressing her breasts into my hands while rubbing her delectable ass against my cock.

Already panting, I yank her bra down just enough to free her breasts, palming one as I grind against her. Then I shove my hand into the front of her jeans to cup her pussy.

She huffs playfully at the rough treatment, reaching back to twist one arm around my head — as if I'm going anywhere — while she scores her blunt-cut nails up my other forearm.

Light-headed and so fucking hard that I'm slightly worried I'm going to fucking come before I even get Mirth's pants off, I swiftly readjust, snagging both of her wrists and drawing them, captured in one hand, to her own chest, keeping her pinned to me.

With my free hand, I yank her pants and her lacy white underwear down to her ankles.

She writhes in my hold, playing at fighting me.

But I can feel that frayed cord of energy churning in my chest.

I can feel it reaching for her.

And I need ...

I need to be inside her. That will fortify our connection.

And I need that between us. We need to start healing. Together.

"Mirth?" I ask, not really able to articulate myself but just making sure she's actually with me.

"Don't stop, Bolan," she snarls.

I lower her to the ground on her knees, going down on my own knees behind her. Until I'm holding her as I did at the pond. She arches her back for me, presenting her ass.

"So fucking perfect," I groan, grabbing her hip even as I keep her wrists pinned to her chest. Thankful that my last transformation ensures I'm not totally covered in mud — my hands or my cock — I line myself up. Sliding my cock against her warm pussy from behind, coating my tip in her wetness. And somehow — rather heroically, it feels — I manage to not just blindly thrust all the way into her like the fucking beast I am.

She moans, arching even more to try to give me better access. I hold her still, crowding over her back, and carefully coat my entire length in her warmth. Cognizant of her little gasps when I rub against her clit, I try to hold off just a little longer. But she begins to writhe against me in need, so I notch my tip within her, gently easing into her — slowly in and out — until I'm fully seated, fully encased.

She's tight, and so fucking warm and wet. I squeeze my eyes shut, trying to slow my breathing, to focus. Then I realize ...

"Mirth ... I don't have a condom —"

She responds to that by shifting slightly away, slightly forward, then settling back even deeper on my cock. Then she clenches all her internal muscles around me, deliberately, demandingly.

Fuck. Fuck.

I'm holding her too tightly for her to ride me. And that

isn't what she wanted. She wanted me to fight for her, take her, make her mine.

I guide her hands to my knees on either side of her legs, then press between her shoulder blades, forcing her to lean more forward. It's still an awkward angle. But unable to hold myself back any longer, I start fucking her.

She moans, then almost shrieks when I find her breast and pinch her nipple with one hand, seeking out her clit with the other.

"Can you come like this?" I ask, panting the words between hard, steady thrusts, barely pulling out before bottoming out over and over again. As if I can't actually bear to move more than a few centimeters away from her.

"I don't …" she groans. "I don't … know."

"We can —" I try to slow my pace, but Mirth's nails dig into my knees, letting me know exactly what she wants. For me to continue. "I've … I've never been bare like this … and it's you, it's you, and I'm not …"

Pleasure stretches up my legs, exploding across my tailbone, as my orgasm hits fast and hard. Literally out of nowhere. I don't know how I manage to do so, but I pull out — Mirth shouting in dismay — and ejaculate half into the churned mud and half onto my own leg.

I'm still fucking coming when Mirth twists to get her hand wrapped around my cock and strokes out the last few spurts.

"That was my fucking come," she snarls.

Before I can respond — still shaking from ejaculating so hard — she captures my mouth with hers and grabs my hand, guiding it between her legs.

I press kisses along her jaw and neck, letting her show me how she wants to be fingered — two fingers, pressed on either side of her clit and at a rapid pace. I'm still fucking high, high on Mirth, when she stiffens, then relaxes completely in my arms. Her head lolls back on my shoulder, neck stretched and open toward me. She arcs up, pressing herself into my fingers. Her hand tightens on my wrist. Her breath catches, mouth dropping open with a groan. Then she shudders against my chest, cradled against me, as she orgasms.

Energy pours from Mirth, and all I can do is try to watch her, watch her face, as I tease the lingering quivers of pleasure from her.

I soften my touch, switching up the rhythm, until her perfect fucking teeth pinch down on her lush lower lip and she shudders out a second orgasm, having never completely come down from her first.

Utter satisfaction, utter contentment floods from her into me as I cup her pussy, brushing my lips up and down her neck. A bruise is slowly forming where I've bitten her. And I'm a fucking asshole because it satisfies me that I've marked her so overtly.

The tightness in my chest eases. I know this is just a step taken toward each other, but I ... I'm not quite so wounded anymore, and I hope ...

Mirth reaches to cup my face, and I realize that I've been crying. She curls her fingers over mine on her pussy, pressing her ass firmly against my groin. And yes, I'm already hardening again.

"I love you," I whisper, shamelessly sucking on that bruised bit of skin. "Don't say it back. Not yet. But I've loved you for a very long time, and I tried to be your friend. I tried to keep it that way. You and Armin. I never wanted to be anywhere but with the two of you ..."

My voice breaks as I struggle, just for a breath, with the utter loss of my soul brother, Armin.

Mirth takes in a shuddering breath, battling her own grief.

"I've been such an idiot." I clear my throat. "I convinced myself, when you finally came back to school, that the kiss meant nothing to you. You were so sweet and nice, and I ..."

"It had to mean nothing, Bolan," she whispers. "I had to shut down all of it ... to control my powers."

She snuggles back into me. Still cupping her pussy with one hand, I cinch my arms around her in a firm cuddle.

I should straighten her clothes, salvage what I can of mine, and get her out of the cold. But I need just a moment longer. I suddenly have too much to say and not any of the words I need to articulate it all.

"Those were the longest six months of my life," I confess. "Without you. And I knew why. I didn't want to acknowledge it. Because you'd ... moved on, and that was right. That was the right thing to do. To keep it clear between us. I could be friends with Armin, but you're a fucking princess! And I —"

"That's not how I ever saw it." The post-orgasm contentment leeches from her tone as I piss her off. Again. As always. "You think I thought I was somehow better than you? Better than everyone else?"

"That's not what I meant," I say lamely. "Of course you didn't —"

She huffs.

But she doesn't push my hand away from her pussy. She doesn't move her perfect fucking ass away from my hard cock.

"I should just keep my mouth shut and fuck you again," I croon into her skin just behind her ear.

She shudders, then quietly giggles.

That laugh is like a hit of ecstasy. It filters through into my chest, surrounds my heart, and ... and ...

"I'm yours," I say, more stupid tears dripping down my

face. "I'm yours, Mirth. I'm sorry I fucked it all up. And I'm sorry I haven't been with you … helped you through losing Armin."

"We could have … should have helped each other," she says sadly.

I slide my hand away from her pussy, wrap my arm around her hips, and rock her against my chest. She turns her head, pressing her face into my neck.

"Let me try now?" I ask.

"Okay," she says.

She doesn't tell me she loves me. Or that she belongs to me as much as I do to her. But she's giving me a chance. And that's more than I thought I'd ever have with her again.

I feel her smile against my neck. "Now that we aren't actually fucking, it's a little weird to have my pants around my ankles and you completely naked."

I chuckle. "Is your pussy getting cold, Mirth? I'm happy to warm it."

She snorts a delicate laugh. "Your mother promised me pancakes."

"Well, that's a mood killer."

She laughs again. Then I let her go just enough to get her clothing straightened, even as mud crusted as it is. My jeans, shredded by my transformation, aren't remotely salvageable, so I don't bother dressing. I'm not fucking walking back to the house in only a sweater and boots.

Naked, I carry everything clutched in one hand and capture Mirth's hand in the other, guiding her back toward the house. We retrieve her abandoned backpack, Armin's urn still safely tucked within it, at the edge of the pond.

Armin could be just as impetuous and self-destructive as me. But he wouldn't have been pleased with me fucking his beloved sister in the woods.

I laugh, covering the sob still lodged in my chest.

Mirth twines her fingers through mine. "Armin?" she murmurs, as if she can read my mind. And since my soul is carved from hers, maybe she can.

"Yeah. I was just thinking ... he'd beat the shit out of me, with his actual hands, if he saw us now."

Mirth hums, not denying my assessment. But then she grins, looking at me with a delighted — and yes, satisfied — smile. Her eyes are bright purple. "He'd get over it. He'd never deny me anything I truly wanted."

Me. She wants me. My heart swells painfully, hurting with how much I love her. "I want you," I say, instead of blathering more declarations that she's not ready to match. "In every way, every day."

She flushes prettily. "You just had me."

"I always want you."

She leans into me, tilts her head up, and brushes the lightest of kisses against my lips. Her sweater gapes open at the neck, and my gaze snags on the bruise darkening her shoulder. From my bite. Possessiveness and smug arrogance floods through me. Again.

It isn't a claiming mark. I would have needed to break the skin, and Mirth would need to bite me in return for me to claim her as one shifter claims another. Not that I know if that sort of essence connection would even work between an awry and a shifter. But I brush an answering kiss over the bruise nonetheless — along with a soul-deep, silent promise — then nip lightly at her ear.

Just to get one of those sweet, quiet giggles from her.

Her eyes glinting purple, energy threading between our clasped hands, Mirth keeps flicking her gaze to me as we walk back to the house. I meet that gaze steadily every time she looks — not that I've looked away from her for more than a moment since she goaded me into fucking her.

I want her to know I'll always be here. Any time she looks for me, looks my way, I'll be here.

THANKFULLY, I FIND CLEAN SWEATPANTS IN THE mudroom. They're black like I prefer, even if a little tight. All the shifters in residence — my mother and sisters — are slighter than me, even in my still-near-emaciated state.

Mirth hangs her backpack on one of the empty coat hooks, pouting at me playfully as I pull up the sweats to cover my still fucking half-hard cock.

I've got her pinned back against the wall, inhaling her little gasp of surprise, before I realize I've moved.

"Wolf," she teases, nipping on my lower lip and recognizing who was momentarily in control even before I did.

"Since I so easily captured you again," I rasp into her neck, palming her ass and lifting her up to wrap her legs around me, "I might as well take full advantage."

"Easily?" she teases. Joy practically sparks off her, embedding into me wherever our skin touches. "Maybe I should play harder to get."

I laugh almost involuntarily. Then, once again distracted by the mere sight of it, I languidly lick the bite mark on her shoulder. "I've missed you, love, so much that it —"

"Oh, good! You found each other. Mirth, did you want ..." My mother walks around the corner, her jaw dropping open as she lays eyes on us.

"Maple syrup?" Mirth chirps playfully. Smiling, and still radiating that gentle joy even while pressed against the wall with her limbs tangled around me.

"Oh ..." My mother's smile dies. Her tanned skin pales.

Her bright-blue gaze flicks to me, then to Mirth, and back again. She clenches her hands at her sides. "Bolan ... this is ... not ... what is happening?"

Mirth, now frowning — though not as deeply as I am — presses against my shoulders. I step back just enough to let her slide down my body, but I keep her tucked against me. I'm not certain I'm actually capable of letting her go right now.

My mother's lips twist as she takes in our shared disheveled state. I haven't torn any of Mirth's clothing, but she's covered in dirt and other leafy detritus. Then my mother's nostrils flare — smelling us on each other.

More pissed at her reaction than embarrassed, I open my mouth to tell her off. Because yeah, while I might be shit at staying connected to my own fucking emotions, I know how to be angry, and she's just adding to the things I'm fucking irate about when it comes to her.

Apparently heedless of my ire, my mother snarls — then suddenly darts forward to yank the neck of Mirth's sweater to the side.

To better see the bite mark.

"What have you done?" my mother snarls. Again. At me. As if I'm some young pup.

"I'm pretty certain I don't have to explain how sex works to you," I drawl. "Mother." I tilt my head, all belligerent. "Or consent, for that matter. But I'm also pretty certain you need a lesson in truth telling."

My mother blinks at me, momentarily thrown by my seemingly random accusation. Then her expression firms, eyes narrowing, lips pressed together. "Do you know what you've done?" she hisses. "You do not bite one of the awry. You can't just fuck —"

Mirth wraps her hand around my mother's wrist — skin-to-skin.

With a sickening whoosh through my stomach, I realize that my mother still has Mirth's sweater clutched in her hand. She's still pulling it to the side to expose her neck and shoulder.

No one touches Her Royal Highness without permission.

If Roz had been anywhere nearby, my mother would already be on the ground.

My mother's gaze slowly shifts to where Mirth is now holding her. I see the same realization dawn across her face. Then a flicker of fear in the depths of her blue eyes.

"Is it me specifically?" Mirth asks quietly. "Or all of the awry you hate?"

My mother takes a shaky breath. "That's not ... I could never hate you, Mirth. I'm not ... I'm just shaken ... I love you, darling." She deliberately peels her fingers back, releasing her hold on Mirth's sweater.

But Mirth still holds her wrist.

My mother swallows harshly. "I just ... your friendship was already ..." Her gaze flicks to me, now filled with a remorse I don't understand. "It's always going to be a parent's instinct to protect ... but if Bolan has hurt you ..."

A terrible yawning pain opens up within me. I've mistaken my mother's reaction. "You think —"

"He hasn't," Mirth says firmly. Then her voice cools to skin-blistering levels. "He wouldn't. He's mine. Whether or not you approve." She releases my mother's wrist.

My mother instantly snatches her arm back, cradling it against her chest. I've always found Mirth's energy enticing. But obviously my mother feels much differently.

"You're both adults," she says. "I can't tell you what to do, but this choice is reckless. Bolan, your father died protecting —"

"I'm confused," I say, drawing Mirth tighter against me

when she tries to turn away and reach for her backpack. To leave. "Are you concerned that I raped Mirth, or that she has purple eyes?"

My mother's nostrils flare. "Neither. Of course not! Don't try to twist this, Bolan —"

"Into what?" I ask mockingly. I'm suddenly so fucking angry that I want to snatch Mirth up in my arms, leave the fucking house, the fucking property, and never look back. "The truth?"

"You know I love Mirth. As I loved Armin. But they are ... their friendship has always been ... dangerous. For us all."

Mirth flinches.

I stifle a growl, but it still rumbles unvoiced through my chest. "The friendship you benefited from, you mean? You never turned down all the gifts —"

"Gifts!?" My mother sneers. "Blood money for your father."

"No. I believe that blood money ... for him doing his sworn duty ... came in a lump sum before I ever met Armin or Mirth."

"Bolan," my mother says, visibly trying to calm herself. "A mating bite —"

"Not that it's any of your business, but you can clearly see I didn't break the skin."

"But you still bit her! And that is ..." She inhales deeply. "That's not —"

"You fucking helped me get ready for the fucking matchmaking event! What the fuck did you think would happen?"

My mother sags a little, swaying on her feet.

I fill in the blanks. "You thought I wasn't good enough for Mirth."

"I love you, Bolan, but why must you always have to be so dramatic!? You cannot mate the heir to the United

European Nation. It will never happen. She needs ... Mirth needs ... a prince."

My voice softens under a momentary onslaught of grief. "The prince is dead."

My mother reels back from me, hurt and shocked.

I press her anyway.

"Armin took a chunk of my soul with him when he died. Fortunately, Mirth owns the rest." I swallow, then make an acknowledgement out loud for the first time. "I'm part of the Savoy bond group. It was never just one prince fated to Mirth. It was six of us. Originally."

My mother blinks at us, unable to fully absorb — or, more accurately, to process — my claims.

But it's Mirth's energy that surrounds me, that steadies me, as her eyes turn from my mother to me. I can feel that purple-eyed gaze sliding across my face. And when I turn to her, I see she's gazing up at me with sadness, but with more of that gentle joy as well.

"We're soul bound." Mirth smiles, hesitant. It's the first time she's acknowledged the connection between us. Out loud, at least.

I don't like the sadness, the tentativeness, underlying that smile, so I pull her into me, pivoting so my back is to my mother. So I'm shielding Mirth from her weirdly judge-mental gaze. I cup her face and press my forehead to hers so that I'm all she sees as I whisper, "We were carved out of the same bit of the universe. Soul bound to find each other through each life we spend walking the earth."

Mirth just gazes up at me, capturing what little of me still belongs to me alone in the depths of her eyes. I know I still need to prove myself. I know it will take another life-time to do that, but this moment, right here, is everything I need to —

Behind me, my mother huffs. "Well, at least you're both

just as delusional as the other. And yes, I have maple syrup." She pivots away.

As if that's the end of the conversation.

As if she can freak out, say a bunch of shit, then just walk away.

I keep my forehead pressed against Mirth's, but I raise my voice so my mother knows I'm addressing her. "I can hear Sophia and Emily moving around upstairs. Is Livi around? She's going to want to be here for the next part of this conversation."

My mother hesitates halfway out of the mudroom.

I glance at her over my shoulder, still so fucking angry about what she's kept from me. What she's kept from all my siblings. "You'll never guess who else is part of the Savoy bond group."

Not content to be hidden from view, Mirth shifts slightly to the side. I'll have to get used to that, to not being able to hoard her away from the world.

Mirth's movement draws my mother's gaze, and Adeline Yates Harris finally rallies enough to remember who she's supposed to be in this moment. "Congratulations, Mirth. I'm so pleased you found your … mates."

"You don't believe in such connections?" Mirth says quietly.

My mother's shoulders stiffen. It's subtle, but I catch it.

"I always thought you and dad were chosen mates," I say, unable to adopt as much of Mirth's poise as I would like.

"We were," my mother snaps defensively.

"Is that why the bite mark bothers you?" I ask. "Because you two never exchanged bites?"

"That is none of your business."

"It is when you've been hiding a baby brother from us all."

My mother's eyes widen. I'm not sure what she was expecting, but it wasn't that accusation.

She also knows exactly what I'm talking about.

I press her. "How long have you known? Were you even together when Dad died?"

"Of course we were. We were married, committed to each other."

"He couldn't have gotten another shifter pregnant if you were bite bonded."

"That's ridiculous. A dangerous myth and an utter lie."

"I imagine a DNA test would make it all very clear to you," I say, knowing I'm being nasty but absolutely unable to stop myself. "I imagine the fact that he ... Rian ... that he looks like a fucking replica of Dad —"

"That's enough, Bolan. My relationship with your father isn't in question, and I don't believe for a moment that —"

The sound of rapid footsteps overhead — one of my younger sisters running down the hall — interrupts my mother's impassioned denial. She snaps her mouth shut, levels a warning look at me, and spins away. As if I won't just follow her into the kitchen.

I thread my fingers through Mirth's. Her skin is chilled. But when I pause to check on her, she just regards me with her purple eyes softly glowing and her chin raised — ready to stand where I now need her. At my side.

Still, I need to justify my behavior, so I latch onto just one of the things currently bothering me. "If I had a brother, I had a right to know. I had a right to have him in my life, if he wanted to be. And now ... now I need ..."

"You need Rian to know that," Mirth says softly. "You need him to know that you would have fought for him. Will fight for him."

"I'm tired of letting people down. My people."

"Your bond mates."

I nod at her understanding. At her acceptance. I'm not sure why doing so makes my chest ache, though. Maybe because I don't deserve her. I open my mouth to say some of that, any of that. But Mirth just touches my cheek, then brushes her fingertips across my cheekbone and down my jaw.

"I'm going to fuck up," I murmur. "I know I am, but —"

"I've seen all your so-called fuck-ups, Bolan. Literally witnessed them. My eyes are wide open."

"I'm so sorry —"

"That's not what I meant," Mirth says a little sharply. Calling me so effectively to heel that my wolf presses against my skin, rumbling and pleased. "You say you're mine."

"Yes. Utterly. Devotedly."

"And ... when haven't I been yours? When haven't I taken your side against the world?"

I grin at her. Fuck, I'm changeable today. Like always, maybe. "If you like, I can recount the number of times you've been livid with me just in the last week."

"That's between us. It has nothing to do with this conversation with your mother," she says, all poised and pretty.

As if we haven't just been fucking in the dirt. As if she hadn't taunted me, taunted my wolf, until I claimed her exactly as she wanted to be claimed, harsh and ready. As if she hadn't shoved my hand back between her legs while I was still recovering from coming so hard I could barely stay upright, demanding to come herself and showing me exactly how to help her do it.

And yeah, no matter how mind-altering that orgasm was, I'm never going to forget her snarling 'that was my fucking come' right before she milked my cock.

"What are you thinking?" Mirth murmurs, eyes glinting.

I shake my head, stepping back from her even as I tighten my hold on her hand. "These sweatpants are way too tight for us to follow the path of my thoughts right now."

She flushes, then deliberately drops her gaze to my crotch.

I catch her chin, raising her eyes back to meet mine. Then keeping my eyes wide open, I lean in and brush a gentle kiss across her lips.

She doesn't close her eyes either.

She looks right at me, accepting. I know it's tentative between us. That I'll have to earn her trust. But I'll do anything, anything it takes to be worthy of her friendship and our bond.

LIVI, MY OLDER SISTER, IS STANDING BEFORE THE massive granite kitchen island with her dark-blue eyes fixed to our mother, who is spooning fruit salad into smaller bowls with her back to the rest of us. Barefoot, Livi's thrown an oversized light-brown sweater over her ballet exercise gear. She's tall and slim, her dark-blond hair slicked into a bun on the top of her head.

And she's livid. At Mom. Livid like she overheard a good portion of our conversation.

Livi glances our way as Mirth and I step through from the mudroom. She gives me a cursory once-over — like she might be triaging me for damage — and comes up with a smirk. Then she pivots like the masterful dancer she is as she executes a perfect bow to Mirth.

The princess at my side snorts delicately. Then as mockingly as she can, Mirth flicks her fingers for Livi to rise.

She hates people bowing to her. Always has.

I should do it more often.

"Olivia," Mirth says.

"Your Royal Highness. You look ... well."

Well fucked.

I almost say it out loud. Though my smirk most likely speaks for itself. Because Livi shakes her head at me before turning her attention back to our mother.

"So ..." Livi says. "Who is Rian?"

"Our half-brother," I say, tugging Mirth close enough to the island that I can steal one of the sausages my mother is now plating. I catch the moment she thinks about swatting me with the metal tongs she's using, then stops herself.

"A kid Dad had before he died?" Livi asks, her tone still level like she isn't almost as angry as I am.

I sniff the purloined sausage, confirming it's turkey, then offer it to Mirth. For her to bite. To eat from my hand. My princess gives me a quelling look, then delicately nips the end off the sausage, chewing it.

I chuckle, somewhat amazed that I can be so livid and so fucking overwhelmingly in love at the exact same fucking time.

"Really?" Livi sighs. "I get to watch this unfold right now?"

I stuff the rest of the sausage in my mouth. To stop the cocky, completely inappropriate shit that wants to fall out of it.

"Rian?" Livi prompts.

My mother throws a dark look at me. "Just leave it."

"Rian was born after your father died," Mirth says, her tone edged in defiance. She's just as tired of not speaking her truth as I am.

"You know him?" Livi asks, head tilted.

"Yes." Mirth is calm despite the energy pouring off my mother now. Off all of us. She looks at me, those purple eyes feeding my soul even as they pin me in place. "He's mine. Like Bolan is mine."

I can tell she expects me to protest. To demand that she choose between us.

I'm not that fucking stupid. "Yeah," I say, grinning like the cocky asshole I am. "Catching you straddling him in bed, all naked, made that crystal fucking clear."

Livi's mouth drops.

My mother's cheeks flush. In disapproval.

Some pieces of our past family dynamics start clicking together for me. Like why we were never sworn to a shifter pack.

"There was nothing to catch," Mirth says coolly. "I'm not hiding any of you."

"Any of you?" Livi echoes. "How, um, I mean ... you mean there's more than just Bolan and this Rian?"

"That is also none of your business, Livi," my mother snaps. Her head tilts, listening.

I catch the murmured strains of Sophia and Emily arguing from the front hall a moment later.

"It's called a bond group," I say to Livi, gleefully defying my mother now. Normally, I'm just an absent asshole, literally not around. But apparently, claiming Mirth has already changed me. Because I'm here, and I'm fighting for the family I want now. Whether or not they're blood related to me.

"Not a pack?"

"Nope. Only three of us are shifters."

"And ... all of you are together? But, um ... isn't Rian ..."

"My long-lost brother? Yep. I'm not obligated to get anywhere near his dick, if that's what's bothering you."

Livi slaps me on the shoulder. Hard.

"That's enough," my mother hisses. "The girls don't need to hear this!"

Looking my mother dead in the eye, I add, "It's Mirth who has to juggle us all. Well, as many of us as she wants."

Livi's mouth opens and closes a couple of times. Then a big fucking grin swamps her face, and she giggles. "Right fucking on, Mirth!"

Mirth's face, already a little flushed, goes up in flames.

My younger sisters, Sophia and Emily, chattering excitedly, choose that moment to pretty much tumble into the kitchen. All long limbs and blazing smiles, they rush me, both jostling each other to be first.

They're within reach when their senses catch up to their impulses and they realize that Mirth is in the kitchen as well.

They stumble to a halt, shriek in unison, and slam their hands over their mouths. Then they bow. Deeply.

Livi cackles. Loudly, and as mockingly as only an older sibling can be without saying a word.

Practically panicking, Emily, the elder of the two at fourteen, realizes her mistake first. She quickly curtsies instead and tries to tug Sophia to follow her lead. Instead, Sophia collapses on top of her sister, and they go down in a tangle of arms and legs.

I side-eye Mirth, noting that she's actually struggling to maintain a straight face.

My mother slams the hot plate of pancakes down on the kitchen island so hard the plate cracks in two. A few pancakes slide onto the floor, tumbling to land at Mirth's feet.

Silence settles over the kitchen. The girls peer up at all of us, slowly straightening.

"What's wrong?" Sophia asks.

"What's going on?" Emily says, overlapping her sister's question.

Livi crosses her arms, abruptly irate though she was laughing her ass off a moment before. She leans against the kitchen island and all but snarls, "Mirth and Bolan are soul bound. They're part of a bond group that includes our half-brother, Bolan and my dad's kid, who Mom knew all about and hid from us all."

Emily and Sophia turn wide eyes from Mirth and me to Livi, and then to our mother. A look of utter betrayal filters across Sophia's face even as Emily's energy shifts to match Livi's.

"A brother!" Emily explodes.

My mother throws her oven mitts on the counter, one at a time, then she sweeps a look over us all. Her voice is cold and full of vitriol when she finally speaks.

"Bond groups are unnatural. A true commitment can only happen between one man and one woman. James wanted to bring another, younger woman here. He insisted she belonged with us. That she was his chosen, like I should be. When she was really just another wolf willing to whore herself out for position. It's her own fault she cheated and got herself pregnant."

Every word that falls from my mother's lips completely alters my perception of her, of my childhood.

A terrible, heavy silence threads through the room. It's full of confusion and a deep sadness. Mostly from Mirth, I think, because it's my darling perfect princess who speaks first.

"I'm sorry you feel that way, Adeline."

My mother swallows, her icy demeanor faltering a little.

As if it's okay to spew that shit to her children, but not to Her Royal Highness. "I ... I understand that you are awry, Mirth. The rules are different for you."

"Different how?" Livi asks. "Lots of wolves are polyamorous."

My mother clenches her teeth. "The awry are ... different than us."

"Different? As in somehow incapable of making true commitments?" Livi says disdainfully. "You think Armin and Mirth haven't cared for us all these years?"

"They've done their duty to you both," my mother says stiffly. "Their friendship is very valuable."

"Valuable," Livi mockingly echoes.

"That's not what I —"

"And ..." Sophia interrupts our mother with a firm whisper, "I don't understand the man-and-woman thing? Some people don't identify with a singular gender or even the gender they were born with. You ... Mom ... you think nonbinary people aren't capable of making a true commitment?"

"What about queer people?" Emily asks, her tone harsher than her sister's. "Where do they fit into your tidy little world view?"

"That's ..." My mother clenches her hands into fists at her sides, looking between all of us — except for Mirth. "That's not what I meant. Don't twist my words."

Emily and Sophia glance at each other. Some silent communication passes between them, and they nod practically in unison.

"We're heading over to our dad's," Sophia says.

"Don't be silly," my mother says. "Bolan just got home —"

I open my mouth, but Livi interrupts me.

"I'll drive you." My older sister eyes our mother pointedly, then says, "Just in case anyone is wondering where I stand on all of this, I'm currently fucking three people. My dance instructor, a mage friend from school, and the woman who runs the fucking dance academy. Yep, not only is she a woman, but she's fifteen fucking years older than me."

My mother's mouth drops open.

Livi continues, "And after I drop the girls to their dad's, I'm going to introduce them all in a group text and see if they all want to fuck me at the same time."

My mother turns on her heel and walks out of the room.

After a moment, the front door opens, then slams closed. A beat later, a car engine engages.

Roz, Mirth's royal guard, pokes her head into the kitchen from the direction of the mudroom. "Everything okay in here?"

No one answers her, so she nods, then retreats back the way she came.

Livi glances at me. "Did that go the way you thought it would?"

"Not remotely. But you don't seem all that surprised. About the discriminatory shit."

Livi sighs, opening her arms toward Emily and Sophia. They both lurch forward to be enfolded in her embrace. "There's a reason I haven't mentioned who I'm dating."

"I had no idea."

"You haven't been here, Bolan," my sister says. "I'm not blaming you, but ..." Her eyes flick to Mirth for a moment. "You found your soul family at age nine."

"You've barely lived here yourself," I say defensively.

"Yeah, I missed it until I moved back. After I finally ditched Edward."

Emily peers up at Livi, then over toward Mirth and me. "How cold do you think the pancakes are?"

"Do you care?" Sophia asks.

"Nope!"

Trust a wolf to default to the yearnings of her stomach in the middle of a family crisis.

Emily and Sophia grab a stack of plates from the cupboard, then start serving themselves.

"I'm so sorry," Mirth whispers to me.

"I'm shocked." I press a kiss to her forehead, then tug her toward the breakfast to see what we can salvage. "But I'm not sorry."

4

$\mathcal{M}$IRTH

THE YATES-HARRIS HOUSEHOLD IS IN SUCH AN uproar after the confrontation with Adeline that, after eating only a few bites of breakfast, I blow way past the emotional onslaught I've been attempting to ignore until I'm actually swaying in my seat. Bolan, in the middle of an agreeable rant with Livi about their mother's past misdeeds, sees this, then promptly scoops me up and carries me the three flights into his attic room.

I fall asleep snuggled in his arms in his single bed. Just as I had fantasized about doing almost every time we visited in our youth.

I sleep hard, but the light hasn't shifted much when I wake. I blink up into the open rafters as the edges of the small room slowly come into focus. The walls around the low bed are lined in decades-old glam-rock posters, including one directly overhead with a scantily clad, big-haired, extremely sexy woman surrounded by likewise big-haired, bare-chested skinny men in gold leather pants and heeled boots.

All the posters were hung by a much younger Bolan. But the wall above the long, low bureau and the top of the bureau itself have been turned into a shrine of sorts for Bolan's band, the Blitz. Band posters, photos, magazine articles, and ticket stubs are pinned to the wall, with all sorts of memorabilia cluttering the furniture.

A tiny ache takes up residence in my chest. Adeline's reaction to finding Bolan and me all tangled up in the mudroom was … unexpected. But still … she loves Bolan so much, and I've damaged their relationship in a way I know can never be fixed. Not without a fundamental shift in beliefs — namely Adeline's.

Rian is in Dublin and about to confront his own mother. Or he has already …

I reach for my phone, only just then realizing that I'm wearing nothing but a printed black tank top and my panties. My backpack, with my phone, is all the way downstairs. A glance around the cluttered but tidy room informs me that other than my bra, which is hanging on the desk chair, the rest of my clothing is nowhere in the immediate vicinity.

Shifting out from under the bedding, including a patchwork quilt made out of old band T-shirts that I immediately wrap around me, I pad barefoot into the tiny bathroom. After relieving myself, I brush my teeth with Bolan's toothbrush and try to sort out my hair. I'm unsuccessful. But I flush — all pink-cheeked and more than a little pleased — when I catch sight of myself in the reflection and realize that the top I'm wearing is from the Blitz's first European tour, well-worn with age and use. I've coveted it for years.

Around the corner from the bathroom, the door to the

rest of the attic space has been drawn partially closed. Catching a rhythmic pluck of guitar strings, I pause before opening it all the way.

The guitar fades. I peek around the doorframe to catch a side view of Bolan as he leans over, the old Brazilian rosewood Martin guitar that Armin and I bought him for his fifteenth birthday in his lap as he crosses something out in an open notebook. The Martin is the guitar he used to play me the song in the rowboat, right before I kissed him as a teenager. Bolan jots something down, likely an edit to whatever he crossed out.

I can really only see his left side from this angle, but my heart skips a couple of beats, then picks up, as I lay eyes on him. As it always does.

I can't quite believe that ... Bolan is mine now. More than just a friend I keep a careful distance from, more than a first love that my heart could never shake. He's mine. He's always been mine.

He believes we're soul bound. Carved from the same section of the universe and fated to search for each other in every lifetime.

I'm ... I'm still concerned that I've somehow stolen that bond connection from Armin. But I want ... I want to be Bolan's ... fate.

His fingers dance over the strings of the guitar, as quiet as he can be as he finds a rhythm that satisfies him, mouthing words as he reads from the notebook.

Trying to not wake me.

With the quilt still draped over my shoulders, I slip around the door as quietly as possible, bringing more of the room into view. Dozens of notebooks have been pulled out of the worn steamer trunk that also serves as a coffee table in a seating area excavated from the rest of the box-and-furniture-filled attic. The old brown corduroy couch slumps so deeply under Bolan's weight that he's practically sitting on the floor.

Bolan looks up, unsurprised at my approach. His expression is shockingly serious — not even a hint of a smirk in sight. Not until he runs his eyes over me. Twice. Then his gaze heats up, just a little pleased with himself.

"My clothes?" I ask.

"Laundry. Except the long sweater. Livi said it needed to be hand-washed and hung to dry, so I just spot-cleaned it."

Unable to hide my surprise, I raise both eyebrows.

Bolan flashes me a grin, seemingly enamored with my bare legs.

Slightly flushed myself — he's still wearing only the tight black sweatpants, and the lyric tattoos twining around his arms and chest, of course — I force myself to drop my gaze to the pile of notebooks.

Because more words between us, instead of giving in to the need to climb all over him, might be prudent.

We've known each other for almost two decades. So maybe the stages of our relationship are all actually moving glacially slow, and we're just now at the point where I want to be constantly touching him.

"Sully texted," Bolan says, seemingly oblivious to my train of thought. "Just checking in when he couldn't reach you. I told him your phone was in your bag, that you were napping. But that we were okay. That we'd be back in London for dinner. Together."

"Okay. Thank you." I smile a little at the possessive inclusiveness in that 'together.' Sully and Bolan are going to have to navigate their own relationship now instead of just continually shoving Armin or me in the middle of it. But I'm glad Bolan wants to make the effort.

I catch myself staring at him again. And he, seemingly

happy, stares right back. So I force my gaze back to his notebook. "You're writing?"

"Playing around. It's something old … that I …" Bolan swallows, dropping his gaze to the open page of the notebook as he teases notes from the guitar. Almost as if he's nervous. Then he looks up at me with that serious expression etched across his face again. He's not nervous. He's worried.

"Can I … play it for you? It's rough, but … ah … it's for you. Always meant for you, but … trapped in the pages of this notebook."

I understand the worry now. I reacted badly the last time he attempted to play for me, during the epically awkward matchmaking formal presentation of gifts. I close the space between us, lowering myself into the dusty burnt-orange armchair across from him with the notebook-strewn steamer trunk between us. I tuck my bare feet under me, pulling the T-shirt quilt snugly around me.

A smile ghosts over Bolan's face. His still newly dyed black hair falls over his brow as he settles his cobalt eyes on the lyrics and musical notes scribbled across the page sitting open before him. Without looking up, he starts playing. Louder now that he's not worried about waking me.

He works through the opening bars twice, as if still getting a feel for them. Then he starts to sing.

I'm in a magical trance
A mystic charm has filled my every sense
It's a mystery to me
But all I see
Is her

I'm instantly frozen in place, but not in a suffocating way. No, I'm warmed from within, hanging in the moment and barely wanting to breathe for fear of it ending.

She cast a powerful spell

Every wall I'd built trembled and fell
Crumbling into dust on the earth between us
Me and my magic girl

The song is about me. He said it was so. A love song from teenaged him to teenaged me. Almost forever doomed to be hidden within the pages of an old notebook.

Because he didn't kiss me back.

And no matter that he regretted it, he had let me pretend it never happened. He let me protect myself.

And we lost all those years.

We lost all those years and ... maybe ... maybe even Armin.

My magic girl manipulates time
I've seen it stop with a wink of her eye
My magic girl reads my mind
She knows my heart better than I
And now I find she's made me blind to everyone but her
I confess I'm happily possessed by my magic girl

Maybe ... maybe I was supposed to be more for both of them. Stronger, stable. Maybe I could have held Armin in this life.

If I'd been enough.

If we were actually soul bound, if I'd had Bolan, and even Sully ... if I'd claimed them. Maybe I would have been — we would have been — enough to balance Armin.

Bolan looks up from the notebook. His eyes are red rimmed. He presses his hand against the strings to mute the guitar.

I take a shuddering breath, unable to stop the tears snaking down my cheeks.

"You hate it," he whispers.

I shake my head, sobbing just once before I get it under control. "Armin," I gasp. "I just ... I just wish I'd been enough for Armin."

Bolan's chest heaves as he also strangles back a sob. "He wanted something we couldn't give him. We, Mirth. It was just a stupid, fucked-up accident."

"You don't think ... if he had the support of a fully realized bond group —"

"No!" Bolan says harshly. "He still would have made the same choice."

I take another shuddering breath. I wipe my face with my borrowed tank top as I take a deeper breath. Then I whisper, "Play the rest for me?"

Bolan watches me for a moment. Then he nods and starts playing again.

She transformed my soul
Vanquished my fears and gave me strength unknown
My invisible shield
When life gets real
She is my magic girl

I rest my head back and just listen this time, willing my mind to empty, then to fill up with Bolan's voice and words.

This was always enough for me. This was always where I ached to be. And I'm here now.

The last notes linger between us for a moment. Then Bolan leans over, plucks up his pen, and scribbles more notes across the page, crossing out lyrics and subbing in other thoughts.

"I haven't written in over eighteen months," he says, not looking up at me. "Haven't played since Armin died."

But he picked up the guitar for me. Once in an attempt to woo me, and now because he wanted to play. For me. For us. For our future.

I rise from the chair, leaving the quilt behind me.

I take those last couple of steps to Bolan.

He sets the guitar to the side, gazing up at me.

I place my hands on his shoulders.

I lean over him.

He lifts his face to mine.

I brush my lips against his, softly — a question.

He presses up into my kiss, sealing our lips together — an answer.

Mine.

Always and forever.

5

SALVATORE

THE RAINY, COBBLED STREETS OF DUBLIN SPEED past beyond the fog-edged windows of the armored vehicle masquerading as an SUV that was waiting for us at the airport. Bulletproof glass is raised between the back seat and the driver. Greg, the royal guard cat shifter now begrudgingly dogging my every step, essentially interrogated the local royal guard recruit about his background and qualifications before settling in with me.

I've cracked the window despite the rain, itching to lower it even further for the fresh air. The commercial flight to Dublin was utter chaos for my senses. I already didn't want to leave Mirth. I understand why she needs to work through her grief, as much as doing so is even possible, but I still want to be forever at her side.

I've been doing a lot of things I don't necessarily want to do, just in the last forty-eight hours alone. Such as giving Bolan a heads-up that Mirth was heading out to his family property. So maybe that's all just a shock to my bratty, self-centered system. But my meds aren't helping, and I can't smoke one of my joints in public.

And yes, I tried to book a private flight. I barely managed to secure two seats in what passed for first class on the pond hopper between London and Dublin. Fucking Greg insisted on not only sitting together, so I couldn't book a row to myself, but also taking the aisle seat. For security reasons.

I'm already sick of that phrase — *for security reasons* — which I've heard a half-dozen times in the last day. But according to Mirth, I can't just 'gad about town' if I'm also going to accept my title. Hence the security detail.

I suppose it's my fault for not actually outright owning a fucking plane. But I don't really want to own anything. As soon as I had a chance to liquidate everything my father had accumulated, I had done so.

Greg, stuffed into the seat to my left, angles the screen of his phone. I read the headline — *Lord Savoy Uncovered!* — and don't bother scanning anything else.

"Eli is going to be pissed," I murmur, looking out the window again as we pass through a Georgian-era-inspired section of the city. "He wanted to control the narrative. And the timing."

"He'll get used to it." As the car slows to a stop at a light, Greg's energy gathers tightly around him for a moment. Then he does that thing where he checks the immediate area — in this case, beyond the vehicle — for any threats without moving from his seat, barely moving his head, and without making it at all obvious that's what he's doing.

"Where are they now?" I ask, even though I'm certain the shifter is sick of me nagging him, and not at all accustomed to my habit of rapidly changing the subject.

"Safe," he says. The first few times I asked, he gave me more details about Mirth and Roz and showed me the last text message he received from his fellow royal guard. But he quickly figured out that too many details aren't what I need to feel settled. Well, as settled as I can be when completely out of my comfort zone with my meds failing.

At the very least, my meds aren't doing what I want them to do right now, which is focus me without smothering all my senses. Instead, I keep getting jolts to my system — including vicious, stabbing-pain headaches — even as everything feels all muffled in wool batting. It's a fucked-up combo.

"We don't know each other very well," I say.

"I know my duty, Lord Savoy," Greg says stiffly.

That's not what I meant at all. "You were on Armin's detail."

Greg's shoulders tighten, and he nods stiffly. Not looking at me. But then, when paired one-on-one like this, a royal guard usually watches everything but the person they're guarding.

"You weren't with him. On the ski trip," I say, not certain if I'm prying or trying to make him feel better about losing Armin.

"No." He clears his throat, glances at me quickly, then looks away. I wonder if the driver can feel Greg's gaze drilling into the back of his head through the bulletproof glass. Or if the pilots felt it all the way into the cockpit, which Greg made certain he had in his line of sight during the flight.

"Can you fly?"

"It's a requirement. At this level, at least."

I laugh quietly to myself. Of course he can fly a plane, even though all the Royal Highnesses have their own planes and crew. Unfortunately, Mirth's plane wasn't in London.

Plus, if I took off in it, then she would have known I wasn't dutifully checking things off the stupid list that Eli keeps updating.

Every time I glance at my phone, there's another fucking thing he wants me to buy. The last text was about some art installation that needs a donation or a fucking patron or fuck knows. I barely looked at it. Plus I'm getting dozens of other text messages and emails from people I barely know — and I have no idea how they got my contact info — all of them piling up on my notification screen.

"Do you know how to make it so only the text messages I want come through?" I ask, even though I fucking loathe asking anyone I don't know well for help. "Like, as a priority? It's ... it's not helpful right now."

Greg doesn't even blink at the request. "One of the royal guard tech mages can completely reorganize your phone and add extra security measures at the same time."

"Remotely? Like, right now?"

He nods. "Just need to give them access."

I unlock my phone, then eagerly drop it into his open palm. It was starting to feel like an explosive device in my hand. "Just Mirth, please. Bolan, Christoph, and Elias. I ... I don't have Rian's number yet."

"I can get it for you."

"No. That's for me to do."

Greg just nods, translating my directions into text message form.

"And Fluff and Fizz, my assistants. Everyone else can just ... wait. Or reach me through F&F."

Greg's thumbs are flying across the screen, texting someone not in my contacts list. The tech, I assume.

"And Eli has that note document thing he keeps updating," I say, gazing back out the window and already feeling lighter. "I can't outright block him this early in our relationship. Oh, and my fucking law firm. I suppose I can't block them either. They're seriously freaking out. Like, in glee, ever since I had them make that lump-sum investment in Christoph's vineyard. Plus I'm buying all this shit that Eli thinks I need to own now. We need to own. For the bond group."

"And your socials?" Greg asks, clearly reading the question off the text chain he's now got going on my phone.

"Fluff and Fizz run them. Mostly. So they'll still need access. Why the fuck doesn't the archduke of Austria have a security detail?" I ask, fairly caustically. "Christoph is, like, fifth in line for the fucking throne, isn't he?"

"He's monitored, but refused a personal detail," Greg says. "That wasn't an option for you."

The cat shifter sounds just a little smug about that. But if Mirth needs to know I'm as safe as I can be, then I don't give a shit if the royal guard thinks I'm a pushover for her. Christoph will fold just as fast if given the chance.

Silence stretches between us until a cloud-shrouded university campus comes into view, then we start winding through the narrow streets that stretch between buildings. Unlike the city center of Dublin, the campus of the University College Dublin is mostly mid-twentieth-century architecture.

"You know exactly where he is?" I ask, meaning Rian — and knowing I shouldn't be surprised at the response.

"We do."

"Since I asked you to take me to him?"

Greg smirks, just a little. "Since he stepped off the property."

Left Lake Thun Castle, he means. "So you track all of us?"

Greg hands my phone back to me. "Anyone important

to Her Royal Highness always has some kind of overwatch."

"The kids? You got Tommy that phone Mirth wanted him to have?"

"I did. Had to practically blackmail him to get him to take it from me."

I bark out an involuntary laugh, already liking the little asshole way too much for someone I haven't even met yet. But then, I'd probably love anyone Mirth picked. My soul is aligned with hers, after all.

"So you're tracking the kids too?"

Greg grimaces. "The phone is rigged with all the same security, plus tracking hardware and software, but ... they're minors. And we don't really have any jurisdiction. Not legally."

"But Mirth feels like she has some connection to them."

"She does." He hesitates for a moment. Again, we don't know each other very well. "I haven't been on Mirth's detail for long, and she's been ... deep in mourning for most of our time together. But I ... I already know to trust her, to trust her instincts. She's not just ..."

"Some pampered princess," I say, just a little mockingly. "Or some wildcard. Not like Armin."

Greg checks his own phone, swiping through a few notifications, so I let the topic drop until the SUV pulls to a stop at the back entrance to one of the university buildings. A smooth, near-white concrete block speckled with perfectly matching square windows, which are barred on the lowest level. Three or so storeys tall.

Greg reaches for the handle of his door.

"I don't want to be dragging you with me into every conversation," I say.

He nods curtly. "I'll see you to where you need to go, then give you as much space as the situation allows."

So 'always within sight,' he means. And definitely within hearing — for a cat shifter, at least. I doubt that any of it is negotiable. Being around Armin and Mirth since we were kids has made me accustomed to that type of oversight when in public spaces, but having my movements curtailed, and the lack of privacy, is already chafing me.

"Also," Greg adds just before he steps out of the vehicle, "you'll meet the rest of your security detail when we get back to London, Lord Savoy." He's intentionally rubbing it in a bit, like a dominant asshole.

Yeah, I'm fourth in line to the fucking throne now. I always was, but now everyone else knows it too.

"I get Mirth," I whisper to myself, waiting like a good little boy for Greg to secure the entrances and exits, then open my door. "I get Mirth. I can handle all of this because it comes with Mirth."

Rian Callaghan is leaning against an aged wooden door in a long, otherwise empty corridor. The lower level of the building, as well as the stairwell, was thronged with students dashing between morning classes, so the empty upper hall is a welcome relief.

Mixed-race, the wolf shifter is a ridiculously pretty, green-eyed boy on the verge of becoming a stupidly gorgeous male specimen. I had noted it offhandedly when I briefly met him outside the Lake Thun stables. But it's understanding his connection to Mirth — and by exten-sion, his connection to me — that makes me look closer, see more, now.

Not that I can't handle the competition. I never did give a shit about my own looks, and they never attracted anything of value for me anyway. Mirth loves me despite the way I look. She never was big on drawing attention, and that's all my face does.

I already know that Rian doesn't swing my way, not even a little. Not that I'm particularly attracted to him. My main concern — especially because I'm certain that Mirth, who so easily accepts people at face value, didn't pick this up from our last joint conversation — is that I'm not sure Rian's going to be great at sharing either.

That's a complication. Because Mirth needs him. Therefore, the fledgling Savoy bond group needs him.

Oddly, though — because it's unusual for me to attempt to juggle multiple complications at once — none of that is actually why I've abandoned Eli's shopping list and hopped on a plane to Dublin.

Dressed in worn jeans, not-so-worn work boots, and a white T-shirt under his black sweater, Rian looks up as I approach. Arms crossed protectively across his chest, he clearly hopes I'm someone else but already knows I'm not. An old black leather backpack, barely half full, slumps against the wall at his feet.

"It's rare that people frown at the first sight of me," I say like a complete asshole, smoothing a hand and a touch of my essence down my dark-navy suit jacket. I count the buttons — thankfully just in my head — before I can quash the impulse. Four. Only the top button done up.

"Sully." Rian offers me a conciliatory smile, straightening away from the door. His Irish lilt is more pronounced than it had been over the phone or at Lake Thun, maybe from being back in Ireland.

I'm pleased he doesn't give a shit about titles, though his gaze flicks to Greg hovering at the entrance to the corridor behind me, and a bit of his frown returns.

"Mirth insisted," I say. "Though she thought I was

going to be wandering around London all day, yammering on about being Lord Savoy and buying expensive shit. Either way, she decided that poor Greg here should keep me safe."

Rian raises an eyebrow. "What expensive shit?"

I shrug. "Like a house. And art to put in it. How many houses do we need in London?"

"We?" Rian asks, just a little edged.

I grin at him, just a little snarky myself. Because he should know that I'm cool to let him fuck around, feign ignorance, or avoid shit, but only until it bores or bothers me. He'll have a difficult time outplaying me anyway, if I'm in the mood. To make that clear, I deliberately glance at the name plaque beside the door he's been holding up — *Professor Trina Callaghan.*

He's staked out his psychologist mother's campus office.

"Is she in class or dodging you?"

"Both," he huffs. "Maybe."

"Let's grab a coffee or whatever while we wait."

"While *we* wait?"

"Yeah, we."

Rian takes a deep breath, then finally drops his arms to his sides with a somewhat doubtful nod of agreement.

I get that the situation is overwhelming. So reminding myself I'm here for a reason, I drop my selfish-prick mask, stepping just close enough to grasp the top of his shoulder.

I don't touch easily. Not like this, but ... I want to make this work.

I'm not certain what I bring to this bond group yet, other than mountainous piles of dirty money. And ... Mirth doesn't need my money. Bolan doesn't give a fuck about assets or other such shit. Depending on how the earl's assets are tied up, Eli probably could have bailed Christoph out himself, so the duke didn't have to sell land to maintain his inherited estate. Or start his winery.

But I still don't want to just be an unlimited bank account to everyone but Mirth.

Rian looks me steadily in the eye — he's about ten centimeters taller — then grasps the side of my shoulder. "Thank you," he murmurs. "For coming. I know you'd rather be with Mirth."

"She didn't send me."

"I know."

"Eli says we need more horses. Did he send you a shopping list?"

Rian swallows, presumably at the mention of Eli, not the prospect of buying horses. But then he laughs, still sounding just a little overwhelmed. "Not to me."

"All right, then. You can help me with mine."

I drop my hold on him. Rian picks up and swings his backpack over his shoulder, and we turn back down the empty corridor. Greg hovers near the exit to the stairs, looking everywhere but directly at us.

"So ... Mirth, you, and me ..." Rian prompts. "And Lord Elias Hereford? Just the three of us?"

I glance over at him. "No. Though nothing has been solidified yet."

"I guess that's a conversation for Mirth and me," he murmurs.

"Some of it," I say. "But this, today, is about you getting some answers you need, right? About your dad?"

Hands shoved into the front pockets of his jeans, head slightly bowed, Rian nods. But he doesn't continue the conversation.

"Coffee shop?" I ask Greg as we near.

The cat shifter nods, types something into his phone, then opens the door to the stairs. Rian and I trail behind

Greg down to the first floor, crossing toward the main entrance. Classes must have started because fewer students than before traverse these lower corridors, barely glancing our way. My suit, rather than my blue hair, likely stands out more on campus.

Rian brushes his shoulder against mine in that tactilely casual shifter way.

And I know, no matter how much I want to be Mirth's shadow right now, that I've made the right choice in coming to support him.

Armin should be with us too.

Maybe all of this wouldn't feel so disjointed, so rushed, if Armin were still with us. Mirth wouldn't have been forced to choose anything at all. All of our relationships — as lovers and friends — could have unfolded more naturally.

Hot tears spike behind my lashes, my cheeks flushing with restrained emotion, restrained grief.

Rian brushes his shoulder against mine again, intentionally this time. He presumably can smell my grief, though he doesn't know me all that well yet.

I clear my throat, and we don't acknowledge it further. Neither of us can do anything about any sense of what should have been involving Armin anyway.

According to the map Greg has pulled up on his phone, the University College Dublin has a few small coffee shops spread throughout the campus. Rian matches my stride, not bothering to hurry or to duck or cover his head in the rain, driven now by a rising wind, any more than I do as we cross from the building that houses his mother's offices to a nearby bustling cafe.

As we push through the glass doors, students in a range of ages take one look at Rian and me and get a little stuck.

A hush momentarily falls throughout the space.

It's enough to unnerve Greg just a bit. The cat shifter had fallen slightly back to give us an illusion of privacy, but now he slips forward to place himself between us and the seating area as we join the line at the counter.

Understandably, really. Mirth doesn't have a few million followers on her socials, then make a habit of wandering into college-campus cafes.

Heroically, both Rian and I attempt to ignore Greg as the cat shifter continues to stay between the two of us and everyone else as we order, while also trying to blend in. He's unsuccessful. But then, so am I.

"Spanish latte," I say to the cashier, not bothering to scan the menu.

Sporting an adorable septum piercing, she just gulps and nods before turning wide brown eyes on Rian.

"Triple espresso," he says. "Straight."

I give him a little amused look at the pointed 'straight,' but he doesn't catch it. Or he deliberately ignores it. "Greg?" I ask.

"I'm fine," the cat shifter says, his back to me.

Rian scans his phone over the card reader and inputs a generous tip. I should be pleased he doesn't expect me to pay, but it bothers me instead.

I smile at the cashier. "Thank you."

She smashes her lips together as if frantically suppressing a massive smile, muttering something that might be, "You're very welcome," while barely opening her mouth. I turn to scan the seating area.

All the tables are occupied, but a trio of women sitting in the corner by the window — and obviously eyeing us — stand up, giggling quietly and grinning among themselves as they heft backpacks over their shoulders.

"We've got a class," a brunette with her long hair partly twisted back from her temples calls out, waving us over.

"Thanks." I flash her a grin, causing more giggles to erupt from the next table and from two more over.

I turn back to pick up my latte, ignoring the whispers of "Do you know who that is?" and "That's Salvatore!" and "Fuck, he's even tastier in person!" Then, as the group moves to the exit, the first brunette says, "Who is that other guy? He's adorable. Should we know him too?"

Rian rolls his eyes at me. "Really?"

Greg huffs, muttering under his breath, "Really."

"You've only been with me for a few hours," I say snippily to the cat shifter.

"You think you don't have a reputation among the royal guard?" Greg snips back. Well, as snippy as he gets. "Think of the insanity of you, Bolan, Armin, and Mirth all in one place at a time."

I've never really thought about it before. But I never really had any sort of infamy until after leaving school anyway. I stayed until I was twenty-one because Mirth stayed. I can barely remember what advanced degrees I accumulated enough credits to complete.

"It's not going to get easier now," I say. "But there will be more expendable bodies between an attacker and Mirth, so that'll make you happy."

"None of you are expendable," Greg practically growls.

I've finally managed to piss him off.

Rian knocks my shoulder with his — a little harder than is polite — grabbing his triple espresso and crossing toward the table. The women cleared their plates and mugs, which is cool of them.

Just like that, the wolf shifter has put me in my place.

Normally, I'm not a fan of being managed by anyone but Mirth. But Rian feeling comfortable enough to make an attempt at it is more amusing than annoying.

We sit. Me with my back to the rest of the cafe and Rian across from me. Greg removes the two extra chairs, placing them along the far wall, where they're certain to be a tripping hazard on the way to the washrooms until someone else steals them for their own tables.

Only then does the cat shifter step back to the counter and order himself a drink.

Rian eyes me over the lip of his mug.

"I don't do it deliberately," I say, speaking in generalities because I'm not certain what to read from his expression.

"Sure you don't," he says. But then he flashes me another of those sort-of-sad grins, so I get that we're being friendly.

My phone vibrates in my suit pocket. I fish it out just in case it's Mirth.

It's Eli.

> *Just checking in.*

"I've never had anyone check up on me as many times as Eli has in the last forty-eight hours," I grouse. Then I dutifully send back a mini report.

In Dublin. With Rian. Waiting on his mom.

"You don't seem to actually mind," Rian says.

It isn't a question. And he's right.

Another text pops up.

Ah, good. I didn't think of that after Bolan's revelation. Thank you, Salvatore.

I stare at that message for a bit, mostly at the thank you, and slightly displeased that I'm feeling a little flushed at the praise. I didn't think that was a kink of mine.

"Anything wrong?"

I shake my head, passing the phone over to Rian so he can read it for himself. He does, then he taps the screen with two fingers, as if thinking about what he wants to say.

"Just ask." I take a sip of my latte. It's good. Sweet and creamy, with just the right level of bitter.

"You're forming a bond group. So you can ... ask Mirth to join you. Like, all of you."

"And you." My heart thumps a little, as if I'm about to ask him to be exclusive and I'm still just a little uncertain about the answer. An odd reaction because I've never wanted to be exclusive in my life. Not sexually, at least. My heart always belonged to Armin and Mirth — as has my soul, apparently. Which explains a lot about my lack of interest in exclusivity. "We need you as well."

Rian glances out the window. He could be keeping watch for his mother, but I think he's conflicted in multiple ways right now.

"You love Mirth," I say.

Rian looks at me sharply, as if I'd made that a question. I hadn't. Then he nods.

I shrug, taking another sip of coffee. "So what is the issue? Me? The rest of us? Or is it just your long-lost half-brother, Bolan?"

"Was he born with that name? Bolan?"

"No. He was Oliver for the first seventeen years of his life. Ollie Yates."

"And you're just Salvatore. No last name either."

"My birth name never meant anything to me, though I suppose it must be on some early school records. If you wanted to go digging."

"Your mother was that famous model, Zsa."

"Murdered by my father. For trying to leave him, I think. My memory is rather hazy about it all. A few months before his past caught up to him. I was seven. Armin and Mirth made me theirs, and I never gave a shit about anything or anyone else."

Rian blinks at me for a long moment, then shakes his head. "I can't figure out if you're a brilliant liar or …"

"Utterly truthful all of the time?"

"Yes."

"Your nose should tell you."

"Your essence … cloaks you. And … you smell a bit like Mirth now."

I raise both eyebrows at that. Because no matter how much I hated doing so, I very deliberately washed Mirth off me before leaving the apartments.

Rian clears his throat. "I think … it might be in the same way I occasionally smell of Mirth now."

"Soul deep," I whisper, smiling a little to myself.

"Stronger. On you."

I shrug. Mirth and I have known and loved each other for two decades. Having sex just formalized and strengthened a bond that already existed.

"And you and Armin?" Rian asks, slightly hesitant.

"On and off. Mostly off." I smirk at him, already knowing the answer to my next question but wanting to nudge him a little in the direction I think is worrying him. "And you and Armin?"

"Business. Horses. And barely that before …"

"The skiing accident."

"Yes."

"But he made an impression," I say. "Eli says you were being wooed from multiple directions. But Armin felt … right?"

Rian regards me steadily.

For a moment, I think he's trying to see beneath my skin. Into my soul. Into the truth of me. Or …

"Can you feel that between us?" My voice is a little thin, my heart thumping again.

He nods, just once. "Like I've known you for a lot longer than I actually have. Like it's ... easy between us."

Relief steadies my heart. "Yes. Same. So ask me everything you're worried about asking Mirth."

He flushes a little, eyes on his neglected espresso now. "I don't ... I've been surrounded by shifters my entire life. And sex with multiple partners is just either fun or a biological impulse."

"But not with Mirth."

"No. It's different with Mirth." He finally meets my gaze. "I want to know how it's supposed to work in a bond group. Some shifters are polyamorous, but I never saw that as ... never thought of it —"

"Are you worried that you're going to have to suck dick? Or that you're going to have to share Mirth?"

Rian reels back a bit at my bluntness. But then he just grimaces and nods. "The jealousy."

"Listen, I don't come from a bond group. Not like Mirth does, with her father having multiple chosen mates. Neither does Bolan, Eli, or Christoph."

Rian shifts in his seat, then takes a deliberate sip of his triple shot. Presumably because I just outlined the full extent of the bond group for the first time. I should have left this all to Eli. But I followed my impulses, and here we are.

"But I do know that Mirth is our crux," I say, quietly but with utter resolve. "We revolve around her. Our only true role within the relationship is to love and balance Mirth. It doesn't have to be sexual. This isn't about incest, if that has you worried?"

"I'm not that much of an idiot," Rian says, clearly

feeling like a complete idiot. "Siblings are bonded by blood and sometimes ... soul."

So it's the soul bond he's questioning. If he's been skin-to-skin with Mirth, as I know he has, I have no idea how he can question that connection.

I can't fix that for him. All I can do is address the concern he's outlined for me.

"Right. So, say if Armin were still ..." Grief cracks through my voice, but I get it under control quickly. "There's a good chance it might have been on and off again between Armin and me for our entire lives together, even as I'm full on with Mirth."

"And the others?"

"Am I fucking them?"

Rian huffs, then exasperatedly asks, "Am I expected to fuck any of them? Or you?"

I bark out a laugh, drawing even more attention than before. Greg, leaning back against a standing-height table, sipping a coffee, straightens warily as if I'm about to be assaulted.

Rian grimaces. "I just want Mirth."

"Right. Well, you understand consent, right?"

"Of course."

"The rest of us understand it as well. No one is going to be grabbing your cock or sticking a thumb up your ass without you asking."

Rian blushes deeply, taking another sip of his coffee. "That wasn't actually my concern, really."

"Jealousy."

He nods, gaze downcast.

"Is it all of us? Or just Bolan who worries you?"

"Well, I don't really know the rest of you."

I nod. I don't have a concise answer for him. "That's

something we work through. Together. If it comes up. And we keep it away from Mirth."

"Will Bolan keep it away from Mirth?" Rian asks wryly.

I lean over the table toward him, smirking. "Bolan has been pressed against a reinforced glass barrier of his own making for over a decade. If he finally breaks through to the other side, he's doing nothing, absolutely nothing, to jeopardize it."

"How do you know?"

"Are you willing to walk away?"

"No."

"But you've only known Mirth for a few weeks."

"No," he says again.

I shrug. That's his answer, then. "Tell me about this shit with your mom. Is she dodging your calls?"

"All after the first one."

"Pretty sure Bolan's about to be in the middle of it with his mother as well. Mirth has gone to their place to scatter some of Armin's ashes."

"And Bolan?"

"I gave him a heads-up."

"For Mirth."

I nod. "Maybe you and he can compare notes."

"Yeah. Though ... I have to decide if it even matters."

"You have a half-sister as well. Olivia, Livi. She's, like, a famous dancer."

Rian looks surprised, then pained all over again.

"So some part of it matters."

"Yeah."

"You want me to be with you for the conversation with your mother? I can wait here. Just, you know, be here."

Rian stares at me for a long while. Then he smiles, radiating an amused joy. "Well, as the head of my potential bond group, I guess I should introduce you, Lord Savoy."

Oh, fuck.

I'm the fucking head of the fucking bond group.

Rian laughs at whatever he sees on my face, then he pushes my phone back toward me. "I've got a list of horses I've been keeping an eye on. Mostly breeding stock. That should keep Elias happy."

"For a few minutes, at least." I swallow as much of my trepidation as I can, because I seriously thought that Elias or Christoph would be the public head of the bond group. "After you talk with your mom, we'll ... I'll introduce you to the others."

Rian shakes his head. "That's between Mirth and me. I go with her."

"I'm not going anywhere, Rian. Neither is Bolan unless Mirth rejects their bond."

He raises his hand placatingly. "That's not what I'm saying. But we made our own promises to each other. Mirth makes a decision first."

I open my mouth to try to pitch the idea of being stronger as a group, just like Elias and Christoph pitched it to Bolan and me. But Rian's gaze shoots out the window, and his shoulders tense.

I follow his gaze.

A dark-haired, dark-skinned woman in a sleek black wool coat, plaid scarf tucked under the collar, and wedge heels has paused at the edge of the building across the way. Her umbrella is angled back just enough to give her a clear view of the cafe — specifically of Rian sitting in the window.

She flares her nostrils, likely having already scented her son in the vicinity. Then she purses her lips.

Rian has frozen, seriously tense, across from me.

"This isn't just about your parentage," I say slowly, piecing it together. "Or that you're bonded to Mirth. Is it?"

"No," he says. "I'm already not living the life my mother wanted for me. I haven't been since I sued for emancipation."

"Normally, other people's lives are ridiculously boring to me," I say, smirking like the smart-ass I am. "But you might be an exception, Rian Callaghan."

He barks an involuntary laugh, then finally drops his mother's gaze to flash me an appreciative smile. Then, instead of charging out after her like most shifters would, he calmly picks up his coffee and takes a sip.

Intrigued despite my usual lack of interest for any relationships beyond the few I maintain, possibly badly, for myself, I watch Trina Callaghan visibly struggle between marching into the cafe or fleeing the looming confrontation with her son.

It takes only a few moments, and another steady sip of his coffee, for Rian before getting the confrontation over with wins out for his mother. Trina crosses to the entrance, where a student holds the door open for her to enter, then leers appreciatively at her back, along with two of his friends. More shifters.

That insignificant interaction tells me a lot about Rian's mother. First, she doesn't notice. She studiously ignores her son to tuck her umbrella into the rack by the door, then delicately pulls off her thin leather gloves, crossing to the counter to order a drink. Second, Trina is definitely young enough to be pulling looks from her college-aged students, which means she likely wasn't much older than Rian is now — almost nineteen — when she had him.

Rian's father, aka Bolan and Livi's father, would have been at least ten years older than her. Probably more like fifteen. Age gaps within bonded groups aren't necessarily a nefarious thing. But still, the idea makes my stomach ache. Just a bit.

Still blatantly twisted in my seat and watching Trina, I take a sip of my cooled latte to cover my discomfort.

My third thought — as Trina's gaze slides over me as if I'm of no consequence — is that she must not be formally bonded to a chosen mate or mates herself. College-aged or not, the shifters at the entrance wouldn't have leered at a bonded professor. They'd have scented that connection — typically the exchange of essence through bite marks.

"Bonded shifters don't normally cheat," I murmur, low enough that I hope only Rian can hear me. "It's a scent thing, right?"

He doesn't answer me. But when I turn back to look at him, his expression is still smooth. Thoughtful, not angry.

"Is that put on?" I ask, strangely serious. "That calm demeanor? Because if so, can you teach it to me?"

Rian blinks at me, then cracks a surprised smile. It's an almost sweet expression. "I've always been ... levelheaded. And you don't need to be taught calming techniques, Sully. Things already don't bother you like they bother most people. Why would you want to be any different?"

Surprised in return, I sit back in my chair and stare at Rian.

He takes another sip of his espresso, grinning back at me.

"I get it," I murmur. "I get what you bring. Why you are necessary. For all of us."

That wipes the smile from Rian's face, and an emotion I'm not adept at reading flits across it instead. Just for a breath. Need? But not sexual desire. Because I know those sorts of looks well, at least when directed my way.

It's gone a second later, when his gaze flicks over my shoulder to Trina approaching the table.

Greg gets there ahead of Rian's mother, sliding an empty chair into place at the end of the table as an excuse to make eye contact with her.

Trina falters for a moment. Her slight smile — an involuntary thank you for the proffered chair — fades, then is overtaken by a frown.

Greg isn't in uniform. But shifter to shifter, I'm certain Trina knows a royal guard when she scents one. Or at least she knows that something more is going on than a polite gesture.

Her free hand falls to the back of the chair as her gaze sweeps from Greg to Rian, then finally to me. She's carrying an extra-large cappuccino in her other hand and a black leather satchel on her hip, under her open jacket, presumably to keep it out of the rain.

I stretch back in my chair, smirking at the mother of one of my bond mates. Rian might be all about staying calm in all situations — and yeah, I can feel a bit of that attempting to rub off on me — but I'm a fucking asshole when I want to be. Trina Callaghan is on my naughty list. And not in a good way.

Greg — also a huge, unhelpful asshole — undermines me completely by saying, "Your guard has sourced a private plane for you, Lord Savoy. It is at your disposal."

I can practically hear the capital letters in my title. "No need to piss on me, Gregory," I say. "Ms. Callaghan isn't a threat."

He huffs in that cat shifter way. Then, completely unprofessionally, he side-eyes Trina a moment too long before withdrawing back to his watchful post.

I look at Rian, raising one eyebrow because I'm aware that Trina is still absorbing the info Greg just dumped on her, and I have to maintain my facade. "The royal guard must be all abuzz about you. Seems the protective mode isn't just for me. Or Mirth."

It makes sense. Rian's father, Bolan and Livi's father, would still be revered among the royal guard. For giving his life to save Armin and his mother. I didn't even need to be all that dialed in to know that. There is absolutely no way, no matter how professional they may strive to be, that Roz and Greg haven't overheard and then shared the revelation about Rian's parentage, at least with each other. But I'd be surprised if there wasn't an actual memo going around.

Rian simply nods, his gaze mostly on his mother. Trina seems frozen in place, still gripping the back of the chair with one hand.

So, proper gentleman that I am — and also, annoyingly, the highest ranked among us now that fucking Greg has outed me — I slide my chair back just enough to partly stand, smooth a hand down my suit jacket to keep it from flapping forward unbecomingly, and gesture toward the still-empty seat. "Please join us, Ms. Callaghan."

Trina blinks at me, then finally offers a slight dip of her chin instead of the more formal curtsy. "Thank you, my lord."

The chin dip is fine because technically I haven't filed all the paperwork and formally accepted my position as lord of the House of Savoy. It hasn't occurred to me before, but I'm now hyperaware that upon doing all of that, then formally bonding with Mirth, I might actually be His Royal Highness, the Duke of Savoy.

That thought makes me feel slightly ill. Enough so that, even though I manage to find my seat, I lose a bit of time obsessing about it in my head.

In the interim, Trina has removed her coat, sat down, and taken a couple of sips of her cappuccino in silence.

Am I supposed to be the one to speak again? Rian

wouldn't hold me to that formality in the presence of his mother, would he?

I flick my gaze from Trina's hands, still wrapped around her large ceramic mug, to Rian questioningly.

He doesn't acknowledge me, gazing steadily — and still so calmly — at his mother.

So I'm not expected — by him at least — to advance the conversation. And Rian has already indicated he wants me to stay.

The cafe is filled with murmured conversation and the sounds of hot drinks being brewed and frothed, but silence stretches taut over the table. If I didn't know better, which of course I do, I would have thought it was some essence spell stifling us all.

I'm literally seconds away from squirming to dispel the hold that silence has on me — or blurting out something completely inappropriate — when Rian finally breaks it.

"You can't even look at me?" he asks softly.

Relief floods through me, freeing my lungs. I'm aware that only a minute has passed, but again, my meds aren't being terribly helpful today. Though oddly, I've been highly functional and fairly focused with Rian.

Like I am with Mirth.

Trina visibly braces herself as she steadily meets her son's eyes. She lifts her coffee as if to take a sip, but then angles her gaze toward me. Pointedly.

Rian snorts quietly. "Salvatore, this is my mother, Trina. Mother, this is Salvatore. He's ... my bond mate."

I don't like the momentary hesitation in Rian's introduction, but I understand that he thinks those particulars are for him and Mirth to work out. "Pleased to meet you, Rian's mom," I drawl.

Trina doesn't quite look at me, still waiting, stiff in her

seat, for further explanation from Rian. As if it isn't her who owes him information.

It occurs to me that this might be some sort of typical parental interaction. Maybe Trina is trying to exert her authority over her son? To get the upper hand in the conversation?

Having never had parents, not that I can really remember, I have no frame of reference.

Rian just waits.

Which is crazy, because after only a few more seconds, I'm ready to blurt out anything just to get the conversation moving forward to where everyone can apologize and we can go back to Mirth whole and happy.

Trina breaks first. "Why is Lord Savoy in Dublin?" she asks. "With you? And who is Mirth?"

Satisfaction flits over Rian's face — like maybe he's won something? Seriously, all these games are just annoying. And confusing.

I hate all of it.

But I'm here for Rian.

I'm here to just support Rian.

That reminder loosens something in me. Steadies me. "Rian and I belong to Mirth," I say easily. "She is our crux."

Trina blinks, then whispers, "What do ... but you are ..." She looks to her son for clarification.

Rian tilts his head, watching her. Marking her reactions.

She huffs, finally getting a little peeved.

She's a pretty woman. Handsome, I think, is the correct term. Tall, slim in that strong, taut way of shifters, with a slightly round face. Her makeup looks minimal, but my own experience tells me that it takes her time to make it appear that way. Her hair is straightened to her shoulders, not a strand out of place despite the rain and the wind.

Being peeved suits her far better than the restrained demeanor she was feigning earlier. She is not a submissive. She can't even pretend to be for long.

"Which part is most shocking? That I'm a mage?" I ask almost teasingly. "Or because I'm royalty? Or is it because I'm male-presenting?"

Trina doesn't answer. But I can see all the thoughts whirling in her mind, just behind her eyes, before she glances away.

"Did you know ..." Rian asks, still in that calm, almost gentle tone that I have no idea how he maintains, "that Bolan is my half-brother?"

Bolan is famous enough to need no introduction other than his chosen name.

Trina swallows, opening her mouth just slightly as if to speak. Then she shakes her head just as slightly.

It's not a no, though.

Even I can read that.

"You need to tell me," Rian says, his tone firming, "for us to continue to have any sort of relationship."

Trina's head snaps up, fingers flexing around her mug. "That's emotional blackmail, Rian. We've already had this discussion. Just because I'm your mother, just because I love you, doesn't mean I owe you all the parts of me, all the parts of my past."

Rian leans forward. A sharp ire cracks through his calm, though he keeps his voice so low that I have to listen closely to catch the words. "You owe me the parts of myself. Parts I didn't even know were missing. Have you deliberately kept me from my brother?"

Her hands finally leave her mug as Trina presses one of them to her chest, taking a shaky breath.

"You said my father abandoned you," Rian continues.

"That you had no family to turn to. All you had to do was reach out!"

"I did!" Trina whispers harshly, almost crying out. Then she moderates her tone. "I did reach out."

"To the royal family?" I ask, completely surprised.

"Of course not."

"To the royal guard?" Rian asks, frowning as deeply as I am.

Trina swallows again, her voice hollow when she speaks. "No, no ... I ... didn't want to ... ruin ... his reputation. And I did ... I did think he'd abandoned me. It was three weeks later that I worked out he'd died, that he was just ... just ..."

More of that sick feeling twists through my stomach. For a pregnant eighteen-year-old shifter. For her falling for an older shifter with an important, dangerous position.

"The royal guard would have taken care of you," I say quietly. "Rian's father died protecting Prince Armin and his mother."

Trina just shakes her head. I'm not certain if she's denying my assertion, or if her loyalty to her deceased chosen mate simply extends that far.

"Who, then?" Rian asks.

"I ... I had to figure things out quickly after I ... found out he wasn't coming back. I was ... he'd started an account for me, enough in it to cover my first year of university. He said that she ... that Adeline would need time to accept me ... that I should focus on getting my degree ..."

"Adeline?" Rian asks, his voice a low rasp.

"Bolan and Livi's mother," I say.

"So you knew?" Rian's voice is pained now. "That he had another family?"

"I was part of that family," Trina says, still quiet. But edged and fierce now. "I was ... his. And he was mine. I knew it the moment I saw him. And he knew it. He ... his ties were to the royal guard, not to a pack. It had to be that way, that's ... he explained that it worked like that. He wanted to bite me into his family pack."

"He hadn't bitten Adeline," I murmur, voicing the conclusion I'd already come to.

"They must have been married," Rian says, getting just a little pissed. "Under law. You still cheated with a married man."

Trina clenches her hands into fists, leaning toward her son. "You must know. You must know what it feels like, if you're sitting here letting a pretty mage claim you before your mother."

Rian blinks, a little taken aback.

"She's got you there, wolf," I say. "Though Rian's connection to the bond group is through Mirth. He and I have only just met."

Rian takes a deep breath, then lets it all go with his next exhalation. It's seriously impressive. "Who did you reach out to, Mom? I need to know. You made it seem like we were on our own, but I have half-siblings I never knew about."

Trina nods, mostly to herself. It's obvious that she's running through how to deliver the bit of Rian's past she's chosen to keep from him all these years.

"You were almost three ..." She takes a breath, deeply but steadily, then meets his gaze. "I ... it took me that long to get my first degree. I stretched the money James had given me, working nights before you were born and living on campus. I couldn't afford rent in the apartment he'd found for me off campus. We'd ... we'd found for me. And then there was you ... and it was a lot to balance."

"Understandably," I murmur.

Rian dips his chin slightly in acknowledgment. Maybe he knows this part — all the struggle. But maybe it's not enough anymore, hence all the questions. Hence getting emancipated instead of waiting until he was eighteen to take control of his choices and his finances.

Trina sighs quietly. "I went to the house. The manor in the country. I took you with me, and maybe that was a mistake, but ..." She shakes her head. "I knew that Oliver and Olivia should be in school. I had my degree, and I had you, and I thought ... that even without James ... we were supposed to be pack! But Adeline ..."

She presses her lips together, but not in sorrow. As though even now, she doesn't want to speak badly about someone who she thought was supposed to be her chosen family.

"She knew about you?" Rian asks. The question is a quiet, pained rasp. "She knew about me?"

"James ... yes ... she knew about me. James told her. But not you. I never got a chance to tell James about you. I've never lied to you about that. About any of it, Rian. Yes, I could have texted him when I started throwing up and I took the test, but I wanted to tell him in person."

"Because the plan was for you to get your degree while Adeline ... adjusted," I say. Clarifying things, because I'm not certain Rian, for all his calmness, is absorbing everything his mother is telling him. "Not to have a kid. Not before formalizing your bond."

Some emotion, some form of tension, flickers over Trina's face. But she simply says, "Yes."

"And what did Adeline do when confronted with her dead husband's lover and bastard child on her front porch?" Rian's tone has chilled, but he is still way too calm. Completely contrary to the words that fall like blows from his lips.

"She refused to acknowledge any of it." Trina doesn't drop her son's gaze. "She said she never would have accepted me into her marriage. And she refused to even look at you."

"You could have told me. About my siblings, at least."

Trina shakes her head again. "She said that ... she'd have me arrested if I went near her children, that she'd ... sue me for ... slander if I spread my lies. And she'd make sure that ..."

Her gaze drops, and she twists her fingers together.

"That she'd make sure you lost Rian," I finish for her, my world vision shifting far too much and far too quickly for my comfort. Adeline might not have been my mother, or even a mother figure for me, but ... "Bolan is going to be fucking pissed."

"You left me anyway," Trina murmurs. "You chose your horses over your education."

Rian snorts, leaning back in his chair.

Just a little bit of emotional blackmail from mother to son.

"When were you going to tell me?" Rian asks.

Trina looks him steadily in the eye. "Never."

"Never? I have two —"

"Sharing some DNA with someone doesn't guarantee anything," Trina says.

"You didn't give me a choice!"

A few of the nearby customers glance our way, then look away just as quickly when Greg deliberately shifts, folding his arms across his chest and radiating menace.

"Well, I never had a choice either!" Trina blasts back. "Not one choice from the moment I found out James was dead. I had circumstances and decisions to make and not a single person to rely on. Not all of us are bequeathed with a bond group who want us." She casts a look my way.

Rian takes a deep breath. But instead of voicing any of

whatever has to be whirling around in his mind, he crosses his arms, looking away from his mother.

Trina's face crumples. She opens her mouth to say something, her hand twitching as if she wants to reach out to her son. She does neither.

My own chest is aching. And I'm getting itchy again, from so much secondhand emotion, from being surrounded by people. I'm way out of my comfort zone. I want to pull out my phone and text Mirth. Bolan needs to hear Trina's version of what went down, because I have no doubt that Adeline isn't going to confess to even half it. And maybe the real truth lies somewhere in the middle.

But I just sit. I sit and weather that silence with my bond mate and his mother.

Trina sighs softly, taking a sip of her cappuccino. Her hand is steady, as is her voice, when she asks, "Now ... who is Mirth?"

I can see where Rian gets his composure from. I open my mouth, already grinning madly, just at the chance to —

Rian, expression placid though he's still got his arms crossed, throws me a quelling look.

I raise my hands, playfully placating. But still pouting about it, of course.

Rian shifts in his seat — the first sight of blatant discomfort I've seen from him. "My ... potential ... bond group is the next conversation we will have."

And my stomach squelches at the implied rejection.

The disconcerting feeling resolves into a level of disappointment — it scrapes at my insides — that I haven't felt in a very long time. I don't get invested in people, in relationships. Certainly not this quickly. And in a single sentence, Rian has reminded me why.

"Potential?" Trina echoes, glancing toward me, then at her son, brow furrowed. "You're still ... courting?"

Rian looks at me. Guiltily, I think.

I glance away, out the rain-speckled window. The building across the street is slightly blurry. A light fog clings to the brick.

This isn't about me. Rian has already made that clear. He goes where Mirth goes. He's not choosing the bond group per se.

Maybe he and Adeline have more in common than I would have thought.

I shouldn't have come to Dublin. I have a list of things that Eli needs me to do. That, and wooing Mirth, is where I should be focused.

"Some of us are courting," I say into the silence that has once again stretched over all of us, smoothing my hand down my suit jacket as I stand so it doesn't drag across the table. "Please excuse me. I'm wanted elsewhere."

Rian half rises out of his chair. His hand shoots across the table to grasp my wrist. "Sully —"

I still at the contact, partially turned away from the table. I can feel Rian's warmth — and his shifter energy — even through the two layers of fabric between us.

In my peripheral vision, Greg lurches into motion, as surprised as I am. The royal guard crosses the space between us with that shifter swiftness.

A hush falls over the other customers, with us as the epicenter. I raise my free hand to stop Greg's advance.

I twist my wrist to break Rian's easy hold.

Trina, now all but pinned to her chair with the three of us looming around her — Greg at her back, Rian and me to either side — flinches and swallows a disconcerted cry.

"You do not touch a member of the royal household without permission." The quiet but coldly delivered command rumbles through Greg's chest as he looms over us. "And even courting …" He sneers the word rather unprofessionally, clearly implying he heard every word of our conversation. "You certainly don't do it in public."

Rian swallows, looking young and unsure of himself for the first time since I've known him. Which, granted, is all of three meetings now, and only two of those in person.

I tug down my sleeve, smoothing out any hint of crease in the jacket cuff with a touch of my essence.

Trina's nostrils flare. She leans slightly away from me.

She can scent or sense my power. And I'm an unknown mage to her.

I could be deadly.

I can, in fact, be deadly.

I just never choose to be so.

"My apologies," Rian says — to me, not Greg.

I interrupt before he can continue. "I'm the one who foisted myself upon you," I say coolly, even though I don't feel at all steady or poised. "I'll leave you to your conversation. It was lovely to meet you, Trina. Though I'm sorry about the circumstances."

See? I can remember some of my fucking etiquette lessons. Enough to get me out of this very public and very uncomfortable situation.

"Sully," Rian says, pained.

But I'm pissed now — whether or not it's appropriate to be mad — so I just lift my chin and smirk at the wolf shifter. "Your mother is right, Rian. I have courting to do. And you've already made your intentions clear."

"But I haven't made ... Mirth is my choice."

I just nod stiffly, turning away. Greg steps just ahead of me to clear a path through the still-quiet cafe. A light murmur of voices rises behind me. I think Trina says something to Rian, but I don't hear the exact words.

The glass door swings shut. The cool, damp air is a welcome relief on my face.

Greg glances back to see if I'm still following him like a good boy. His eyes glow softly with his essence.

"What did Trina say?" I ask despite myself. Despite me hating this sort of drama, mostly because I don't know how to navigate it without tearing out hunks of my own soul.

"She said, 'Oh, Rian. That's not how bond groups work. You can't just choose whoever this Mirth is.'"

"And what did he say?" I sound like a lovesick schoolboy, even though I have no romantic interest in Rian at all. Or attraction, for that matter.

Greg frowns slightly. "He didn't answer."

I nod. "Right. Let's get home to Mirth."

He nods in agreement, directing us toward the SUV waiting around the side of the building. The cobblestones are slick underfoot. I also should have worn a coat.

The driver steps out to open the back passenger door for me.

"Greg," I murmur, slowing. Thinking suddenly about something I should have thought about much earlier.

The royal guard shakes his head once, still scanning the immediate area for threats even as he anticipates me. "Your conversations are private."

"You don't include them in your reports?"

"No."

"And Mirth? You're friendly with Mirth."

Greg glances at me. "I know my duty, Lord Savoy. I protect you. And Her Royal Highness."

His implication is clear. Mirth doesn't need to know even a hint of any doubt Rian might be navigating. We're in agreement on that.

I climb into the car. Greg takes the front passenger seat after a murmured conversation with the driver.

I glance back toward the cafe as we pull away.

Rian is outside, standing in the rain. Hands in his pockets, shoulders slumped.

We didn't get around to exchanging numbers. Or making plans to introduce him, formally, to the others.

Maybe that was the way he wanted it all along.

I have no idea what I'm going to tell Mirth. Or Bolan, for that matter. Maybe it's not my place to say anything at all.

Except my bond group is fundamentally mine to protect. Even from someone who is supposed to be ours. Supposed to want to be ours.

6

$\mathcal{M}$IRTH

"LORD HEREFORD IS NOT TO BE DISTURBED."

Roz has insisted on accompanying me through the all-but-deserted corridors of the World Council. Well, the offices of the World Council. In Zurich. And my guard now completely blocks me from the view of the assistant standing between me and the next step in letting just a little more of Armin go.

Not that I'm feeling overly dramatic this morning. Not at all.

I slept restlessly, even while comfortably nestled between Sully and Bolan, then took the royal helicopter to Zurich from London after an early breakfast together. Yes, there's a landing pad on the roof of my apartment building, though I generally avoid using it for the sake of the neighbors.

Along with our royal guards, I also haven't managed to entirely shake my two bedmates, who insisted on accompanying me. Even though Sully hates flying by helicopter, and Bolan was supposed to meet with some lawyers about a conflict of interest with his current recording contract. I left the two of them — accompanied by Greg, of course — wandering the city after we arrived. Though I don't expect they'll stay away for long.

"Lord Hereford's instructions are explicit." The assistant stands a little taller, smoothing back her already perfectly smooth, pretty blond hair.

I peek over Roz's shoulder. Though my guard isn't much taller than me, she has a talent for occupying all the space she desires. It might be an intimidation tactic — brought into play because once again, I've insisted that she not wear her royal guard uniform. But I wouldn't mind being able to emulate it just a little bit more in my everyday life.

"I simply need to pass through the offices," I say gently. "I'm sure the earl won't mind —"

"The councilor is a busy man," the assistant snaps, hands on her slim hips now. "If you need to speak with him, we can make an appointment for next month —"

I step to Roz's side. My guard is a moment away from giving Lord Hereford's assistant a little essence-fueled nudge.

The assistant flicks her gaze to me, dismissing me in an instant with a twist of her lips. Granted, Roz does appear to be more intimidating at first glance. But ...

The assistant goes very still. Her eyes widen as she slowly returns her gaze to me, as if she's actually in fear of what her eyes see even as her brain takes a moment to process it. Her face pales.

I offer her a polite smile. Though I don't remove my sunglasses. I probably should have when we entered the building, just to be polite, but I haven't slept well, and my head is aching just a little.

My heart is aching just a little.

My soul is aching a little more.

The assistant drops into as deep a curtsy as her pencil skirt allows.

Roz snorts, then tries to cover her inappropriate reaction by clearing her throat.

"I'm not here in an official capacity," I say, trying to not let Roz's amusement bleed into my own reaction or tone. "You're just doing your job."

She straightens, keeping her gaze downcast. "My ... Your Royal Highness ... I had no idea —"

"Paying attention to your surroundings might be a smart idea, shifter," Roz says.

It's a mild rebuke, but the poor assistant flinches. "The council is not in session, and Lord Hereford doesn't have anything on his public schedule."

Roz gives her another once-over, unimpressed. "Then why are you here, Lia? Still sniffing around?"

Lia goes still, wary.

Okay, there's clearly more going on here than I'm aware of. But honestly, it's not my concern. I shouldn't be surprised that Roz knows Lia, or at least knows of Lia. The aforementioned Lord Hereford, aka Elias, went through weeks of security background checks, alongside jumping through all the other ridiculous hoops my father dreamed up for the matchmaking event.

"If you'll excuse me," I murmur, crossing for the heavy wooden doors that lead into the inner offices. "I know the way."

"Oh!" Lia cries. "Please don't touch —"

My hand closes around the carved brass handle, easily passing through the intricate, yet somehow delicate, warding that seals the doors. But the essence-fueled protections don't collapse under my touch, as per usual. They accept me, accept my essence, instead.

It's an odd sensation. I'm not certain I've ever felt the like.

I turn the handle freely, then push through the door.

Lia gasps behind me.

But my gaze is already tracking across the room, beyond the brown leather and dark wood that fills the seating area to my immediate left, toward the huge desk situated closer to the far windows.

The wood-slat shades are partially open, allowing angled slashes of late-morning light to filter across the all-but-bare bookshelves lining the walls, then play out across the hardwood floor.

But the slim, blond, pale-skinned man rising from behind the desk to greet me isn't washed out at all. His light-blue eyes blaze, capturing all my attention.

Elias. Lord Hereford. He's removed his suit jacket, loosened his tie, opened his collar, and rolled up the sleeves of his dress shirt.

And yes, there is something perfectly scandalous about the amount of skin Lord Hereford is displaying. But then, he didn't expect a visitor to barge into his office.

Then I notice the sharp-edged weapon, carved purely from light, resting in the palm of his raised hand. Held at the ready, set to stab me through the heart with a mere flick of those slim, perfectly manicured fingers.

Apparently, I didn't slide through his outer wards as easily as I thought. And he's not rising to greet me. A strange sort of thrill shivers through me, and I find myself biting back a most inappropriate grin.

Elias's gaze snaps to my mouth. To my lower lip caught in my teeth.

"Think you can take me?" I say, my voice low and playfully taunting. My own power shivers over me again — I recognize the energy the second time it happens, but it's still a completely unusual feeling. "My lord?"

I've misplaced my brain somewhere, willfully abandoning the polite princess in the outer halls and momentarily forgetting —

Roz's presence shifts behind me, just beyond the wards I can still feel sealing the doorway. Wariness laces through her voice. "Your Highness?"

Elias's gaze levels over my shoulder. He raises both of his hands slightly, palms outward and now empty. The weapon constructed out of light has dissipated. At the same time, the wards on the door through which I easily passed fade away.

I glance at Roz with a polite smile.

She grimaces, looking steadily and intently at Elias for a moment. Then she deliberately casts her gaze around the entire office. With a stiff nod to me, she snags the door handle and steps back into the outer hall to pull the door closed.

She's not going to be pleased that I don't plan to actually stay within the confines of the office she's just deemed safe enough to momentarily house me.

Removing my sunglasses, I turn back to Elias. He doesn't meet my gaze, looking everywhere but at me as he rolls down the cuffs of his shirt.

A sliver of disappointment runs through me. "I don't mean to disturb you."

"Not at all." He retrieves the carefully folded suit jacket slung over the back of his chair, pulling it on. His posture is stiff. "Please forgive me. I have ..." He casts his gaze across his paper-strewn desk. "I was deeply focused, and ..."

More disappointment etches its way through me at his

formal tone. A silly, irrational reaction. We're not friends or lovers, after all. We barely know each other.

I take a few more steps into the office until I'm standing before the desk. I fold my hands together around my sunglasses, ever so politely. My backpack, the marble urn within it, is oddly heavy across my shoulders, even though the urn is two handfuls lighter than it had been.

Elias straightens his tie, then taps the screen of his phone to check for recent messages.

Such as the one I should have sent before assuming I could just pop in. I … I should have expected that he'd be in his own office. But I hadn't.

After another glance at the piles of paperwork on his desk, his fingers twitching as if he wants to tidy them, he finally raises his gaze to meet mine.

Light-blue eyes to violet.

The tips of his ears are slightly pink.

I've misunderstood his reaction to my arrival. He's … embarrassed? Under all the composure, all the formality. But why would me showing up unannounced be embarrassing?

Roz's comment about Lia still sniffing around comes back to me. And I click it all together, though perhaps a little haphazardly.

I really have interrupted Elias. Or caught him in the middle of doing something he … something private? Maybe his state of undress wasn't just the earl making himself comfortable? Maybe Lia's presence … was …

"I'm sorry, my lord," I say, my own cheeks flaming. "I should have known these were your offices now that you're occupying your familial council seat. I truly didn't mean to interrupt. I thought I could slip in and out."

Elias blinks rapidly. "You aren't here to see me? Ah, I

mean, you could never be an interruption, Your Highness. It's always a pleasure ..."

He swallows.

Possibly because I'm just staring at him. My odd sense of disappointment is now all riled up and warring with the embarrassment. I pointedly don't glance down at the papers. Just in case it's whatever he's working on, and not just Lia's presence, that he's embarrassed for me to witness. I would have thought the guard on the main doors would have announced us ... perhaps that was why Lia was in the outer hall? Answering the phone?

No. She seemed genuinely shocked by my presence.

Elias tries again. "I was hoping that I could meet you for ... lunch sometime this week, Your Highness."

"Lunch, my lord?" My voice is more thin than politely reserved.

Elias glances down at his phone again.

I'm not certain if he's checking the time or expecting a message. But either way, I'm obviously truly interrupting him. And truly unwanted. Though I've stumbled into this situation, and I really should have no expectations of my reception, I feel just a little ... dejected ... rejected?

Sully has led me to believe that —

Elias shifts slightly, clearly waiting on me to continue the stilted conversation. That's protocol.

Because I haven't properly responded to his lunch request. Another flash of pure disappointment runs through me, visceral and sharp. I thought we had dispensed with all the stupid protocol and ...

The urn is heavy on my back. The backpack straps dig into my shoulders. I need to just get through this awkwardness. I need to set aside whatever expectations I had and keep moving forward.

Hands still clasped before me, I paste on a perfect-princess smile, imbuing my voice with a lightness I don't feel. "We used to come here, Armin and I." My tone is once again lilt-ingly pleasant. "Mostly on school breaks, around visits with our father. I think it must have been something Anne tried to enforce for a few years. Bonding time. He'd get called away … and we'd be …" I shrug and tilt my head, perfectly prettily.

Elias is just staring at me now, his expression on the cool edge of refined. His light-blue eyes are sharp. And slightly darkened with some emotion. It looks a little like anger, but could also just be a product of the windows being at his back, not perfectly illuminating his face.

"Your father likely regretted showing us something this intriguing …" I continue with my little story, stepping to the side as I speak until I can rest my hand on one of the bare dark-wood bookshelves. "Because every time we visited the council offices afterward, we always pestered him to …"

I press a touch of my essence to the switch hidden underneath the shelf nearest my shoulder. I'd been too short to reach it the first time the former Lord Hereford had shown us the secret door and the staircase beyond it, hidden behind his bookshelves.

The latch clicks under my fingers. Released from the essence holding it in place, the entire bookshelf slides a few centimeters forward, hinged on one side. I glance at Elias.

His shoulders have slumped, expression fallen. Or maybe it's opened up? Either way, and somewhat oddly, it doesn't soften the carved lines of his face in the least. No, his sadness or … grief makes him seem older. Possibly exhausted.

Perhaps my unannounced presence is just another burden.

The piles of paperwork already tell me he's one of the

few world councilors holding hereditary seats who don't simply see their position as nominal. Even ceremonial.

I can feel it now. Feel him now. His grief, combined with everything I'm already holding, slices through my chest. Harshly enough that I can't stop myself from quietly gasping under the onslaught.

Elias's expression completely shutters. He offers me a stiff smile as his essence shifts around him. All the light in the office, including the daylight slashed through the wooden shades, dims ever so slightly.

Then I can't feel him, or his grief, anymore.

After almost staggering under the weight of our combined sorrow, I'm momentarily rudderless at its withdrawal, swaying on my feet. I grip the half-open bookshelf for support.

Elias's eyes widen.

I turn away, pushing the section of bookshelf open wider. My voice is shaky as I murmur, "I won't be a moment."

Then I'm moving again, opening the fire door that was likely installed when the seventeenth-century building was retrofitted for more modern offices. It was easier to hide the staircase than to tear it out, I suppose. Plus, it provides an emergency exit.

Though the stairs lead up, not down.

Leaving Elias without another word, I resist a childish impulse to slam the bookshelf closed behind me. I'm certain he can get it open if he wants it open.

I quickly ascend the twist of heavily worn hardwood stairs. A modern metal railing has been installed, making the passage tighter than it felt when I was a child. I don't think I've traversed these stairs since I was ... thirteen or fourteen ...

I've also never walked them alone.

Some firsts should never be. And for me, climbing these stairs without Armin is a first that I never, ever wanted to experience. I know that's a tiny change, a minuscule moment, in the grand scheme of things, but …

I pause at the top landing to press a hand to the center of my chest, still gripping the railing with my other hand. My heart beats against my rib cage — rapid but somehow heavy at the same time. And not because I've practically just run up dozens of steep stairs, though that's obviously a factor.

I bow my head and just weather the moment. Thick curls of my hair, which I allowed Sully to play with this morning before we climbed aboard the helicopter, fall forward all around my face. I just need a breath, another breath, before I once again rally.

I should have known I might run into Elias. And therefore I really should have called ahead and made certain I was welcome. But I … I thought, so stupidly, that some level of friendship had been growing between us. And on top of my grief and the reason I'm here, that has thrown me.

Ultimately, despite all my best intentions, I am that selfish.

Selfish, completely self-centered, not to have called ahead. And now selfish to be shocked that I'm really not welcome. That I'm actually … intrusive.

The scuff of a shoe on the stairs just below me tells me I'm not alone. Though I'm not certain how Elias has followed me so closely without my knowing.

He can shield himself from me somehow. Here in his offices, at least. He hadn't been doing so at Lake Thun.

I lift my head, get the door to the balcony open, and step out into the cool of the late morning before I'm actually ready to be moving. It's an acquired skill — doing things I don't want to do, fueled only by pure, willful determination.

A stone parapet and balustrade sweeps around the curve of the upper tower, though the offices below have been carved out in straight lines. If I walked to the far left and peered back, I'd see the modern glass edifice that the World Council built behind the traditional council seat about twenty years ago.

I do walk to the left, but I don't bother peering up at the ridiculous monument. Not that I think the World Council, led by my father, is ridiculous. I just disagree with the need for so much ... flash.

Maybe it's just me.

Still, plenty of the council's members choose to retain their offices in the original building, so perhaps I'm not the only one who doesn't feel a need to throw away all tradition in order to be perceived as relevant in the modern world.

I shrug my backpack off, retrieving Armin's urn from its depths. I set the urn on the low balustrade, cupping it in both hands as I look out over the city. Zurich spreads out in three directions from this vantage point, though I'm not situated quite high enough to see across all the rooftops. There's a green space at the base of the World Council buildings. Set up for security purposes, mostly, but it's also pretty. Even with the trees barely in bud and the display of spring flowers still to come.

Elias hesitates in the open doorway behind and to my right. His gaze is on me, not the view.

And yes, I can feel that intent from him again.

A chill breeze plays with my hair, and my hands grow colder and colder against the marble of Armin's urn. But now that I've achieved my primary goal, I'm stuck in the moment. My thoughts are disorganized. I haven't forgotten why I'm here, of course, but my plan suddenly seems ... so trite. So indulgent.

Wandering around to places of some significance to my childhood with Armin, to spread his ashes?

My brother would have accused me of hiding behind that self-imposed ritual. Of wasting precious time. And he'd have been bored out of his mind.

The school. The pond. And now the balcony where we played and pretended to hide from our parental figures, even though they always knew exactly where we were at all times.

Elias clears his throat gently.

I flinch. The urn, despite its size and weight, wobbles in my hands. I'm gripping it too tightly, even as it feels as though I don't have a good enough hold on it at all. It feels like it could tumble over the edge, falling many meters to smash on the stone pathway that meanders through the park below.

Elias lunges forward, but a literal rope of his essence gets to me first, twining around my hands and the urn. Gently cinching my hands in place while steadying the urn. Then the earl is next to me, close enough to brush his chest against my shoulder as he closes his hand over the top of the urn.

"The parapet is lower than I remember," I say, like an utter idiot.

"It does seem terribly unsafe up here," Elias murmurs.

I don't look up at him. I keep my gaze on the urn. On his hand pressed to the lid. We aren't touching at all now, but we're close enough to be breathing in each other's essence.

I take a deep, utterly greedy breath. Then another.

"I'd forgotten this place existed," Elias says quietly. "I haven't been up here, not once since ..."

"... your father died?"

I catch his nod in my peripheral vision, neither of us looking at the other.

"He'd come up here with a cigar," Elias says. "Even though he wasn't supposed to smoke them." He hesitates. "He died of an essence-wasting sickness."

"I know," I say. "He weathered it for years. I could feel it."

Elias closes his eyes and huffs quietly. Like he thought his father's condition was a big secret and now feels stupid that it wasn't. "I had a plan ..."

"Lunch?" I say, both a little cool and a little peeved.

He shakes his head, then rubs his free hand across his face. "Yes. Lunch." He clears his throat, pointedly looking at Armin's urn.

I sigh. Heavily. Not simply internally as a perfect princess should. "I had a plan."

"Not lunch."

I snort, completely unbecomingly. "Not lunch."

Elias carefully peels his fingers and palm off the urn. "You're spreading Armin's ashes in all the places that meant something to the two of you."

"Silly, right?" I say weakly. "Using Armin's death as an excuse to avoid my responsibilities."

Elias is silent for long enough that I feel myself getting all twisted up inside. Again. Then he leans into me, still not quite touching, and brushes a kiss across my temple. "I think ..." His voice is husky with contained emotion. "My father would be honored that he ... could be a part of ..."

"He used to make us these ..." I sob, just once. And not just from grief. Because there is joy embedded in this memory. "These little animal figurines, but out of light. He'd line them up ..."

Elias places his cupped hand on the balustrade next to

the urn. My words catch in my throat as he lifts his hand to reveal a tiny cat figure created from pure light. Then he places his hand down again and manifests a puppy, then a horse, then a songbird.

A few tears snake down my cheeks, though I try to blink the bulk of them back. Maybe I'm mourning more than just Armin.

Maybe I'm mourning, so utterly selfishly, the parts of me that I've lost … the part of my soul?

Elias gently brushes his finger along one of the bird's wings. In a flutter of light, the bird takes flight, flitting around our heads and shoulders.

I laugh, though I'm still crying.

"I didn't know that you knew my father," Elias says. "I've been obsessing over the proper order of things. And that's important, but I …" He looks at me then. Finally. Tears shining within the blue of his eyes. "I didn't know you knew my father. He took his position very seriously, and I suppose any contact with you and the prince would have felt … sacred to him. Sacred enough to not tell anyone else."

I can feel him again. Whatever barrier he placed between us in the office is gone, stripped away.

I turn my head. I raise my chin. I look Elias in the eye; then I wait. I wait to see what he wants. Because I already know I want him in my life. It doesn't have to be sexual. It doesn't have to be some possibly mystical connection — like what Bolan and Sully believe exists between us. But I want his friendship.

"Someone has to keep us all organized, focused," I say. It's a challenge, not a tease.

Elias reaches up and smooths his thumb across my cheek, wiping an errant tear away. "I agree. You're all terribly prone to disorganization."

I laugh involuntarily. Then I turn back to the urn, remove the lid, and reach in for a handful of ashes. This time, my fingers brush the bottom of the urn, and I try to settle within that feeling, that looming end. Spreading Armin's ashes was the point, after all.

Elias steps slightly away, giving me a bit of room but not completely withdrawing.

The chill wind catches the ashes the moment I pull my hand free.

I open my palm, not thinking about anything in particular.

The little songbird of light lands on my open thumb, perched on my knuckle for the entire time it takes for the wind to spread Armin's ashes over the balustrade and beyond.

Until only a dusting across my skin remains.

I place the lid back on the urn, sealing it.

I turn my head toward Elias and raise my chin. It's not a challenge this time, though. It's a request.

The bird takes flight. The essence fueling it and the other light-constructed animals dissipates as Elias moves close enough to hover his lips over mine.

I lift up on my toes to close the kiss, brushing my lips against his, just once. Then again.

We hover in that moment, not otherwise touching. Just lips smoothing over lips, breathing in each other's essence.

Until Elias sighs, lightly pressing his forehead to mine. "You're cold, Mirth."

I open my mouth to protest, but he grabs my backpack and tucks the urn safely within it. Then, with a hand firmly pressed to the small of my back, he coaxes me toward the stairs.

And maybe — just in this moment — I don't mind his controlling tendencies. I don't mind giving up the lead. It's possible it's a bit of a relief. No matter that I also liked the gentle kisses.

7

$\mathcal{E}$LIAS

I SETTLE MIRTH ON THE COUCH. SHE CURLS HER legs under her, carefully keeping the soles of her boots off the sleek brown leather. She raises an eyebrow and offers me a tiny smirk when I retrieve a hand-knit afghan blanket from the lower cupboard of the side table. But she doesn't ask why I have a blanket in my office, simply allowing me to tuck it over her legs.

Mirth brushes her fingers across mine as I'm withdrawing my hand — the touch and the tingle of her power as intimate as kissing, even as intense as having someone else's mouth wrapped around my cock. But I'm hovering on the precipice of being overwhelmed by the soul-encompassing intimacy I found with her on the balcony, and ... I'm not certain she feels it all as intensely as I do. So I don't reach back for her.

"You inherited your father's power," Mirth murmurs, her breath tickling my neck.

"Yes."

I could turn my head and kiss her again. Except even I understand that the kisses on the balcony weren't meant to be sexual. Not carnally, at least. That's not what Mirth needed from me at that moment. And closing my mouth over hers now would be carnal.

But I want it to be, more sharply than I've ever wanted anything. More than I've wanted anyone. I already know, I can already sense, that even the moment Armin stole in the back room of the nightclub all those months ago, kissing me without warning, and as shocking as that was, is a barest hint of the desire I already feel for Mirth.

We haven't had that discussion.

I've barely started formally courting her.

Now that the thought has flitted through my mind — the comparison of the touch of both of them, their power against my skin, and the simple fact that the last carnal kiss I participated in was with Armin — well, I don't want to be thinking of her brother while kissing Mirth.

Ironically, Armin hadn't asked for consent. Though it wasn't his rank or position that stopped me from pushing him away.

I want things crystal clear between Mirth and me.

Mirth smooths a hand over the blanket. The ostentatious emerald-and-platinum ring on the ring finger of her right hand catches a slice of the daylight filtering in through the half-shuttered windows.

"But your mother was a fabricator mage. Like Sully."

I laugh quietly. "No one is like Sully."

Lord Savoy is yet another subject I don't feel at all ready to dissect, which just adds to my verging-on-being-overwhelmed state. I gave him that ridiculous to-do list so I have an excuse to check in with him whenever I want. A contract with his name on it is one of the many documents currently on my desk. One I'm hoping Mirth's keen eyes didn't note before I can broach the subject with her.

Her first, then Sully.

Sully is not going to like anything contractual between us. Sully won't be contained by any of the terms I would put on those pages.

I already know I can't ask Mirth to abide by any of my regular rules around sexual contact. Not only does she outrank me in society, in the bond group — and no doubt in sheer power. I still don't have a firm grasp on what her purple eyes denote, though I do know it's more than mere empathy. But also, I don't want any rules etched across a page between Mirth and me. And that mere thought, that mere desire, has shaken me as well.

"Fabricator mage is a broad classification." Mirth grins up at me.

Her violet eyes are shockingly vibrant. I wonder if I could capture the light from within them — not diminishing it in the least by doing so — and harness it. What blade of power could I create with that mere glint? What shield?

Mirth blinks, her grin dimming.

I haven't kept up my side of the conversation.

"The blanket is my mother's work," I say, forcing myself to stop tucking it in around her. It's perfectly tucked already, but doing so again is an excuse to hover around Mirth but not quite touch her. As if another touch might send me to my knees, reaching to pull her down on top of me. "Textiles were just a hobby for her, though. She always complained that my father's office was too chilly."

Mirth casts a deliberate look around the room, freeing me from her gaze. "You haven't redecorated. Just removed all the …"

"Clutter?" I say mockingly, straightening but now

feeling a little unmoored. I had all these lists, plans, on how to properly court Mirth —

"I'm sure a councilor is always in need of … books," Mirth says primly, defending my father though he has no need of it now.

I want to retreat behind my desk. To place a firm barrier between us. To collect myself. But I've bungled this entire interaction. Though Mirth did trigger all of my disconcertion by walking unannounced through my wards with only the barest whisper of her passage. No one — not even my father, my earliest mentor, with whom I shared essence on a primary, DNA-encoded level — could do that.

Aware of Mirth watching me, I cast my gaze over the paperwork covering almost every centimeter of my desk. None of it is for Mirth's signature, though. It's up to me, to all of us, to establish a bond group worthy of her consideration. The ties between her bonded must be unbreakable, unquestionable, so that she'll never doubt us. So her father will never doubt us.

"Do you mind if I watch you work for a few more moments?" Mirth asks sweetly, nothing remotely demanding in the question.

I glance at her, too many responses whirling in my head to address at once. I pluck up my phone and cross back to the seating area. I want to sit on the couch, in the hopes that Mirth will cuddle into me like she did on the terrace at Lake Thun. But it was Christoph, and Sully for that matter, who had smoothed that into a possibility. So I take the matching leather chair, unbutton my suit jacket as I sit — and at the last moment, tug the chair just a little closer to Mirth.

I set my phone on the arm of the chair. "These I replaced."

"Same color leather, though," Mirth says teasingly.

I narrow my eyes at her, understanding that she wants to play for a bit, even though the touch of her grief is still heavy within my chest. And I'm no empath. I'm the opposite of empathic. A defense mechanism, I believe. From watching my father slowly die for over a decade.

"Am I interrupting?"

"I'm actually almost done," I say, knowing that Sully, and maybe even Bolan, has already mentioned what all this planning is about. "There are a few lingering contracts, but the structure is in place for the formation of the bond group."

"The Savoy bond group."

"Yes."

"And how did you get Sully to agree to that?"

"Why would you assume it was me?"

Mirth laughs. The heaviness in my chest eases a little. Her hold on her power has loosened, but I'm fairly certain that's not why I can feel her in my chest. Christoph mentioned the same connection.

I can block it, though. Mirth is already distracting. In a way that I suddenly, continually, want to be distracted for the rest of my life. But rationally, it's far too soon to be contemplating, or even requesting for that matter, a lifetime commitment. Not on an individual level, at least.

"I had no idea that Sully was Lord Savoy," I say, addressing only one part of Mirth's question. "The reveal was ... a shock."

"He wanted it that way."

"But you knew."

"Of course."

"Always?"

"Always."

I nod thoughtfully.

"Sully hasn't been very forthcoming about the bond

group you've decided to form," Mirth says. "Other than you giving him a to-do list and that he literally loathes just about everything you've asked him to do."

"If he's going to claim his title," I say mildly, "then Lord Savoy must establish a presence in the nation."

"Sully already has a presence."

Mirth is teasing. But doing this properly, all of us forming, establishing, the bond group properly, is exceedingly important to me. Mirth needs us, and we need her. It's more than just proving that we're a fit for her — powerful enough, rich enough, skilled enough. The world needs to know it too. There must be no question that we as a bond group can stand beside Mirth.

Too many conversations still need to be had, though, and Sully and Bolan have no time for conversations. Or contracts. Or proper protocol.

"You're worried," Mirth says gently. "About ... me?"

"No. I'm simply tired. My apologies."

"Maybe we should get some lunch ordered in?" She tilts her head playfully. "Then take a nap?"

I swallow. Then I find the strength deep within myself to relax enough to take the gift she's so generously offering me, and I fucking flirt back.

"I don't think I'm napping around you, Mirth."

Her smile widens. "I'm sure there's something I can do to help you sleep ... I could read to you? That helps the twins. Though I suspect that with you, the book would need to be terribly boring."

I laugh involuntarily.

Mirth looks momentarily startled. I feel her essence shift, tightening around her.

"What about some warm milk?" I tease back.

She smiles, though still slightly hesitant.

I'm not certain what startled her, but ...

"I do think you can help me with some of the research I've been doing." I get up and cross around my desk.

Mirth's brow furrows, utterly becomingly. "With ... contract law?"

I laugh quietly to myself, though I get that she's a touch dismayed at the thought I might actually talk about contracts with her. From a locked drawer, I retrieve three books — purloined from my father's personal library, and which I've been combing through in between drafting contracts — along with my notebook. I rarely set pen to paper these days. It's too inefficient. But it felt right for this particular area of research.

These two areas, more accurately. But for the Savoy bond group, they are one and the same.

I set the books on the side table beside Mirth, keeping my notebook on my knee.

She glances at the titles stamped across the spines, then paraphrases the contents of the worn leather tomes without even opening the top book. "Intersection points. Soul-bound bonds. And ... the awry."

"You've read them."

She taps a French-manicured fingertip to the book on top of the pile — *The Potent History of the Soul Bound*.

"I've skimmed this, but the other two were ... required reading. For a time. I imagine Armin had a better grasp of the text than I do." She looks me in the eye, her violet gaze drilling into me. Then she says, without a hint of grief or anger, "I was the spare heir. Not powerful enough."

"Not 'not powerful enough'," I say, trying to be considerate while broaching a complicated subject. "I've spent the last four weeks finding out every little thing I could about you. Other than what appears readily enough on the surface, such as your charities and your public appearances as the so-called face of the royal family, more-personal information was somewhat ... difficult to obtain."

Mirth nods, still perfectly agreeable. "I'm not 'not powerful.' Tell me how you know. Besides the eyes."

"These books, and what other research I managed to accumulate before the matchmaking event, reenforce the ... perception of the awry, in general. Things such as the brighter or lighter the eye color, the more access an awry has to their essence ... to all essence."

"And my eyes are almost as bright as my father's. As bright as Armin's. Both known to be exceedingly powerful telekinetics. I could still be a dud, though. A genetic anomaly."

I nod, deliberately settling back in my seat in an attempt to defuse some of the tension now lightly threading through our conversation. "The public consensus is that you're simply more circumspect than your brother or father."

"Than my brother was," Mirth says.

"Yes."

"But you know differently."

"Yes."

I hesitate, but for just a moment. I don't want any secrets between us, between any of us. I want all of us within the bond group to be able to trust each other. Otherwise, I'm fairly certain we won't function in the way I now know — from my research — that we will need to function.

I suspect Mirth's trust will be the most difficult to nurture. Mirth might have the most to hide. Just as she usually tucks all her power away.

"The records of the royal guard aren't generally open to public purview," I say, starting by stating the obvious so Mirth can understand how I retrieved the information I now think I possess. "And anything having to do with the royal family isn't subject to warrant or court order."

"It's rare that the family denies such requests, though," Mirth says, perfectly pleasant. "From any governing or law-enforcement entities."

I nod to acknowledge that caveat, even as I continue with my main line of thought. "The presence of such a record indicates that an investigation took place, though. Or that charges were made that required supporting documentation."

"Of course ..." Mirth frowns, still unaware of the connections I've already made. "But you aren't the public, Lord Hereford. You can request any and all of the royal guard's records. Though ... you also aren't one to advertise your intent."

"No." I smirk, just a bit pleased that Mirth has me at least partially figured out. "I'm not."

She taps the stack of books with her fingers, as if she needs to keep me focused. She doesn't. I'm near obsessed with the topic, with her. "But we were speaking of the awry and my power specifically. I'm not seeing the connection to the royal guard?"

I nod. "I was ... annoyed that I missed the connection between Bolan and Rian Callaghan. It's common knowledge, if not publicly known, that Bolan's father, James Yates, died protecting Prince Armin and his mother. The statement issued by the royal guard to the public was officially released three weeks after the incident."

"That's an extra security precaution."

"I know. But the families involved, whether they lost a father, like Bolan and Livi, or if their family member was wounded in the attack, were informed immediately. And taken care of immediately. The records of such compensations or other considerations are meticulously organized.

However, they hold no mention of Rian's mother. There are two later mentions of Rian. That he'd taken the position of head horse breeder and was run through the corresponding security assessment, and then a ... shift in his security level about a month before the matchmaking event."

Mirth flushes prettily, confirming what I already guessed — that she started her relationship with Rian then, and the royal guard had done their due diligence behind the scenes. Both putting him through another level of scrutiny, then opening the ease of access between them. I wonder if either of them noticed.

I continue, "While the royal guard is circumspect, a mother and child in need of funds or other help isn't the sort of thing that would be wiped from their records."

"What is the sort of thing that gets wiped from their records?" Mirth's question is cool and calm, but it still slices through me.

I hesitate again. I can get fixated on puzzles and problems, and this conversation can easily wait for weeks or even months. For when everything is much, much more settled. But my instincts say this is important.

I hesitate only because in my desire to know everything there is to know about Mirth, I might be crossing a plethora of boundaries.

"I blinded my trainer when my powers first came in," I say bluntly, seemingly changing the subject. "I was a late bloomer. For my bloodline, at least. My parents weren't yet certain whether I would wield light or not."

"How old?"

"Thirteen. I could manipulate essence enough to attend the Phrontistery but hadn't specialized."

"It was fifteen for me," Mirth says, her gaze on me still steady — not remotely shying away from the topic.

It's possible that I'm wrong. That the pieces of the incident I've uncovered have nothing to do with Mirth. "I was angry and frustrated about losing the football division," I continue. "Childish."

"You were just a child."

"My father collapsed for the first time when I was sixteen. I haven't been a child since he was diagnosed. Since I understood the responsibilities I would need to take on decades before they should have been mine to bear."

Mirth takes a slow breath. "I harmed at least a half-dozen people when my power manifested. And I'm fairly certain I killed three of them, including ... including someone who was just trying to help us."

I don't react. Or at least I try not to react. I had uncovered only one of those deaths. "Another kidnapping attempt?"

"Yes." She hesitates this time. Just for a moment. Perhaps in remembrance. Or perhaps in not wanting to remember it at all. "An inside job. Armin and I were ... convenient, not targeted. I believe so, at least. An ... extraction unit was seemingly waiting nearby, tipped off by one of the school security guards. Presumably watching for anyone worthy of ransom to leave the protection of the school grounds. There would have been no way for them to anticipate that it would be Armin and me leaving."

"I don't think either of you make for a convenient kidnapping."

Mirth laughs involuntarily, then sobers quickly. "How did you know?"

I give her a moment to work it out for herself.

Her lips twist. "The royal guard memorial fund. You didn't just look at who the beneficiaries were from Armin's kidnapping."

"After I did that bit of digging about Bolan's father, I

was surprised by how many guards refuse a full payout. It's always enough that they likely wouldn't have to work another day in their lives. But most take the disability aid, then return to duty in some capacity within a few months."

"The royal guard are loyal. It's a calling, not an occupation."

"It would have to be. There were lots of injuries between Armin's attempted kidnapping and the sudden death of a guard who'd been assigned to your and prince Armin's school detail. But oddly, no other fatalities."

"So you found a record of the guard's death benefits?" Mirth asks quietly. "Just that? Nothing of the incident itself?"

"Not a whisper. Not a single notation."

She twists her lips. "The royal guard records aren't as meticulous as you thought."

"Were there more royal guard witnesses? Or any other witnesses at all?"

She opens her mouth ... then pauses, thinking. "In the end ... I suppose there was just my father, me, and Armin left. And only two of us were standing. Anyone who stumbled upon us in the aftermath, who dealt with the clean-up, would have had no idea that it wasn't my father's carnage strewn across the street. Or Armin's ..."

Mirth drops her gaze, brushing her fingers across the blanket as if using its texture to ground herself. Or perhaps she's just thoughtful, and I have an obsessive need to read into everything she's doing and saying. "Though ... my essence would read differently than a telekinetic's, for anyone sensitive to that sort of thing."

I need more. I understand her reluctance to divulge the full details. We're still practically strangers, after all. And even then, she has no idea what I would already do in order to protect her. But the Mirth who could harm a half-dozen people, including killing one of her guards, is at odds with the perfect princess I've had in my peripheral vision for her entire life. I'm looking right at that Mirth, *the* Mirth, right now. I know my life is meant to be threaded through hers.

"It's never happened again?"

"No. I've never voluntarily or involuntarily killed anyone again. You?"

I inhale deeply. Oddly, not relieved by her answer. Perhaps because I didn't need to be. "I've had a few ... close calls. Training accidents. But no, I haven't inadvertently maimed anyone else."

"It takes a lot of power to blind an essence-wielder so badly that a healer can't restore at least some of their sight."

I don't answer that. It's not a question, and Mirth already knows that she's correct. I rather desperately want to ask her what triggered her. But if she wanted me to know, she would have already told me. It's an easy guess, though, that it was the kidnapping attempt itself, the need to protect Armin, that caused her primary talent to manifest.

Mirth redirects the subject with another tap to the books on the side table. "So ... that confirms what this book tells you. I'm as dangerous as an awry can be." She's watching me closely. "I believe there's an entire chapter in this book on how the awry were hunted, are still hunted, and condemned for their twisted, uncontrollable essence. I'm the sort of awry that fueled the fever for those hunts."

I try to match her dispassionate tone, though I know I fail even before I open my mouth. "And yet it would have been those with purple eyes but none of the power who were beheaded or stoned or burned."

"Or those who willingly walked to their deaths, fearing what they were capable of destroying."

I'm barely breathing now. The twist in the conversation

— from playful banter about Mirth reading me to sleep, to the weariness that comes from holding, holding tightly, to immense power — is challenging what little equilibrium I have around Mirth. Mirth, who normally holds her power so tightly that she seems without any at all.

"Are you scared of me, Lord Hereford?"

Not realizing that my gaze has settled on her hand atop the books, I lock my gaze to Mirth's, holding her blazing purple eyes steadily.

This question — playfully and lightly posed — is perhaps the most important thing she's asked of me.

I cannot equivocate. I cannot wait for the proper moment to address this.

"I'm not scared of you, Mirth. I belong to you. I was put on this earth to balance you. To help you hold the inter-section point."

She holds my gaze, all her power once again tightly tucked away. But she doesn't otherwise respond.

I lean forward, deliberate intent threading through every one of my words. "I think … I've been researching this as well, and I've questioned the others, as much as they're willing to articulate themselves." I can't stop from twisting my lips at recalling just how stubborn Bolan is, specifically. And Sully isn't much better. "And I believe that whether or not we were all formally bonded, or even acknowledged the possibility of a bond between us, that Armin's death created … a fissure. A chasm that, in order to continue forward, to continue to … live, we needed to come together to try to heal."

Mirth blinks back a flush of emotion.

"I … I'm so sorry that it took Armin's death for us to rally, to find each other. To find you."

"You believe, then. In soul-bound mates. That the universe has … nudged us together because we lost Armin?"

Some emotion all but aches at the heart of Mirth's question. It isn't grief, though. And with that unknown still hanging between us — even as I sense it's the same thing, or at least part of the thing, that drove her away from us at Lake Thun — I don't know how to fix it. Not head-on, at least.

I'm still a little overcome, overwhelmed about it all myself. Burying myself in paperwork has been my only relief for days.

"My parents were soul bound," I say. "Just the two of them. They ... never needed anyone else to complete their bond group. Or maybe there weren't any more bonds for them."

"Same with my father," Mirth says. "Before his soul-bound mate and their child died. Years before he had Armin and me, before he took chosen mates, because ..."

"The intersection point," I say, tipping my chin toward the pile of books.

"Mostly, yes. I think."

"You'll explain that to me more? Yes?"

"Not now, but yes."

I nod agreeably, but only because I think the topic of the nascent connection between us and the others is more important. I suspect it's also the cause of the distance Mirth has placed between us.

This is why I wanted to do this all properly, perfectly timed. Then Sully and Bolan went running after Mirth, and —

I clear my throat. "My mother lasted two years after my father's death. It's not that they didn't both love me. Want me. But ... I think ... I think she held him here, on this plane, for longer ... longer than she should have. The pain he —"

I take a breath. I haven't really acknowledged that truth

out loud before, not allowed myself to truly articulate it in my own head. "She burned through her own essence, her life force, to do so. My father sent her away on a spa vacation with her sisters the weekend he summoned me out to the estate. Summoned me to make me Lord Hereford. But he ... needed help at that point. Needed help to transition to the next plane of existence. And my mother wouldn't help him."

Mirth gasps, quietly pained. Then she leans closer, offering her hand.

I take it. I take the comfort, though I know it should be the other way around. That my grief is old and tired while hers is still fresh. But the chance to be skin-to-skin ...

"Maybe she couldn't do it," Mirth says, her eyes shining. "Maybe the bond between a brother and sister could never compare ... but I don't think I could ever have helped Armin leave me. I don't think I could have been strong enough to let him go. Not even if he was in pain ..." Renewed tears roll down her creamy cheeks. "I think maybe ... maybe he was already in pain, and I wasn't enough —"

She shakes her head, still gripping my hand as she dashes the tears off her face with her free hand. "We're talking about you."

"We're talking about us," I say, my chest once again aching with our combined grief. Mirth must be an empath. Or it's the fundamental nature of the bond we share, as tentative as it currently is.

"Yes. Okay." She takes a shuddery breath and pulls one of those perfect-princess smiles out to shine on me. "Your mother?"

I should hate that she feels the need to smile at me like that. But selfishly, I adore her for keeping us on point. "My mother never forgave me. Not even with her dying breath. Not that I was allowed to witness it. I was banned from the estate. I never bother visiting even now. The aunts have the running of it."

"You're Lord Hereford," Mirth says with a bit of an edge. "No one tells you that you can't set foot on any of your properties."

I chuckle at her unfettered belief ... in me. When she really doesn't know me at all. And I suddenly want ...

I want to be that person for her.

She squeezes my hand, then her gaze drops to my mouth. She tilts her head becomingly. "Shall I make you feel better? Maybe in the same way you eased ..."

Then she trails off and glances toward the closed door. "Oh, too late. Shall I apologize ahead of time for not warning you, Lord Hereford? Or will you make me grovel later?"

I raise both eyebrows, somewhat confused — and also somewhat disturbed at the idea of making Mirth do anything as degrading as groveling.

Then I hear the raised voices beyond the door. The almost-fevered clamor of excitement. It's more contained and muted than it was the last time he made an entrance, but I would have sworn there weren't that many people in the offices. Plus the guards and admins who are working while the council isn't in session really should be more circumspect.

"I'm not traveling alone today," Mirth says, completely unnecessarily. And definitely belatedly.

The door to the outer office is yanked open. I catch a glimpse of Roz and Mirth's other guard, Greg, looking extremely peeved. Then Bolan is all but tumbling into the room. Black hair falls across his brow, and a massive smirk stretches across his face. He's clad in his regular worn-black aesthetic.

It's Greg's presence that prepares me for who follows the normally belligerent rock star.

Lord Savoy. Salvatore. Sully.

He's kept his hair blue since Lake Thun. His suit is only a few shades darker, paired with a pinstriped white dress shirt that looks practically mundane for him. One too many buttons are undone at the collar.

I knew that Sully had returned to London and spent the evening with Bolan and Mirth, though his responses to my text messages haven't been at all forthcoming since he met with Rian and his mother. But I had no idea that Sully and Bolan had accompanied Mirth to Zurich — hence my verging-on-obsessive need to check my text messages all morning. Though I do hope their presence means they've actually filed the remaining paperwork formalizing Sully's claim to the Savoy title.

Sully's light-gray eyes lock to Mirth, as if he's been looking in her direction before he even cleared the doorway. But his presence still hits me like a wallop to the chest. Not as hard as when Mirth is near, though. And the tenor is different. Tense and tight, while Mirth is more like coming home. Maybe it's all intensified by the tenor of my conversation with her. Or maybe it's the perpetually overwhelming situation. But whatever is between the fabricator mage and me, it's not about comforting kisses and creating a support system.

I'm honestly not certain that Sully has eyes for anyone but Mirth. I'm not certain I should even be contemplating looking his way either. Not yet. Not until everything else is settled.

Conversations need to be had. Many conversations.

Mirth huffs playfully. "What have you done!?"

Bolan, still with that shit-eating grin and all the swagger he can muster, raises both hands. "It's Sully's fault. He made me a bet. I won." The grin shifts into a smirk, and Bolan's lax body language sharpens as he stalks toward Mirth — completely ignoring everything else.

Mirth puts it together before I do. "I'm not a prize!"

"Oh, baby," Bolan croons, now looming over her. "You are so much a prize."

Roz yanks the door shut behind Sully, closing us all in together. The far-too-large office suddenly feels very full.

Bolan leans over the couch, hands braced on either side of Mirth's shoulders. Laughing but shaking her head, she shoves him away. He falls in a heap beside her, pouting.

Much more composed, Sully passes his gaze over me, freezing me in place in my chair. Then he saunters over to Mirth's other side, leans over the arm of the couch, threads a hand through her hair, and lays a blistering kiss on her. A kiss Mirth leans deeply back to completely accept.

Bolan and I just watch them both. Not a flicker of jealousy in either of us, though. Just pure contentment. And as the kiss continues, more than a little want. A need.

Breaking the kiss, Sully edges himself onto the couch, pulling Mirth into his lap. She protests playfully but doesn't push him away. Bolan snags one of her long curls between two fingers and presses it to his face, inhaling.

Can he scent her desire for Sully? If so, I'm suddenly and irrationally jealous of that ability.

"No, wolf," Mirth says, though she's smiling at him sweetly. And just a little provocatively. Or that might be the slight puffiness her lips have gained from Sully kissing her hello.

Salvatore grasps Mirth's hips, positioning her exactly where he wants her in his lap. Then he levels an impassive look over her shoulder. At me. No playful brat in sight. Sully is pissed about something. Fed up.

"You have contracts to sign?"

I hesitate. "First drafts."

"I'm tired of this shit."

"Me too," Bolan huffs dramatically. He throws himself back to rest his head on the other arm of the couch, then slings an arm over his eyes. Without kicking Sully and Mirth, he only fits lengthwise with one foot on the ground and one leg bent against the back of the couch. Legs splayed, groin pointed toward his soul-bound mate. Presumably with intention.

"There will still be changes," I say cautiously. "We haven't discussed everything that needs —"

"Then add … addendums or codicils or whatever," Sully says. "I want Mirth to know we want her, that we're doing all of this for her. Now. Not three days from now."

"Sully," Mirth murmurs, "I have to make responsible choices. I have to think of —"

Sully covers Mirth's mouth with his hand, tugging her head back so they're pressed cheek to cheek. Her eyes go round with indignation. The rest of her protest is muffled in his palm.

Clearly peeved at being silenced, after already being displaced from her seat, she grabs Sully's forearm, then squirms to get away.

Thus wiggling her delectable ass on Sully's lap.

He groans, openly and loudly. Then he sucks on Mirth's earlobe, whispering, "Just like that, Mir."

She stills, eyes narrowing, both hands still gripping Sully's forearm.

Bolan, peeking at the two of them from under his arm, grins saucily. The shifter's emotion and intent are always easy to read, both worn like an epic chip on his shoulder. And his heart beats blatantly, solely, for Mirth. I can see that every time they're anywhere near each other.

Even having only really known Mirth and the bond I'm

convinced we share for a few days, I understand Bolan's life-style choices — all the numbing agents he once needed to continue functioning — far better. At least he had Armin and Sully.

I've been adrift since my father died. Since before that, really, but I let all my responsibilities distract me. I understand the rush, though. The need to —

"I want to sign now," Sully reiterates between planting light kisses on Mirth's neck. "If I have to be Lord fucking Savoy, I want Mirth. Mirth is my prize whether or not Bolan won the last bet."

"And what bet was that?" I ask, unable to tear my gaze off Mirth as she twists to try to get a look at Sully.

He grips one of her plush hips and visibly, though slowly, grinds into her ass from below.

Her protest sounds a lot more like a muffled moan this time.

"The bet ..." Bolan's eyes, bright with his wolf, remain fixed to Mirth. "The bet isn't important. The wager is."

"And what is the wager?" I know I'm just playing into Bolan and Sully's game, the power play between them. But I desperately want to see where they think they're taking it.

Bolan laughs huskily. "Dibs."

Mirth shrieks indignantly behind Sully's hand. Then she bites him. Hard.

He shouts, releasing her to shake his hand out.

She's on her feet, twisting to face them both, hands on her hips. "This is entirely inappropriate. We're interrupting Lord —"

Bolan practically slides off the couch to kneel before her, head falling back. To her, it likely looks as though he's groveling, but I know the pose for what it truly is. Prayer.

Ever helpful, I casually lean over and drag the coffee

table away a few steps so Mirth doesn't accidentally stumble over or around it.

Sully meets my gaze around Mirth's lush hips, smirking. "Lord Hereford doesn't appear to be minding the interruption, Mir." His gaze drops to my groin. An impertinent eyebrow rises to match his smirk.

I was interested, even enticed while watching Mirth and him, of course. But not yet erect. Not enough to be obvious. Sully's look changes that, though. I lounge back in my chair, and I ignore my hardening cock.

I ignore him.

I don't like being played with.

I won't be played with.

Something shutters in Sully's gaze. "Fine," he says. "Let's talk about contracts. Have you drafted one for Mirth yet?"

I know exactly what he's implying. What he's heard. Clearly, I'm not the only one who has been doing research this week.

"Does Mirth know all about your little ... predilection, Eli?" Sully says, pushing. "That one of your little contract fucks is still hanging around outside this office, waiting to see if —"

"Enough, Sully," Bolan snaps, standing as effortlessly as he'd slid to the ground.

Sully levels a fierce look at Bolan. "I'm protecting Mirth. If I have to be Lord fucking Savoy, then —"

"Then don't be," Mirth says. Her cool, quiet statement instantly blankets all the rising tension in the room. "Don't be Lord Savoy, Sully."

Sully's face falls. His shoulders slump. All the pent-up frustration and burbling anger just drains from him.

My heart pinches in a way I've never felt before. At

Sully's devastation, and at Mirth's cool pronouncement, and at everything she's rightfully read into his ire.

How is all of this hinging on such a delicate balance?

I believe what I said to Mirth — that Armin's death was obviously a catalyst. But it's also obvious that we weren't all ready to come together, to fully commit to each other, to a bond group. And to our roles within that group.

This is why I had a plan. This is why I wanted a solid foundation. We don't even know each other. So how are we going to convince Mirth that we can support her in every way she needs?

"Princess ..." Bolan reaches for Mirth, but she pivots, perfectly steady on her feet. She easily sidesteps the coffee table, crossing to retrieve her backpack.

"Mirth ..." Sully closes his eyes and hangs his head. But he's utterly deflated, almost flat. Pushed too far out of his comfort zone.

And maybe that's partly my fault. With the lists and contracts.

Backpack in hand, the urn heavy within it, Mirth turns to take us in with a sweep of violet-hued eyes — which don't look at any of us at all. Her expression is once again perfectly serene.

A numb sensation slowly spreads through my chest as I stand, buttoning my suit jacket by rote. Is that sensation the absence of Mirth? She's gathered all her essence tightly again.

Sully stumbles to his feet as if he feels the same — perhaps even more acutely, given how pale his naturally tanned skin has become. "Please. That's not ... that's not what I meant, Mirth."

"It's exactly what you meant, Sully. And it's perfectly fine. Perfectly understandable, in fact." She flicks her gaze to me, smiling without exposing her teeth. Without it reaching her eyes. "I apologize again for interrupting you, Lord Hereford. Thank you for indulging my ... whims. I'll leave you to your paperwork."

Bolan steps forward with that shifter swiftness, touching Mirth's jaw. Just lightly, but it seems to break her free of the facade she's pulled around herself like a physical barrier between us and her. The rock star's eyes glow with his wolf. Her gaze snaps to meet his as he looms over her, like he's completely ensnared her.

"You know that's not what Sully meant, Mirth." Bolan's voice rumbles through his chest.

All the hair on my arms stands up as Bolan's innate dominance coils around Mirth.

She bares her teeth at him in a blatant challenge. "It's too much, Bolan. I'm too much!"

"Which is it?" he asks, darkly intent.

I have no idea where the sullen, belligerent, self-centered rock star has suddenly disappeared to. Even Sully is staring at Bolan as if truly seeing him for the first time.

"What?!"

"We'll address both those statements, Mirth. Pick which one bothers you the most, and we'll start there."

She huffs. "Bolan!"

"We're not going anywhere. None of us." His words are low and measured.

"You're being a bully, Bolan," Mirth says, her gaze still riveted to him. "I'm allowed to have feelings. I'm allowed time to think. I don't have to accept —"

"You know what happens when you run."

They've bonded, I realize.

I've been so focused on Mirth, then distracted by Sully, that I didn't feel the shift in the tenor of energy that threads between Bolan and Mirth. It's not the robust connection that anchored my parents together, and is therefore far easier to miss, even with my general sensitivity to essence. But still, utter relief floods through me, cracking the numbness threatening to take up residence in my chest.

As erratic and self-centered as the rock star seems on the surface, I know now that he's all in — to the bond group and to Mirth.

"Don't run," Bolan says.

Pure unfettered defiance brightens Mirth's eyes. She raises her chin, then completely and utterly dismisses Bolan, taking a single step to the side and striding past him, past us all. As if none of us exist.

She heads straight for the door.

I expect Bolan to grab her. Sully was already pushing her around.

I'd have to stop him, I realize. I don't want to get between them. Yes, each of us must navigate our own connections with the others, but we can't force any of those connections, especially not physically. I should have curtailed Sully's handling of Mirth earlier as well.

The princess lays her fingers across the handle of the door.

Bolan sinks to his knees. He doesn't take a step first or make a sound. He simply kneels and waits, staring after Mirth. There is absolutely nothing playful in the gesture this time.

Mirth stills, staring at the door for a moment before she slowly looks back at him over her shoulder. Energy gently shifts between them. She pivots just as slowly, presses her back against the door, and closes her eyes. The backpack dangles from her fingers.

"I'm not playing games," she murmurs, seemingly to herself.

Bolan doesn't move a muscle. "I know."

"You're acting like I'm a game. Like this is a game."

She means more than just Bolan kneeling or the bet. 'Dibs.' I didn't realize that bothered her. I know Mirth isn't the simple, perfect-princess persona she wears with seeming ease, but I had no inkling ...

I tear my gaze off her, watching Bolan instead. Is it just his heightened senses that help him assess Mirth's emotional state? Or is their bond growing stronger, even in this moment?

I want that connection so badly I can fucking taste it.

"It won't happen again," Bolan says, steady as a fucking rock while my heart still beats wildly in my chest. "You're mine, and I'm yours. Sully doesn't give a fuck about a stupid fucking title. His meds aren't working well, and something pissed him off yesterday. He's not talking to me about it either. Elias isn't fucking the shifter in the front office. I would smell sex on them. You aren't an inconvenience or an obligation. To any of us. And Elias, specifically, wants any part of you that you're willing to share with him."

Well, that was perfectly concise.

Maybe Bolan should speak for us all more often. Maybe I've completely underestimated the rock star.

Mirth raises her chin a little higher. Though her bright eyes betray the molten core of her emotional state, she's all poised and cool toned as she says, "Elias can fuck whoever he wants. And Sully never wanted the title." Her blazing gaze slides toward the devastated mage hanging on her every word, her every breath.

All three of us are desperate to move past this awkward, soul-wrenching moment.

Now who's the dramatic one?

Bolan chuckles, dark edged. "Eli can fuck whoever, hey?"

Tension runs through Mirth's jaw. Her gaze flicks to me, and she clarifies, "Whoever he wants."

I smile tightly at that. Then I follow Bolan's blunt lead. "I never really wanted, truly wanted anyone before. Before you, Mirth. Before this bond group. Sex was just a ... necessity, not a desire. And companionship, deep friendship was ... unnecessary."

Mirth listens to every word, tilting her head in acknowledgment once she's absorbed them. I hope. Then she flicks her gaze to Sully. He jerks as if meeting her gaze is like grabbing a live wire.

A perfectly understandable reaction.

"The title means nothing," Sully says dully. "It was nothing to my mother. It was nothing to my father. And they ultimately were nothing to me, weren't they?"

Mirth swallows. I feel the history between her and Sully yawn open. So much love and consideration. Acceptance.

"So ... the title is nothing," Sully whispers. "The money is nothing. Except for what it might help secure. Because you mean everything. You and Armin ..." His voice cracks. "And even fucking Bolan are my entire fucking world. You took my hand, literally. Do you remember that first day, moving into the dorms? When I was a seven-year-old with an obscene expense account and a hired driver dropping me off with only the clothing on my back? My own mother's blood on the cuffs of those jeans? And you and Armin had all the books and boxes and guards, all the hushed whispers following you around. You took my hand. And Armin figured out the way to the dining hall. Remember?"

Mirth nods.

"I say the wrong things. I don't process information like other people. I —"

"I know, Sully."

He takes a shaky breath. "I ... saw Rian yesterday."

Mirth steps away from the door, and all the tension in the room — good and bad — snaps into nothing. "What? When?"

"I went to him, to Rian. In Dublin. And now I'm pissed. Or I was pissed. Now I'm just … numb. But I'm also still pissed, mostly at myself, because … maybe … maybe I shouldn't have gone." He closes his eyes for a moment. "I don't want to talk about it with you, Mirth. But I think … I probably need to talk about it, don't I? Otherwise, I wouldn't have been … but it shouldn't be with you. Because what if I misunderstood? Or I'm just overwhelmed about everything else? I don't want to fuck up anything. Between us or in the bond group. Or with you and Rian."

The rush of words stops, and Sully takes another shaky breath. His right hand smooths down his suit jacket, pausing at each button.

"Me," I say after waiting a moment so I don't interrupt him if he wishes to continue. "You'll talk to me, Sully. And I'll help you sort through your reactions. Then we take to Mirth whatever needs to be taken."

Sully opens his eyes, raises his head, and looks directly at me. "All right."

Mirth glances between us, reluctantly nodding though she looks as though she wants to protest.

"Good." I reach for my phone. "I'll order lunch in. While we're waiting for it to be delivered, we'll go over the bond group contracts, make any amendments needed, and sign them. If Bolan and Sully are still amenable. And whenever you want, we'll discuss Rian."

We all level our attention on Mirth. She presses her lips together, clearly wanting to push — though what subject still needs clarification, I'm not certain. Instead, she steps away from the door, crossing to thread her fingers through Bolan's hair.

I suppress a moan of relief.

"Please order enough for Roz and Greg, Elias." Mirth slides an arch look my way. "And Lia, of course."

"Lia," I say steadily, "doesn't need to be here today. I'm sure she'll appreciate the rest of the week off."

"Find her a better placement," Sully demands.

Mirth frowns at him. Bolan seems to have slipped into some sort of meditative state, likely from Mirth combing her fingers through his hair. He's still on his knees, but not touching her in return.

"Do you have a personal issue with Lia, Salvatore?" Mirth asks.

Sully turns his sharp gray eyes on me, still riled despite his awareness that he's taking it out where he doesn't intend to. Though he honestly might be as pissed about Lia as he seems. "I do. No one fucks around outside the bond group. Not on Mirth ... and not on me."

"Fine," I say, cutting off any possible extension of the argument. "Most bond groups are faithful to each other, whether or not that includes a sexual component. But I'll add it to the bond group contract." I look pointedly at Sully. "Just for your comfort, Salvatore."

"Fine."

"Good."

"I'm thinking ..." Bolan drawls, eyes still closed. "Pizza. With lots of meat and cheese."

Mirth shakes her head and sighs. Then she twists her fingers through the back of Bolan's hair, tugs his head back with a fair bit of force, and brushes a kiss across his lips. If that's supposed to be a punishment on her part, I'll gladly be naughty enough to require it. And I've never liked anyone's fingers in my hair. In fact, I barely tolerate kissing.

"I don't like it when you're upset, Mirth," Bolan murmurs. "I don't like it when you've been crying. But if you need to do or be either of those things, let me at least be there with you? No more going off on your own."

"Bolan ..."

"Mirth," he growls, "how many more trips with the ashes are you planning?"

"One more stop."

"You will take me."

"And me," Sully interjects.

"All right. Anyone who wants to come with me can come. Okay? Yes."

The promise is barely past her lips before Bolan is surging up, flipping her over his shoulder, and striding toward the door that leads to the connecting conference room.

"That room isn't soundproof," I say.

Bolan whirls around, surveying the office — and almost clipping Mirth's forehead on the side of the bookshelves in the process.

She squeals, pummeling him with her fists. "Bolan! I can barely breathe!"

The rock star homes in on the other all-but-hidden door between the built-in bookshelves, striding toward it instead. The bathroom. He flings open the door with Mirth still huffing in protest over his shoulder. Then he strides in without turning on the light. Just kicking the door shut behind him and once again owning everything and everyone around him.

All the energy drains from the room.

Sully and I just stare blankly at the closed door.

I'm not certain if I want an invitation to watch, or to participate — or if I just wish Bolan hadn't felt the need to cart Mirth away.

"Dibs," Sully mutters, running a hand through his hair so that it sticks up at all sorts of adorable angles. Then he pivots and flings himself into the chair across from my desk, clearly defining the parameters of our conversation. "Plus, you know, he's not as much of an asshole as he seems."

I step around my desk, sitting down in my chair. "He is just as much of an asshole. But ... he's our asshole."

Sully flicks his gray eyes up to meet mine. Then he nods, almost curtly. "Yeah."

"Tell me about Rian."

Sully looks away, over my shoulder and out the windows. "I might have overreacted."

"I doubt it."

He blinks, surprised.

"Why did you decide to go to Dublin? Shouldn't Rian be overseeing the transport of Perseus to London? There's a major qualifying race on Thursday." Perseus, Armin's ridiculously expensive prize stallion, was a late addition to the schedule at Regal Park Racecourse. "I believe this race is one of the last chances to qualify for this season. Unless Mirth wants to race Perseus overseas."

Sully shifts in his chair. He's rumpling his suit, but I already know he doesn't care. "Rian's mother is in Dublin."

I nod, already knowing this part. The connection between Bolan and Rian was annoyingly shocking news, but I've done my due diligence since hearing it.

"I thought Rian might need support. I thought that was ... something I should do. You know, as Lord Savoy." He clears his throat, still not looking directly at me. "Bolan went home as well. For a chat with Adeline."

Ah. "How did that go?"

"Ask Bolan." Sully sighs, softening his tone. "Not well, I surmise. But I was being a close-mouthed, pissy asshole about my own shit, so I didn't really ask why."

"Is Rian ... reluctant?"

Sully swallows harshly, then whispers throatily, "Not about Mirth."

I settle back in my chair, disappointment making me pause.

"Yeah," Sully says. "That. Maybe it's just me that he —"

"I doubt it," I snap, halting that train of thought.

"No. You're right. He doesn't want to share."

"He's young. But he won't risk losing Mirth."

Sully nods, obviously running the conversation with Rian over in his head. Then he says quietly, "What if …"

"Mirth isn't leaving you. Or Bolan."

"She might … try to keep Rian, like, on the side …"

A dull sensation settles in my stomach. "If he's part of the bond group —"

"He is."

"You felt it?"

Sully nods. "It's not as solid as it is between Bolan and me, or even … you and me … but it's there. A friendship, at least. I … wouldn't have gone to him, right? I fucking traveled commercial on the way there."

"That is a commitment," I say wryly, even as I completely understand what he's saying.

The mage attempts to murder me with just a look.

I offer him a twisted smile, then I lean forward and extract Rian's copy of the contract from the pile on my desk. I gaze at it for a moment, then say, "We'll court him."

"Court him? He's already scared as fuck that one or more of us are going to want to suck his dick."

I snort, tapping the contract on my desk. "That's for him and Mirth to sort out. You don't have a problem with boundaries, do you, Sully?"

"Well, I don't need to have a contract written up just to have sex with someone," he snaps back caustically.

I raise an eyebrow at him and just wait. I've done as

much research on Salvatore as he's done on me. Likely more. He's had very specific tastes for the last couple of years.

Though for both of us, the need to be with Mirth — our crux — is going to play havoc on the boundaries we've erected for ourselves.

"Fine," he says. "Of course I don't have a problem with it. Maybe I'll never suck another dick again."

I laugh quietly, turning my attention to Rian's contract. "We'll see. Now ... maybe we need to make a welcoming gesture. Horses ... not under the Savoy name, but as a gift to Rian, specifically. He wants independence."

"How do you know?"

"He doesn't have a problem with sucking dick, Sully. That's easily solved in a single conversation. He has a problem with losing Mirth. To us. And he has a problem with not being enough. No title, lands, money ..."

"Bolan doesn't have titles or lands."

"He's a rock god. And to Rian, he's also suddenly the big brother who had a father ... for the first nine years of his life, at least. Plus a stable home and siblings."

"Fuck," Sully groans. "Rian got emancipated when he was just a kid."

"That's generally when emancipation occurs."

"Fuck you."

"Not right now, Sully."

Oh, yes. I'm in my element now. This is something I can fix. I pick up my phone to start making lists.

Sully snorts, then sighs. "Being the youngest in a bond group filled with powerful people isn't remotely independent." He eyes my phone. "Spending more of my money?"

I shrug. "What were you going to do with it?"

"Well, order lunch first ..." He tilts his head toward the

closed door of the bathroom. "Mirth is going to be hungry."

It takes me a moment, but the muted sounds of Mirth's cries of pleasure eventually filter through the thick wooden door. I flush. My cock instantly hardens, compressing almost uncomfortably against the zipper of my pants.

Sully smirks at me. "Wait until she comes. I hope you have another suit on hand."

I blink at him, phone forgotten in my hand. "The bond?"

He laughs, letting his head fall back. "Yeah, the bond is pretty hard to resist. Though why would you want to?"

MIRTH

I SHOULD PULL THE BLINDS AGAINST THE DARK night sky. Bolan has crashed out on the floor next to my living room couch like the degenerate rock star he is. But it's exhaustion, not drugs or alcohol, that's caught up with him. Sully is curled up next to me on the couch, also asleep, and making it difficult for me to reach my phone. Mostly because I don't want to acknowledge more of my day ... evening ... night ... both the overwhelmingly good and the achingly bad.

But three text messages in a row flashing up on my screen are hard to ignore, especially when only a limited few of my contacts are tagged to send notifications through.

I'm both hoping it's Rian and worried what he's going to say. I don't know anything yet about what happened between him and Sully, except that I've never seen Sully take his anger — his hurting? — out on anyone it wasn't primarily directed at. Though that could be because there are few people who wield that sort of power over the fabricator mage. He doesn't let many people that far into his life.

The same could be said for every one of the current occupants of the apartment.

The apartments.

After lunch in Zurich, Sully dragged Elias to London with us. Multiple laptops, devices, contracts, and all. Hence the need for more bedrooms. Unceremoniously flinging open the doors to Armin's side of the building, Sully had wandered into my brother's space as if he had no idea I hadn't opened those doors in seven months.

He did know, of course. And that was how he dealt with it.

I attempt to slide out from under Sully's sleep-heavy arm. He shifts in his slumber in protest, and I freeze in place. When he doesn't wake, I reach out for my phone and snag it off the coffee table with my fingertips.

The screen lights up at my touch. The earlier text messages are from Anne checking up on me, but the last text is from Greg. Not Rian.

I frown. I know the royal guard are scrambling to expand my protection. Roz wants Greg back with me, and other guards specifically assigned to Sully, but she's extremely picky about whom she's even willing to interview.

>When was the last time you heard from Thomas Walsh?

Flummoxed by the question, I open my messages. Ignoring that my last text to Rian has gone unread at the top of the list, I open the thread right below containing Kitty's pictures and texts from earlier in the day. From those messages, I now know all about Tommy's little sister's favorite breakfast — oatmeal with brown sugar and cinnamon. Her least favorite class — gym. And what she's drawing during her afternoon art class. She also sent a short and very shaky video of Tommy racing around a football field. If he was doing anything of significance at the time, I couldn't tell. But I was later informed that their school won the game. And there was sprinkle cake with white frosting to celebrate. Not Kitty's favorite.

I check the time on the picture of the cake: 4:45 p.m. We were still in the air between Zurich and London when it came in. I text Greg back.

It's mostly Kitty who checks in. Last photo she sent was taken around 4:45 p.m. Or at least that's when she sent it.

Greg replies almost instantly.

>*Would you forward it to me?*

I do.

Is everything okay?

Staring down at my screen for an answer, I carefully slide around Sully so as not to wake him, then get up off the couch. After stepping over Bolan, I pause to pick his Martin guitar up off the floor and place it on the credenza behind the couch.

>*Just on the phone with tech right now.*

Picking up the lit peaches-and-cream candle that Christoph sent me from the side table, I cross through the living room and kitchen, ignoring the complete mess from dinner scattered across the countertops. I send a text to Tommy's phone — so to Kitty — even though it's way past her bedtime.

I'm in the hall that bisects the two upper halves of the apartment building, ready to head down the stairs to the royal guard quarters and talk to Greg face-to-face when I look up, momentarily startled. Because not only is there a light on in Armin's apartment, hanging low over the large, rough-hewn trestle dining table on the far side of the space. But through the still-open main doors, I can see someone moving around, deep within the shadows of the darkened kitchen.

And for just a breath, I think it's Armin.

I nearly lose hold of my phone. I must make a noise. Because Elias's head snaps up, and all the low light around me dims even further under a sharp tug of his essence. The candle in my hand almost gutters.

"Sorry," I murmur, stepping into the apartment proper. "I didn't mean to startle you."

I quietly pad through the shadowy great room toward him, placing the candle on the far corner of the wide counter that stretches between the dining area and the kitchen. Within the kitchen, Elias sets the kettle aside. He was making himself tea. In the dark. Presumably, a mage who can wield light has amazing night vision. I don't, though, hence my momentary confusion.

Beside and behind me, the trestle table is strewn with paperwork and electronic devices. After we tumbled free from the helicopter still perched on the reinforced roof, and once he had commandeered the space, Elias conducted individual meetings with Bolan and Sully, then got Christoph on the phone.

During that time, I had a much-needed shower, answered a few neglected text messages and emails, and ordered dinner. And three Savoy bond group contracts were quietly, but seemingly definitively, signed. With plans made for Christoph to come by in the early morning to sign the fourth. Or, more specifically, to add his signature to four of the five accepted contracts.

I'm not quite certain what I'm feeling about any of it — the paperwork and the life-altering promises passing between them all. Except ... hopeful?

And ... concerned about the fifth unsigned contract.

"You should be sleeping, Mirth," Elias says, skirting the kitchen counter.

"You should be sleeping," I say, trying to be playful. But now that my heart rate has returned to normal, most of my attention is back on the text messages from Greg. Both Tommy and Kitty are likely happily tucked in bed, I remind myself.

"What's wrong?" Elias asks, crossing to me, close enough to touch but not actually touching. "Do you need anything? Where is Sully?"

"He's sleeping —"

My phone buzzes in my hand. A new text from Greg appears on the screen.

>The tracking software has been disabled or blocked on the kids' phone. The techs noticed during their regular late-evening ping.

Pure fear streaks through me. There is nothing at all logical about the extreme nature of that reaction, but —

"Mirth!" Elias's hands close around my upper arms. "Tell me."

I shake my head. "I don't know anything yet. The kids ..." Elias has no idea whom I'm talking about. "I ... met a young boy at my last literacy charity event. He ... he's Tommy, and his sister is Kitty. I ..."

I flush a little. The fact that I have the royal guard tracking children I'm not related to or responsible for isn't something I should probably just blurt out. Not even to someone in the process of forming a bond group with the specific intent to woo me into joining them.

Elias gently takes my phone from me. He scans the texts, swiping his thumb over the screen. And I just ... I let him.

I just need a moment.

The phone buzzes in Eli's hand. His light-blue eyes flick

over the screen to read it. "Last known location was their apartment. Greg already has the locals doing a drive-by." He sets the phone back into my hand. Then, still holding that hand cradled in his own, he guides me over to the kitchen table. "The kids probably accidentally broke their phone."

I slump into a chair. "Of course." I exhale heavily, placing my phone face up on the table. "I'm overreacting."

"I didn't say that." Elias steps to reach across the counter to pull the tea strainer from his mug, depositing it in the sink. "I don't think that." He places the steaming mug in front of me, then steps back around the table to settle in the seat he's already claimed for himself.

I wrap my hands around the mug, inhaling deeply. I don't drink tea. And Elias knows that. So I just accept the comforting gesture for what it is.

I watch him work for a few minutes. That too is calming. Tucked into this pocket of light within the dark of my beloved brother's apartments. It feels ... oddly right.

I lean forward far enough to push the unsipped tea toward Elias. He picks the mug up without looking away from whatever he's typing on his laptop, taking a sip.

I tap the screen of my phone even though it would have lit up if there was a message.

"Are the children ours?" Elias asks, his tone even.

"Ours?" I echo stupidly.

He turns his head just enough to pin me with a sharp light-blue gaze. "Do they belong to you? To our bond group?"

"I ... don't ..." My heart rate picks up a little, and another shiver of fear snakes down my spine. "They're just children. I was concerned about something Tommy said about purple eyes ... I have a responsibility as an awry."

"Your reaction indicates it's more than that."

"Isn't that enough?"

Elias simply raises an eyebrow. Then when I don't cave under his scrutiny, he turns his attention back to his work.

It's just that there isn't anything to cave in to ...

And ... now I can't stop thinking about it, thinking about how blind I might have been ... about so many things.

"What if ..." I whisper. "What if they are ... ours? They have parents, lives. They're just kids."

"Tommy and Kitty are why you're establishing the scholarship," Elias says, still perfectly steady and apparently perfectly informed about everything I've done in the last three days. "Yes? We'll start with that."

My stomach sours at the implications. "They deserve to be ... normal. Have a normal life."

Elias grimaces, just a little. "If they're ours, then they're already not normal. Look at the configuration of the bond group already. You and Armin, awry. Three shifters, all with a little extra mixed in due to an awry-blooded parent or grandparent. Yes? A dual-specialized fabricator mage, and me with a rare affinity. Have you ever heard of one bond group containing two awry before? Let alone the rest of us?"

Elias lets that question linger between us. I don't respond right away because I don't actually have an answer.

"If you feel a pull toward them, it's likely that Tommy and Kitty are already not normal," he finally says gently. "And even if they aren't ours, we'll protect them."

My screen lights up before I can respond. I read the text messages from Greg as they come in, one after another.

>*No one answering the buzzer at the apartment.*

>*Lock on the exterior front door is busted. Not necessarily related, looks like older issue.*

>*No answer at the door. Need probable cause to enter.*

Elias gets up, crosses around the table, and pulls the

neighboring chair closer to me. He leans over to read the messages, then gently takes the phone from me and types:

Send them in. I'll take responsibility. – Elias

>They're in. Used a prior noise complaint as cause.

Elias rests his hand on my knee. I clasp it tightly.

We wait. My screen goes black multiple times, with me lurching forward to wake it. In the end, Elias turns off the automated sleep function.

The time passing aches through me.

Then finally Greg texts again.

>I'm on site. Apartment empty. Could be trashed. Could always look like this. No sight of the kids. Beds unmade.

Elias texts back. *Have they been taken?*

>No blood. No overt signs of a struggle. We're checking local hospitals.

>I've got the locals going door to door.

>The techs are trying to trace the phone again. Any phone.

Feeling as though I'm moving oh so slowly, I take the phone from Elias and text Greg.

I need contact information for Miller Hernandez, please.

Miller, of the California-based Hernandez bond group, is the tech genius who conceived and designed the tech we all use in our everyday lives, including the phone I gave the kids. And even though I abruptly ended my matchmaking event and didn't choose the Hernandezes, I already know Miller will help me if they can.

>I'll get you a direct line.

Elias touches my cheek gently.

I smile at him reassuringly. "Don't worry," I say, feeling perfectly calm — but also as if I'm not wholly inhabiting my body. "They're mine. I'll find them. I'll protect them."

He swallows at whatever he sees in my gaze. "We'd better wake Sully and Bolan."

"And Christoph," I say, speaking without thinking through the request ahead of time. Without even thinking of the why behind it. Why does it feel like I'm going to need all of them, even if they aren't yet mine? "He's in the city, yes?"

Elias nods. "I'll text the duke as well. He's staying at the club, though. They have a no-phone policy throughout the common rooms."

"Thank you," I murmur, settling my attention back on my phone.

Elias crosses through the great room, heading through the main hall to wake Sully and Bolan, but I linger in that pocket of light over the dining room table, surrounded by the yawning darkness of Armin's apartments.

No. My apartments now.

Our apartments now?

It's only been a few days since my conversation with my father, a few days since I walked away from the match-making event. Walked away with what I thought was a firm understanding of the *why*. Why I wrote that list of names under the influence of the intersection point. Why I was drawn to the men who were clearly Armin's soul-bound mates — because my name wasn't on the list.

After further revelations about the responsibility of holding and stabilizing the intersection point, I'd come to another understanding — a resolution — that I would have to choose the Merton bond group. That they, with their strong generational bond, were my only option. It wouldn't be a love match, of course. But I have no doubt that I could have formed a solid friendship with Isla and Noah and maybe even Archie.

But that resolution — the idea of accepting the Mertons just because their generational bond group is so well established — seems like ... an evasion now. The path of least resistance.

I tug one of Elias's contracts across the table toward me. It's open to the final page with his, Bolan's, and Sully's signatures set in black ink, plus two empty spots for Christoph and Rian.

My name isn't on it because they all think I'm their crux.

They think they're meant to revolve around me. Just as I had always wanted to revolve around Armin. Had needed to revolve around Armin. He grounded me, made me feel safe within my own skin.

Because the other choice? Accepting what I was capable of? That was too much, too hard. Too scary.

Even before my primary power exerted itself, I was always happy in Armin's shadow. Happiest when I was tucked right behind him. And after my mind-destroying ability manifested, it was easier to subvert it when I was within Armin's powerful sphere. Easier to let him be the heir and to shoulder all the expectations that came with that role as well.

That too was the path of least resistance.

I didn't want to be a murderer. To wield an ability that gave nothing back to the world. It was easier to tuck it away, to hide it, creating a bubble around myself that just grew thicker through the years.

The screen of my phone flashes with the switchboard number, and I know that when I accept the call, Miller Hernandez will be on the other end of the line. When I accept the call, I'll be accepting whatever happens next. Whatever it takes to protect those who belong to me.

I'm a princess of the realm. The heir to one of the seven intersection points. So the list of people I owe my protection to is actually staggeringly long.

I'll think about that later. Much, much later.

I tap the screen, accepting the connected call and putting it on speaker at the same time. Even with his shifter hearing, I doubt Bolan can pick up much of the conversation all the way through both apartments. But I'm not hiding any of it from my ... my suitors.

"Mx. Hernandez," I say, my tone perfectly smooth, "I do apologize for disturbing you." I'm actually not certain if the Hernandezes are back in California or still in Europe. I'm either waking Miller or interrupting them at work.

Their voice is as steady as mine, though, and warmer than I expected. "It's wonderful to hear from you, Mirth."

I smile, happily surprised at the tech shifter's use of my nickname. "I have an issue that I'm hoping you can help me with."

"A phone you're trying to track."

"Yes. It's an older model of yours, I believe." I rest my gaze on the phone. Miller's personal contact photo is displayed on the screen. A sunset across a sandy beach with two figures in the background holding hands. I don't have to lean closer to know it's a shot of Miller and his chosen, the model-actress Taylor. "I'm not certain what you can do that the royal guard techs haven't already done ..."

"Your techs have sent me what data they have. Their tracking software is very advanced. Even if the phone was simply powered off, or just broken, they should still be able to pick up a final location. My understanding is that they're getting nothing at all from it?"

"I don't know the particulars. Simply that I've been concerned about the children I gave the phone to, and one of the techs noticed it was offline. For lack of a better way to put it. They've done an on-site visit, and the children aren't at home."

"Some evidence that the house might have been broken into," Miller murmurs, as if they're talking while only half listening. "Or at least not all that secure."

"Yes."

"I'm running everything through my software and our satellites as well, but ..."

"You see exactly what the royal guard techs see." I sigh. "I just ... this is perhaps an overreaction ... but is it possible for you to track the children in other ways?"

Miller laughs quietly. "Not legally. And likely not any better than your royal guard techs, who have more jurisdiction than I do. I assume they're currently looking for the children's guardians as well?"

"I'm sorry for even asking. I'm ... I was hoping you'd have ... a backdoor, to the phone tech, at least."

"Also highly illegal."

I sigh again. "I'm not sure why I'm bothering you. I just ... you came to mind."

"I'm glad I did." There's a pause. Then Miller speaks almost hesitantly. "Are ... are the children like you? Is that why you think they've been taken? Are they awry?"

"I'm not certain. I think ... they might be. As far as I know, they haven't manifested yet."

Silence stretches between us before Miller speaks again. "There is ... someone else."

All the hair on my arms stands up, as if the energy of the universe has just ever-so-lightly brushed up against me. It's a tiny touch of the intensity I felt before writing that list of names — my possible soul-bound mates — under the influence of the intersection point. I don't know how it's possible to feel it now at my apartments in London.

"Maybe I shouldn't even mention it," Miller murmurs. "I stay out of that world now. Unless there's something I can do from the sidelines without jeopardizing my bond group ..."

This is why I reached out. I just *know* it, even though that type of essence-wielding isn't among my abilities. "I would appreciate the introduction."

Miller clears their throat. "It doesn't quite work like that. I can reach out to this person. And if they want to reach you, to help you, they will."

"All right."

"And Mirth?"

"Yes."

"They won't recognize your position, your rank." Another beat of hesitation. "And you'll owe them."

"Money isn't an issue."

"They trade in favors."

Now I'm the one to hesitate.

"You understand what I mean?" Miller says in response to my silence.

"I believe so. Is this other person also one of the awry?"

"Yes."

So the favor they demand might be binding on an essence level. And open ended. "They'll help me find the kids."

"I believe so, yes. They specialize in this sort of thing. But if they do agree to work with you, it will be you and you only."

"The purple eyes," I murmur softly.

"Yes. Plus the societal norm that the royal guard represents is an anathema to them."

"I understand. Thank you, Miller."

"I'll keep working with the royal techs to see if I can help them with the phone."

"I appreciate it."

Miller takes a breath, then says, "Will you be happy, Mirth? It's ... you haven't chosen the Mertons, have you? It's Sully, yes? And maybe ... Bolan?"

"Nothing has been formalized. But it's not the Mertons." It's the first time I've acknowledged that out loud. "Is there something that concerns you, more specifically than simply who I've chosen?"

Miller clears their throat. "Just completely unsubstantiated rumors."

My stomach sinks. Something about the Mertons? "Perhaps a conversation for later? After I secure the children?"

"Yes. And again, the person I'm hoping to connect you to might be an ... ongoing resource ... in that sort of area. If you wish."

I have absolutely no idea what Miller is referring to. Or whom the tech shifter might be about to get me tangled up with. "I'll need a name for your contact so I can ask the royal guard to transfer the call to me."

"It ... that's not going to be an issue. I've sent them a message already, along with a ... data package."

A data package. "All the info you have on the children?"

"All the info I have on you." Miller clears their throat. "Routing a skilled tech through the switchboard isn't much of a ... barrier, Mirth."

I laugh quietly. "Of course it isn't."

"Not that I tried to get through the other protections on your phone, but I have enough information that I could contact you again."

"Please do."

"Best of luck, Mirth. We'd better clear the line now. My

contact is very ... insular. It's better if you're alone for the first meeting."

"Thank you, Miller. My regards to the Hernandezes."

"Right back at you."

I tap the screen to end the call. Silence falls around me. After a mere moment, I find I'm unable to sit within it. My mind whirls through the conversation with Miller, in anticipation of the conversation to come. Assuming Miller's contact reaches out at all.

I have no context, no experience, with ... well, any of this. So I can't even guess what my next steps should be, let alone what they will be.

Bolan pads into the great room, moving almost silently on bare feet. His eyes are bright with the essence of his wolf, presumably to see better in the low light.

"Anything more about the kids?" he asks quietly, crouching next to my chair but not touching me.

I allow myself the moment, reaching out to lightly run my fingers through his hair. "I'm waiting on another call. You and the others can't be here for it."

He frowns. "Why not?"

"Those are the rules."

He huffs. "How would anyone know?"

"They will know."

He narrows his eyes. "No one tells you what to do."

"Including you, Bolan."

His energy spikes around him in a way that actually feels belligerent. I lean over him and brush a kiss across his lips before he can turn all of this into an argument. "I'll come find you when I know more."

He grumbles under his breath, then nips lightly at my lower lip as if he thinks that's a punishment. It's not.

Huffing, he straightens, crossing back the way he came.

But he pauses in the outer hall, looking back over his shoulder at me, just a little smugly.

"You might not answer to us, Mirth. But you don't have to tackle everything alone anymore. We can shoulder some of the responsibility. Just like we can help you protect the kids. If you let us in. That's how this is all supposed to work."

I hold Bolan's gaze. He doesn't just mean this situation with the kids. He doesn't just mean how I segregated myself in my grief over losing Armin. Even before my brother died, even when I tucked myself into his shadow or trailed along in his wake, I was ... oddly alone.

"I'm ... let's just find the kids, okay?"

Bolan nods, shoving his hands in the front pockets of his low-slung jeans and bowing his head. "I'm going to head out with Sully. Elias will stay with you. We haven't gotten hold of Christoph yet. Maybe ... if the kids are ours, we can track them on the ground better than the royal guard can."

"You haven't even met them yet, Bolan."

He shrugs belligerently, still not quite looking at me.

"Just ... wait?" I ask quietly. "Just wait for me, please."

His head snaps up, eyes bright in the low light. "For as long as it takes, Mirth. Forever."

"So dramatic, wolf," I say, trying for a light teasing tone and actually managing it. Mostly.

He flashes a toothy grin at me, then steps through the hall into my apartment beyond.

Taking my phone, I slide out of my seat, crossing through the darkness and down the hall into Armin's bedroom. Everything is neat and tidy throughout the apartment. I might not have done my sisterly duty over the last seven months and taken care of my brother's more personal items. Paying any lingering bills, packing up, or donating his possessions. But the staff have kept everything dust-free since Armin's death.

In the massive main bedroom, moonlight filters in through narrow floor-to-ceiling windows cut into the original brick. The heritage restoration of the building required that the architects retain as much of the original facade as possible, while also making certain that all seismic upgrades and other improvements were in place.

The filtered light does little to penetrate Armin's walk-in closet, but I navigate to the row of neatly folded sweaters easily enough. Setting my phone on the shelf, I find the oversized black cashmere sweater I want by feel. A well-worn favorite of Armin's, and fashionably oversized even on him, the sweater is thick and comforting on me.

I retrieve a silk handkerchief from Armin's drawer — he never used them for anything other than pocket squares — and pull my hair back. Quickly and messily braiding it, I all but knot it into a loose bun, using the silk handkerchief to secure it. Sloppily.

I'll need sensible shoes as well ... though for what, I have no idea. I'm trying not to think too far —

The screen of my phone glows in a way it never has before. Like black neon. Without even a hint of hesitation, I swipe my thumb across it as I would to accept a call.

Deadened air fills the space around me. As if this tiny pocket of the universe is suddenly waiting, listening for ... something. Waiting on me?

"This is Mirth," I say.

That feeling of waiting flexes around me for a moment, just long enough for me to wonder if it's an energy actually emanating from the phone itself. Is the tech on the other end powerful enough to reach through my phone ...?

Then I remember they're a purple-eyed tech. Of course they're powerful enough.

And I blithely answered the call.

For the kids.

But also in acknowledgement of all the responsibility I've shirked for far too long.

Tapping ... lots and lots of tapping, like fingers flying over a keyboard, filters through the phone's speakers. Maybe multiple keyboards.

"Her Royal Highness Euphrosyne. Heir to the United European Nation." A low voice murmurs through the energy most definitely emanating from the phone now. North American accent. "I've been hoping you'd call. A lot of us have been hoping you ... or before he died, that brother of yours ... would reach out. Powerful friends in powerful places, am I right?"

"Who am I speaking to?"

A low laugh filters through the phone's speakers. "You can call me Coda. Let's find your missing kids, shall we?"

"Yes. Please."

"Good," Coda says. "But first things first. I now have complete access to your phone and everything that comes with that. Miller and your techs haven't found your missing kids." More keyboard tapping. "They don't even have a trail yet, not even a cold one. But I, having pulled that bit of vid from your phone and matching it with multiple other feeds from that game, I've already got eyes on both kids at the soccer game earlier today. So we'll start our trace there ..."

I close my eyes, relief already trickling through me. "Football."

"Yep, right. So ... point is, I suspect I'll need to see what you are seeing. And once I'm in your phone, I can't be easily removed. No matter how skilled your techs are."

"I understand. The second thing?"

The keyboard tapping intensifies. "Let's track where

your kids went after the game. Then we'll figure out where to go from there."

I wait. The darkness and the tap of Coda's fingers on their keyboards is a comforting cocoon. But just a gossamer layer, easily torn through when I need to move again.

"So … seems no one knows exactly what you can do, Princess. But an awry's eyes don't get much lighter than yours without that awry being able to take care of themselves."

"Is that pertinent?" Yes, I'm peeved that the tech awry is apparently researching me when they should be solely focused on the kids.

Coda chuckles smugly. As if they can read my mind. I glance at the phone screen still glowing that neon black. The tech isn't a mind reader, but no matter how level I've kept my tone, I'm not guarding my expressions.

Coda huffs, amused. Presumably at me just catching on that they're already tapped into my camera. "It's pertinent if you're going to need to ditch your guard."

"Am I ditching my guard?"

There's a long beat, more keyboard tapping, then a quietly murmured, "Fuck. Give me a moment …"

My stomach twists. But I grab my phone, and I'm already moving, away from the comforting darkness, back through the apartment, across the hall and into my own main living space.

Elias, Sully, and Bolan are deep into a quiet conversation near the couch, their phones in hand like they're coordinating something. Presumably the plan to head out themselves. They all look up as I enter.

"Miller?" Elias asks, quietly frowning. "Again?"

I shake my head. Holding my phone in my palm before me, I don't pause to fill them in. "Am I ditching my guard?" I repeat, speaking to Coda.

I don't wait for a reaction from the others, crossing through to my bedroom.

Elias and Sully take off toward the other apartment, but Bolan follows me, keeping close enough that I can feel the heat of his body.

I push into my walk-in closet, not bothering with the lights to grab a pair of well-worn gray sneakers. Instead of stepping back to the built-in bench, I sit down on the floor right where I am, setting my phone beside me to pull on the shoes.

Bolan crouches beside me, eyes narrowed on the phone.

"Hello, rock star. I'm Coda," the tech says, clearly able to see my wolf shifter through the camera on the phone. "Do you belong to the princess?"

"I do."

"And the two mages in the other room?"

"Them as well," Bolan growls.

Coda laughs quietly. "Well, this is going to be a fun friendship, Mirth. Normally, I don't play well with strangers. But you already come with the best party favors."

"The kids?" I prompt, catching sight of myself in the mirror as I grab the phone and stand. Except for the sneakers, I've dressed all in black without realizing it.

Stepping back into my bedroom to grab his boots, Bolan is swathed in black as well. "We're going after the kids? Together?" he asks. He's clearly confused but also clearly standing at my side, not in my way. "Without the guards?"

"They draw too much attention," I say grimly. "Right, Coda?"

"Oh, yeah, we're definitely about to break some ... societal rules."

Elias's cool voice comes from the closet doorway. "How do you propose we get past them?"

The earl is now wearing a long black wool coat over his already dark suit — something from Armin's closet that my brother never actually wore. At his side, Sully has swapped his suit jacket for a black peacoat.

Bolan pops up from tying his boots.

"This way." I lead them all farther into my closet, raising my hand and placing it over a section of the wall at about shoulder height.

"Wait," Coda says over the phone. "Lesson one. When working with me, I do all the tech. Hold your phone up."

I oblige, having no idea how the tech awry even knew there was a palm reader hidden in the wall paneling.

"I thought this was the panic room," Sully says, pulling a thin-ribbed black scarf out of his pocket and twining it around my neck. A touch of his essence keeps it pinned perfectly in place.

Energy shifts through the phone in my hand, still held up to the wall. Thankfully, my own power doesn't rise to try to thwart it. A hidden door slides open before us, revealing a well-lit, steel-walled room. "It is. It's also a second egress."

"The royal guard are tied to all these security measures," Elias says.

Coda pipes up from my phone. "Not right now they aren't."

Blinking against the brightly lit interior, I step through the door into the luxury panic room, ignoring everything as I cross toward the second concealed door.

"What's the second lesson, tech?" Elias asks coolly.

"That's between Mirth and me, Lord Hereford," Coda says tersely. "You're just along for the ride. I'll happily ditch you if needed."

Elias throws me a look. But I just hold my phone up to

the second hidden palm reader and say, "The kids are in trouble."

"What kind of trouble?" Sully asks. "More than the phone being broken and the apartment empty?"

"Coda?" I prompt.

There's a long pause. The second concealed doorway slides open, beyond which a well-lit stairwell, also of steel construction, stretches downward.

"The kind of trouble that comes with cages," Coda says.

Bolan slips around me, taking the stairs first. Heart pounding at Coda's characterization of what the kids might be experiencing, I follow. Sully is at my back, Elias just behind.

"But don't worry." Coda's fingers clatter over their keyboards. "It might be a new playground, but I'm pretty certain I know these assholes. Turn right in the alley. I've already got a car waiting for you."

"We should inform the royal guard," Elias says behind me.

"I'll keep them in the loop," Coda says. "But just a few minutes behind. Mirth and I have an agreement."

"The favor?" I ask. "We didn't specify."

Elias huffs behind me, totally peeved and not at all cool about it. But still with us.

Bolan unlocks the door at the base of the stairs — it's physically bolted in five separate places — and we step out into the alley. The light over the door winks out, as do the rest of the lights punctuating the alley's darkness. Elias's contribution to our sneaking away from my sure-to-be-pissed guards, even while protesting.

"Ah, you are handy, Earl," Coda says. "And I think you'll like our friendship, Princess."

"That's the favor, then? Open-ended friendship?"

"No. The friendship is a bonus."

"You'll help me rescue the kids."

"I will. And you'll get me access. The block on your kids' phone should have made it obvious to your techs. I need someone to get me into their system, and this is a perfect opportunity."

"Who?" Sully asks. "Into whose system?"

"The Möbius Group. If I'm right, that's who has your kids. It's too fucking clean a snatch. The lack of fingerprints all over it is a dead giveaway."

A chill runs through me. "Awry hunters," I whisper, only in partial disbelief. The other part of me already understands the truth of it all.

"Operating unchecked in the United European Nation in the twenty-first century?" Elias scoffs. "Ridiculous."

"These rotten roots run deep and dark," Coda says ominously. "Just because this is the first mistake they've made in this century doesn't mean they're not embedded deep into the fabric of every society."

The first mistake. "They don't know," I murmur.

"Don't know what?" Sully asks.

"That the kids are under my protection."

Bolan looks back at me over his shoulder, eyes blazing bright. "Our protection."

Coda cackles through the speaker of my phone. "Well, this is going to be fun."

"Children are involved," Elias snaps.

"Oh, Earl," Coda croons nastily. "Children are always involved. Ask your beloved princess. How many times has someone or some group tried to snatch her?"

A car idles at the mouth of the alley. Bolan opens the back passenger door. Sully climbs in first, then reaches a hand back for me.

No one responds to Coda. Because the tech awry is correct, after all.

9

———

 ’m not certain I’ve ever been in the part of London that Coda directs us toward, but I recognize the three-storey building. It helps that the tech awry likes to gloat, and they pull the very first selfie the kids sent me from my phone and flash it on my screen just as we arrive. I don’t yet have any idea what connection Tommy and Kitty have to this building, or why they would have been outside it that late at night, but their apartment is only a few streets away.

The vehicle Coda delivered to us came with keys but no driver, so Elias is at the wheel when Coda asks him to circle the block slowly. Bolan is in the passenger seat, with Sully in the back seat with me. The streets are quiet, traffic sparse, the streetlights set fairly far apart. A few businesses, including a pub or perhaps a restaurant, occupy the ground floor. No cars are parked out front of the main building, but two men in dark suits are posted at a side door. Halfway down a narrow alley.

“See the mark or stamp or whatever on the corner of the building there?” Coda says tersely. “That’s not a builder’s mark.”

We're not close enough for me to see the stamp Coda is referencing, but I can see it at the edge of the frame on the selfie the kids sent.

On our second pass down the street that fronts the building, a car ahead of us turns into the narrow alley, pulling up to the side door. The driver steps out, crossing through the side door and barely even acknowledging the two men posted there. Not turning his head in our direction. One of the men — the guards? — gets into the car.

"Valet?" Sully murmurs. "That doesn't suit the neighborhood at all."

"Did anyone else recognize the driver?" Elias asks tensely.

There's no response except for the quiet tapping emanating over the phone speakers.

"Maybe I was mistaken," he murmurs.

"Follow the car," Coda says quietly. "At a distance."

It isn't a long trip. The valet backs out of the alley, rounds the block, then pulls into an underground car park. The site is unmarked but gated.

"Do we know for certain the kids are in that building?" Bolan asks.

"Nothing is for certain until you get eyes on them," Coda says. "But I haven't picked up any other movement to suggest they've left this area."

"There are underground tunnels all through this section of London," Elias says tightly. "There could be multiple egresses."

"I have a map," Coda says coolly.

"With cameras on all the tunnels? And every exit?"

The tech doesn't answer. Which I've already learned is answer enough.

The gate to the car park starts to close. Elias abruptly

guns the car, sliding through and down into the darkness without warning.

"What the fuck?" Bolan growls.

"We need to park, don't we?" Elias flicks off the headlights. Then a touch of his power shivers through the car, and I know without asking that he's doused all the automated lights on the vehicle as well.

The interior of the car park is dark and utterly silent as Elias slides the vehicle into the first available spot, just off the entrance ramp. There aren't any other cars parked nearby, but Bolan tilts his head and says, "Other guy just parked, down a level."

"No cameras," Coda says over the phone. "And I don't have a schematic to the building yet."

"We should head back up to street level," Bolan says.

"And just walk in the alley door?" Sully asks rhetorically. "Even if no one recognizes me or Eli, how far do you think you and Mirth will get?"

"Then we split up," Bolan says.

"Absolutely not," Elias snaps.

"Four of us separated can cover more ground," I say, though I'm not actually all that keen about running around in a darkened car park alone. But not because I'm worried about getting hurt myself. I already know I'm the most dangerous person in the immediate vicinity, maybe even in all of London. And not only because I have Coda on my phone.

"Mirth." Sully grabs my free hand. "We need to call in the royal guard. Or the police."

"Not yet," Elias says. "This might be nothing. Or ... we might have to move faster than is exactly ... appropriate."

Legally, he means. The United European Nation is a constitutional monarchy. A democracy, not a dictatorship. Unless reacting to a direct attack on a royal subject, the royal guard can't charge around busting into buildings. The police need reasonable cause to do the same. Coda might be able to compile enough evidence to convince the locals that the kids were kidnapped, but by the time it worked its way through the system …

I open my door and practically tumble out of the vehicle, heading farther into the dimly lit underground space around us.

"Mirth!" Elias hisses, though he follows on my heels. Under a touch of his essence, the lights dim around us, keeping us in shadow. Bolan and Sully are only a step behind.

"The valet isn't going to head back through the gates, then walk all the way back around the block," I say quietly. "They use this garage for a reason."

"An underground connection," Bolan murmurs.

"License plates," Coda says over my phone.

I keep walking, pointing the phone camera toward the cars as we pass them, letting Coda's control of the camera capture whatever the tech wants. Elias takes my slightly slowed pace as an opportunity to get ahead of me, Sully at his shoulder.

Bolan keeps pace with me, close enough that our shoulders brush together. My sneakers are nearly silent on the smooth concrete underfoot, but I have no doubt a shifter would be able to hear my approach. I loosen my hold on my power just a little, actively trying to pick up the energy of the valet. If he's an essence-wielder, I should be able to feel him nearby.

"These are some pricy rides," Bolan mutters.

"Yes," Elias says tensely. "I wouldn't mind getting another look at the Aston-Martin as well. Custom paint."

I know very little about cars, but as we cross deeper into

the car park, we're slowly surrounded by luxury vehicles, including a few Rolls-Royces and Bentleys.

Yes, I recognize those.

"Someone is smoking up ahead," Bolan murmurs. "Weed laced with essence. Similar to Sully's joints. You don't have a side business going, do you, Lord Savoy? Now that you've got so many mouths to feed?"

Sully shoots Bolan a disparaging look over his shoulder but doesn't bother with a clever retort.

We skirt around the end of the row of cars, heading even deeper underground. Elias and Sully come to a sudden stop, and I nearly run into the earl's back. Sully angles his shoulders, lining up with Elias and keeping me tucked out of sight behind them.

Bolan curls his hand around my wrist, his hold loose but intense.

I peek around the well-dressed barricade now blocking my path. The valet is leaning against a concrete wall next to a large steel door with a fancy electronic lock. The lock is as out of place as the luxury vehicles.

I don't like the contrast. I don't like that we're here at all, that the kids are missing, and that Coda traced them to anywhere other than sleeping peacefully in their beds. I don't like that Coda thinks an underground awry-hunting-and-trafficking group might be involved.

The valet pauses midtoke, blinking at Elias and Sully's sudden appearance, Bolan and I still out of sight behind them. While smoking his joint, the valet appears to be taking pictures or vid of the nearby cars.

"Elias Fitzbern," Elias says smoothly. "Earl of Hereford. This is Lord Savoy." Then he waits expectantly. As if the valet is just another employee. As if he has every right to go wherever he wills.

Bolan's fingers flex around my wrist. I turn the phone off speaker and press it to my ear.

"You're supposed to check in at the entrance, my lord," the valet says, lowering both his phone and the joint. I can't place his accent. Watered-down Slavic? He's wearing some sort of essence charm. I can feel it now, but not his own power. Which is presumably why Bolan picked up the scent of the joint first. "Supposed to let me park for you."

Either the valet is a mage, or he has a powerful employer. Any charm that can fool my senses is rare. And expensive. Similar to the unusually powerful block currently on the kids' phone. While we drove here, Coda informed me snootily that even if the phone were broken, the awry tech would have been able to trace it — meaning it has to be essence-blocked.

Elias sniffs offishly. "I knew the way, of course. And I loathe anyone driving my car but me."

The valet looks behind us, perhaps to see what car would be worth walking through the garage for. Elias is still controlling all the light around us, though, keeping the upscale vehicles illuminated but Bolan and me in shadow.

That's when I realize that the valet can't see Bolan or me at all. Can't apparently sense us in any way. His eyes skim right over us, looking only at Elias and Sully.

He snuffs out the joint, then gestures toward the door with a mocking bow. Elias and Sully step forward. Bolan holds me back.

"Don't worry, Princess," Coda murmurs in my ear so quietly that I barely pick up the words. "I've got them tagged and tracked."

The screen reader built into the wall scans the valet's face instead of his palm. Then he grabs a large lever and disengages the metal lock strapped across the door in two places with a slight grunt, making me wonder if the weight or the awkwardness of the maneuver is part of the security measures.

Elias and Sully pass through the steel door without looking back. What appears to be a long concrete corridor stretches out beyond them. The guard follows, turning back to shove the door closed with his shoulder. The clunk of the lock and a shiver of essence follows, presumably sealing the door again.

"Tech and essence protections on the door leading through into the tunnels," I whisper, just in case Coda missed it with the phone being pressed to my ear.

They don't answer. I get the sense that the tech awry has a half-dozen things currently going on at any time, maybe more. Bolan and I wait for another moment. My heart is racing more than I would like — seeing as how any nearby shifter would be able to hear it, including Bolan.

"The Aston-Martin." Bolan nods his chin toward the car in question.

I put the phone on speaker again, pointing the camera toward the vehicle that bothered Elias and stepping forward just enough to get a clear view of it.

"Got it," Coda says.

"So ... do we bust through the door?" I ask Bolan. It's fairly clear that Coda can get us through the tech. My essence usually cancels out all other essence, even when I don't want it to. And Bolan is more than strong enough for the manual locks. "Or find another entrance?"

"Option two," Bolan says, threading his fingers through mine and tugging me lightly back the way we've just come. "We don't know if it's wired to their main security."

I blink up at him.

"What?" He flashes me a grin. "You think I haven't gone where I'm technically not wanted before?"

"Breaking and entering, you mean?"

"Please. Is it really breaking anything when your accomplice can just slide the locks open?"

He means Armin. And my brother's telekinetic abilities.

I laugh, quietly pleased.

Bolan squeezes my hand.

For one of the very few times since Armin died, my thinking of him — and the tiny glimpse of him I never had before — doesn't hurt my soul.

"He would have just sauntered in through the front door," I say, a little ruefully.

"No, Mirth," Bolan says, deadly serious suddenly. "He never would have risked the kids like that. Or you."

"Only himself."

Bolan sighs, raising our joined hands and pressing a kiss to the back of my hand. "Yeah."

We retrace our route through the garage and step back out through a door alongside the gate, keeping tight to the shadows at the edge of the building. Bolan sniffs the air, head cocked. "Clear."

Coda pipes up over the phone speaker. "Blake Evans."

"Blake Evans," I repeat, racking my brain. Then it hits me. "That's ... Viscount Boyne. He's ... he's ... one of the members of the Merton bond group. A few years older than Archie."

"Fuck. That's how Elias knew the car," Bolan mutters quietly. "They probably play fucking polo together." He glances around again, his eyes glowing with his wolf. "Get us another entrance to that building, Coda."

"Already on it," the tech awry chirps, sounding practically cheerful now. "And it's racquetball every second Saturday afternoon, not polo."

Bolan finds a secondary entrance to what now appears to be a series of interconnected buildings, a full block away from the well-guarded door in the alley. He does this much to Coda's chagrin, but apparently the maps the tech awry has access to aren't terribly detailed. Or more specifically, not terribly current.

Though London's streets were laid down centuries ago, the hidden passages and tiny gardens between those streets are often secrets known only to locals. But as a wolf, and even while in human form, Bolan has no trouble following the collection of overlapping scents that eventually leads us around the opposite side of the complex.

We're silent and watchful as Coda cracks the security on the door, somehow once again reaching through my phone to do so.

"This isn't connected to the security mainframe," the tech grumbles. "I can't take over the system from here. Or even the cameras. I need you to find me a security hub."

"We're here for the kids, Coda," Bolan says, opening the door and stepping into a dark hall ahead of me.

"Don't worry your pretty head about it, rock star," Coda says. "Mirth understands that we're doing each other a favor."

I close the door, encasing myself in darkness. Coda toggles something on their end, and the locks click into place behind me. I take the phone off speaker, pressing it to my ear instead.

I feel Bolan the moment before he reaches back for me, holding my hand to guide me through the dark. Even after my eyes adjust, I can barely see more than the edges of the hall.

"Right," Coda murmurs.

Bolan pauses — keeping me behind him — at the next intersecting corridor. He waits for a moment, then heads in the direction Coda indicated, proving how easily he can hear the awry tech even when I have the phone pressed to my ear.

We continue like that for ten minutes. Yes, I check the time on my phone more than once. As we weave through the building, Bolan's nose guides us away from any recent human scents, heading back the way we've just come along the streets.

Coda corrects the wolf twice, guiding us to other security panels and ending up even more annoyed every time they can't gain access to the security hub for the building. Presumably it's because these corridors are running between separate businesses.

From the exterior, the complex — which is to say, the half-dozen older buildings within the same block — appears only a few storeys high, with various businesses occupying the ground floor. But ten minutes in, mapping the interior has already becoming a frustrating experience, and not just for me. Coda gets increasingly edgy the longer it takes for us to find something to 'plug into.' That's the tech's phrasing, not mine.

We bypass more security panels and locks, poking our heads into a garage that's filled with luxury cars in various stages of repair. Farther along, the next back door leads to a pub with a beauty salon next to it. Everything is long closed this late, edging into early morning.

Oddly, all the back sections of the interconnected buildings appear to be mostly large empty rooms.

We keep moving forward.

"Turn right up ahead. Again," Coda says in my ear, getting seriously pissy now. "And pick up the pace. If I can't get into their main security system, assuming there is one, the other two aren't going to be able to keep bluffing."

"What?" I ask, following Bolan around the corner and breaking into a jog. "Bluffing? Are Elias and Sully in trouble?"

Coda doesn't offer any clarification other than more rapid typing in the background.

"You're the one who's been leading us," Bolan snaps.

"Get me access to the cameras," Coda snarls, "instead of making me fog them one at a time, and this will go much smoother."

There has been an odd lack of security cameras. And most of what we've happened upon and quickly moved past have been focused on the back entrances to the businesses.

I know I'm not the only one worried about the incongruencies piling up. High tech is mixed with no tech at all. As if some activities that take place in this complex should never be recorded. Pair that with the expensive and powerful essence wards on the doors and on the kids' phone, but with a lack of wards or other essence-based —

"Stop!" Coda shouts in my ear.

Bolan and I freeze in place.

"Scan with the phone, Princess. Slowly."

I put Coda back on speaker. We haven't accidentally happened upon a single other person yet, so I'm likely being too cautious keeping them at my ear anyway. I move my phone left to right along the corridor wall, then turn around and scan the camera along the other wall in the opposite direction until I've executed a full circle.

I see nothing on the walls. No signs, no marks, no doors. There's barely a single layer of white paint on the drywall … as if these walls have been quickly built in place to section off certain parts of the interior …

"Next left, then stop. There's a concentration of energy." Coda finally sounds a little pleased. "Assholes are trying to hide it."

"Like they know you're coming," Bolan mutters.

"They've been fucking hunting us awry for centuries, wolf," Coda says. "They've learned a few tricks."

"If it is this so-called Möbius Group at all."

"It's got their fingerprints all over it."

We turn left, and the minimally painted walls abruptly transform into a worn red-brick corridor.

A small seating area opens to the immediate left. It's empty, excepting the modern and expensive furniture and a scattering of mostly empty champagne glasses. Two silver ice buckets that could have come from any of my father's numerous castles are set on a low sideboard. Open bottles of champagne are shoved into the half-melted ice.

"Cigars," Bolan says, nostrils flaring. "Expensive."

"Someone was celebrating," I say. Emotion flares in my chest, settling to seethe with each measured breath I take to try to keep myself focused. "An achievement?"

"Or an acquisition," Coda says. "Get me through those doors. Now."

On our right, ornate antique double doors are set into the brick wall. Not original to the building. But also, at first glance, not reproductions.

I wrap my hand around the handle.

Bolan cries, "Wait!"

Too late. The essence sealing the doors tries to grab me, searing across my palm, then streaking up my arm and over my shoulder. I stifle a moan of pain.

"Fuck, Mirth!"

Bolan reaches for me, but I raise my other hand, phone and all. "Stop! It will jump from me to you."

I loosen my hold on my essence. It surges up and through me, then simply nullifies the essence spell warding the door. The ward collapses with a fizzle of energy, and the latch clicks under my hand.

Bolan grasps my shoulders, holding me back gently so he can tug my hand free of the door. He turns that hand over. My skin is seared a deep pink. Heaving a panicked breath, he shoves up the sleeve of my purloined sweater. More streaks mar my creamy skin, tracing my veins.

"Sully will soothe it," I say calmly. Though honestly, my hand feels like it's literally on fire. Fine beads of sweat have broken out along my hairline. I'm not quite certain I've ever experienced this level of physical pain … not in a long time, at least.

"Whatever mage is tied to the ward will know we're here," Coda says, clearly exasperated by the lack of stealth in our breaking-and-entering abilities. "If they're in the area …"

"They'll be heading this way," Bolan mutters.

Still crowding in behind me, the rock star reaches around and shoves open the door.

It swings open to reveal a young girl with dark-blond, slightly curly hair and dark-blue eyes. Half-hiding behind a barrel chair, she's wearing cat-print pajamas and only one sock. Her eyes are red, her nose swollen. From crying.

"Mirth …" she whispers, completely dismissing Bolan.

Kitty.

I'm across the room — a plush office of some sort — and crouching to sweep the nine-year-old into my arms before Bolan can hold me back. She presses her face into my neck and takes a shuddering breath.

"Take the phone to the computer, rock star," Coda

says, voice distant through the phone speakers and the panicked buzzing in my ears.

Bolan hesitates, throwing a manual lock on the door behind us before gently tugging the phone from my hand and hustling out of my line of sight.

I just let Kitty hold me.

She doesn't cry again, though. She sniffs, then says quietly, "I knew you'd come."

I hear it then. The shift in the essence surrounding us. That isn't, wasn't, simply some childish wish to be rescued by the most powerful person she knew.

Kitty *knew* I was coming for her.

Though there still isn't any hint of purple in her eyes, she is awry. A seer of some sort.

"Where's Tommy?" I ask, still holding Kitty tightly.

"They took him," she sobs, then presses her face into my shoulder to stifle herself. "They ... took us."

"Who, Kitty?" I ask. "Did you recognize them?"

She steps back from my hold, pressing her lips together and avoiding my gaze now. She shakes her head.

Unable to lie to me out loud.

My heart pinches. "It doesn't matter. We'll find Tommy, and we'll go somewhere safe." I tune in to the murmur of conversation between Bolan and Coda. The tech is talking the wolf through hardwiring my phone to the desktop computer.

"Here, Mirth," Kitty says, pointing toward the lower half of a built-in bookshelf. "Your friend on the phone needs some of the things in here. And they stole my phone ..." Her voice wobbles. "That you gave me."

I don't correct her on the original ownership of the phone, having no doubt that Tommy handed it over to his sister at first demand. A dark wooden panel has been partially pried off the bottom section of the bookshelf, revealing an inset safe.

A fireplace poker lies on the ground next to it, though a quick glance at the fireplace in the seating area confirms that the tool is just decorative. It's been retrofitted, of course. No open fires in central London. A criminal enterprise that kidnaps children isn't going to get exposed by willfully violating building codes.

"I'm in!" Coda cries gleefully through my phone speakers. "Finally, fuck."

"We're going," Bolan says. "We've got Kitty. That's enough to get the police involved."

"But Tommy!" Kitty cries, clutching at my arm. "We have to go get him first."

Bolan steps around the huge wooden desk, trying to soften his expression. "We haven't met —"

"I don't wanna know you, wolf," Kitty spits, surprisingly vicious.

Bolan snaps his mouth shut, then looks to me. More than a little chastised.

"That's got to sting, rock star," Coda muses, punctuated by a plethora of keyboard tapping. It's possible the tech has more than ten fingers. "When was the last time someone didn't want to know you. Plus ... I just need a second ..."

"And Kitty says we need to get into the safe," I add.
Bolan huffs.

Kitty folds her arms across her chest and glowers at him. "You're supposed to help me. And we're supposed to help the others."

Bolan frowns, narrowing his eyes at her. Then his nostrils flare, and his gaze snaps to me.

I nod just once. Yes, Kitty is awry. Not even partially

manifested yet, but what threads of power she does have access to sleepily stir around her.

I want to ask her all the questions churning in my head, but I also get the sense that she's been pushed way beyond her limits. I don't want to force her to face more, not just yet.

"I'm here to help," Bolan says.

"Good," Coda says. "Because I need you to go get the pretty but stupid lords who've gotten themselves detained."

"What?!" I cry.

"It's fine," Coda says dismissively. "If they were okay with dropping a few bodies, it wouldn't even be an issue."

"We're being circumspect," Bolan says indignantly, more pissed at the not-so-subtle charge of incompetence than the suggestion that we should have murdered our way into the building.

Of course, now that we've confirmed these people kidnapped Tommy and Kitty —

"Answer your phone, rock star," Coda says.

Bolan tugs his phone out of his pocket, sighing dramatically at the black-neon glowing screen.

"I need Mirth's phone plugged in for now," Coda says, caustically cajoling. "I'm grabbing as much data as I can before we meet more interference."

"More interference?" Bolan growls.

"Mirth and the kid are safe here with me," Coda says. "I control all the cameras and most of the security system now. You go collect your playmates. I'll find the boy."

Bolan wavers, clearly torn.

Arms still folded, glower firmly in place, Kitty taps her foot impatiently.

Bolan steps over to me, kissing me almost bruisingly, then nipping my bottom lip before growling, "Don't fucking go anywhere."

He stomps to the door, unlocking and flinging it open dramatically.

"Go right," Coda says, through Bolan's phone speaker now.

Bolan yanks the door closed, snarling, "Lock this," before shutting it completely.

Kitty practically skips over to slip the lock into place.

"Possessive asshole," Coda mutters through my phone speaker rather gleefully.

"He has a dirty mouth," Kitty says, her tone chastising.

"Oh, I hope so." Coda cackles. "For the princess's sake."

"Kitty is nine years old," I say coolly. "Please act accordingly, Coda."

A beat of silence stretches between me and the phone still tethered to the computer on the desk.

Then Coda says, "You're right. I'm sorry."

Unfazed, or maybe just ignoring us, Kitty crosses back to the safe, hunkering down to look at the keypad. "I can't get in." She looks back at me over her shoulder, blinking her still-reddened eyes.

"That's what you have me for," Coda says. "Grab the phone."

"I thought you still needed it plugged in," I say.

"Nah, I'm downloading direct now." Coda chuckles darkly. "This chapter ain't ever dodging me again."

Kitty jumps up, running over to the desk and grabbing the phone.

"Press the screen against the keypad," Coda instructs her through the speakers. "And hold it there."

Energy shifts around the phone.

"That tickles," Kitty whispers.

"How did you *know*, Kitty?" I ask quietly, crouched next to the young girl. "About me coming for you? Did you see ... pictures in your head? Or maybe it was a whisper in your mind, or just a sense of need?"

Kitty blinks at me for a moment, staring deeply into my eyes. My violet eyes. "Do you see too, Mirth?"

"I don't. But I ... get feelings sometimes. I knew you needed me." I try to smile at her, but I can't quite pull off the expression right now.

"I saw you ..." Kitty's eyes fill with tears. "I saw ... I saw you and Tommy and a cage, and ... I shouldn't have said anything. Tommy told me never to tell anyone about the things I see, not even my dreams. Not even my ..." She whispers so quietly I almost miss the next words. "My mom. I think ... they weren't supposed to take Tommy. Just me. He tried to run with me. But I ... I can't run as fast as he can ... and ... and ... they ..." Her breath hitches. "They ... they grabbed us both ... and ... and what if they took Mom too? Or ... what if they hurt her? And that's why ... that's why she didn't help us?"

"We're going to figure it all out," I say. I could tell her that no one was home when the royal guard went looking for her, and that there were no signs that anyone was hurt in the apartment. But she doesn't need extra or exact details now.

She needs her brother. To know Tommy is safe and to feel safe herself.

I know. Because I always needed Armin in the same way.

"You can open it now," Coda says in as gentle a tone as I've heard so far from the tech awry. "Take everything, please."

I open the safe, revealing more paper money, in multiple currencies, than I've ever seen in one place. Plus thin one-ounce gold and silver bars and stacks of actual paper bonds. What looks like three portable hard drives are tucked between the money and the gold bars. A narrow shelf at the top of the safe holds a half-dozen phones.

"There we go," Coda mutters gleefully. "Grab the hard drives first. The baby girl needs to carry the drives, Mirth."

Because of my energy. It doesn't usually affect tech, but the portable drives might also be essence protected.

"Got it!" Kitty runs back toward the couch and retrieves a brand-new-looking pink backpack. She unceremoniously dumps its contents — books, crayons, and a doll — and brings it to me. "My phone?"

The bag sports a designer label. The toys and treats ... are bribes? To keep Kitty mollified? Anger flashes through me, hot and pervasive. I almost lose hold of my essence. I almost wipe every living person in the building from existence. By melting each of their brains.

Taking Kitty wasn't a simple snatching of a convenient target. This was planned. The presence of the pink bag tells me so.

"Mirth?" Kitty asks almost meekly. "My phone?"

I take a steadying breath. I meet Kitty's questioning gaze. She's not scared of the energy that has to be rolling off me now, but she is wary.

And I smile.

I smile, and I know. I know what I'm capable of. And that I will do what is necessary to protect not only those I love, but those who don't have anyone else to protect them.

"You have to be willing to hurt others to save yourself, to save those you love." That was my father's challenge, wasn't it? When he completely overreacted to Radek and Lukas's feigned kidnapping because he didn't think I was capable of doing what was necessary to rescue myself.

So, yes. Challenge accepted. I smile, and so I don't keep

worrying the little awry at my side, I reach into the safe for her phone. An interior essence ward of some kind dissipates under my touch. "Whoever set the protections on this safe really knows we're here now." My voice is calm, measured.

"Not a problem," Coda says without further elaboration.

From the top shelf, I pick up the phone covered in sparkly pink and purple decals and hand it to Kitty. She grabs it in both hands, carefully checking it over for damage.

A trickle of disconcertion cuts through my calm acceptance. "Coda ..."

"Press your phone, back-to-back, to Mirth's phone, baby girl," the tech commands. "Let's check it for tracking software."

Kitty follows Coda's instructions. Energy passes between the two phones, and she gasps sweetly, wiggling her fingers as if they're tingling.

"Can you tell if it's the phone that drew their attention?" I ask quietly, focused on grabbing the other phones while pointing Kitty toward the hard drives. All of it gets zipped into the various pockets in Kitty's backpack.

"It wasn't you, Mirth." Coda's tone has darkened again. "Give me a couple of hours and I'll get you a detailed report of how the kids came to the attention of the Möbius Group."

Coda clearly doesn't want to elaborate yet. I glance at Kitty, but she's looking through the photos on her phone — lots of selfies, a few containing Tommy — and I don't know her well enough to know if she's shut us out or is listening to everything we say. Either way, if Kitty's slip about her mother potentially being involved in their kidnapping is true, it's best we don't discuss it.

"Have you got the guardianship paperwork in place yet?" Coda asks.

I swallow. "I can't just —"

"The awry protect awry. You can. And solely on that basis alone."

Kitty looks up at me. She's holding my phone now, and I realize she's found the first picture Tommy ever sent me. The one with the building in the background — and the stamp on the brick just over their shoulder.

"Can I send this picture to my phone?" Kitty asks.

Tommy deleted the earliest messages and photos he'd sent me, as if afraid of someone seeing them. "Yes."

She doesn't look away, so I just hold her gaze steadily and wait.

"Tommy too, right, Mirth?" she asks in a whisper. "Even if he doesn't have purple eyes? You'll look after Tommy too? That's what guardianship means, right?"

"Yes."

Kitty frowns deeply. "The wolf is going to be very bossy."

I laugh involuntarily, opening my mouth to tell her that wild, carefree Bolan is the last person who would tell anyone what to do with their lives. Then I see a shimmer of light behind Kitty's eyes — a shift in essence within those dark-blue depths.

I close my mouth, knowing she's right. Bolan is going to be a crazy strict parent. Sully and Elias are going to be the pushovers.

Oddly, the idea of all that — building a life together and all it entails — doesn't concern me. Whether or not I understand every last nuance of what's going on between us all, I've already made my choice. My choices.

Kitty huffs, my silence only confirming her assessment

of Bolan, and returns her attention to the phones, transferring more photos between them.

I eye the rest of the contents of the safe. "Coda. Do you really need all the money and —"

"If I'm going to trace it," Coda says. "So yes. Also, I'm pretty certain you aren't going to agree to just burning the building down, so I need to plunder what assets I can. To fund our cause, you know."

Awry protecting awry.

Giving in, I look around for something to cart around the remainder of the safe's contents. I'm not sure how much that many stacks of paper money and bonds combined with the one-ounce gold and silver bars weigh, but they'll need to be carried in something solid. Spotting a trashcan with a liner in it, I straighten and step away from the safe to see if —

"Now ..." Coda murmurs thoughtfully. "Where does this go?"

A section of the paneled wall behind the desk slides open, revealing a doorway and a sporadically lit, brick-walled passageway beyond.

I blink at the gaping hole in the back wall. "Well ... cutting through the brick was definitely not permitted under the heritage restoration bylaws."

Coda cackles.

Kitty, still hovering by the safe, whimpers quietly, drawing my attention. She presses her phone to her chest, eyes wide and fear shimmering off her in waves. "That's where they took Tommy," she whispers.

"All right," I say, stepping back to pick up her backpack and help her get it settled on her back. I retrieve my phone, ignoring the rest of what's in the safe. "Then that's where we're headed."

"I don't have access to the cameras through there, Princess," Coda says, sounding actually cautious.

"We'll come back for the money."

"That is so not the point," Coda mutters.

I take Kitty's hand. She clutches her phone in her other hand.

"These people ..." Coda's fingers are flying over their keyboards again, likely trying to gain access to whatever tech is beyond the passageway. "They care more about your purple eyes than your rank or, like, the societal standards or whatever normally keep you relatively safe. You don't have your entourage to protect you, Mirth. Wait for them, then we'll all look for the boy."

"I never actually needed anyone to protect me, Coda." I squeeze Kitty's hand. "I'm in disguise, you see. The pearls, the perfect smile, the sweet demeanor. The crown. Underneath, slumbering deep, deep down, I'm the one to be truly feared. And there's only one way to wake me ..."

Kitty squeezes my hand back, not the least bit scared of me.

Together, we cross around the ostentatious desk, stepping into the passage and the shadow beyond.

HAND IN HAND, KITTY AND I PAD ALONG THE DARK hall. Just past a short side corridor, we cross into a large, low-ceilinged room. Minimal light sources, all filtering down from above, carve a spotty path through to a dark area that might be another egress on the far wall. A large electronic control board is situated against the wall at the mouth of the office corridor. I have no idea what it controls, but with its many levers, it looks a little like one of the sound boards I've seen in Bolan's recording studios.

Still hand in hand, and with Coda exceptionally silent on the phone, Kitty and I cross deeper into the room. Despite the sporadic pools of yellow-white light, it's dim enough that we almost stumble upon a low round platform. It's empty. But as we continue on, it's easier to see at least a dozen other similar platforms that contain some type of display.

We cross by the art first. I'm not in any way an expert, but I think the first is a blue-and-green-toned Monet I've never laid eyes on. The second is a Picasso that I'm certain is supposed to be housed at the National Gallery. A large chunk of concrete, clearly having been somehow removed from the foundation of a building, sits on a larger platform. On it, etched in thick lines of black spray paint, is a Banksy portrait of an angel-winged girl in a bulletproof vest. The angel's eyes are a purple hue.

"Fuckers," Coda snarls over my phone speakers. "That's supposed to be in New York. We're fucking taking that with us."

I don't correct Coda's language. Mostly because the angel-winged girl reminds me — terrifyingly so — of the girl currently holding my hand.

Heart aching in my chest, I know for certain what I'm looking at now. Jewelry and other antiques that should be in museums are set on another half-dozen pedestals. Including a carved and painted mask that clearly belongs to the Salish people, and a flawless step-cut vivid blue diamond practically the size of Kitty's palm.

But this isn't a gallery. There's no proper lighting, and the ceiling is low enough to feel oppressive. It's not conducive to —

A murmur of voices filters through to us from up

ahead, near the dark space that I thought might be another exit. Followed by laughter, then a defiant, pained cry.

Maybe the shadow is a dark-colored divider or ... a thick curtain?

I press my hand over Kitty's mouth the moment I realize who has voiced that cry, then I tug her into the deeper shadows behind the Banksy angel.

Kitty struggles against my hold. In protest, not in a serious bid to get away from me.

I let my essence unfurl. I've been holding it loosely for a few days now, and it stretches around me almost gleefully when I slacken my hold further.

Kitty stills in my arms, but she doesn't flinch or try to pull away from my touch.

She doesn't start laughing as she would if I were melting her brain.

I remove my hand from her mouth, offering it for her to hold again. She blinks up at me in the darkness, then takes that hand.

She doesn't voice a single laugh, not even a giggle from the touch of my power.

And I knew that would happen. Didn't I?

Logically, I knew it couldn't just be my brother and father who were immune to me. At least immune without me specifically targeting them.

Two men suddenly appear on our far left, from the direction we were going. Movement behind them confirms they've stepped through from a curtained-off area. Or we're in the curtained-off area. Still chuckling to themselves, they head toward the control panel by the corridor to the office. Both are brown-haired, and bulky like shifters. I can't immediately read their essence, though, and I've never seen either of them before.

"That little shit actually thought someone would come for him," the taller of the two says.

The short one scoffs. "Crying like a baby now."

Kitty stiffens. But in defiance, not fear.

The shorter of the two checks his phone. "They're ready."

The taller flips a few levers or switches on the control panel, and a section of the ceiling slides open above the Monet.

The sound of a crowd amicably chatting — celebrating, even — filters down to us.

"Fucking toffs." The tall male flips a third lever, peering down at some gauge or readout on the control panel.

A motor whirls underneath the Monet. Then the platform begins to rise, becoming a pedestal that lifts the painting toward the opening in the low ceiling.

We're in some sort of theater space. Below the stage, at best guess.

This is an illegal auction of rarities. But not just antiquities and art.

Kitty is on offer as well. The young awry might even have been intended as the main event.

I've never attended such an atrocity. But I know that it didn't get thrown together at the last minute.

Sick to my stomach at all the thoughts I'm cobbling together in my head, I tuck Kitty closer to me. Snatching the kids on this specific night had to already have been planned. Was someone waiting until one of them manifested as awry? Was it their mother? That's what Kitty wouldn't outright say, wasn't it? They weren't supposed to take Tommy, she said.

Just Kitty.

But Tommy was already ready, waiting. He had been since even before he approached me at the literacy event and repeated what he'd once heard somewhere, from someone.

That people with purple eyes are locked away for their own protection.

"Now," Coda murmurs through my phone speakers.

The tech awry is right. We need to move.

More platforms are rising. The grating churn of the mech that powers the pedestals should cover our retreat if we're careful. The Banksy angel starts to lift even as we move away.

Transferring my hold to Kitty's wrist so I don't lose my grip on her hand if we need to run, I keep as much to the shadows as possible. Trying not to blindly bump into more displays. The way to the office is blocked now, and we haven't yet found Tommy, so I head to where the men came from, toward where we heard the pained cry.

Instead of trying to find the opening, we skirt the thick black velveteen curtain that I wasn't close enough to see from deeper in the room. On the other side of the curtain, only one much larger platform occupies this section beneath the stage.

This platform is large enough to hold a metal cage. The steel bars of the cage are so thick I'd have trouble closing my hand around them, but with enough space between them that the slight figure huddled within is clearly discernible.

Tommy.

And Tommy isn't an awry.

He's something … else …

With my own essence loosely twined around me, I can sense the tenor of Tommy's power even through the heavy-duty protective essence entwined around the cage.

Kitty twists free of my hold, dashing toward her brother before I can caution her. Fortunately, my fear makes my own reaction quick enough that I'm up on the platform only a moment after her, snatching her back before she makes contact with the bars.

She opens her mouth to shriek. But Tommy's hand, thrust through the bars, closes over her mouth to muffle her indignation. Tommy, who is shirtless, hisses in pain. The skin on his bare arm sears, then blisters, from the essence coating the metal bars. His hiss isn't human at all, and neither is his malformed jaw.

Kitty cries out a second time, grabbing Tommy's arm and trying to shove the limb back through the bars.

He withdraws, cradling the seared arm against his chest. His other shoulder is clearly dislocated. The bruise capping that shoulder deepens further in color, as do the blisters on his arm. Yes, even as I watch.

Tommy is healing, and too quickly for a not-wholly-manifested eleven-year-old. He's barefoot, his toes misshapen and partially clawed. He's wearing only jeans, torn at the knees and frayed at the hems. Though they might have been that way before he was kidnapped.

He's definitely not an awry but a shifter of some sort — and seemingly stuck in the middle of a transformation. I can't get a solid read on the energy underlying this partial shift. Perhaps the protections coating the cage are fucking with my senses. But it feels as if an ancient power, completely different than the essence that fuels me and Kitty, pulses through his veins.

"You came," he rasps through his misaligned vocal cords. His eyes are bright with fever, or with the power of his beast. "Mirth. You came for us."

"I did," I say, perfectly steady. "Always ... we'll make sure this never happens again, but I'll always come when you need me."

"Okay." Tommy closes his eyes, slumping in the center of the cage and carefully avoiding the bars.

"What have they done to you?" Kitty sobs.

"Shot me up with something," Tommy says wearily. "It triggered me ... my essence. They thought maybe I was awry. Like you." He laughs harshly. "Boy, were they wrong."

"They could have fixed your arm. Clothed you," I say, completely pissed, and not quite certain why I'm fixating on those details over the kidnapping itself.

Maybe because I've nearly been kidnapped — or at least solid attempts have been made to kidnap me — so I'm used to it ...

It's probably best to not pick at that bit of possible psychosis right now, though.

"They said I should fix it myself," Tommy murmurs. "That it would make me more valuable to fully reveal my beast."

"Not forced like this," I snap. "You're still too young. Your body might handle it, but your mind will ..."

Tommy offers me a twisted smile. It looks like it hurts. "Maybe ... you can worry about that for me, hey? I'm ... I don't want to hurt anyone, but the cage is making me sick."

"Stay here, darling," I say to Kitty.

She hunkers down on her heels obligingly. Then she raises her phone and takes a picture of Tommy hunched and partially transformed in the cage.

"Hey!" he protests.

"Evidence," she says with a shrug.

I skirt the cage, looking for the latch. When I find it, it appears completely manual. But it's coated in the essence that burned Tommy so badly.

"Out of my realm," Coda says. The tech has been very quiet, though I have no doubt they've also been continually working in the background.

Aware of the children watching me, I take the phone off

speaker and press it to my ear. "There's a powerful mage involved."

"Multiple mages," Coda says. "But don't worry, your men are on their way to you now. There was ... an incident, but it gave the earl a chance to flex, knocking everyone out with one of his light tricks. He just, ah, inadvertently blinded Bolan at the same time. So the healer had to step up."

"Permanently blinded?" I ask, completely cool. But remembering Elias's story about how his power first manifested.

I'm not numb. Just perfectly in control, focused.

"Ah, no. The wolf keeps shaking his head and grumbling about it. But like I said, they're only a few minutes away now." Coda suddenly hoots, completely distracted. Then they add, "I'm in!"

"Who the fuck are you!" a deep voice shouts.

I glance over my shoulder.

The shorter of the two backstage crew members is moving toward us. The second guy is behind him a moment later. Both definitely shifters, judging by their speed.

Kitty cries out.

Coda says something in my ear, but my hands are already falling to my sides, my phone tumbling to the pedestal.

I straighten. My already awoken power pours from me, lapping around my ankles and curling around my hands, eager but obedient. Because I'm not a fifteen-year-old girl who's just been rejected by her soul-bound mate. I'm not in fear for my brother's life.

I'm not scared of the responsibility that comes with this power anymore. Not concerned about what my father will demand of me, demand I do with it.

I'm a princess with a sworn duty.

I'm an awry with an inherent responsibility and the sheer power to protect other purple-eyed essence-wielders like me. Like Kitty.

I am Mirth.

I apply all that intent, all my focus, to the two charging shifters.

The shifter farther away from me has a phone to his ear. I rotate my wrists, unfurling the power curled around my forearms. With another casual flick of my fingers, and a long whip of pure essence for each, I wallop the two men directly in their chests.

Their eyes widen.

They stumble, their phones clattering to the ground.

Then they laugh.

The sound burbles up within them, pouring out of their mouths completely involuntarily.

They clutch their throats, falling to their knees while roaring with peals of gleeful laughter. Clutching their bellies, then their heads, in extreme, unfettered, mind-melting joy.

The nearest guard falls face-first to the floor, convulsing. Still laughing.

"What the fuck?!" Coda shouts — darkly delighted and talking over the speakers of Kitty's phone now.

Both of the kids just look at me, wide-eyed and a touch fearful. Not even a hint of amusement in their gazes.

"It's all right," I say. My voice isn't gentle or sweet or all that cool anymore. "You belong to me. I would never, I could never, hurt you."

Kitty, pointedly not looking at the still-convulsing shifters, skirts the cage. She pauses to pick up my phone but is already reaching for my hand as she straightens.

I take the phone from her, then I take her hand. Her

skin is a little cool to the touch, so I rub my thumb across the back of her hand.

She blinks up at me, intently holding my gaze. "Tommy. The cage. And you … Mirth," she whispers.

Her vision, she means. She's just seen her vision realized. She smiles.

"Let's go home," I say, my tone a little softer.

"Yeah," Tommy says. His voice is ragged with pain. "We … Kitty and me … our mom … she … we can't go … home."

"I'm going to get you out of the cage. I'm going to get you healed. Then you'll both come to my apartments here in London, and you're going to eat and sleep. In whatever order feels best. Tomorrow, we will start sorting out all the rest, okay?"

"Okay," Tommy says gruffly. His gaze flicks to his sister.

Kitty, still gripping my hand, just grins back at him. No doubt still ecstatic at seeing her vision realized.

He huffs, exasperated. In that way that only an older sibling can be exasperated at a younger.

And I smile. I smile at the remembrance of Armin huffing like that at me.

It still hurts. It's always going to hurt, but it's not debilitating.

I wind a thick tendril of my essence around my hand, then grasp the latch of the cage.

But before the essence protections sealing the cage dissipate under my touch, the sound of motors rumble awake all around us, above and below.

A section of ceiling directly above us slides open.

The pedestal underneath us jerks into motion.

Kitty stumbles into me.

Tommy shouts.

"Fuck!" Coda cries through Kitty's phone speakers. "That's not me!"

I could grab Kitty and jump from the pedestal, abandoning Tommy.

But I don't.

I wrap my power around myself, around Kitty — who clutches at my hand even harder — and around the cage. I peer upward as the mechanical pedestal carries us into the theater overhead.

We're propelled through the floor and thrust onto the stage above, the platform fully sealing the hole that appeared overhead. I close my eyes against the bright lights flooding the area. But I can still sense the space open up around us.

A heavy hush falls over the crowd gathered beyond those bright lights. A silence so deep I swear I can hear Kitty's quick, panicked breaths and Tommy's heart racing.

I open my eyes, blinking against the lights for a moment. Thankfully the main spots are focused on the display — no doubt in the process of being auctioned off — to my right.

The Banksy. With the purple-eyed angel in the bullet-proof vest.

Just a little ironic.

I sweep my gaze across the crowd before me. If this was once a traditional theater, the raked seats have been removed, though the golden gilding and deep-red velvet curtains remain along the walls, pillars, and sconces. The patrons of the illegal auction are arrayed at round tables, six or seven people at each. Deep, large booths are set along the sides of the room, and a few upper balconies fan out alongside the stage.

Every single patron, all of them decked out in suits and pretty dresses and expensive jewelry, stares at me, frozen in uncertainty that quickly edges over into unrestrained fear.

Because my eyes blaze with the power writhing around

me and the children. My unfettered essence undulates across the raised stage, primed to cascade over the edge and into the audience.

I smile, fierce and biting.

When I open my mouth, it's not my sweet princess tone that gently flows through my words.

"I'll deal with the rest of you entitled, soulless assholes in a moment. But which of you sick fucks thought you could kidnap children in my fucking realm?"

10

———

CHRISTOPH

Mirth, her eyes blazing violet orbs of power, stands on the raised stage. Next to a Banksy these privileged assholes have stolen — I saw the installation in New York when it first appeared — and are now auctioning off to the highest bidder. She holds a young blond girl in cute pajamas, maybe eight or nine, by the hand. All the immense power that Her Highness carries, usually so tightly that I can barely scent it, wraps around them both, as well as a metal cage that contains an older boy. The boy is painfully stuck mid-shifter transformation. And appears too young for that transformation to not have been forced upon him.

I jerk to my feet, knocking the table of the booth tucked in the back corner of the theater enough to slosh posh drinks over a half-dozen nauseatingly expensive cigars. The rest of the table's occupants — the assholes who invited me to the auction — don't even notice.

Mirth has them completely enthralled.

Not one of the three fuckers at my table displays even a hint of surprise at the appearance of a child in a fucking cage. An auction for rarities and magical antiquities, they said when they sidled up to me at the club. Presuming that I'd be amenable to it all because not only am I a low-born bastard, shipped off to the United States by my duke father, but I'm now also well-known among the asshole toffs — thanks to Eli — for running an exceedingly profitable underground, illegal fight ring.

Apparently, the auctioning of children as one of the 'rarities' wasn't even worth an offhand remark.

At my movement, the awry goddess on the stage snaps her radiant purple gaze to me, narrowing her eyes as if sighting prey.

That mere look slices through me, instantly scarring my soul. I open my mouth to explain my presence ... or to declare my utter devotion ... or to demand that she get the fuck off the stage, to stop exposing herself to a theater full of stupidly powerful essence-wielders.

She offers me a twist of a smile, reaching for me with all that intense power. Her energy teases over and along a binding that I can now clearly feel, hooked just under my rib cage, near my heart. That mutely felt but previously unseen bond — our soul connection. A soul-deep bond that my seer mother murmured about when I was much, much younger.

The princess that my mother's long sight, normally tuned to financial prognostication, promised to me ... but I didn't believe, couldn't believe. Not literally, anyway. I was only the bastard son of a duke, with a line of heirs before me. And how many actual princesses even exist?

But my mother saw true.

I never understood why she stayed with my asshole of a

father, tucked away in that cottage and treated like a precious commodity when it suited him, and like a convenient fuck when he couldn't get it elsewhere.

Mirth and I were forged from the same pocket of the universe. Everything my mother did to protect me, to care for me, steered me toward the destiny unfolding before me. My path tweaked and prodded according to my mother's sight, enough for me to be standing here and now.

The revelation is overwhelming.

Mirth tugs on the bond between us. Just lightly. But it definitely snaps my attention back where it belongs. Had she been blocking that connection? Shutting it down along with the immense, intense power that now pours from her?

It doesn't matter. Because now I know for certain it's there. Now I know for certain why the burgeoning friendships with my other bond mates are so ... unburdened of expectation. Now I know why other relationships were, are, difficult for me. Why I never really bothered to look for anything more than the most casual of connections.

Why I held Mirth in the garden at Lake Thun.

Why I gave her the peaches.

I can see all the strands of essence between us now, including the power spilling over the edge of the stage, creeping across the floor toward the nearest audience members. I've always had a sight for essence — a genetic gift from my awry mother — but it's never been this intense, this exact before.

The *why* of that twists through my chest. As if Mirth herself is reaching within to grab hold of my heart. And my lungs, because I'm not certain I'm breathing at all.

We strengthen each other, our gifts, just by being in close proximity.

The bond between us thickens, then grows taut.

"Lord Williams," Mirth says. It's an outright claim,

thrumming with power. "You're standing on the wrong side of this."

Centuries of seeking the missing sections of our souls stretch between us, but only seconds have actually passed.

I push away from the table, heading for the stage before I even decide to do so. But I'm not beguiled. No, I'm moving toward my soul-bound mate with pure need, pure protective intent.

The momentary hush that fell over the audience cracks wide open. Toffs start jumping up from their seats, scrambling for their belongings.

Getting in my way.

Mirth's blazing gaze runs over all of them a second time. They literally freeze in place, mouths agape. Hands clutching at clothing or chairs or each other. All that power at their fingertips, all the privilege in the world, and Mirth's mere presence has them too fearful to even flee. Let alone fight back.

And Mirth isn't compelling anyone to do anything. Not yet.

A form of empathy, she called it.

I chuckle to myself, elbowing the assholes who've stumbled into the aisle out of my way. Empathy. That was the fucking understatement of the fucking century.

"Hold the phone a little higher," a voice says from the stage. "Scan to the right …"

The young girl raises her phone obligingly, arm shaking.

The realization that they're being filmed breaks the hold Mirth has on the audience. Essence begins to spark all around me. Most of the spells the mages are conjuring are defensive in nature, protection wards and the like. But some asshole mage in a three-piece suit and a flashy gold watch raises a hand toward Mirth.

I punch him in the back of the head. Hopefully not hard enough to kill him.

He goes down.

Then the screaming and the scrambling start.

Not unusual, honestly — at least not after I start throwing punches in the ring. Though the tenor here is more terror-filled than titillated.

A few more mages start flinging their essence all over the place, most of it hitting me as I shove my way toward Mirth on the stage. Being a giant of a shifter comes with pros and cons, but at least I partially block Mirth and the kids. My stupid suit gets singed. I'm fairly essence-proof, though, and well adapted to functioning under intense pain, so it doesn't much register.

Mostly because I can't really take my gaze off the awry goddess awaiting me.

Mirth's nostrils flare in indignation — a response to me taking hits. The power that's been protectively undulating around her, spilling over the edge of the stage but not reaching for any of the nearby idiots, now snaps out in multiple directions.

The screaming and scrambling shifts ... into laughter.

Ignoring whatever the fuck is happening behind me, I vault onto the stage, easily passing through the energy churning between us. I hesitate, but only for a moment, before meeting Mirth's gaze.

She smiles up at me sweetly, the expression a disconcerting contrast to the immense power still twined all around her. And the kids.

"Christoph," a voice purrs over the girl's phone speaker, "I haven't seen you since our last raid in New York. You could have called."

I recognize the voice now. Coda. How the awry hacker and Mirth know each other is something I don't take the time to worry about, and I don't break my gaze from Mirth when I respond to the not-so-veiled accusation. "It was a last-minute invitation. And I didn't know for certain it was them. Not until I saw the kids."

"Tommy needs your help," Mirth says, seemingly not at all concerned about my presence at what appears to be a gathering, perhaps even a full branch, of an underground trafficking faction. The Möbius Group. "Please, my lord."

The gentle request, threaded through with the weight of all the power at Mirth's command, shudders through me. Still ignoring the stifled laughter and the chaos behind me, I instantly bend a knee and wrap my hand around the bar at the center of the cage door.

Essence protections sear across my palm, over my hand. Pain blazes in its wake, aching through my bones. I ignore it, steadily meeting the boy's terrified blue eyes through the bars.

Tommy.

I know he is mine to protect the moment our gazes lock. Just like the others in my bond group are mine. I can see the thread-thin bond shimmering between us. It looks ... fragile.

Tommy's jaw is distended. Fingers clawed. He's partly transformed into some beast, the nature of which I cannot discern. Maybe the protective coating on the cage is fucking with my senses? His left shoulder is dislocated. Scarring from half-healed burns marks his hands and forearms. His ribs are darkly bruised.

I tear the steel cage door off its fucking hinges, ripping a hole through the protections sealing it at the same time.

Tommy valiantly tries to get to his feet. The cage is high enough that he should be able to stand, but I'm fairly certain there's something wrong with at least one of his knees. So I reach into the cage, the protections I've ripped through still active enough to sear through my suit and blaze across my upper arms and shoulders. Yes, I'm too big to fit through the cage door without twisting sideways.

Tommy reaches for me with one arm, cradling the other to his chest. I awkwardly pull him closer. My heart wrenches at the sharp cry of pain and distress he valiantly tries to swallow.

Then I have him huddled against my chest. Dark-blond hair that wants to be curly falls across his brow as he chokes back more pained sobs. From all the places I'm certain that I've inadvertently hurt him just while getting him in my arms.

Still crouched, I pivot so I don't have the audience at my back. Phone still in hand, the girl runs to me. I raise my elbow to gently block her from throwing herself on her injured brother. She hesitates, tears streaking her face. But when she leans over my arm, using it to support herself, her dark-blue eyes are fierce and determined.

"He'll heal quicker now." My words come out in a dark rumble that I'm unable to soften. "Now that he's not in the cage."

"I'm okay, Kitty," Tommy says.

Kitty reaches for him, laying a trembling hand on his uninjured shoulder.

"Sully is near," Mirth says casually. Her gaze is fixed to the panicking audience. Well, anyone not laughing as if they're utterly mad is panicking. "I can feel him now. I can feel all of you." She sounds relieved and peaceful, even while half the people in the crowd clutch at their sides, gasping for air and weeping with laughter under the mere touch of her essence.

"There aren't any cameras in here," Coda grumbles through Kitty's phone speaker.

Kitty straightens with renewed purpose, pointing her

forgotten phone and its camera back out at the room. She leans against my shoulder without fear, as near as she can be to Tommy. The little one is ours as well, like her brother. It's another thread-thin connection, but it's steady. Her power, the tiniest tickle next to the tsunami that is Mirth, marks her as awry.

Tommy stifles another pained moan.

"It's the partial shift that's hurting the most," I say to him. "You're going to listen to my voice, listen to my heart, and breathe with me and remember your wholly human form."

"They gave me something," Tommy says.

"Close your eyes," I say steadily. "With each breath, imagine whatever shit they gave you dissolving in the power of your blood."

Tommy looks at me with fear-blown eyes.

I get in his face so that all he can see is me. "You are so powerful, so unique, that you scare all these rich fucks, Tommy."

"How ... how do you know?" he croaks.

"Because you belong to me. Understand? You belong to Mirth, so you're mine as well. And look at Mirth ..."

He glances past my shoulder.

"Feel her power?"

He nods, pained.

"Feel how strong she is? She's yours. Not only is her strength, my strength, yours, but you are carved from the same portion of the universe as we were. You're younger and still learning, and that's okay. But whatever those fucks gave you? It's nothing compared to the power already in your blood."

The pained fear in Tommy's eyes darkens into a fierce anger.

"Good," I say. "Now, close your eyes, take a deep

breath, and exhale any remaining shit." I inhale, then slowly exhale.

Tommy mimics me.

As does Kitty. "I'm more powerful than these rich fucks," she says on her exhale.

Coda cackles gleefully through the phone speakers.

Mirth huffs.

And Tommy laughs. He laughs, shouts in pain, and shifts back into his wholly human form.

"Oh!" Kitty cries. "You did it, Tommy!"

The boy in my arms shakes from the effort, and he's still wounded enough that he needs a healer. But he meets my gaze steadily.

"Good," I say. Then I finally look up to address the next issue.

Not that Mirth isn't in complete control, but I'm fairly certain all this manic laughter isn't healthy for the inflicted. Not that I care. But Mirth wouldn't normally hold her power so tightly if she was cool with just going around murdering people.

Three elders of the Merton bond group — the ones who invited me here, and whom I left behind at the table — stand before the stage in the center aisle, seemingly locked in a contest of wills. With Mirth.

It's a one-sided contest.

Mirth appears equal parts amused and annoyed, but in that detached way that peerage has of making everyone feel beneath them.

I'm thankful she's never looked at me like that.

To be fair, ranking among peerage is often a nebulous thing. No one but her father outranks Mirth, no one but Mirth outranks me. In this room, at any rate. Lord Savoy, Sully, who is supposedly nearby, completely outranks me.

The Merton bond group as a whole outrank just about

everyone they come into contact with. And others tend to treat them accordingly.

But one on one?

There's no contest of wills they could hope to win, not by rank or by power, when faced with Mirth.

Evans, aka Viscount Boyne, situated between the other two Mertons, is a powerful shield mage, and his power flickers over the trio now. Apparently he plays squash or who-the-fuck-knows-what with Eli. I was barely listening to him tonight, to be honest. DeVere, a baron who attended school with my much older deceased brothers, invited me to the auction. We ran into each other at a totally rigged poker game at the archaic gentleman's club where Eli suggested I stay whenever I'm in London. I made my first appearance at the club tonight instead of showing up on Mirth's doorstep uninvited.

Then there's the head of their bond group. The elder Lord Merton himself. Vincent. Isla and Archie's father.

All three Mertons look smug as fuck. Presumably because they think they're withstanding the onslaught that's bringing down over half the other toffs in the theater now. But I can clearly see that Mirth isn't even trying to affect the Mertons ... to infect them? I'm not entirely certain what her power is, not even with it spread out before me in all its glory.

Honestly, it's possible she's holding back even now, having crafted a protective perimeter all around us and only lashing out initially to protect me. The farther away the audience members are from the stage, the less they appear affected.

The main doors also appear to be sealed. Likely a security measure by the auction coordinators, but it's working against them now.

"That's enough, Mirth!" Lord Merton snaps. As if he

has any right to speak to the princess in that tone, let alone address her without her titles while in public.

"Do you think I've made my position clear, Lord Merton?" Mirth asks, utterly amused.

Lord Merton huffs, glancing at me with a deep frown. He doesn't bother looking at the kids at all as he shifts his imperious attention back to Mirth. "Just take the children and go. I'll clean up your mess."

"Your mess," Mirth says. "Unless you'd like to try to convince me that my soul-bound mate is the head of this chapter of the Möbius Group?"

The other two mages glance at each other. It's a quick but guilty-as-fuck look.

"Don't be silly, Mirth. You obviously can't penetrate Viscount Boyne's shield, and you certainly can't stand against me should I decide you need ... quelling," Merton says, angry but trying to hide it. "And even if I do let you go, allowing you to take the children with you, you can't prove that we knew anything about this ..." He nods toward the cage at my back, as if unwilling to lower himself to even say the words 'child trafficking.' "Or this ... so-called Möbius Group."

He doesn't fool my nose. Or the reach of Mirth's weaponized empathy essence, presumably.

"I'll take that as a challenge," Mirth says, smiling.

Coda cackles over Kitty's phone speakers. "Grandpa has no idea what any of us are capable of. I've already got his financials at my fingertips. Give me a couple of hours and I'll start excavating the centuries of fucked-up shit his family trades in."

That's a promise, not just a boast, for a tech as skilled as Coda.

"Yes, very short-sighted of him." Mirth laughs, quietly gleeful.

In sharp contrast to the power threaded through every word that passes her lush lips, Mirth's laugh is charming and sweet.

Birds sing, flowers bloom, and the heavens bathe us in joy.

I have no idea if my reaction is from our shared bond. Or from her complete support despite the initial appearance that I might have been involved with the Möbius Group. Or from her earlier claiming of me. Even though we barely know each other.

So I ignore it, straightening to my full height, then shifting Tommy in my arms enough that I can tuck Kitty against my leg with my other hand.

Mirth tilts her head. "But I don't think you deserve to die laughing, Lord Merton. I also don't think you deserve something as easy as Coda destroying your financials with a click of a couple of buttons."

Lord Merton's face reddens. He huffs again, angrily, through his nose.

His bond mates glance at each other again, openly rattled now. It's possible they're contemplating abandoning the head of their bond group. If they were soul bound, their loyalty would be unquestionable — even when faced with the level of danger Mirth represents.

"No ..." Mirth muses. "The great and powerful Lord Merton wouldn't be here at the behest of anyone else. If you aren't the head of this chapter, then you're near to it. So I will ensure that you're completely miserable and alive to be stripped of it all. It won't take me more than a single phone call. But perhaps a lunch date would be more polite." She flashes him a perfect-princess smile. "One must always be polite. Yes, Lord Merton? But I can make those arrangements after I get the children safely home."

Apparently too angry to respond with words, Lord

Merton raises his hands toward Mirth. He's a mage, specializing in potent poisons. Undetectable poisons, according to rumors.

I move, pivoting to protect one child in my arms and the other beside me, even as I step in front of Mirth to take Merton's hit.

Light suddenly blazes around the edges of the main doors, erupting as sharp, bright beams that shred the thick velvet curtains covering the walls to either side.

The previously sealed heavy wooden doors drop forward.

The nearest toffs, previously trying to get the doors open between debilitating bouts of laughter, scream. A few mages throw up whatever shields they can muster as they bodily fling themselves out of the way.

Then Lord fucking Hereford stalks into the theater as if he owns the place.

So, a completely normal attitude for the earl.

Elias is flanked by Sully and Bolan. The earl has a bloody slash across his forehead, the wolf shifter's clothing is torn and bloody, and the fabricator mage looks as though he's just wandered off the pages of a fashion magazine. As always.

The Merton trio pivots to take in the new threat.

"Close your eyes," Mirth murmurs to me, closing her own eyes and reaching to cover Kitty's.

I close my eyes as I press Tommy's face to my chest.

A bright light flashes through the room.

Many bodies drop — hard — to the ground.

I open my eyes.

Every single rich fuck is down, including the three Mertons.

Eli tugs impatiently on his shirt cuffs, striding down the central aisle toward the stage and looking absolutely livid.

Sully and Bolan follow. The rock star grins, half-crazed. The blue-haired mage appears completely disinterested.

"I thought the Mertons' shield mage was supposed to be one of the most powerful in the realm?" I murmur to Mirth.

She flashes me a grin. "It's a light trick. Harnessed by essence, yes, but it's still pure light. Focused properly, Elias can knock just about anyone out, for a couple of minutes at least. It doesn't need to get through a shield, just screw with a target's eyesight. Well, more specifically the brain, through the eyes."

Eli reaches the miasma of Mirth's power, which is still undulating over the edge of the stage. He hesitates. Just for a moment.

"That was perfect timing, my lord," Mirth says in that measured tone. Her gaze is on Eli, but she doesn't withdraw her power to allow him passage. The challenge is clear. "I was close to completely melting at least a dozen brains."

Eli steps into Mirth's unleashed energy, fists clenched at his sides. It's the most emotional display I've ever seen from him — and I once completely pummeled him in the ring — as he climbs onto the stage. His light-blue gaze, pinned to Mirth, is still completely livid.

For a moment, I'm concerned that the earl has snapped under the stress of the situation. I worry I'm going to have to step between him and Mirth. Betraying his trust and potentially undermining his place in the bond group.

Mirth just grins at him. "Did you come to rescue us, my lord?"

He all but lunges to close the remaining space between them, sliding his hand around her neck and tugging her closer to slam his mouth over hers. It's a possessive, scared-out-of-his-mind kiss.

Mirth sways into him, tilting her head to give him better access.

"Oh!" Kitty squeaks.

Startled, Eli pulls back from the kiss, glancing disconcertedly at the young girl tucked against my leg. Kitty stares, wide-eyed, right back at him.

Eli didn't even notice her. Maybe he didn't notice anyone but Mirth.

The earl clears his throat, visibly trying to rein himself in. Until he meets Mirth's delighted gaze. "You will not do that again," he commands.

Mirth just hums, perfectly content. Then she smiles over Eli's shoulder. "Sully, love, Tommy is hurt."

The pretty-boy mage jerks as if just waking up, then instantly moves for the boy in my arms.

I blink as well, realizing that Sully, Bolan, and I have all gotten caught up watching Eli kiss Mirth.

The fallen bodies beyond the stage begin to stir. Disconcerted moans and pained groans fill the theater.

"Can we move the boy, Sully?" Eli asks, scanning the immediate area. "The shortest way out is through the main doors, I believe."

Mirth, the only one of us who entered the space from another direction, doesn't suggest an alternative.

Sully presses a hand to Tommy's forehead. The boy's eyes flutter, and he relaxes in my arms. "Just quick pain relief," Sully says. "It won't last."

"The Banksy!" Coda cries through Kitty's phone speakers.

"The royal guard are on their way," Eli says grimly.

"And pissed as fuck," Bolan adds.

Mirth huffs quietly. "Language, please —"

Bolan lunges for Mirth, throwing her over his shoulder.

She shrieks indignantly. "This is not going to be a thing, Bolan!"

The wolf, laughing like a maniac, pivots, jumps off the stage, and dashes up the aisle, dodging the rich, morally bankrupt fucks slowly waking up from Eli's incapacitating light show.

Kitty tugs at Eli's sleeve. Sweetly, she says, "I know I'm a big girl, but could you hold my hand?"

Eli doesn't hesitate to grab her hand. Then, after jumping off the stage himself, he carefully lifts the girl down. Weaving through the bodies littering the floor, the two of them follow the crazed wolf out of the theater.

I, with Tommy in my arms and Sully at my side, jog after them as best I can without jostling the injured boy in my arms. If not for my concern about the kids, I'm not certain I'd walk away so readily. These sick toff fucks don't deserve to —

"Well, that was a blast!" Coda's cackle echoes through the theater from the speaker of Kitty's phone. "So much pretty vid of so many upstanding people."

The awry tech is reading my mind.

No one is walking away from this unscathed. And I'm rabidly excited to witness whatever Mirth is going to do to the Mertons. With her promised single phone call.

11

MIRTH

Tommy falls asleep shockingly fast while eating his fourth slice of pizza. One moment, he's on the couch next to me, interrogating Kitty about every aspect of every moment they spent apart in the last day. The next, Bolan is lunging forward and catching him right before his head hits the hardwood floor.

On the opposite side of me from her brother, Kitty, snuggling into my shoulder as if my energy doesn't remotely bother her, jerks upright with a tiny shriek.

"It's all right," Bolan says soothingly as he shifts Tommy back onto the couch, carefully setting his head down on a velvet throw pillow. "Took him longer than I thought."

"Adrenaline," Christoph says quietly. Arms crossed and face in deep shadow, the bear shifter has posted himself at the street-side windows. And not for the view. "He needed to know Kitty was safe ... with us."

Bolan stares down at Tommy thoughtfully. "You get a read on his beast?"

Christoph flicks a look at Kitty. She huffs, crossing her arms to mimic his stance, then stares right back at him. Christoph huffs playfully in return, allowing his arms to fall to his sides as he steps closer.

Through the window, the sun begins to flush across the tops of neighboring buildings as it rises.

"Cath palug," I say. "A gigantic cat shifter. Like Anne."

Bolan tilts his head thoughtfully, nostrils flaring. "A cath palug? Really. I caught the feline scent but couldn't place it. It's retreated now."

"The shit they pumped into him has flushed from his system. That was mostly what I could scent." Christoph steps over to stare down at Tommy alongside Bolan. "A monstrous cat shifter. Rare enough to be practically mythical. No wonder those assholes threw him in a cage. They collect all unusually powerful creatures, not just those with purple eyes."

"He'll be fine now," I say, mostly to soothe myself.

Christoph shifts his attention to Kitty. "Bedtime now."

Kitty juts her chin out at the huge bear shifter. Christoph's been trying to get us all to bed since we arrived back at the apartments. "Then why wasn't I in a cage?" she asks challengingly.

Christoph bares his teeth at her. "They'd get a better price for you once your powers have settled. Maximizing profit. Or maybe the Mertons were just going to keep you for themselves, little seer."

The twist of emotion that runs through that weaponized term of endearment finally makes Christoph's reaction to Kitty much clearer. His mother was a purple-eyed seer, and though her cage was far more gilded than Tommy's had been —

Kitty scrambles up onto the couch, which really doesn't do anything to even her height out against Christoph. "Mirth won't let you hurt me," she spits viciously.

He looks startled, actually taking a step back.

Kitty points her finger at the duke. "I saw you! I saw you!"

All of us adults hesitate for a moment. Then I speak tentatively, my stomach souring. "In your head, Kitty?"

"No." She sobs once, then stamps her foot on the couch, defiant. "He was sitting out there with all the others staring at us. He's the reason they put Tommy in a cage."

Christoph takes another step back, then another. At the last moment, before tripping over it, he sinks down into one of the large leather chairs. Making himself less threatening — but also in shock, I think.

"You …" I clear my throat. "You trust Coda, don't you, Kitty?"

"No," she says with utter conviction. "Coda can only be trusted to do what Coda wants."

More of that shaky silence stretches around us. I meet Bolan's gaze, but Christoph has his eyes on the ground.

"I think …" I whisper. "I think that is actually very wise. But you trust me, yes?"

Kitty pivots to stare down at me. "I trust you, Mirth."

"And I trust Christoph."

The duke takes a deep, shaky breath.

Kitty narrows her eyes on him. "Why?"

"Because he's mine," I say steadily. "And you saw what I did to those people in the theater?"

"And the two guys below."

"Yes, well, I think I might have killed those two." Now it's my turn to take a shaky breath. "But that … power …"

"Making people laugh so hard it kills them?"

That's the simplest explanation, so I just add to it.

"That's a form of empathy. I can feel emotions, and I can ... twist those emotions. When someone is lying to me ... I can feel it. If I try."

Kitty's eyes widen, then narrow again. "Well, I don't know, do I?"

Bolan tries to swallow a laugh and ends up coughing.

"I am not funny," Kitty says to him.

Christoph finally raises his head, looking at Kitty. "I'm sorry you saw me like that, in that situation. I would never hurt you or allow anyone else to hurt you. Or Tommy. If Mirth hadn't come for you, I would have busted Tommy out of that cage the moment I saw him. So ... I can't say sorry for being there, or sorry for accepting the invitation in the first place. Because I'm glad I was there. But if you can't believe any of that of me just yet, that's okay."

Kitty blinks at Christoph for a moment. Then she climbs down off the couch and steps closer to Tommy. She touches her brother's shoulder lightly, not wanting to wake him but making certain he's safe.

Before we can continue the conversation, Elias and Sully step through from the hall connecting the two upper suites of my apartments. Finally.

My royal guard attempted to sequester us all separately once they got their hands on us again. Elias volunteered to take on the brunt of their interrogation and to oversee the aftermath of the mayhem I caused. After healing Tommy as much as the boy's system could handle in the first session, Sully joined the earl. Insisting, without any hint of the anger or frustration on display earlier in the day — well, yesterday now — that as the head of the Savoy bond group, he should make his presence and support known.

I deferred to both of them because I thought it far more important to be with the kids. Though the still-irate earl is certain to use his sacrifice against me in some fashion in the future.

The paperwork will presumably be mountainous.

And I'm a little concerned that Roz is going to outright quit on me. She was so incensed outside the theater that she couldn't look at me.

But it's also possible that with my power now unleashed, I really scare the shit out of everyone. Explaining why no one, other than the people currently in the apartment with me, could manage to look at me in the aftermath. Or question me directly.

Elias's cool facade dissolves upon seeing all of us arrayed in the living room. He pointedly looks out the windows, at the dawn encroaching on the city. I know he's truly pissed because the few lights in the room dim for a moment.

Sully just grins at us all, tired.

"You should all be sleeping," Elias snaps, yanking at his tie.

Kitty pivots away from Tommy, running toward the vexed mage before I can respond. She slides to a stop before him, head falling all the way back to gaze up at him earnestly. "We've been waiting for you!"

Elias blinks down at Kitty, completely confused that anyone would still be up at dawn waiting on him.

"Did you ... did you find Mama?"

"Not yet," he rasps. "The police are looking —"

"They don't care!" Kitty cries. "Mom says we don't mean anything to anyone like that!"

Elias goes down on one knee, raising his hands. Kitty is in his arms before he even gets them fully open. She presses her face into his neck, clinging to him.

His hands spasm. In utter shock, I think. Then he wraps his arms around her and just rocks her gently, side to side. "You mean something, kitty cat," he murmurs. "You and Tommy, you mean everything to us. To all of us."

My heart pinches harshly, then warmth floods my chest.

Kitty sobs into the collar of Elias's rumpled suit. He presses his hand against the back of her head and just holds her. "I'm sorry, Kitty. We're here now. We're here now. We'll figure it all out together."

Sully appears frozen in shock. Not by Kitty's emotional display, but by Elias's response to her. He shakes off his confusion, stepping closer to press his hand over Elias's on the back of Kitty's head, holding them both for a moment. Elias lifts his gaze to meet Sully's.

"Everything will hurt a little less, feel a little less uncertain," Sully says gently, "after a few hours of sleep."

Bolan scoops Tommy off the couch. The fledgling cath palug shifter is still sleeping extremely heavily, but if the two shifters aren't concerned, then I'm not going to fret. Much. Bolan carries Tommy back through the apartment to the guest room beside my suite. Between the two apartments, we have six bedrooms, which seemed like too many when Armin and I first had the suites renovated.

Of course, I also own an entire castle now. Lake Thun. Gifted to me by my father during the matchmaking event ... for me and my bond group.

Elias straightens with Kitty in his arms. Her eyes are closed now, head resting on his shoulder. She's been waiting for him and Sully, I think. Something about Elias's energy makes her feel steadier.

I slip off the couch to follow the kids to bed, pausing to hold my hand out to Christoph. He looks up at me, old pain etched through his gaze.

"We rescued them," I say gently, knowing without asking that Christoph worked with Coda in New York because of how trapped his mother felt with his father.

Knowing that his realization that Kitty is a seer might have triggered the old wound of not being able to rescue his mother.

I know barely anything about the bear shifter, but I know that.

I continue holding my hand out to him.

Christoph takes it, straightening to his feet to loom over me. I'm utterly comfortable in his shadow, though.

"I didn't doubt you for a moment," I whisper. "Not one second."

He exhales harshly.

I reach up and touch his cheek, then I turn to follow Bolan and Elias back through the apartment. Sully slides his arm around my waist, not pulling me away from Christoph but cuddling us all together.

"We'll let them sleep," I say. "For as long as they want."

ME ACTUALLY SLEEPING IS APPARENTLY impossible, though. Too many questions are still whirling around in my head, even while cuddled between Sully and Bolan, and with the kids safely tucked away in the next room. Though I do try for a couple of hours.

The early-morning sun is flooding through the main room of the apartment as I slip on a new dark-purple silk robe over the long black silk nightgown that Sully swathed me in before snuggling me next to him and promptly falling asleep. The hardwood floor is slightly cool under my bare feet as I wander farther down the hall to check on the kids.

Neither of them stir when I poke my head into their room. But Christoph unfolds himself from a chaise in the corner where he's been keeping vigil, soundlessly following me as I step back out.

Elias stands on the far side of my sleek, dark-wood dining table. What appears to be a completely different set of neatly organized paperwork is on the table before him, along with one of his laptops. His dress shirt is untucked, the collar open and the sleeves rolled up. With his phone pressed to his ear and in the middle of a murmured conversation, the earl gazes out the side windows at the sea of restored Victorian and Edwardian red-brick townhouses predominant in my neighborhood.

Christoph steps past me, heading for the kitchen area. And the already brewed pot of coffee.

Elias glances over his shoulder, his light-blue eyes instantly pinning themselves to me even as he asks the duke, "The kids?"

"Sleeping," Christoph says. "Tommy's energy has settled."

"You were worried he might transform again?"

"Mildly," Christoph says, pouring himself a cup of coffee, then pushing it toward me.

"Mirth doesn't drink coffee," Elias says. "Or tea." His attention is pulled back to whomever he's on the phone with. "Yes? Thank you. We will inform you when we're ready to leave. Yes." He disengages from the call and tosses the phone onto a pile of papers on the table.

"The locals are still pushing the royal guard for access to the kids?" Christoph asks, leaning back against the far counter with the steaming mug of coffee in hand. He doesn't sip from it, though.

"You might have to ... intercede there, Mirth," Elias says. "I've bought them twenty-four hours, but the guard are getting some push to involve the authorities."

"Intercede?" I ask playfully, slowly padding over to the

table. The earl's gaze drops to my bare feet, the silk robe and gown swishing around my ankles. "By royal decree? I'm fairly certain only my father can do that."

"I've rewritten the guardianship papers," Elias says, tearing his gaze away from me to shuffle some documents on the table. "Coda sent through some ... suggestions. Additions. I've got calls in to ensure we can file them as soon as possible. Today. This morning. I just need your signature. I'll witness, so we don't have to haul you in front of a judge."

I skirt the table to join him. He stiffens as I near, so I pause just out of reach.

"Are you still mad at me?" I ask.

"At the situation," he says gruffly. "I'm more unbalanced than I wish to be. And ... yes, utterly and irrationally, I'm completely furious with you. My ..." He shakes his head, rubbing the center of his chest.

"That's not anger," Christoph says mildly, pausing to take an actual sip of his coffee before offering clarification. "That's fear turned inward. Mirth scared you last night —"

Elias visibly bristles at that. "I'm not scared of my —"

Christoph raises a hand, more placating than demanding. "Seeing Mirth on that stage, protecting the kids, scared the fuck out of you. Out of all of us."

"Mirth is obviously more than capable —"

"Doesn't change the fear," Christoph says.

I lean a little closer to Elias, brushing against his arm. "I'm sorry if I —"

Elias's mouth closes over mine before I can finish the apology. Then his hands are on my hips and hauling me up to sit on the table. I gasp, opening my legs so he can settle against me — core to core. Thankful for the long slits up either side of my nightgown.

Christoph simply watches us, as he watched me kiss

Sully in the hot tub. I can feel his grounding energy. And maybe it's selfish or even wanton of me, but we … fit … we all just fit together.

Plus, let's be honest, all of us being here is also fucking sexy.

Elias's tongue invades my mouth, so I open that to him as well. Energy twines and twists between us, cinching us together tighter and tighter.

I feel his cock harden against my inner thigh. I wrap my legs around his hips to pull him closer, arching my lower back until I have him right where I want him, to press, to rub into me. He moans into my mouth.

Then he suddenly stiffens, as if realizing where he is and what he's doing.

He pulls back, leaving me panting.

I don't want to stumble stupidly through his boundaries. But also …

"Do you need to stop?" I ask, my words brushing across his lips.

"We … we don't know each other very well …" He doesn't pull back, though. Doesn't look away from me.

"Am I … is this uncomfortable? Too much?"

He inhales deeply. "I'm trying to not overwhelm you. I want my mouth on you. I want to be kissing you and making you pant and moan. I want you coming on my fingers, on my lips, and on my cock."

"Okay," I pant, a little unhinged myself. "Okay, yes." I slip my hands into the collar of his dress shirt, needing to be skin-to-skin with him.

"But … there are things to sort out," Elias protests mildly. "With the clean-up and the kids. The Mertons. I …"

Pretending that I'm being far more sly than I can possibly be while directly under his gaze — he sees every little thing I do — I get a few more of his shirt buttons undone, unintentionally skimming his nipple with my pinky.

He jerks like I've shocked him. His blue eyes meet mine, questioning.

"Do you like that?" I ask, doing it again. Intentionally.

His hips press forward into me, grinding against me. "Fuck, yes. Apparently. When you do it."

"What about this?" I ask, feeling bold now. I tuck his shirt to the side and flick my tongue where my fingers have been.

Elias trembles under my touch.

He's barely touching me. But turning him on, making him shake, already has me insanely wet. Christoph is still a steady presence, not moving from the kitchen.

Being watched is apparently stupidly hot as well.

So I flick my tongue over Elias's nipple again. And again. But when I go to switch to his other nipple, he takes control back, sliding his hands up my legs.

Under my silk gown, he snags the sides of my panties. Gazing into my eyes, perhaps gauging my reaction, he tugs the scrap of lace down my legs, leaving it hanging off one of my ankles. He glances down as he does so, looking just a touch smug.

I laugh breathlessly, reaching for the rest of his buttons, but he snags my wrists lightly, guiding my hands back to the table as he crowds over me — pushing me down, crumpling and scattering all his paperwork.

The laptop goes flying but somehow doesn't hit the floor.

Elias buries his face between my legs, holding my thighs pressed against his ears and with my silk gown still mostly covering me.

He licks me, once, twice, before focusing on my clit. And sucking. Before he's even touched me anywhere else.

I cry out, arching up into him, grabbing handfuls of his short hair. My head falls back. Panting, I realize that the reason the laptop didn't hit the floor is that Christoph caught it.

Elias presses my legs open wider, pinning one thigh down as he alternates between flicking and sucking my clit with his tongue and mouth.

I writhe under his ministrations, worrying for a moment that I'm actually too turned on, too overwhelmed, to relax enough to come.

Elias guides my free leg up over his shoulder, then slides a hand up my body to pinch my peaked nipple through my silk gown.

Christoph sets the laptop on the sideboard, stepping fully into my eyeline. "He needs this, Mirth." His gaze rakes over me, over Elias going down on me, his voice rumbling in his chest. "Let him pleasure you, little awry. That will settle you and help us all get some sleep."

Caught in Christoph's golden-eyed gaze, I relax onto the table.

He quirks a smile. He leans all the way over to brush a gentle kiss against my lips.

Then I'm coming. Pure pleasure explodes under Elias's tongue, streaking across my stomach and down my legs. The orgasm crashes through me, whiting out every other thought or feeling.

Christoph catches my moan in his mouth with the barest pressure on my lips.

The utter bliss of release flushes through me. And though simply taking pleasure is still a foreign concept to me, I allow myself to sink into it.

Elias replaces his tongue with his fingers, straightening so he can gaze down at me. At my pussy.

Christoph steps out of my sightline, then out of the room. Going back to check on the kids, presumably.

Elias reaches down and unzips his pants with one hand. He frees his hard cock with the same hand. His thumb continues circling my sensitive clit. "Come for me again, Mirth. And then I'm going to come all over your pretty pink pussy."

I lick my lips, drawing his attention there. "Okay."

"Quickly," he growls, stroking his cock. "I nearly fucking came when you orgasmed the first time."

I can't look away from his hand on his cock. "I want it," I all but whine. "In my mouth, in me, buried deep in me."

"Not yet." Elias's gaze is fixed to my pussy. He sounds as if he's really trying to convince himself.

Then his thumb falters on my clit.

His movements become jerky. His hips buck. Then, suppressing a deep groan, he shoots warm ropes of come all over my bare thigh.

"Oh, fuck," I breathe.

Energy contracts between us, then my second orgasm is shuddering through me. "Elias," I pant. "Oh, fuck. That was so ... that was so ..."

I'm still coming as his tongue replaces his thumb, sliding over my clit, gently but possessively. As if he's trying to taste my orgasm, claim it for himself.

"Good girl," he murmurs against that sensitive flesh. "Such a good girl to come for me. Both times." He teases another half-dozen aftershocks from me before stepping away and wetting a clean tea towel in the kitchen sink.

My heart is still trying to pound its way out of my chest as he comes back. He gently cleans his come from my thigh with the warm towel, then the table. He wipes his still-half-hard cock off with a clean corner.

Then he leans in and presses a light, seemingly reverent

kiss to my clit. My pussy is still on full display. My body clenches, feeling empty.

He smooths his hand up my leg. But instead of continuing anything sexual, he lays his cheek on my stomach, just resting his head on me and breathing.

I comb my fingers through his hair. I already know him well enough to understand that in a moment, he'll be tidying my clothing, then guiding me back into bed with Bolan and Sully. Then each of us will deal with the fallout from rescuing the kids in our own way.

Elias will make certain everyone is protected on paper, building an ever-stronger shield of legalese around us until it's insurmountable. And I'll do my perfect-princess thing, flexing the other power I would never wield unless I need to protect people. The power that has nothing to do with my purple eyes and everything to do with the role I was bred for.

But before all of that, I allow myself to hover in a moment of relaxed bliss, and I breathe in Elias. His head is a comforting weight on my stomach. His essence twines gently through my own.

12

Lunch with anyone at Regal Park Clubhouse is normally an engagement I would studiously avoid, because the clubhouse is one of the snobbiest places in London. Even the food is uptight. And honestly, usually served at the wrong temperature. The patrons dine here to rub shoulders, not to eat. Even the waitstaff is pretentious. Though perhaps that's demanded of them.

But I'm on a tight timeline, and the clubhouse is conveniently situated on the upper level of Regal Park Racecourse, more commonly referred to simply as the Racetrack. Where Rian is racing Perseus today. The series of flat races being run aren't for a title or a cup, but it's a perfect qualifying race for a horse with a new trainer. A new jockey as well. Apparently, a member of Rian's main staff also rides competitively.

My text messages from Rian this morning are filled with all sorts of stats and assurances as to why, even as a late entry, it's a good choice of race to start off Perseus's season. But nowhere among all that politely delivered info is an explanation of the distance growing between us. No sexy selfies. Not even a suggestive emoji.

So ... my return texts have been just as polite. No mention of the kids or our run-in with the Möbius Group. Between Elias and the royal guard actively keeping a lid on everything, the illegal auction at the theater hasn't been reported by any mainstream news outlets. And hopefully it never will be. I doubt that any of the figures involved are going to out themselves willingly.

I also haven't mentioned to Rian my now-undeniable connection to the rest of our bond group. Instead, I've asked him to join all of us, including the kids, in the Royal Household Box during the race.

He hasn't replied to that last message.

I tell myself he's busy with preparation, and that I should focus on my main task for the day. Retribution.

Well, really, ensuring that the kids are protected.

But also, retribution.

By my request, because I think he'll be the most level-headed in this situation, Christoph accompanies me to lunch. Even though I know without discussing it that he'd rather stay with the kids. He grumbled through all the adjustments Sully made to his now-perfectly-tailored suit. Then he glowered at all the notes — about who might be in the room and what their presence signified — that Elias had inundated him with all the way out the door and into the car.

I had tuned all of that out, to be honest. The duke was seriously done with the earl's 'helpful tips' for navigating the society that congregated at the Racetrack after less than fifteen minutes of it as well.

Forced back into perfect-princess mode, whether my power was tucked politely away or not, I would have preferred to be alone to tackle this disturbing issue. But apparently, I will never, ever again be allowed out of sight of at least one of my bond mates — never mind a full contingent of royal guards — while in public.

That last part is according to Raoul. And Anne.

Yes, everyone tattled on me. Okay, Roz and Elias tattled.

Roz still isn't speaking to me unless directly and pointedly addressed.

Our armored Rolls-Royce pulls to a stop, deliberately blocking access to the elevator in the car park under the Racetrack clubhouse. Christoph slips out of the car and quickly moves around to my side, where I take his offered hand to get out of the vehicle. Then I tuck a hand into his elbow, allowing myself a little moment of pleasure because I'm so tiny next to the bear shifter. Another armored car idles just ahead of ours, with another behind for extra security even though we're in a gated section of the underground parking. Royal guards in dark-navy suits slip around us, securing our passage.

"There's no going back now," I say. I mean it as a joke — I can feel the tension radiating from Christoph — but it comes out flat. And a little whiney. I wince.

Christoph steps around me, placing the vehicle at my back, and standing so close that all I can see is him. He gazes down at me with warm golden eyes.

"Mirth," he murmurs. "None of this shit means anything to me. You can walk through it all, and I'll be at your side any time you need me. You could choose to walk away from it all, abandon all your worldly goods and titles, and I'd happily hold your hand." He squeezes my hand for emphasis. "How about I just keep ignoring everyone but you, and you do your thing, knowing I'll be at your side wherever and whenever?"

I blink at him.

He flushes. That shouldn't be sexy. Honestly, with how

he left the dining room earlier that morning during my tryst with Elias, I'm not certain Christoph is actually interested in being sexy to me. So my reaction to that flush could be entirely inappropriate —

"You're thinking a lot today," he says.

"Every day," I murmur, leaning into him just a little and enjoying the pocket of respite his sheer presence effortlessly carves out of the space around us.

"The bond is intense."

I nod. "For you as well?"

"Yes. Have you spoken to Elias about it? He's been doing some research."

"Yes. And his parents were soul bound."

"He said."

I step a little closer, then give in to the impulse to run my hand down Christoph's already perfectly straight lapel. The dark brown of his suit is a perfect color on him, highlighting his dark-blond hair and golden eyes against his light-brown skin. His muscles shift under my touch.

Yes, all right. I'm petting him.

I sigh, stepping back and allowing my hand to fall.

Christoph grabs it, flattening my palm against his chest. His heart beats steadily under my hand. "Are you worried that we're being manipulated by the bond?"

I meet his gaze, startled. And I'm suddenly worried about exactly that. "I wasn't. Are you?"

"Nope." He chuckles, the noise rumbling under my palm, bringing an involuntary smile to my face. "I think we choose what we do with that connection. I'm not lost within you. I'm … home. And not just with you."

I inhale deeply. "It's not … it's Rian. I think he's pulling away."

"Some bond groups take decades to form, especially if they're generational."

"Like the Mertons," I murmur.

"Yes." Christoph's smile fades back to his typical inscrutable visage. He wears as much of a mask as I do. "My point is that Rian is ... young —"

"He's accomplished more in —"

"You know that's not what I mean. You and Sully are young as well."

"Maybe you're just old," I snark back.

"Maybe."

His eyes gleam with amusement. Completely idiotically, I feel as if I've performed some impossible feat. But acting like an idiot or not, I grin up at him.

"Do you know why Sully picked this dress for you today?" he asks, all low and rumbly.

And just like that, I feel settled back in my skin. Not overwhelmed in the least. Focused, steady.

Christoph strokes his free hand lightly down my spine, flattening it over the small of my back. Then, looming over me, he fully palms my ass. "It looks like a peach."

I laugh.

Christoph strokes my ass some more, angling his head to whisper in my ear, "Rian isn't going anywhere, Mirth. I haven't even had a taste of you, and I'm already addicted. The boy isn't walking away."

With the warm flush across my cheeks threatening to pool elsewhere, I focus on the fact that we're technically in public. My royal guards might be skilled at pretending not to watch us, but they still see everything. "I don't think it's my ... taste that's the problem. I ... I won't force him, Christoph."

Christoph pulls back, frowning. "You think it's that serious?"

I nod, swallowing tightly. "Sully does. And Sully

doesn't usually ... Sully doesn't care about ... anyone, really. Or what anyone thinks."

"Just you ... and Bolan."

I nod, but then add, "He'll eventually get around to Elias as well. It's obvious they're already physically attracted to each other. The caring part will come in ..." I blink up at Christoph. "That was your point about Rian. We just need to give him time ..."

He nods, but I can see him thinking. Perhaps giving my concerns more weight than before.

"I don't want ... I don't expect all, or even any, of us within the main bond to fuck each other," I say bluntly, because I just want to get the words out and then move forward. "I really never thought much about having multiple partners." Now I'm the one flushing. "But I won't sneak around with Rian either. I won't treat him like that. He doesn't deserve it. You ... you weren't uncomfortable this morning, with Elias and me, right? I read that correctly, yes?"

"Yes."

I nod. "I understand that polyamory just might not be what Rian wants, no matter how much he might want me personally. And ... I'm never, ever just going to be alone. Even if it wasn't ... even if I'd never found the rest of you ... I'm not really a person. I have a place in this world. Responsibilities. And I accept that destiny whether I choose it for myself or not."

"Again, he's young, Mirth." Christoph rests his finger under my chin gently, then he brushes a kiss across my cheek. "He's overwhelmed. We all are. But we have each other, in some form, for support. I've never texted so much in my life."

I smile at his sweet attempt to soothe me. But I have to focus elsewhere now. I have to be the princess now. In a much fuller sense of that role than I've ever embraced before.

"I should have brought my crown," I murmur, tucking my hand around Christoph's elbow, turning us as we move toward the elevator.

The rest of the world rushes back in. The royal guards shift around us, Roz and Greg flanking us while another guard secures the elevator. Two more guards have already gone up to secure the clubhouse level.

"You're always wearing it, Mirth," Christoph says, completely serious. "A wreath of purple vines and flowers across your brow, little goddess. Myrtle, I think. Like the first-century fresco they uncovered in Pompeii." He notices me staring up at him, mouth unbecomingly agape. "Is it the art reference that's throwing you, or ...?"

My breath rushes out of me, and for a moment, I can't get it back. "You can see ... essence?"

"I can see essence," he says, as if it's a regular everyday thing. "I just couldn't see yours until ..."

Until I unleashed my power in the theater. "My mother can see essence," I say, feeling weirdly hollow in my core, yet perfectly stable on my feet.

I catch Christoph's confused frown in the reflection of the mirrored elevator doors right before they whoosh open. Roz and another royal guard whose name I haven't retained precede us within.

"Anne?" he says. "Is that a cath palug trait?"

"No. My birth mother," I murmur as we step into the elevator. Greg follows us, pressing the button for the upper level. "She ... named me. Insisted on it. I thought it was just some odd family thing, even though I was ... you know, bred for a purpose."

"Ah ..." Christoph tucks me tighter against his side in

the somewhat crowded elevator. "Euphrosyne ... the goddess of joy. Or mirth."

"One of the Greek Charites," I murmur.

"Maybe it is a family thing," Christoph says, still perfectly matter-of-fact about it all. "Maybe it runs in your blood or comes with the purple eyes."

"Please." I laugh, a little sharply. "If my father thought my mother's bloodline was descended from ..."

I trail off, mind whirling. Because my father had always been clear about what was expected of me, from me. And when my power manifested ... I refused it. I refused it so utterly that I lost access to most of my secondary abilities as well. "But ... my mother is no great power."

Christoph shrugs. "These things skip generations."

The doors whoosh open. I didn't even notice the elevator moving. Christoph twitches right before the three royal guards step around us and into the quiet corridor beyond. The twitch was subtle — just him stopping himself from stepping out and pulling me with him — but I squeeze his elbow, reminding myself that I'm not the only one currently navigating life-changing events ... hour by hour.

Situated behind a dark wooden lectern emblazoned with the Racetrack logo, the host glances up from her tablet in the barest of acknowledgments. "Do you have a reservation?"

"No," I say, already glancing behind her into the crowded dining room.

"I'm sorry, we're very full —"

"Not to worry," I say. "We're meeting someone."

A brown-haired woman in a pale-blue dress straightens from a table next to the windows overlooking the track below, raising her hand to wave. Her hair is smoothed back into a pretty French twist today, makeup flawless and covering her previously-more-obvious ski tan, bright-blue eyes welcoming.

Isla Merton.

A dark-blond, slim, tan-skinned male in a light-gray designer suit sits on her left. Isla and Archie's chosen, Noah.

Every patron between Isla and me pivots to see whom the Merton heir has waved to so enthusiastically.

I raise my own hand in acknowledgment. Just not as high.

"Name?" the host asks, getting just a touch irritated.

A hush begins to muffle the vigorous chatter that normally fills the clubhouse dining room, radiating out from Isla into the far corners.

"That's not for you to ask," the royal guard whose name I still don't know snaps.

The young woman's head jerks up, eyes flashing with ire. Her reply dies on her lips, face paling as she truly looks at me. She gasps, then starts to stutter. "I ... I ... I'm ... so ... sorry ..."

I sigh, though only inwardly. Then I turn, remove my sunglasses, and deliberately make eye contact with Roz. Roz, who should be the guard standing just ahead to my left, no matter how pissed she is at me for sneaking out last night. I deserve her ire, of course. But the host doesn't deserve to be put in her so-called place this way.

Roz actually flinches under my look. Then she tilts her head pointedly toward the offending guard. He, looking completely confused, switches places with her.

I slide my sunglasses back on, facing the host with a

perfectly pleased smile in place. "Not a concern. I see my friend Isla."

I don't wait for her to recover. She can do that far easier without me standing in front of her. I stride around the lectern, sliding my hand down Christoph's arm until I'm holding his hand. He keeps pace with me unquestioningly.

The other patrons start removing their napkins from their laps, trying to hastily rise from their seats.

"Please," I say pleasantly, but projecting my voice through the room. "Don't let me disturb your lunch."

Most of the patrons settle back into their chairs. A whisper of conversations start behind us as we pass.

Isla remains standing, with Noah rising to her side as I near. Lots of questions about who Christoph is float around us, but the duke at my side doesn't acknowledge any of them. His expression is once again forbiddingly inscrutable.

One of the staff attempts to dart ahead to pull out a chair for me, only to be deftly intercepted and redirected by Roz — no snapping needed. Christoph pulls the chair out for me instead.

I pause to smile at Isla, then Noah. "Thank you for accommodating me."

Noah just flashes me a saucy grin, but Isla clasps her hands tightly. "We were so pleased that you even wanted to see us ..." Her gaze flicks to Christoph, but she quashes the question she obviously wants to ask.

"It's never a problem to ditch the oldies," Noah drawls, his accent still flavored by that hint of non-European French. The light gray of his suit brings out the awry purple in his dark-blue eyes.

"Father wasn't planning on attending anyway," Isla says.

"I imagine not," Christoph mutters under his breath,

pressing a hand to the small of my back to encourage me to sit down.

Isla hesitates at the comment, then ignores it. "Though if we'd known one of your horses was racing, Mirth, all of us would have happily attended. It was just announced."

I slide into my seat. Christoph steps around me and takes the chair between me and Noah. Isla and the other awry both sit as well.

"Perseus," Noah says. "That's the magnificent beast you were riding the other day, yes?"

"Armin's newest horse," I say. The pinch of pain that accompanies the mention of my brother is just a tiny touch of agony today. "It's the first race for the new … team." Not proudly mentioning, acknowledging, Rian is a different sort of discomfort. "We wish them well, of course."

"Of course," Isla murmurs, smoothing her napkin over her lap.

Servers step in around us in a flash, filling the tall crystal tumblers with water and setting champagne down for Christoph and me.

"I ordered ahead," Isla says. "As your guard prefers."

"Thank you."

An amuse-bouche is placed in front of the four of us, the servers' moves coordinated and swift. They withdraw the moment the plate settles before me. The bite-sized appetizer appears to be tiny cubes of seared ahi tuna arranged on a single leaf of Belgian endive.

Isla plucks up her knife and fork, opening her mouth to continue the conversation.

Christoph scoops up the amuse-bouche with his fingers and pops the entire thing in his mouth, barely chewing and quickly swallowing. Then he flashes me a grin and holds his hand out for my plate.

Isla's mouth drops open, her eyes wide and aghast.

If that shocks her, then this conversation isn't going to go at all smoothly.

I pass my plate to Christoph. He eats the second amuse-bouche, then drops the fine china onto his empty plate.

Noah is struggling not to smile. Though when his gaze settles on Isla, it becomes somewhat wary. The Merton heir appears to be slowly melting down internally.

Isla's nostrils flare as anger and frustration overtake her manners. "I selected that dish based on Her Highness's preferences. You cannot —"

Christoph interrupts smoothly. "Mirth doesn't eat in public." He flicks his golden eyes between Isla and Noah. "Or hadn't you noticed?"

Maybe Christoph isn't as coolheaded as I presumed. That was the primary reason I asked him to join me.

Unsurprisingly, Isla gets huffy. "We are not public," she snaps.

Christoph leans back in his seat, then deliberately casts his gaze around the room.

Isla dismisses the duke with an offish tilt of her chin, turning to me. "I know I owe you an apology, Your Highness. I just ... when you asked to join us for lunch ... I thought ... and now ..." She looks pointedly at Christoph.

"You would have preferred Sully or Bolan, no doubt," Christoph says.

Isla's shoulders stiffen, but she keeps her gaze on me. "It's true that, during the picnic, I didn't express myself terribly well —"

"You mauled Mirth's soul-bound mate," Christoph says flatly, derisively. "In front of her. And that's the least of your family's indiscretions."

Isla takes a shaky breath. "Soul bound ... Bolan ... but ... I mean, it was obvious that ..."

"That what?" Christoph snaps.

I reach over and lay my hand on his wrist. The tension threaded under his skin instantly eases. He turns his hand over, offering me his palm.

"Apologies, Mirth," he whispers, his gaze on our hands. He twines his fingers through mine, then draws our clasped hands under the table, under the cover of the white linen tablecloth. His dark-golden eyes meet mine. "I did listen to some of Elias's protocol notes. Some."

"I needed that remedial course at Lake Thun myself," Noah says, trying to lighten the mood. "Too many years playing around with Archie behind the scenes, as it were. Not enough time managing public-facing relationships."

"You've chosen, then," Isla whispers tonelessly.

"It wasn't a choice," Christoph says, his gaze still on me. "The universe tells me I belong to Mirth."

"The duke ...?" Isla shifts in her seat. "And Bolan and ... Sully too?"

"Worried that you'll never get the chance to fuck the pretty Lord Savoy?" Christoph says mockingly.

Isla reels back.

I slowly remove my sunglasses. The bright light pouring in the windows is seriously uncomfortable, but I set the glasses down next to my water and just look at Christoph. His fingers twitch in my hand.

"Sorry, fuck," he says, clearing his throat. "I'm just here for support. Just ... at least three of the tables behind you are filled with the assholes in attendance last night. Plus ..." He jerks his head in Isla's direction.

Isla's eyes are wide, her expression wounded now.

Noah leans across the table, lowering his voice and no longer playful. "What is it, Mirth? What's wrong?"

I've been thinking, on repeat really, of how to broach this subject with Isla since before I made the call to have the lunch arranged.

"Is ... Sully actually Lord Savoy?" Isla asks meekly, as if she knows she should probably keep quiet but can't help herself.

That kind of knowledge, and the connections it potentially represents, is powerful in our world.

Christoph huffs.

Noah's hand comes down on Isla's knee. Heavily. I can't see his arm or hand under the table, but she all but leaps out of her chair in response, then looks just a touch chagrined.

"Do you recall an incident that took place at school when you were ... thirteen or fourteen, Isla? Noah, you would have been ..."

He laughs. "Much older."

I smile genuinely at the other awry's attempt to smooth the tense conversation. "That year, Armin and I left school abruptly, about a week before summer break."

"And you didn't come back ..." Isla says in a rush of remembrance. And just a bit of anticipation. "Not until second semester the next year."

Again, knowledge is power in our world. Unfortunately, Isla isn't going to like what I'm about to tell her, for one of two reasons. Either she already knows, or she doesn't.

"You were younger than me. I wasn't certain it was even something you'd noticed."

Isla laughs sharply. "Mirth, we all revolved around you and Armin. We ranked ourselves according to who was in your classes, how closely they sat next to you, who you talked to in the corridors or in the dining hall. Being selected to be your partner in class, or even better, with a joint assignment outside of regular hours? That elevated your partner's status for the rest of the year!"

I blink at her.

"And ... you had no idea we even existed."

"Hey," Christoph interjects.

Flustered, Isla raises a hand. "That's not ... that's not what I meant." She takes a breath. "So yes, I noticed. The rumors were rampant. No one knew why you left early." She glances at Noah for confirmation.

Her awry chosen shakes his head, keeping his now deeply wary gaze fixed on me. "After my time, dou-dou. Way after."

"When you didn't come back, we heard that ..." Isla glances around, dropping into a whisper, "I mean, of course, these sorts of rumors always follow ..."

"The awry?" I interject ever so helpfully.

Noah snorts.

Isla huffs. "I'm just reporting what I heard, not what I thought. Even though it wasn't in the papers or anything, the rumor was that you were attacked, that Armin was wounded, and maybe even other people died."

"They did."

"Goodness ... everyone thought maybe Armin killed them, defending you. Was it a kidnapping?" Isla rears back, eyes widening as she covers her mouth in dismay. "Did you ... did they succeed?"

I raise my hand to stop her from panicking. "It was an attempted kidnapping. I wasn't ... harmed. Armin didn't kill anyone."

Isla smiles, relieved. Then she transitions from concerned to slightly smug at uncovering the truth in almost an instant.

Until I add, "I did."

Isla's eyes widen. "But you ... you ..." She clamps her mouth shut.

I give her a moment more, but she shakes her head, just listening now.

"The timing seemed odd," I say. "But if I'm honest, I barely gave it any thought in the aftermath. It's only after a conversation with Elias and an incident that occurred last night that I'm starting to piece a bit more of it together." My gaze drops to my abandoned sunglasses, and I resist the urge to put them back on as I recollect the evening. To hide my purple eyes as I continue hiding from my past, from what I'm truly capable of. Even from myself.

But I don't. I don't put the glasses back on.

"I was out unsupervised with Bolan that night at school. We had a ... misunderstanding, and I headed back to the dorm alone. My power manifested, and I was ... concerned about controlling it."

"Happens to all of us," Noah murmurs quietly.

I nod. "When one of the school security guards approached me outside the dorms, I ran instead of going back to my room. Armin eventually found me. But the guard must have been working with the kidnappers and watching for exactly that opportunity. They made an attempt to grab Armin and me."

"Ridiculous," Isla mutters. "To try to take you at the school. Plus everyone knows, knew, what Armin was capable of. And you, you, Mirth, have always been an unknown. That's even more disconcerting."

Christoph tugs his phone out of his suit jacket and slowly raises it, as if filming over my shoulder.

I glance in that direction. The occupants of the table two over and three across from us are in the process of leaving. Their food sits uneaten.

"What are you doing?" Isla hisses at Christoph. Then she cries, "Ouch!" and slaps Noah's shoulder. Presumably, he's squeezed her knee a little too firmly.

"Last night?" I ask Christoph.

He nods.

"What have you put together, Mirth?" Noah asks quietly.

"Have you had any dealings with the Möbius Group?"

His lips thin. "No. Thankfully."

"The Möbius Group?" Isla asks, not moderating her tone at all now. "But they're —"

Christoph shifts his camera as the diners at the table right behind Isla abruptly get up and leave. Their gazes are firmly fixed on the exit, away from us.

Isla snarls under her breath. "What is going on here?! The Möbius Group is just a modern-day legend, right? Like the Illuminati."

"Not a legend," Noah says tersely. "What happened last night?"

I look him in the eye. "Can you guarantee that Archie isn't involved?"

"What?!" Isla cries.

Another table of diners gets up in unison, all of them hustling out of the dining room.

"A sound shield?" Christoph prompts Noah.

The other awry bristles. "It's impolite in public. Plus I'm not the only awry here."

Christoph chuckles, darkly amused. "You really don't want Mirth casting anything in your vicinity."

"But that was Tegan and Amanda Bristol," Isla says. "And I play tennis with Christina Dunworth on Tuesdays. What are you suggesting?"

Noah keeps his gaze fixed on mine. "You're saying that the Möbius Group was behind your attempted kidnapping at the school."

"Unconfirmed," I admit. "I ... ah ... I wasn't asking questions at the time. And anyone I left alive was summarily taken care of by my father. And the royal guard, I suppose."

Isla moans quietly, then slaps her hand over her mouth.

I'm starting to feel as if I'm torturing the both of them. Noah suddenly looks drained, and Isla is barely hanging onto her composure. But I continue, "Last night, the Möbius Group kidnapped two children under my protection. The children might have been drawn to the attention of this group by my ... interest in them."

"Unlikely," Christoph says.

"It's possible," I say stiffly.

"You're not to blame yourself," he says. "And it will not happen again."

I turn my attention to Noah. Of the two of them, he's the only one following the path I'm about to connect.

"Awry children?" he asks.

"Kitty is awry. But her brother, Tommy, is a rare shifter breed."

He nods, as if all this information lines up perfectly with whatever he already knows about the Möbius Group.

"I took the children back."

Noah's jaw clenches. "Archie was with me all night. Besides that, I know him. He's mine. Bound to me like you two are bound to each other."

"What?" Isla asks, quietly pained. "You and Archie? But ..." She shakes her head, straightening her back. "That's not ... important right now. Please, Mirth. Continue."

"In the process of finding and retrieving the children, we made certain discoveries last night. Investigations are ongoing."

"And then you asked us for lunch," Isla says, chin held stiffly but her voice thin. "You think the Mertons are involved ... somehow."

"I know they are," I say gently. "I stood face-to-face with your father and allowed him to walk away because the children were hurt, and that was more important in the moment."

Christoph tilts his head in Noah's direction. "You could also be complicit. It's not unusual for an awry to turn on another awry."

Instead of exploding at the accusation, Noah just looks at me calmly. "Hence, lunch."

I nod.

"I'm ... not really following," Isla breathes.

"Mirth knows when we're lying," Noah says matter-of-factly. "A minor ability among other much more ... robust talents, I presume."

Isla sways slightly, as if she might faint.

"A drink of water, perhaps?" I say.

Noah pushes the glass into Isla's hand, then helps her sip from it. "What are you proposing, Mirth? Will there be an official investigation?"

"Oh, universe," Isla mutters, sounding sick.

"The Möbius Group is too powerful for anything quite so mundane," Christoph says. "The fact that a chapter this robust has operated here, where the awry have ruled for centuries, is ... a little unbelievable."

"Where have you come across them?" Noah asks.

"New York. You?"

Noah shakes his head. "Just ... rumors. And that one wrongful death of another awry at school. At least ten years before Mirth's time there. But ... some things make a lot more sense now. About the ... structure of the Merton bond group."

"What do you mean?" Isla asks shakily. "This ... you can't all be serious. What are you saying? Speak plainly."

"Your father and at least two of your elder bond mates," I say, "are directly involved with kidnapping and trafficking children with powerful potential."

Christoph adds, "As well as black-market art and antiquities."

"No," Isla says, swallowing a whimper.

"It's possible … by the way he positioned himself last night," I say, just trying to get it all out now, "it's possible your father is actually the head of the European chapter of the Möbius Group."

"The United Kingdom at least," Noah mutters.

"You can't be believing any of this?" Isla cries, helpless but clearly beginning to believe it herself. "Noah?"

He leans in and gently kisses her, murmuring against her lips, "We need to listen now, dou-dou. Mirth is giving us a chance to salvage as much as possible."

Isla leans into her chosen for a moment, then nods.

They both turn back to me.

"Archie will have to take the seat on the council," I say steadily.

"Father will never give it up, Mirth."

"You will force him out. You'll bring in a forensic accountant."

"I'm perfectly qualified to —"

"There are other people involved now, Isla."

"You need to clean house," Christoph says.

"And reparations will have to be made," I say. "Large, public displays of philanthropy."

Isla opens her mouth again, but I keep going.

"Every stolen piece of art," I say. Then, more darkly, "Every child sold into slavery at your father's behest."

Isla presses a shaky hand over her mouth.

"I'm not the only one watching," I say. "And I can't guarantee that I can control what this other party will do if they aren't satisfied that the rest of you aren't involved. Though the wanton destruction of anything accessible through tech comes to mind."

Isla meeps in terror behind her hand.

I try to soften my tone. "The realm needs stability. What else are we here for, born into all of this ... the money and the titles ... but to protect everyone else? That's why I've come to you, Isla. That's why I'm asking you to accept responsibility. To do what needs to be done."

Isla's hand falls to the table. Her eyes, wide and filled with tears, lock to mine. "You're right, Mirth."

Noah tugs his phone out of his pocket. He presses a single button, then holds it to his ear. He then clearly interrupts whoever answers. "We need you. Meet us in the Racetrack box. It's easier for you to come to us and ... easier to secure that space." He pauses for a moment, his tone softening. "I'm sorry. We'll explain. Come now. Don't speak to anyone else." He hangs up the call.

"But ..." Isla's hand flutters over the silver cutlery set to the side of her plate, fingertips plucking at the edges of the napkin there. Her eyes are an even brighter blue than usual, flushed with unshed tears. "I'm not ... I'm not certain I'm absorbing this ..."

Noah takes her hand, leaning close enough to press it to his chest, over his heart. Her gaze crashes into his. But instead of completely melting down, Isla's back straightens, and her breathing steadies.

The connection between them is real. No matter that it's been forced along by the matchmaking event and Lord Merton's attempt to woo me into his bond group through the younger generation.

Isla's thumb brushes against Noah's shirt, offering comfort even while taking it.

Then she abruptly leans into her chosen — as if something has just become perfectly clear to her. Her voice is low but fierce. "I'll fight, Noah. You're not ... you're not just a prize to me, to be wooed or won or even bought. I'm ... I might be overwhelmed, but if this is who my father truly is …”

“It’s okay,” Noah says soothingly.

“It’s not okay!” Isla snaps. “None of this is okay. What if Mirth never found out any of this? What if she did but never came to us? I would have just continued to … to … I’m not my father! If this is who he truly is … I’m … sickened … and …”

“I know.”

“You don’t, really. We barely know each other. But I’ll spend the rest of my life making it right, Noah. I don’t give a fuck what color your eyes are or what power you wield. I love you.”

Noah’s eyes widen, mouth dropping open slightly.

“I love you, Noah,” Isla repeats firmly. Then, seeming to realize that fierce declarations of love are a little out of place in the clubhouse dining room, she tilts her head prettily to the side and smirks. “And not just because of that thing you do so well with your tongue.”

Noah laughs, still slightly overwhelmed. “Well, keep that on the list because it’s also a favorite of mine.”

With a blush warming her cheeks and still quietly smirking, Isla angles her gaze back to catch mine. “May I ask for … this is going to sound like I’m doubting you, but I’m not.”

“Proof?” I offer her a smirk of my own. “How much do you want?”

“All of it.”

“That can be arranged,” Christoph says. “As quickly as you need. Likely on a secure hard drive, by courier. Mirth cannot be further involved.”

I chafe at that last bit, but he isn’t wrong. No matter what I did last night to secure the children, my position doesn’t really allow for such vigilante justice. I’m supposed to forever be a neutral unifying figurehead, in fact.

"Understandably," Isla says.

"We'll be in the Merton box," Noah says, glancing at his phone screen. "Please give your contact my details. If I'm understanding the dynamics here, I might be the best point of contact for them?"

Awry to awry, he means. Noah knows enough about the Möbius Group to know that our contact is very likely awry. He's right, of course. I don't need to see Coda's purple eyes to know that definitively myself.

"Thank you, Mirth." Isla, hesitating for just a moment and giving me plenty of time to pull away, touches the back of my hand lightly. "Thank you for trusting us, trusting me."

I nod, squeezing Christoph's fingers under the table just a little. "The impulsive destruction of anything and anyone connected to this group would be easier, even more satisfying, than prioritizing stability and slow, steady change." My voice hardens. "But please don't doubt that I am more than capable of indulging my inner need to destroy anyone connected to this Möbius Group. I could do it while I sat here and sipped my tea."

Isla's fear curls around me. And for one of the only times in my life, I don't hate that reaction.

"You don't even like tea, Mirth," Christoph says.

I flick my gaze to meet his. His eyes are warm, inviting — and maybe laughing at me, just a little. "The next time I'm in a great-and-terrible princess mindset, perhaps I won't invite you along."

"Archie's parking," Noah says quietly, placing his napkin next to his untouched plate. "You don't mind if we leave you to your lunch, do you, Mirth?"

"Of course not."

Isla straightens from her chair. "We'll do a proper lunch next?"

"Just to check in," Christoph says warningly.

This time both Isla and I throw peeved looks the duke's way.

He grins. But grimly, not warmly. At Isla and Noah specifically. "Just following my own set of directives handed to me by those more into this politics shit than I ever will be. I personally would have chosen Mirth's path of impulsive destruction the moment I set eyes on those kids."

"We understand you perfectly," Isla says.

"Keep it that way."

I huff under my breath, nodding as Noah and Isla bow and curtsy in my direction. Then they flee the clubhouse dining room as quickly as they can without actually picking up their pace. I'm thankful, just this once, for the snooty reputation of the remaining clubhouse patrons and the staff, all of whom pointedly ignore the odd goings-on.

"Keep it that way." I mock Christoph's words back at him.

Christoph flashes me a blazing bright grin that is so out of character it momentarily shocks me dumb. He hooks his hand under my chair, yanking me closer before I can even think to stop him. Though I'm honestly not certain I would even if given the chance.

Looping his arm over the back of my chair, as if we're some normal couple in some normal restaurant, he raises two fingers to flag down the nearest server.

That server apparently isn't ignoring us so much that he misses the summons, almost stumbling over his feet getting to our table.

"Clear these extra settings, would you?" Christoph says. "And do you have a chef capable of making proper sushi on staff?"

"Yes, sir. I mean, my lord." The server flags down another of the waitstaff, and together they efficiently and expertly start clearing Isla's and Noah's settings. "I'll quickly have the chef write out a menu proposal, shall I?"

"Nah," Christoph says. "I like just about anything, as long as it's fresh. Do you have sashimi? Sockeye, specifically? Anything with prawns or scallops. Do you like sunomono, Mirth?"

"I do," I murmur, completely and utterly beguiled by something as simple as Christoph … taking care of me. "Miso soup as well."

Christoph flashes an affable grin. "You heard the princess. Thank you."

Thusly dismissed, the servers spin away in different directions.

Christoph takes a swig of his water, then catches me watching him.

"I like you."

"That's good." His voice rumbles through his chest. "Because I'm yours."

THE SO-CALLED ROYAL HOUSEHOLD BOX IS EMPTY when Christoph and I arrive. Roz still insists on doing a walkthrough while we wait, surrounded by other guards in the hall that leads to all the other boxes along the upper level of the stadium racecourse.

"Give us a moment, would you?" Christoph murmurs to Roz as she circles back from checking the bathroom and we step into the box.

My guard's gaze flicks to me, and I offer her a smile

instead of the nod she'd get in public. She smiles back, smirking just a little inappropriately.

Christoph clears his throat, glancing around the box. A small kitchen lies to our immediate right, replete with a sideboard currently overflowing with snacks and drinks. Monitors with active live feeds to the track below are situated on each wall, with a small seating area under each. Two rows of bench-style seating edge the far windows with direct views of the track below. The box is completely glassed-in, layered in protection spells, and currently darkened for privacy.

"Mirth." Christoph touches my back gently.

I wanted to continue holding his hand as we walked from the clubhouse, but didn't. I meet Christoph's steady, verging-on-intense gaze, stepping just a little closer than appropriate. Because I like the way he looms over me. I try to match his serious tone, but with just a little lightness. "Christoph."

His brow furrows, then smooths when he picks up my teasing tenor. He presses his fingertips into my back a little more firmly, then flattens his hand so it covers my entire lower back.

I know it's not terribly progressive of me, but I still love, absolutely adore, that I'm so tiny next to him.

"I've never …" He clears his throat quietly. Again.

"You've never?" I echo playfully. I like watching his throat move when he swallows.

"Right, yes. I've never …"

I hear his hesitation then. And finally, it filters into my silly brain what he might be trying to say. My eyes fly up to meet his. "You've never?!"

He flushes. "No. I mean, yes, of course. I've had sex. Tried it a few different … when I wasn't … when it wasn't what I thought it should be ... what everyone else seems to think it ..."

"We don't have to talk about this," I say quietly.

"I want ..." He runs a hand through his hair, his bicep flexing so much that it appears to be about to rip through his suit jacket.

Oh, fuck, I'm ogling him. Again. He's trying to tell me something, about sex, or not being interested in a sexual relationship. And I've completely misunderstood.

Except how could I have misunderstood? With the peaches, the handholding. He stroked my ass in the car park! I've clearly read too much into all of that. Or maybe it's going too fast for him.

I take a step back, leveling my gaze on his chest, then his shoulder, because I'm not sure I can look him in the eye. Mortification floods through me. I take another measured step back. "I ... I'm ... so sorry. I ... would never ..." I press my hands to my face. This is why he asked Roz for a moment alone.

"Mirth?"

I drop my hands. I get a fucking hold on myself. Breathing in, then lifting my chin and smiling. "Christoph?"

"Don't fucking do that," Christoph says, pained.

I narrow my eyes at him because that sounds an awful lot like an order.

"Listen ..." He sighs, shaking his head. "I'm not great with words. I'm not expressing myself very well."

"I understood perfectly. Thank you for clarifying."

"I haven't fucking said anything yet, Mirth. And you're doing that thing, that thing that twists through my chest, so obviously you don't understand what I haven't even said yet."

I blink a little, not completely following.

"See?" he growls. Then, hands on hips, he huffs.

"Why did you watch?" I cry out before I can censor myself.

"Watch?"

"Elias ... and me ... this morning ..." Ugh, now my chest is aching too.

Christoph rears back a bit, blinking at me in disbelief. "Because it was fucking hot! So fucking hot I had to leave to jerk off in the shower. Do you know how long it's been since I've needed to regularly jerk off? Let alone had to remove myself so I didn't just ... whip it out and come all over your tits without invitation?"

I just stare at him, incredibly confused. But also surprisingly aroused.

Christoph cups his hand over his mouth, closes his eyes, and exhales heavily. "Fuck," he mutters. "This ... this is what I don't know how to do. The ... wooing part."

"Well," I say, my voice a little shaky, "it seems slightly rushed, seeing as we've barely kissed. But would you like an open invitation to come all over my tits?"

He drops his hand away from his mouth, pinning me in place with golden eyes that blaze with his inner beast. It's the first I've seen of his bear. Even last night at the theater, Christoph was perfectly in control.

He reaches for me. I step into his hold. He trails his fingers up my spine, applying a little extra pressure to the back of my rib cage and up, so I arch obligingly. His golden gaze drops to my breasts, as tiny as they are, and he hums appreciatively.

"So ..." My words are awfully breathy for someone who's barely been touched. "You were saying ... something ... important ... about sex?"

Those golden eyes flick to meet mine. "You're short, Mirth."

"Maybe you're too tall!"

He chuckles. "Maybe."

"I'm perfectly average sized ... except for some rounder ... areas."

Christoph steps into me, still not quite pulling me flush to his body, and runs his hand down my back again, firmly now, palming my ass.

My knees go just a little weak. Warmth floods through my core. I grip his shoulders to keep upright.

He drops his head, ghosting his nose up my neck. Ever obliging, I open it up to him. He inhales deeply right behind my ear.

Sharp, almost painful desire slices through me. I can't help the gasp that escapes me.

"Wanna make out?" he asks, all playful now.

"Yes."

He guides me with little touches on my hips until I'm up against the wall and he's crowding over me, doing that thing that he probably doesn't even know he does. Blocking out the rest of the world. His hands shift on my hips again, tugging up my dress a little.

"So tiny," he says. "My little awry."

Then he picks me up under my thighs, sliding my back against the wall and helping me hook my legs around his waist. To even up our heights. He doesn't press into me. He hasn't actually pulled my dress up enough to even do so. But he does palm my ass again, with both hands this time, hovering his mouth over mine.

We breathe each other in for a moment. Then I angle my head just enough to kiss him.

And he trembles ...

It's subtle, but he shudders under my touch.

"Is it just the bond, then?" I ask, slightly worried but

totally prepared for his answer. "Are you just reacting to the bond?"

"Don't much feel like kissing any of the others," he says, pressing a firm kiss to my lips this time.

I move my lips against his, over and over. Slow, languid, closed-mouth kisses. I wrap my arms around his neck, threading my hands through his hair as much as I can.

He rumbles in pleasure. So I comb my blunt nails up the back of his neck and through his hair again, sucking on his upper lip.

He teases the seam of my mouth with his tongue, and I open just enough to swipe my own tongue across his. He moans again.

Desire threads through me, thickening between us.

Christoph starts kneading my ass.

I gasp into his mouth. "Oh, fuck. Oh, I ... maybe that's a little ..." I squirm in his hold, trying to get closer, to rub against him, but I'm hampered by my bunched skirt.

He breaks the kiss, panting slightly. "A little ... much?"

He's still got two handfuls of my ass. I'm foggy with desire. "I really want you to fuck me up against this wall."

He swallows harshly. "So ... right. Public space ... the others are near ..."

Now that he's said it, I can feel that through the bond as well. I groan, completely disappointed. Then I flush a little at my utter wantonness.

He chuckles, slowly easing his grip on my ass.

I press forward, needing another kiss before he sets me on my feet. He angles his head, tangling his tongue with mine again. And for far too brief a moment, he presses into me, shoving my dress up just enough to settle between my legs and rub his hard cock ... once, twice ... against my core.

I moan. Loudly.

"Fuck," he groans. "I'm so fucking hard. I don't think I've ever ..."

He shakes his head as if to clear it. Then he gently shifts me down his body and steadies me on my feet.

I resist the urge to palm his hard, huge cock — denying that to myself is actually painful — before he steps away, running both hands through his hair now.

"It's not ... generally like that for you?" I ask quietly. "Because ... it never was like that for me either ... well, before ... before ..."

He flashes me a shaky grin. "I'm not jealous, Mirth. I'm fucking ... ecstatic. Watching you kiss Sully that night in the hot tub, watching you let Eli lick you to orgasm. That's ... even if you didn't want to make out with me, there's a reason for each of us within this bond. So yeah, a bit of it has to be the intensity of the bond, but not all of it."

"Eli thinks losing Armin has forced the timeline a bit."

He nods. "All of us coming together at once is a lot for you to handle."

Rian flits through my mind. "For more than just me."

Christoph sighs, then gently cuddles me against his chest. He's still hard, but I don't wiggle or rub against him. Yes, I'm a fucking saint. "You already had a bond with Sully, didn't you?"

"I pushed him away," I mumble into Christoph's chest. "After Armin died."

"And Bolan?"

"I'm mad at him. Perpetually."

Christoph hums doubtfully. "Doesn't seem to have stopped you two from strengthening the bond."

I hide my smile. "I can fuck him and still be mad."

"Good to know." He chuckles. "The point is, it feels overwhelming because it is sudden. But other than coming together, nothing else needs to be rushed."

I lean back in his arms exaggeratedly, making him hold me upright. "But we can still make out, right?"

He laughs involuntarily, leaning over to kiss me.

Then Bolan and Sully are shoving their way through the door. Without pulling me from Christoph's embrace, both kiss me soundly hello. I'm gasping for breath and pressed up against Christoph — my back to his front — by the time they're done with me.

Then Bolan makes a break for the snack buffet.

His gaze completely amused, Sully quickly runs his hand and a touch of his essence through my hair, then smooths the wrinkles out of my dress. "I'm going to leave the 'thoroughly kissed' color on your lips, Mirth. It's not at all princess-like, but it makes me so fucking hard imagining —"

I slap my hand over his mouth.

He tongues my palm.

And that shouldn't be as sexy as it is.

Then Kitty and Tommy are tumbling into the room with Elias. Roz hovers, then closes the door behind them. Both of the kids' eyes widen as they take in the far windows and the track below. Tommy's arm is in a sling now, hopefully because Sully is being extra protective and not because he's reinjured it. Kitty's wearing her pink designer backpack despite its origins ... and I realize that I'll have to ask Sully to find a replacement for it, because it bothers me that the Möbius Group gave it to her. Both kids are clothed head to toe in brand-new designer clothing.

They don't even notice us, pressing against the no-longer-tinted glass. Roz must have made the adjustment as they entered.

Elias saunters over, his clearly amused gaze settling on my lips and lingering.

"Lord Hereford," I say.

"Your Highness."

He leans over and kisses me, lingering on that as well.

Not wanting to ruin the moment, I whisper against his lips, "Tommy and Kitty's mother?" I glance over toward the kids. "They seem in good … spirits. Is she … have you …?"

"Nothing definitive," he murmurs. "The local authorities are looking into Gail Walsh's disappearance." His cool tone hides everything I can suddenly feel from him through the bond, as if he's opened that connection between us deliberately. He's still so angry at everything that's happened with the kids. "They're … there's enough evidence to treat her as a co-conspirator rather than a victim."

My heart pinches, and I must not hide my grimace terribly well because he nods stiffly. "Do Tommy and Kitty … do they know?"

"Tommy is well aware," Eli says. "Sully distracted Kitty with all the clothing he had delivered while Tommy and I typed up a preliminary statement. Just in case the locals get more aggressive about talking directly to the kids."

I swallow harshly. "Do we … do we have to pursue it? Couldn't we just …"

Elias touches my hip gently. "I think that as new as it is, the bond, and specifically their connection to you, is helping stabilize them right now. But they need to know, Mirth. They'll need to know whatever we uncover."

"Mirth!" Kitty cries, spinning away from the window as if she's only just realized there are other people in the box. "We placed bets on your horse!"

I pull away from the upsetting conversation with Elias, looping my arm through his and crossing toward the children still plastered to the window.

"Bets?" I say, just so Kitty knows I'm listening.

She nods enthusiastically. "With our own money."

"Stolen money," Tommy grumbles.

"It's an allowance," Kitty insists. "That's what Eli said
—"

"Lord Hereford," Tommy interjects, correcting his sister.

Kitty bobs her head in acknowledgment but continues undaunted, "An allowance of the ... principal. Plus those Möbius guys were assholes."

"I'm not quite following," I say, quashing an inappropriate smile at Kitty's concise but blistering summary of the group that kidnapped and harmed her and her brother.

"Miss Kitty presented me with a dozen one-ounce gold bars and a half dozen silver bars this morning," Elias says, epically smoothly. "Purloined, I believe, from the safe you cracked at the auction space."

"Purloined, yes!" Kitty says, as if she couldn't remember the word. "Like pirates."

"Otherwise known as thieves," Tommy says.

"They deserve it! How much money were they going to make, selling you and me?"

"Perhaps not the best conversation," Elias says. "Given our surroundings." He glances around pointedly.

With the windows all clear, the boxes on either side of us have a perfect view of us in the front seating area. As does anyone with sharp eyesight or otherwise enhanced senses in the nearby stands.

Following Eli's gaze, Kitty's eyes widen. She looks utterly chagrined. "Of course, my lord. I understand."

Tommy huffs doubtfully.

Kitty punches him in the chest.

He grunts. Given that his arm is still in a sling, the blow probably did hurt.

"Eli ... Lord Hereford ... said we could get a safe in our bedroom, my bedroom," Kitty says, stepping closer to me and lowering her voice. "The earl said that was better. That he'd give us an allowance based on the principal. He wrote it all down. Like, all the numbers, and downloaded an app on my phone to show me how to track it."

Seriously trying not to laugh about Lord Hereford being put in the position of potentially laundering the Möbius Group's gold and silver, especially because I'd been in the room and not noticed Kitty taking the bars in the first place, I say, "A safe is always a good idea, Kitty." Then I turn toward Eli, throwing a somewhat fake smile at the occupants of the box to our left as I blank on their names. "A bit advanced for a nine-year-old, no?"

"Kitty requested a favor," he says stiffly, not quite looking at me. "I ... obliged."

The tops of his ears are slightly pink. Lord Hereford is way out of his depth, and still utterly amazing. I brush my fingers against the inside of his wrist, out of sight of the neighboring boxes. Before I can withdraw my hand, he loops his fingers through mine, the gesture mostly hidden between our bodies.

Kitty watches the interaction, her brow slightly furrowed. "That's okay, right, Mirth?"

"The safe in your bedroom? Of course."

Kitty's frown deepens, her hands coming up to grip the straps of her backpack. "Yes, but ..."

I've missed something in the conversation. The boxes on either side of us are filling in, as are the crowded stands. I can feel attention shifting onto us from multiple directions. Kitty and Tommy are too exposed like this, next to the windows.

"Eli says we can live at Lake Thun in between semesters," Kitty whispers so quietly that I strain to catch the words. "If we need to. Like ... if Mom doesn't come back?"

Tommy doesn't correct her again about using Eli's title

in public. His attention is riveted to me now, watchful and a little wary.

"That's an entire castle, right?" Kitty mumbles. "That's yours, right?"

I sit down, grateful that I don't misjudge where the bench seat is behind me. I reach my hand toward Kitty. When she takes it, I pull her to sit beside me. Then I pat the seat on my other side for Tommy. He sits, but he doesn't snuggle into me as Kitty does.

I look up at Elias questioningly.

The conversation in the box fades as Bolan, Sully, and Christoph shift to occupy the seats directly behind us. Kitty watches them with wide eyes, then returns her attention to me.

Elias crouches down in front of me.

We've surrounded Tommy and Kitty in whatever comfort the nascent bond between all of us can provide.

"Eli tells me that the authorities are still trying to figure out everything that happened last night, including where your mother might be," I say, easing into the topic.

Tommy snorts derisively, but I can feel uncertainty and guilt pouring off him.

"She could come back," Kitty insists quietly to her brother. "Maybe ... maybe she didn't mean to tell those people about me ...? Maybe they forced her!"

Elias, still crouched before us, clears his throat to pull the kids' attention to him. "Because Mirth already secured places for both of you at the Phrontistery, I thought it best to discuss all of your options. Of which living at Lake Thun Castle with all of us is one."

"You did?" Tommy asks me. "Like, even before ...?"

"Yes," I say, feeling a little shaky. But in anticipation, not fear. "I was going to speak to your mother about allowing you to attend."

"She'll say yes," Kitty declares.

Tommy's grimace isn't as enthusiastic.

"Plus!" Kitty practically grinds her sharp little shoulder into mine in her renewed excitement. "We helped Eli file those guardianship papers on the way here. We gave, um, statements to the judge person about how we're part of, um, we're both part of your bond group. Right? The judge person. In that white wig. Right, Tommy?"

"Right," he huffs. "Eli already explained it all. But the judge asked us questions, then she explained how a guardianship works for children under eighteen in a bond group, who, like, aren't blood related. It's not an adoption or anything." He says that last bit pointedly, to his sister.

"I listened," she says. "It's like ... making sure we're taken care of ... that we have everything we need."

My eyes fly to Elias for clarification.

"That's why we were a little late getting here. An appointment opened up."

I doubt that any lack of openings would ever hinder Elias from doing exactly what he wanted when he wanted it.

"Don't worry," Sully drawls from behind us. "Christoph kept the princess well distracted."

Kitty interjects. "Because I'm awry like you're awry, right, Mirth? That judge person said there was some co-discell in the charter about that. Like, already a law."

"Codicil," Elias corrects. "And yes."

"And Coda says ..."

Elias grimaces almost imperceptibly at that.

Kitty takes a deep breath, as if she hasn't been breathing properly through all the words she's trying to force out. "Coda says all awry protect each other. That it's this big web or weaving or ... something ... like all our power tied together."

"And I'm old enough to sign the bond group papers," Tommy says quietly. "I don't need Mom's signature. I doubt she'd give it anyway. Not, like, without a big cash payout or something."

"That's not true," Kitty says loudly, her bottom lip suddenly quivering.

Tommy swallows and lowers his eyes. "Lord Hereford says no one is going to dispute a claim from the royal household anyway," he mumbles. "It will be ... public record ... by next week."

That probably shouldn't be true — no one disputing a claim from a member of the royal household — but Elias isn't wrong.

I set my hand on top of my knee, palm up. Kitty is already holding my other hand. Tommy looks at my hand for a long while, then he slowly slips his own into my light hold.

"We're going to figure out what is going on with your mom as best we can," I say to the eleven-year-old.

"But ... I'm yours, right?" he mumbles. "Christoph ... Lord Williams ... said ... he said that I'm powerful because you're powerful. Lord Hereford says that ... we have a ... metaphysical connection."

"Yes," I say gently. "I think you belong with us. But that doesn't have to preclude your other family, okay?"

Tommy shrugs, but I can still feel that mixture of sadness and despair simmering within him, especially when he flicks his gaze back to his sister.

Only Kitty was supposed to have been taken last night. That had been the little awry's own admission, her own observation. Tommy wasn't the intended target.

"And ... Kitty is awry," Tommy says, as if building on whatever argument he's got going on in his own head. "She sees stuff, even if the purple in her eyes comes and goes. So she needs to go to a proper school, where she's ... you know ... taught all the stuff she needs to be taught."

"Yes, Kitty is awry."

"Okay."

"Okay?"

Tommy shrugs belligerently. "I'll go to that snobby school and wear a stupid uniform and learn and stuff. Just to look after Kitty. Everyone always thinks she's weird, and I got to watch out for her."

"Hey!" his sister shouts.

Tommy ignores her. "And in between semesters, we'll all live in your castle ... or wherever you are ..." He meets my gaze. "You, Mirth."

"And Mom?" Kitty asks tentatively. "When Mom comes back?"

Tommy squares his shoulders. Then he says definitively, "Mom, too. Right, Mirth?"

Despite the uncertainty leading up to this moment, my heart is so full of joy that I think it might burst. "Yes. I'll make sure you have everyone you love, everyone who loves you, all together. As much as possible."

Tommy darts a grateful look my way, still trying to protect Kitty. Even from their own mother.

I honestly hope that Kitty's belief in Gail Walsh, rather than Tommy's doubt, is closer to the truth.

"I hate to break it to you, kid," Sully drawls. "But your sister isn't going to be ostracized for her weirdness where you're going."

"Hey!" Kitty exclaims, whirling around to glare at Sully.

He just shakes his head at her. "The richer assholes are, the more they want to know when they might die. You know, for estate planning."

"That's a lesson for later, perhaps," Elias snaps, still crouched before me.

Sully ignores him. Pointedly.

Elias touches my cheek to call my attention back to him.

I lean a little closer.

He whispers, just for my ears, "Too fast? I wanted the paperwork in place … in case we have to … fight for them."

I brush my cheek against his, already knowing that his stepping in to help settle the kids is just one part of how a healthy bond group is supposed to function. "A relief, actually. Thank you, my lord."

Behind us, the door opens. We all turn as the missing piece of our soul-bound group enters the room. He falters at the threshold, looking uncomfortable in his dark-gray suit.

Rian.

His hesitation hurts my heart, my soul.

"Hi!" Kitty climbs up on the bench to get a better look at Rian over Sully's head. "We bet on your horse to win!"

Rian flicks his gaze to me, tugging the door closed behind him. Then he throws a smile toward Kitty just before the silence becomes awkward. "That might be a risky bet."

"Way to step up," Sully mutters under his breath. Then he stands, grabbing Kitty under her arms. He swings the little seer over the bench seats, directing her toward the snack table. "Come grab something to eat. We'll be able to see better on those screens there."

Tommy glances between all of us. Then, easily reading the sudden source of tension in the room, he glowers at Rian as he otherwise silently stalks after his sister and Sully.

Christoph also stands to join the kids. I'm not sure whether he and Rian have formally met, but I seem to have momentarily lost my capacity for niceties.

Bolan sprawls out across the bench seat, his gaze on me.

Elias stands, his hand steady under my elbow as I do as well.

"Seems I missed something important," Rian says edgily, still hovering by the door. "Or I've ... interrupted."

"Not at all." Elias steps around the seats, holding his hand out to the younger male. "It's a pleasure to meet you again, Rian." He looks toward the small grouping around the food. Kitty appears to be stuffing her pockets with candy. "And I don't believe you've formally met Lord Williams."

The duke steps just close enough to shake Rian's hand. "Christoph."

"And the two young ones are Kitty and Tommy Walsh," Elias says, still so polite. "We filed guardianship papers this morning."

"You're adopting these kids?" Rian asks bluntly, though not unkindly.

"Technically, it's Her Highness's name on the paperwork, due to the bond —"

"You adopted kids?" Rian looks at me as though he's never seen me before.

And maybe I'm overreacting, but ... "I tried calling you multiple times yesterday. And this morning."

"So it's my fault for being too busy for a prolonged conversation that I'm not even consulted about —"

Bolan stands up, the movement abrupt enough to interrupt Rian. "Check yourself, pup." Even Bolan's whispers carry weight. "Remember who you're talking to."

"I know that Mirth outranks me. That you all outrank me. No reminder needed."

Bolan shakes his head sadly. "No, brother. Mirth is your soul-bound mate. And I shouldn't have to remind you of that."

All of Rian's anger drains from him. Anger that might

just be frustrated confusion, though it hurts my heart either way.

"Is something wrong?" Kitty asks plaintively from across the private box — obviously still listening to everything. "You don't think ..." Her bottom lip quivers. "You think Tommy and me aren't good enough for Mirth to love us?"

Rian visibly takes the emotional blow of Kitty's question straight to the chest. He opens his mouth but doesn't know what to say.

It doesn't matter, really. Because I'm already moving across the room, smiling. "Have you got your treats? Shall I show you where my brother and I used to watch the races from?"

Kitty nods, eyes watering. Tommy openly glares at Rian.

"Is that an ice-cream bar?" I ask brightly, though my heart feels cracked right through the middle. "Where did you get that, love?"

Tommy points me toward the pile of ice-cream bars on a bed of spelled dry ice. I snatch one up, then guide the children toward a small door in the back corner of the room.

Rian must try to follow, because there's suddenly a wall of bodies between us and him.

My smile doesn't slip.

I don't cry.

I take my responsibilities seriously. I always have. I've always put my duty over my personal emotions and strife.

I get the door unlatched. The children — hopefully distracted again — climb up the narrow staircase to the lookout ahead of me.

13

Rian

MIRTH LEAVES. SHE GATHERS THE KIDS TO HER like they need protection from me and just leaves me behind. Me and all the stupid shit coming out of my mouth that I don't even remotely mean. She leaves me facing off with the four others who are supposed to be part of my soul-bonded group.

I've never been so fucking jealous in my life. I'm not actually certain I've even experienced that emotion before, because this heavy weight all across my chest, threatening to suffocate me, is unmistakable.

I'm okay with the idea, the understanding, that Mirth needs a bond group. Our connection is too intense to ignore. Even if I wanted to.

It's the bear shifter, the duke, who breaks the silence. "No one is forcing you, Rian."

Christoph's not gentle about it, but he's not pissed. Nowhere near as pissed as Sully is at me. Though the blue-haired mage is currently watching the screen over my head as if I don't exist.

"I know," I rasp. "That's not … rationally, I know."

"All of us are having our moments," Elias says mildly as he steps over to fix himself a tea.

Even this little slice of Mirth's everyday life is overwhelming. The china, the silverware, all the piles of pretty food on the sideboard. And I've been in these boxes before. Just not this particular one. I know my reaction to it all is ridiculous. Yet I'm still doing it.

"What we don't do," Sully says, still not looking at me, "is take it out on Mirth."

I open my mouth to dispute that charge, but nothing comes out.

"Well …" Sully amends, "except for Bolan."

"Asshole," my newly discovered half-brother mutters around a mouthful of something. "And I never … my devotion to Mirth has never wavered, not for one minute. I'm only unintentionally an asshole in her vicinity."

"That should be the title of your next song," Sully says scathingly. " 'Unintentionally an Asshole.' "

Bolan actually laughs. "Maybe, asshole. Maybe it will be. And Mirth will fucking love listening to me bagging on myself and trampling on my own heart for her entertainment."

The roar of the crowd, even muffled by the thick glass windows, draws all of our attention. The first race has started. Muted or not, maybe that's what Sully finds so much more entertaining on the screen behind me than looking at any of us. Than looking at me.

What the fuck is wrong with me? I've gotten all of this twisted up in my head, in my chest —

"If you give us time, Rian," Elias says, all smooth and cultured, "we'll figure out how we all fit together."

"It's not just about fucking," Sully says.

I flinch as if he's knifed me.

Bolan eyes the suddenly irate mage. "What the fuck, Sully? Are you off your meds?"

Sully closes his eyes, visibly restraining himself.

Elias steps in. "Bolan. While many may appreciate it when you pretend to be dimwitted, perhaps as a way to amuse yourself, that is not helping this situation."

Bolan flashes a charming grin at the earl. "Just antsy, Eli. Sully can handle it."

"We're all uncomfortable," Christoph says. "Talking it out, plainly, is the only way to get through it. Mirth is hurting."

Sully sighs. Then he's briefly startled to discover Elias standing so close to him, like he's actually tuned that far out. The earl offers the blue-haired mage a twist of a smile, along with the cup and saucer he's holding.

Elias wasn't making tea for himself.

Sully blinks down at the proffered teacup. There's a biscuit perched on the edge of the saucer as well.

"You prefer the chocolate-dipped shortbread, yes?" Elias asks, ever so politely.

Moving slowly, as if no one has ever handed him a tea and a biscuit before, Sully takes the offering. "Thank you, Elias," he murmurs. His shoulders visibly relax.

Both Bolan and Christoph have stilled, watching this simple interaction. Engaged, focused ... present.

That's ... that's what this is ... what it's supposed to be ...

This is why Sully came to me in London. This is what I inadvertently rejected when I didn't properly claim him in front of my mother.

Elias steps back to the sideboard and makes another cup of tea.

Some sort of pain cracks through my heart, adding more and more weight to the shit I'm already carrying. "I've fucked up," I gasp. "I'm fucking up."

"It's a lot all at once," Elias says mildly, as if it's nothing. Nothing that can't be easily fixed, anyway.

"Say it all now." Christoph settles against the wall. "Here, with us. Everything you have to sort through, everything you think we might need to hear. Then you can go to Mirth and see ... tell her what she needs to hear to trust that you'll place her first in your heart the next time you hit a rough patch." He takes a breath. "No one is telling you there won't be rough patches. That's fucking life, isn't it?"

"So," I say shakily, "you're the psychologist of the group?"

"Yeah, damn, Chris," Bolan exclaims. "That's the most I've ever heard you say. Like, even if I put everything you've ever said together."

Sully smirks. "Daddy."

"No," Christoph says perfectly mildly. But with a boundary made perfectly clear.

Sully just nibbles on his biscuit, chuckling quietly.

The energy in the room shifts. Lightening, yes. But also somehow twisting around the four of them just a touch tighter.

With me still on the outside.

Because not making a choice is a choice in and of itself. And earlier that morning, I sat there on the edge of my fucking bed, and I watched my phone ring when Mirth called —

I press my fist against my chest. Moving way too quickly for his size, shifter or not, Christoph's hand comes down on my shoulder. His grip is tight, heavy.

He holds me in that moment until the pain of my own fucking betrayal eases just a bit.

"Apparently, I'm not the only fucking dramatic one in the group now," Bolan drawls. "Must run in the blood. Which is good, actually, for the rest of you assholes. Because maybe it means I didn't inherit my mother's brand of crazy."

Sully chuckles again, but doubtfully this time.

Bolan angles his bright-blue gaze on me, not quite looking me in the eye. That's polite, shifter to shifter, but not really necessary. Because however dominant I am, I already know his wolf is more so.

"I thought ..." I just start blurting it all out. "The night we met was ... I'd never had that kind of reaction to another person before. I wanted to burrow under Mirth's skin. To be buried deep within her, yeah, of course. But I also wanted ... needed ... to ease the burden she carried, carries, within her."

"Soul bound." Christoph releases his grip on my shoulder slowly, as if worried I might fall over without him holding me.

Another cheer runs through the crowd in the stadium seats. The first race is over.

"That first morning, I lay there, watching her sleep," I whisper. "I only managed to leave at all because Armin's other horses arrived. I needed an actual excuse. That's ... too fast. And Mirth knew it, because she had no problem walking away, she ... I was the one who reached out, maintained contact ... and when the invitation came to the fucked-up matchmaking thing ... I almost accepted it."

"Why didn't you?" Elias asks.

Lost in my own recollections, I blink at him. "Mirth didn't want me dragged into all of that." I glance at Bolan, then Sully. A hopeless sort of jealousy twists through my words. "She didn't spare you."

"Mirth didn't know we'd been invited," Bolan says.

"Tried to kick me to the curb the moment she saw me, even with that perfect-princess mask firmly in place."

"She practically begged me to stay," Sully says with an affected shrug.

"That's because you weren't a threat," Bolan lashes back. "You're safe, Sully."

Sully just smiles at that, perfectly content. Because he knows Mirth loves him. He's known she's loved him for a very long time.

"I didn't know it would be you," I say, drawing all the attention back to me. "All of you ..."

"Mirth must have explained," Elias says. "That she needed a bond group. That she couldn't choose just one of us, even if she wanted to."

"Of course she fucking explained," I say, so, so angry at myself. "But I just wanted her. I wanted everything she could spare me. Every look, every touch ... I understood that she had to have a bond group. An established bond group. For, like, political reasons or ..." I glance at them all, feeling utterly stupid. Childish. "That it would just be ... like a ... contract. Only on paper. I thought it would be the Mertons."

"You know the Mertons?" Christoph asks.

I can hear a lot I don't understand loaded into the question. "No. They bid for my contract, but they're ... trophy collectors. Not serious about their horses."

The four of them glance between themselves, sharing information that I don't have access to, but it's my own words I hear as they echo through my mind.

Trophy collectors. I knew it within minutes of sitting down with Archie to discuss my heading their then-nonexistent breeding program.

My stomach sinks. Mirth isn't a trophy.

Oh, fuck. I've been looking at this all wrong.

"So," Elias says coolly, "just so I understand your objections to the idea of being soul bound to us, through Mirth. Is it who we are? Our titles and positions? Or is it that you're worried that we're going to want to fuck you?"

Bolan's head whips toward the earl. "Um, excuse me?"

"Way to woo, Earl," Sully says sarcastically.

"We're beyond wooing," Elias says. "We have been since the moment Rian stopped answering Mirth's calls."

"Not even twelve hours' grace?" Sully eyes the earl as if he's seeing him differently. "Does that go for all of us?"

"You know it does," Elias snaps.

"Just checking."

"I'm not interested in fucking anyone but Mirth," Bolan says utterly seriously. "I'm not homophobic. It's sexy as fuck to participate. If you want me there. And I'm happy to lend a helping hand when more than two are desired, or four for that matter. But I can tell you now, I wouldn't be able to get it up with any of you. And my fucking ass is off-limits."

"Everyone knows that, Bolan," Sully says sourly.

Looking at Sully, Bolan points at me. "You just said baby brother didn't know. Baby fucking brother, Sully. There *is* a line."

The intensity of the crowd shifts again. I glance up at the screen to confirm that the second race has begun. "Perseus is in the fifth race," I say numbly.

"Mirth will need to be down here," Elias says. "Visible. We'll keep the children out of camera view. Bolan and Sully, you'll flank Mirth. She'll be more comfortable publicly acknowledging you two than Christoph or me right now."

Sully nods.

Bolan shifts on his feet, looking at me. "It's Rian's race ... his accomplishment. Even if Perseus doesn't win."

Elias side-eyes me for a moment. Then with cool

viciousness, he says, "Rian made his choice. Staff members don't stand at the side of their princess."

"Slow the fuck down, asshole." Bolan raises his hands toward the earl. "Mirth was clear that Rian is part of us, that he —"

"I agree," Sully says, setting down his tea. "With Eli."

Bolan looks conflicted. Then all three of them turn to Christoph. And I realize what's happening. What I've put myself on the outside of ...

They're protecting Mirth. They're putting it to some unvoiced vote. Organizing things now, like who sits where, so that Mirth doesn't have to worry about it later.

Protecting Mirth.

From me.

But ... I'm hers. I'm her safe space. "I haven't ..." I say, addressing Christoph. "I have made a choice. I chose Mirth. I choose Mirth."

Christoph looks at me steadily. His dominance is an actual weight. "Mirth needs balance. We're already struggling to provide that for her, for ourselves. We're all sorting out our own personal shit. Losing Armin has destabilized the bond." He glances over at Elias, as if for confirmation.

"I believe it has, yes," the earl says. "And not just for Mirth. For both Bolan and Sully as well."

"It's not about who is fucking who," Christoph says. "Or feeling jealous or inferior. It's that we are stronger together. And together, we can support Mirth. Just as she unequivocally supports us."

I nod. My heart is pounding.

"You think none of us had better things to do today?" Elias asks caustically. "I'm in the middle of drafting fucking water-conservation legislation that will hopefully impact the fucking world. But I'm here, because you, Rian, are racing Mirth's horse. And this is what bond groups do for each other."

Sully touches the back of Elias's hand. The earl's fingers twitch. But without lessening his glare on me, he tangles his fingers through Sully's, taking the comfort offered.

"I, myself, never have anything better to do," Bolan says. "I totally volunteer to follow Mirth around and attend to her every whim."

"Mirth doesn't have whims," Sully says.

"That's an issue for another day," Christoph says. "First we stabilize. Then when she knows we're devoted to her, the kids, and our life together, Mirth will accept that she can ask for more ... personal things."

I haven't been this lectured and schooled in my entire life. But I've always prided myself on my ability to actually listen, to make corrections when needed.

A sharp knock precedes the door opening behind me. Mirth's main guard, Roz, pokes her head in, immediately scanning the room for Mirth and frowning deeply when she doesn't see her.

"In the lookout," Bolan says.

Roz nods, her tension instantly easing. "Word has gotten around that Her Highness is attending today's events and has a horse in the fifth race. Will you be issuing any invitations?"

I'm seriously confused by the question.

Elias steps in smoothly. "The royal guard may issue a blanket statement. Her Royal Highness is pleased to attend today's races in support of her horse Perseus in the memory of her late brother, Prince Armin. But as she doesn't want to cause any distraction, she will view the race, along with Lord Savoy, Bolan, and her other chosen, from the royal box."

"Her chosen?" Christoph murmurs. "Is it time for that?"

"Mirth isn't hiding any of us," Sully says. He looks at me pointedly. "She made that clear, right?"

My face flames like I'm a fucking child. Like the fucking child I'm being.

"Plus," the blue-haired mage adds, holding up his phone, "there are already pictures of Christoph hand-feeding Mirth pieces of salmon maki an hour ago. So that isn't going back behind closed doors."

Christoph stiffens in surprise.

Bolan whistles. "Someone is so getting fired for taking pictures in the clubhouse. I hope the payout was worth it for them." He leans over to peer at Sully's screen. "Look at you, Duke. Fucking besotted. I seriously thought you were in the no-fucking camp. But Mirth climbing you like the behemoth you are about a half an hour ago made your intentions pretty clear."

"This is information I don't need," Roz says, though she sounds amused under her curt, professional tone. "Are you all happy with that statement?"

"Yes," Elias says.

Roz closes the door behind her.

Cheeks flushing, Christoph pulls his own phone out of his pocket, holding it like it's something he's forced to carry but doesn't really know how to use. "Can you send me those, Sully?"

"I'll do you one better," the blue-haired mage drawls. His thumbs are already flying over his screen. "I'll get the originals."

Then as if they're engaging in some kind of silent communication, but without looking at each other, each of the four steps away from guarding the door Mirth and the kids disappeared through.

I instantly take the opening.

"Tell Tommy and Kitty to come down," Elias says, not looking directly at me. "They haven't eaten enough."

"Yes." Sully's tone is even frostier than the earl's. "I need to see how Tommy's arm is healing."

I understand my place now, and what I need to do to start building trust if this bond group is what I really want.

Understanding doesn't make any of what I might have seriously fucked up easier to fix, though.

M IRTH IS PRACTICALLY HANGING OVER THE TOP of a short balcony, gesturing down toward the track, with the kids standing at the railing to either side of her. I slip through the already open door at the top of the stairs unnoticed and take a moment to do some watching myself — of Mirth and the kids. I barely notice the few empty seats behind them, or any of the other minimalist decor. This perch is purely a way to view the track below without anyone, and everyone, watching right back.

It doesn't take me more than a moment to see how the kids lean into Mirth, how they look at her. But not like they're worshiping a princess or are simply enamored with a pretty woman. They're drawn to her, yes. But they're ... safe with her.

She feels like home to me too.

"Oh, there he is!" the young girl — Kitty — cries, jabbing her finger at a downward angle toward the track. She's got a small pair of binoculars pressed to her face, the straps looped around her neck. "That's him. Number 1. Number 1. That's Perseus, right?"

I understand that they're parading some of the horses

around the track between races to increase the take on the later races. As long as they're kept separate, it's good to let them stretch their legs.

"But who's the rider?" Tommy says distrustfully. "Eli says that Perseus is fast, young but fast. But that the rider will make the difference between first and second place."

"I don't know," Mirth murmurs, glancing toward the stats now scrolling over the huge screen hanging over the center of the stadium. "The rider's name wasn't posted when I last checked."

"We should have asked Rian," Kitty says.

"He wasn't answering Mirth's calls, remember?" Tommy says darkly.

"Oh," Kitty whispers quietly. "Right ..."

Mirth's shoulders stiffen. My heart pounds in my chest as I wait for whatever she's going to say. Even though I need to speak up, step up now ... I wait just a moment more.

"I'm certain," Mirth says, her tone perfectly pleasant, "that had I asked Rian directly, he would have provided us a name. He knew we were coming to see Perseus race. He took time out of his very busy schedule to send me all those stats, remember? I should have forwarded those to Eli, but I didn't know the earl would take you to place bets."

"Okay ..." Kitty says, still a little doubtful. Then her enthusiasm floods right back in. "I mean, truthfully, we kind of begged Eli. And he'd already given us each a draw on our allowance."

Tommy watches Mirth steadily as she completely covers for me. Disappointment — in myself — adds another sharp edge to the maelstrom of painful emotion lodged in my chest. Mirth lying. For me. And Tommy already old enough, smart enough, to see right through it.

The last seventy-two hours have been utter hell on my perception of myself. All of it self-inflicted wounds.

Mirth catches Tommy watching her, offering him a slight smile. "Does your arm hurt?"

"No," he says, also valiantly lying.

"Must be the shoulder, then," she teases back, grinning.

Tommy grins right back. I'm not certain it's possible to not smile back at Mirth when she smiles at you. "It ain't nothing."

I scuff my foot on the floor, already stepping forward so it doesn't seem as though I paused to watch them at all. Mirth straightens from hanging over the edge of the balcony, glancing back but not really looking at me.

Tommy glowers.

Kitty grins, wide and welcoming. For the second time.

And this time, I shove all my other shit away, all the shit I carried with me into the Royal Household Box below, and I grin right back at the young girl.

"How good is your rider?" Kitty asks me, perfectly serious. "Does Perseus like them?"

"It has more to do with trust than like," I say. "I'm not sure Perseus likes many people. Maybe just Mirth and my cousin, Bev."

"We're still working on trust ..." Mirth murmurs. "Perseus and me."

That knifes me through the heart. Because even though she's referencing the night she scared the shit out of both of us, My Highness isn't just talking about the horse.

Only a few weeks ago, I pulled her off Perseus's back before he could slam her into the fencing ...

Only a few weeks.

To fall for Mirth hard and fast, so fast.

Only a few weeks to make a lifetime commitment ...

Actually, that part didn't take more than a minute.

I try to catch Mirth's gaze, but she's an expert at not quite looking where she doesn't want to look. The sunglasses don't help. I've always disliked them, though I know she wears them for more than sun protection.

"Who is the rider, then?" Tommy asks.

"Andrea Quinn," I say, stepping close enough that I can see the central vid display screen and a portion of the track. "Her stats should be up on the screen now. Andi's ridden my horses for just over a year. Only time and a few races will let us know if she's a good pairing with Perseus." I point to the large screen where they're now running the stats on the horses and the jockeys, including pictures of both beast and rider. The betting is still open while each rider does a single slow canter with their horse around the track. "There."

Mirth follows my gesture, then goes very still. "Andrea Quinn," she murmurs. "Andi. I thought she was one of your trainers. I saw her at Waterfell."

"That too," I say, swallowing through a sudden twisting sensation at the base of my throat.

"Are those good stats, then?" Tommy asks.

"Fair," I say, still talking around that odd phantom pain. "Not as experienced as most of the other jockeys racing today. You'll see when you compare. But Andi's win ratio is just as high."

The next horse in the race — a four-year-old black thoroughbred with white points — starts its loop of the track on the opposite side of the stadium from where Andi is exiting on Perseus.

"Oh, pretty!" Kitty exclaims.

"But not as fast as Perseus," I say smugly. "We've only got a few minutes until the race. Elias wants both of you to eat something, and Sully needs to look at your arm, Tommy."

"It's fine," Tommy mumbles even as he's already moving. The idea of some extra pain relief clearly isn't as bad as he's making it seem.

"Mirth and I will be right down." I touch Kitty's shoulder, directing her to follow her brother.

Tommy stops abruptly, looking at Mirth. "We can wait."

"Take the binoculars," Mirth says, perfectly pleasant. "You can watch the replay on the monitors, but you're going to want to focus on the finish line during Perseus's actual race."

Tommy nods a little hesitantly. But when Kitty offers him her hand, he takes it. His little sister drags him through the door, leaving it open.

"Has Andi been at Lake Thun as well?" Mirth asks in that polite tone.

Thrown by the subject change — at least in my mind — I hesitate. Mirth's face is turned to me, chin lifted, so I'm certain she's looking right at me, at my eyes, though her own eyes remain shadowed behind her sunglasses.

"You're lovers," Mirth says. It's not a question. "Her face fell when she saw me coming out of your rooms at Waterfell."

"What? No," I stutter, actually blindsided. "Andi? She ... did she say something? We did ... we were, but not —"

"It's not like you don't know who I'm fucking, right, Rian?" Mirth says, all fucking icy tone and sedate smile.

"Yeah, it's pretty clear who the fuck you're fucking, Mirth. Or who you want to fuck if you haven't quite gotten there yet," I snap. All the words, all the frustration, are out of my mouth before I even know what I'm saying.

The smile slides right off Mirth's face.

My chest feels like there's an anvil on it. I can barely breathe.

"That's good," she says quietly. "I'm glad I was clear from the start."

Oh, fuck, oh fuck, oh fuck. Mirth has been clear. Very,

very clear about what she wants from me, about getting my consent, and —

Oh, fuck. "Mirth, I —"

"I'll release you."

The anvil is replaced with a fucking dull-edged steel sword, skewered right through my chest. "What?"

"Or you can reject me," she says as if the words aren't carving right through my heart. "Actually, that might be easier. On you."

Easier? On me? "Mirth …" I gasp through the pain.

"We haven't formalized the bond, signed any contracts. You don't know the others at all, so your ties to them should be minimal. You can go back to Waterfell. I'll send Perseus with you. With his ownership papers. As a … thank you for … being there for me when I felt like I didn't deserve it."

I sit down hard, vaguely thankful that there's actually a chair behind me.

This twisting in my chest …. I get it … I get it now.

It's Mirth. It's what Mirth is feeling, tangled through everything I'm feeling. It's the opposite of when she orgasms. When she's relaxed and content, and all the things I should be trying to —

Mirth lays her hand on my shoulder. "I'm sorry, Rian. I shouldn't have …" Her voice hitches.

I've let my head drop in my hands. When did I stop looking at her? Trying to connect with her? I snap my head up.

Tears snake down her creamy cheeks from beneath the glasses. "I knew I was asking too much," she says.

Oh, fuck me. The other four weren't just teasing downstairs. About Mirth never having so-called whims. I don't know her well enough to know her like that, but they do.

They do. And they already know that Mirth never asks for anything for herself.

Except me.

She asked me for a ride. And I said yes.

I said fucking yes.

"I don't think it will take any formal words between us for you to reject the bond. But I'll have Elias look that up for you." Mirth's fingers slide across my shoulder as she withdraws her hand, withdraws from me, turning away but lingering on that touch.

That last touch.

My brain restarts. I don't know where the fuck my head has been these last few days. But I'm here now. I'm here.

I lunge for Mirth, going down on my knees where I fucking belong as I grab her hand back.

She gasps, stumbling slightly.

I press her hand to my chest, over my wildly beating heart. "Listen, listen, Highness, please." I take a deep breath, trying to sort through all the words, to find the right ones. But there aren't any.

"I love you," I gasp. "Highness. Princess. Mirth. Euphrosyne. I fucking love you. I know it's only been a few weeks. It's too quick. We've only had these stolen moments together. And maybe we're soul bound, maybe this is fate, and this desire is triggered like that ... but I ... I know it's more than that."

She laughs quietly, wetly. "More than being created for each other by the very universe that sustains us? Sustains the world?"

"Well, when you put it like that?" I shrug, desperately trying to be playful with her. To be her light. Her safe spot. I tug her a little closer, still on my knees and gazing up at her. "I don't know how this is supposed to work. I've been up in my head about it. About where I fit with the others.

What I can possibly give to you that any one of them can't
—"

"You aren't interchangeable parts," she snaps.

I laugh. "I get it now. I get what I bring you. What I want to bring you."

She tilts her head. "And what is that?"

"I'm a blank slate. A new start. We don't have any past together, no baggage. And no expectations. I don't have responsibilities to an important position or an estate. Or even, sad as it is, familial obligations. I'm yours, Highness. I choose to be yours."

Mirth's lips part slightly as she listens to me lay out my epiphany to her, pretty much in real time as I'm experiencing it.

She takes off her sunglasses. Not touching me, she leans over me. I tilt my face up to her, and all her dark hair falls down around us. And I understand. She's taking us back to that moment. That moment in my bed where she asked me to hide away with her.

"I won't falter again," I whisper, aching to kiss her but not closing the space between us.

"At first sight," she says, her violet eyes burning into my soul, claiming me over and over again. "When I thought I was lost. My soul bruised and raw. When I worried I couldn't go on without Armin, that I would never heal the wound of losing him. I saw you. I needed a ride."

"And I gave it to you."

"I loved you, Rian, at first sight. I just didn't think I was going to be able to keep you."

"Keep me, Mirth. Will you let me be yours? Will you let me be part of your bond group?"

"Yes."

I surge up on my feet, taking her face in my hands and

her lips with my mouth. "I'm sorry, I'm sorry," I pant between kisses. "I won't falter again."

She smooths her hands up and down my back, our roles reversed in the moment ...

And that's all a part of it, isn't it? This give and take in a natural flow.

"The race," she murmurs against my lips.

"Fuck," I groan.

She laughs. The vestiges of that suffocating pain in my chest, that emotion clogging my throat and stopping up all my words, disperses. I'm light-headed, high on joy. High on Mirth.

14

$\mathcal{M}$IRTH

"A PLANE!" KITTY GUSHES, GRABBING TOMMY'S arm and jumping in place at the end of the long kitchen counter. "We're going on a plane!"

"I know," her brother grumbles around a mouthful of the pancakes Christoph made us all for breakfast. "I'm right here."

Kitty turns her dark-blue eyes on me where I'm filling the dishwasher. Even highlighted in the light streaming through the side windows of my apartments in London, not even a hint of purple hides in the depths of those eyes this morning. Her hair dances around her neck in perfectly defined curls, courtesy of Sully's fabricator magic.

"Sully ... um, Lord Savoy says we're going to need snow boots and ski jackets."

I nod. "The new clothes will be waiting for you at Waterfell Castle. And it's okay to call us by our names when it's just the family."

Kitty stills for a moment, then she nods almost shyly. "Family," she says, as if testing out the word. Then she looks at Tommy sharply. "I told you."

"In private," he says mildly.

Eli, still seated at the dining room table and reading an actual newspaper — he had six delivered earlier by courier — sets his teacup into its saucer. With a noticeable clink.

Both kids glance over at him.

"Have you packed everything you want to take with you?" the earl asks.

"Yes!" Kitty bounces on her heels.

"Yes, sir," Tommy says.

"Go double-check your bags," Eli says. "We'll all meet at the front door."

Kitty takes off. She wears an adorable skirt-and-sweater combo today, a swirl of light blue and fuchsia pink, with three iridescent rhinestone bracelets on her left wrist.

Tommy, in jeans and a zippered merino top, bumps his shoulder lightly against mine before sauntering off after his sister at a more sedate pace. I touch his back as he passes.

Kitty's voice emanates from up the hall that leads to the bedrooms, sharp and demanding. "The rest of us are all ready to go!"

"I see that," Bolan says, sounding still half asleep.

"You don't even have shoes on!" the young seer says.

"It's Mirth's plane," Bolan says. "It doesn't take off without the princess."

Kitty huffs, then stomps away.

Eli is trying to repress a smile as he neatly folds his paper. He catches me eyeing him and smirks. "You know it's because you're perpetually pissed at Bolan, right? Kitty's picked that up. Just like it's going to take Tommy time to relax around Rian. Though that's likely due to other male figures letting him down. The kids are yours, first and foremost. As it should be."

Bolan wanders into the kitchen, black hair deliciously mussed, T-shirt untucked over his jeans, and yes, barefoot. Partway through making a beeline for the coffee, he spots me. A breath later, I'm pinned up against the kitchen counter and being thoroughly kissed.

When his mouth falls to my neck, which I helpfully tilt back and to the side for him to ravish, I gasp, "You were getting coffee."

He hums contentedly, then whispers in my ear, "Did you sleep well, my Mirth?"

With his warm breath across my ear and his voice rumbling through me, my nipples tighten, and I actively suppress a groan. "Yes, thank you," I say, just a little breathless. I spent the late evening with Rian. But wakeful, and after getting up to check on everyone else, I found Sully and Bolan in my bed in the early-morning hours.

Eli steps into the kitchen. His light-blue eyes are sharp yet still warm as he watches Bolan practically maul me good morning. He rinses his teacup and sets it to the side of the sink.

Bolan pulls away from me with a groan, then steps back to pour the last of the coffee into a mug. I gather myself, then remember to close the door to the dishwasher. The rock star lounges back against the counter, takes a huge swig of coffee, then nods toward Eli. "We're not going to get a better moment," he says.

Eli pulls a blister pack of pills out of the pocket of his suit jacket, holding it in the palm of his hand. "I researched this and picked it up yesterday. The side effects, if there are any, should be minimal, and it won't interact badly with your current birth control." He extends his hand toward me.

I flush. "I'm not due for my shot for another month."

"That's not entirely effective, Mirth," Eli says.

Still flushed, I glance over at Bolan.

He shrugs and takes another sip of his coffee. "You know we haven't been great with the condoms."

Eli moves a little closer to me, lowering his voice. "Mirth. All of this is your choice, but I know the bond is overwhelming right now. I nearly fucked you on the dining room table without a thought about anything except that you asked for my cock, and I wanted nothing more than to give it to you."

I lean against the counter for support because my legs are suddenly a little weak ... at the earl's utterance of 'fuck' and 'cock' ... and the remembrance of him pressing me to the —

Bolan crowds against my other side, leaning close enough to pointedly breathe in my scent. "That's not a helpful train of thought, Princess. Not when we have a plane to catch."

I look down at the blister pack in Eli's palm.

"Just an extra precaution," the earl says.

I meet his gaze, then Bolan's, as a tiny sliver of sadness slashes through me. "You ... you don't want kids? With me?"

"I'll fuck as many kids into you as you want," Bolan says, quietly fierce. "We all will."

"Not me," Eli says gently. "Not with the possibility of passing on the wasting sickness. But I will very happily raise all of our children."

I glance between them both again. "But ... not now."

"It's your choice, Mirth," Bolan says. "But Eli's research says that even on regular birth control, the intensity of the bond clicking in for all of us at once might, like ... override it." He glances at the earl.

"Yes. Perhaps nullify it," Eli says.

I understand why Eli is sensitive to this subject, watching a parent waste away from an illness he might pass on genetically ... so I take the blister pack from the earl, popping the first pill out and into my hand.

"Do you have our timeline all worked out in among your plans and paperwork, Earl?" I ask, trying for teasing but still feeling oddly sad. Or maybe disheartened.

"You don't have to take it, Mirth," Eli says a little stiffly. "But yes, I was thinking ... five years."

"Five years?"

He nods. "That will let the soul bond settle between us, and it will allow you to focus on Kitty and Tommy."

My eyes snap up from the pill in my hand to meet the intensity of Eli's gaze. "What have you uncovered?" I ask him, heart suddenly in my throat. "Their mother ...?"

"Packed," Bolan practically spits, dumping the rest of his coffee in the sink, then putting the mug in the dishwasher.

"Packed?" I echo, confused.

Eli sighs. "There is evidence that Gail Walsh received a large sum of money the afternoon before the kids were taken. She then transferred that sum into an account that she immediately drained and closed. She bought train tickets. With cash."

"Two," Bolan adds. "One adult, one kid. Coda caught Gail on camera at the bank and the train station while initially trying to track the kids."

"According to Greg, who was at the apartment during that first search for the kids, Gail Walsh appears to have emptied her closet, plus packed a bag for Tommy," Eli says. "The bag for Tommy was still there."

I feel a little light-headed. "Kitty did say that Tommy wasn't supposed to have been taken. But I still hoped ... I hoped ... maybe in the panic of it all, that the kids might have been mistaken about ..." I shake my head, swallowing the rest of my useless words.

"I don't think the payout was for Tommy," Eli says, his cool tone only a thin veneer for the anger I can feel simmering underneath. "I think he got in the way. And whatever sniffer they sent to verify that Kitty was awry got a whiff of Tommy when he tried to get Kitty away from them. He was a late addition to the auction. Maybe the cage was set up for Kitty. Or maybe, as Christoph assessed, the plan was to ... let her mature into her power before selling her."

My stomach churns hopelessly even as I remind myself that we got to the kids ...

"And their mother?"

"Used one of the tickets," Bolan says caustically. "Then at one of the stations way before the destination, she got on a different train, then another without a ticket. Maybe she got her hands on other ID, or maybe she disguised herself so well that even Coda couldn't keep track of her. But the trail is cold. For now. She's gone. For now."

I look at Eli. "Or ... or someone already went after her ..."

Eli frowns. "Why would they ..." Then he puts it together. "First-generation awry blooded ..."

"She passed it on to Kitty. Plus the cath palug shifter gene to Tommy. That makes her too valuable to just walk away."

"Coda will keep looking," Elias says.

Bolan rubs his brow. "The kids ..."

"We should tell them," I say quietly. "But ... maybe we give it a little time?" I glance at Eli, then at Bolan. They both nod. "Let's get settled at Lake Thun, but ... before they head off to school. We should have more information by then. Or more clarity, at least. And if the elder Mertons are deeply involved in the Möbius Group, then having Isla dismantle it all from within might ... give Coda more leads?"

Eli and Bolan both nod, then fall thoughtfully silent. I look down at the contraception pill in my palm. Eli is right. This is not the time to add more complications — however welcome they might be — to our lives.

I take the pill.

Eli steps back to pour me a glass of water. I drink it.

Bolan kisses my temple, flashing me a grin. "Apparently, I need shoes." Then he saunters out of the kitchen.

Eli takes the still half-full glass from me, sets it on the counter, then pulls me into his arms. I tilt my head up, face pressed into his neck.

"We'll take care of them," he murmurs.

"I don't doubt it for one second," I whisper back.

I STEP THROUGH THE DOOR TO MY FATHER'S study. He's waiting for me by the windows, through which sunlight glints off the fresh snow dusting the mountain peaks that surround Waterfell Castle. I can't remember the last time I saw my father in casual slacks and a cable-knit sweater. He has no tumbler of whiskey at hand, no chosen flanking him, to mitigate the weight of this conversation.

I carry my backpack with Armin's urn in one hand, and a puffy jacket in the other. The jacket is for my father. I'm already wearing all my winter gear. Though with the sun streaming through the windows, I already know I won't need as many layers as I anticipated.

The flight from London passed quickly. Kitty spent

most of her time rotating between window seats, taking pictures and texting each one to all of us. Tommy slid into the seat next to me — beating out both Bolan and Sully — then stubbornly didn't move from it while playing games on his new tablet and eating from a small mountain of snacks Christoph kept steadily supplied.

"Mirth," my father says, his tone tired — but warmer than he's been with me for a long while.

No doubt he can feel the power contentedly twined around me. But ... I also hope it's more than that. More than just the relief that I've accepted my role, my duties wholly.

"Did you want me to come down?" he asks, without turning to look at me.

I've abandoned my soul-bound mates, along with Tommy and Kitty, to Anne and Eleanor, slipping away to get dressed and grab the jacket before seeking out my father.

Not that I didn't know exactly where he was from the moment I set foot on the property. My sensitivity to that, to the intersection point itself, is strange but not uncomfortable.

"Do you remember the lookout over the river that you took us to as children?"

He turns to me then. Backlit, his face is in shadow. "Of course."

"It's one of Armin's favorite spots. Was. Was one of his favorite spots."

My father's bright-purple gaze falls to my backpack, then to the jacket in my other hand. Then he looks at his empty mantel for a long moment.

I hold the jacket out to him. He steps over to take it, pulling it on and partially zipping it up. I meet his heavy gaze, so much experience churning in those eyes, which are just a shade lighter than my own. Almost a century of life, choices, mistakes, love, grief, regrets.

I don't look away from any of it as I hold my hand out to him.

He grasps it, his touch no warmer than my own.

Then his essence snaps out, slicing into me, burrowing into my skin and pulling me apart.

I close my eyes and just bear it silently.

I'm nowhere. And also everywhere. Disintegrated and shifting, with only my father's hand holding me from being lost forever.

Then my feet crunch through snow. My next breath is icy and crisp. And I'm in one piece again.

Teleportation.

I pull my sunglasses out of my pocket, putting them on before opening my eyes. But the vista is so bright that I need to blink more than a few times to adjust to it.

My father squeezes my hand gently, then releases me.

He's teleported us to a sheltered spot on the sheer face of a mountain. Not a cave, but a niche carved out of the stone. A wide shelf of sorts. There's a proper name for it, no doubt. My father would know, but I don't ask. Because this isn't that sort of moment.

He steps back to a small pile of branches next to the cliff face. The neatness of the pile makes it clear that he still comes up to the viewpoint, collecting fallen branches from the well-treed slopes that surround us while he hikes. More accurately, while he rock-climbs.

I wander closer to the edge of the cliff, allowing the breathtaking view of the swollen river slicing through the craggy mountains to settle me, fill me. The river drops off to the far left into the waterfall that can be seen from one side of the castle, but I can't quite see the castle itself from this vantage point. Armin and my father would often scale the cliff behind this outcropping. From there, on a clear day, the castle and the entire mountain range around it can be seen.

I never enjoyed that climb myself. I never needed to feel as though the entire world was at my feet. And that was okay. As I now understand it.

My father builds a small fire, using three calf-high boulders previously gathered in an arc as a windbreak. He builds the fire by hand, though he could have one blazing in mere minutes if he used his telekinesis.

Still gazing out at the view, I perch on the middle boulder with my back to the firepit, pleased that my jacket is long enough to cover my ass. The sun, reflecting off the snow and the rock, is warm on my face.

"Are you going to tell me why one of my chosen is hiding the details of an incident that took place in London two days ago?" my father asks mildly, striking two rocks together, then using just a touch of essence to enhance the resulting spark. It sets the dry moss alight under a triangle of branches.

"Raoul?" I ask, already knowing the answer while also trying to hide my amusement.

"Who else?" my father grumbles, blowing lightly to coax the tiny licks of fire from the moss to the kindling.

"Perhaps he's still gathering all the intel," I say. "To present it properly."

My father huffs. "And the annoyingly thick stack of paperwork on my desk from Lord Hereford? And the bank draft from Lord Savoy buying out Rian Callaghan's contract? None of it submitted for my input or approval."

I just hum agreeably.

"Eleanor has already sent the staff in to relocate our rooms at Lake Thun," my father continues. "Because you'll apparently need more room now."

"That's lovely of her," I say.

"And the two children you brought with you? The younger is an awry."

"I know."

"A seer?"

"I believe so."

Satisfied that the fire has taken, my father steps over to the edge of the cliff, standing far closer to the sheer drop than I had. He looks out across the winding river, back stiff and hands on his hips. Then with a heavy sigh, he turns and sits down next to me.

"So we're not talking about any of that," he says.

"We'll stay for a few days," I say mildly.

We sit together, taking in the view for long enough that the fire begins to warm my back. Then I take Armin's urn out of my backpack and place it on the ground before us.

"I haven't been here," my father says, "since Armin ... left us. Eleanor asked me to bring the twins last week ... I made an excuse about the snowpack melting too quickly." Plumes of white mist — condensation from the cold — punctuate his words. "She let me get away with the lie."

"Fresh snow last night," I say, not agreeing or disagreeing with him.

He huffs a laugh. "Why is it that the child who didn't inherit my power is the one most like me? Had you ... you I never had to worry about ... you never would have ..." He takes a shuddering breath. "I was hard on Armin. I had to be hard on him. You know what normally happens to awry telepaths or telekinetics."

"They go mad. Or tear themselves apart."

"I thought his mother's blood would dilute my own. When I realized it hadn't, I thought I was going to lose Armin when his powers manifested. I prepared for it. But then, he had you. You as his counterbalance. And he survived his manifestation, then his teens, and ...”

“Almost his twenties.”

We fall silent for a moment, both thinking of Armin.

“Christoph tells me that a crown of purple myrtle appears around my head,” I say, “when I give my power ... freedom.”

My father looks at me then. “I haven’t seen it since the night you saved Armin from those kidnappers. But yes. From your mother’s lineage. Goddess-touched, they call it.”

“The night the Möbius Group tried to take me. And Armin.”

“Likely, but unconfirmed.” He laughs grimly. “They never dared try to take you or Armin again. They couldn’t pay mercenaries enough to even attempt it.”

His gaze falls on the urn sitting on the ground before us. Then he looks at me and nods. I lean over, removing the lid. My father’s essence shifts, curling around my hands, then flooding into the jar.

I sit back as a controlled spiral of Armin’s ashes — the last of them — rises at my father’s behest from the urn. I hold my hand out, and the spiral shifts closer, hovering over my palm.

I look at my father. “I won’t leave you.”

His expression cracks under a wave of utter agony, utter grief. He bows his head over his knees, and he sobs, power and essence pouring from him.

The mountain beneath us shudders under the onslaught of his unfettered grief. Under that same onslaught, the marble urn cracks, then disintegrates, mixing with the now-erratic spiral of Armin’s ashes.

Then the energy that is the intersection point reaches out to my father, to me, and takes everything pouring from him, all of that immense power, absorbing it.

My father takes a deep, shaky breath.

He raises his head.

Then he allows the wind to take the ashes and the marble dust. But not all at once.

I watch it slowly filter away. "I hope Armin's at peace now, once more one with the aether. We'll find each other again."

My father sobs, just once more.

And I'm crying too, silently. I lean against his shoulder, and he reaches for my hand.

I can feel my soul-bound mates all reaching for me as well, soft brushes of comfort and love through our nascent bonds.

Even if they aren't all currently perched on the edge of a mountain, they are with me.

All around us, the bottomless energy of the intersection point settles, as if it too has been purged of grief and despair, of constantly seeking a connection with Armin. Scarred but not mortally wounded.

"Is the weather going to be clear tomorrow?" I ask.

My father scrubs the tears from his face. "Yes. Why?"

"We should bring the twins up. Actually, maybe we should have a family picnic!"

My father huffs disapprovingly. "I'm not going to ferry you all up here like some pack animal. Plus, there's not enough room."

I lean my head against his shoulder, our hands still clasped. "Maybe in the summer."

He laughs, then whispers so quietly that the words are almost lost to the wind, "Anything for you, my goddess-touched daughter. It's already all yours. You and your chosen few."

ACKNOWLEDGMENTS

With thanks to:

<u>My story & line editor</u>
Scott Fitzgerald Gray

<u>My proofreader</u>
Pauline Nolet

<u>My beta readers</u>
Anteia Consorto, Terry Daigle, Gael Fleming

<u>For their continual encouragement, feedback, & general advice</u>
FAROFEB (esp. the Discord crew)
Hailey Edwards
Carrie Ann Ryan

ABOUT THE AUTHOR

Meghan Ciana Doidge is an award-winning writer based out of Salt Spring Island, British Columbia, Canada. She has a penchant for bloody love stories, superheroes, and the supernatural. She also has a thing for chocolate, potatoes, and cashmere.

For recipes, giveaways, news, and glimpses of upcoming stories, please connect with Meghan via:
www.madebymeghan.ca
info@madebymeghan.ca
and
subscribe to her monthly newsletter

facebook.com/MeghanCianaDoidge
instagram.com/meghancianadoidge
tiktok.com/@meghancianadoidge

ALSO BY MEGHAN CIANA DOIDGE

<u>Novels</u>

After the Virus

Spirit Binder

Time Walker

Cupcakes, Trinkets, and Other Deadly Magic (Dowser 1)

Trinkets, Treasures, and Other Bloody Magic (Dowser 2)

Treasures, Demons, and Other Black Magic (Dowser 3)

I See Me (Oracle 1)

Shadows, Maps, and Other Ancient Magic (Dowser 4)

Maps, Artifacts, and Other Arcane Magic (Dowser 5)

I See You (Oracle 2)

Artifacts, Dragons, and Other Lethal Magic (Dowser 6)

I See Us (Oracle 3)

Catching Echoes (Reconstructionist 1)

Tangled Echoes (Reconstructionist 2)

Unleashing Echoes (Reconstructionist 3)

Champagne, Misfits, and Other Shady Magic (Dowser 7)

Misfits, Gemstones, and Other Shattered Magic (Dowser 8)

Gemstones, Elves, and Other Insidious Magic (Dowser 9)

Demons and DNA (Amplifier 1)

Bonds and Broken Dreams (Amplifier 2)

Mystics and Mental Blocks (Amplifier 3)

Idols and Enemies (Amplifier 4)

Instincts and Impostors (Amplifier 5)

Endings and Empathy (Amplifier 6)

Misplaced Souls (Misfits 1)

Awakening Infinity (Archivist 0)

Invoking Infinity (Archivist 1)

Compelling Infinity (Archivist 2)

Awry (Conduit 1)

Grand Romantic Delusions and the Madness of Mirth, Part 1

Grand Romantic Delusions and the Madness of Mirth, Part 2

Novellas/Shorts

Love Lies Bleeding

The Graveyard Kiss (Reconstructionist 0.5)

Dawn Bytes (Reconstructionist 1.5)

An Uncut Key (Reconstructionist 2.5)

Graveyards, Visions, and Other Things that Byte (Dowser 8.5)

The Amplifier Protocol (Amplifier 0)

Close to Home (Amplifier 0.5)

The Music Box (Amplifier 4.5)

Moments of the Adept Universe 1

Misson Recon: Bee (Amplifier 5.5)

Soulmates, Doorways, and Other Unruly Magic (Dowser 9.5)

www.madebymeghan.ca

www.ingramcontent.com/pod-product-compliance
Lightning Source LLC
Chambersburg PA
CBHW030742310726
48969CB00005B/1289